# The Gem
# and the Star

48-HOLD

# THE GEM

# AND THE STAR

## LINDA KILGREN

To order additional copies of this book, contact:
Xlibris Corporation
1-888-7-XLIBRIS
www.Xlibris.com
Orders@Xlibris.com

# CONTENTS

Acknowledgements ...................................................... 11

Prologue ................................................................... 13

Chapter 1 ................................................................. 21

Chapter 2 ................................................................. 32

Chapter 3 ................................................................. 41

Chapter 4 ................................................................. 52

Chapter 5 ................................................................. 62

Chapter 6 ................................................................. 75

Chapter 7 ................................................................. 87

Chapter 8 ................................................................. 96

Chapter 9 ............................................................... 113

Chapter 10 ............................................................. 124

Chapter 11 ............................................................. 140

Chapter 12 ............................................................. 151

Chapter 13 ................................................................... 162

Chapter 14 ................................................................ 174

Chapter 15 ................................................................ 184

Chapter 16 ............................................................... 196

Chapter 17 ................................................................ 209

Chapter 18 ................................................................ 219

Chapter 19 ............................................................... 227

Chapter 20 ................................................................ 240

Chapter 21 ................................................................ 251

Chapter 22 ................................................................ 261

Chapter 23 ................................................................ 276

Chapter 24 ................................................................ 287

Chapter 25 ................................................................ 301

Chapter 26 ................................................................ 310

Chapter 27 ................................................................ 325

Chapter 28 ................................................................ 339

Chapter 29 ................................................................ 354

Chapter 30 ................................................................ 363

Chapter 31 .......................................................... 373

Chapter 32 .......................................................... 383

Chapter 33 .......................................................... 397

Chapter 34 .......................................................... 410

Liambria Two ...................................................... 410

Chapter 35 .......................................................... 422

Chapter 36 .......................................................... 431

Epilogue ............................................................. 445

*For, Peggy Holder, my mother, who said,*
*"Write something romantic."*

# Acknowledgements

T hanks to the MOB girls: Joyce Brown, your knowledge of trivia was most useful; Richelle Matli, Anita Langlois, and Renee Menchhofer, your feedback on the first draft was right on and I'm glad you liked it. Special thanks to Shirley Lui, my CAT Scan partner, your logic about the manuscript was on the mark, and thank you for understanding about my hypoglycemia attacks. And finally to Ernest Lee, for telling me exactly where this planet is sitting in the Milky Way.

# Prologue

# Earth, October, 2000A.D., San Francisco

Sparks flew like shooting stars as the clang of the swords reverberated around the exercise room. Cwen grunted as she deflected an incredibly hard swing aimed at her head by Vlad. The swords were not toys. They were capable of decapitating a person, which made Cwen wonder why her trainer was acting like such a crazed berserker.

"You've had that damn dream again, haven't you?" Vlad sneered, swinging the blade toward her middle.

Anger sizzled through her as she twisted to the side, clashing her sword on Vlad's, his nasty remark festering like a boil. But he was right, her mind was not on the exercise. Her phantom lover had come to her again, making Cwen feel a burning and yearning in her insides she had never felt before. The man's face was always shadowed in darkness, yet she was sure she would recognize him on scent alone; earth, grass, and male.

Vlad's blade was a silver blur as it sliced through Cwen's protective padding, cutting a long ribbon in her left arm. Cwen stumbled back, her sword hanging idle in her right hand as she gazed at the blood spilling down her arm with surprise. The hot sting was just reaching her brain when Vlad growled in disgust.

"How many times do I have to tell you not to get distracted! I could have killed you just now!"

Cwen looked at him with murder in her own eyes because she knew the tirade was just beginning. Vlad was a magnificent male specimen, towering over her own five-ten to six-four. Solid muscles on his sweat-shined bare chest rippled with every movement. His brown eyes slanted dramatically, giving him an exotic look. The smooth gold collar set with a large emerald and the matching bracelets added to Vlad's mystique. Yet, she felt no attraction for him because he was her tormentor.

Vlad began to pace, shaking sweat from his brown ponytail as if he'd just come in out of a downpour. "This is what I get for trying to train a female in combat." He threw up his hands. "It's your Aunt Amma's fault. Letting you read all those trashy romance novels about knights, fair damsels and—God-give-me-strength—love."

Cwen's breath quickened as her rage became blinding.

"No one is going to come and rescue you but yourself! You don't dare wait around for some—"

His words were cut off by Cwen's scream and her maniacal attack on his person. Suddenly, all of her body was thrown into the battle. She used her feet and legs, all the while hammering blows on Vlad's sword so fast that he barely had time to fend them off.

Cwen pressed her attack, knocking Vlad's sword from his grip, oblivious to the clattering it made as it skidded across the floor. With every ounce of strength she possessed she kicked him in the gut, laying him flat on his back, pressing the tip of her blade to his throat.

Vlad didn't have the time to wonder at the pain in his belly for his eyes were locked with her smoke-green ones. He had never seen such danger in their depths, or the prospect of death.

Cwen's chest heaved with the need for air in her lungs.

She began to shake as she glared down into Vlad's startled brown eyes.

"You could have killed me just now," Vlad stated. "What stopped you?"

Cwen blinked twice, gazing down at her sword pressing Vlad's neck. She flung the sword aside with a loud metallic bang, spinning so fast her long, thick braid snapped like a whip. Her long strides carried her to the door of the room. With her hand on the knob she flung back at him, "Aunt Amma would have complained about the mess."

Cwen jerked the door open and found her Aunt Amma, who was dressed in her usual outfit of white blouse and black skirt, staring at her with concern. Cwen said nothing, brushing past her aunt and heading up the stairs.

Amma walked in the room toward Vlad, who was leaning on his elbows. Amma reached down a hand and hauled him to his feet. "Well?"

Vlad rubbed at the pain in his belly. "There's nothing else I can teach her."

"But when it's time, will she kill?"

Vlad recalled the deadly look in Cwen's green eyes. "Of that I have no doubt."

As she entered the bedroom Cwen's anger had so reached maximum intensity her face was flushed, her body vibrated in intermittent shakes, and tears welled in her eyes but stubbornness stopped them from falling. She never cried. Anymore, that is. The last time she had wailed like a baby was when Sashna had disappeared. Cwen had been seven-years-old then. Sashna was the only friend she had ever had. A little girl as herself to share her secrets with, to play with, and to fall into fits of giggles with. Cwen let out a sigh, remembering that was the last time she had really laughed.

It seemed that little time had passed after her friend's disappearance and along came Vlad. Nothing had ever been the same since the brown-haired giant's arrival. At that time, the Training had begun.

Cwen's fists curled into tight balls. The child she had been was terrified of the mysterious man. But Aunt Amma was deaf to her pleas, insisting that Cwen follow Vlad's every order. She was immediately snatched out of public school, her lessons taught to her by the implacable Professor Pimbleton in the massive library of their Pacific Heights mansion. When Pimbleton wasn't pounding science, mathematics, English, physics, history, theology, astronomy, and theories of rocket propulsion into her brain, Vlad was pounding the fighting skills into her body. Her aunt was wealthy, but the lessons Cwen had endured went beyond the eccentric wishes of a guardian. Cwen had a black belt in karate, the muscles in her body had been sculpted into beauty of form and strength through constant trips to the gym. She was swift on her feet and now, she supposed with a grim smile on her face, proficient with a sword.

It reminded her of the burning pain in her arm. Slowly, she slipped the padded suit from her body, slowing even more when she reached her injured arm. She slid the padding back as if she were peeling an overripe banana. Cwen grimaced at the sight of the long gash on her upper arm. Removing the suit had caused fresh blood to flow.

She padded nude into the bathroom, wrapping a hand towel around her arm. She was sure she'd left a trail of blood along the plush blue carpeting, but at the moment she didn't give a damn.

Her gaze lifted to her reflection in the bathroom mirror. Her green eyes still held a trace of smoke from her anger. Wisps of black tendrils had escaped her long braid. A slight pallor glazed her bronzed, angled cheekbones.

As always, Cwen couldn't believe she was related to Aunt Amma, their coloring being so different. Her aunt had hair of spun gold, the length of which matched her own, worn always in a long ponytail, and her sparkling eyes were the color of pale sapphires. The woman's face was ageless, not a wrinkle in sight. Aunt Amma and Cwen could have easily passed for the same age.

Suddenly Aunt Amma touched a hand to her shoulder. Vlad would be furious with her if he knew she had let her aunt sneak up on her undetected. Aunt Amma moved as if she were a mist, making no sound. Vlad had taught Cwen to walk just as quietly.

"Vlad told me he winged you. Let me have a look." It was an order, not a request.

Cwen turned to face Amma, intending to be recalcitrant, but the look of concern in her aunt's eyes stopped her. Silently, she lowered the towel. Amma lifted her arm to have a close look, pursing her lips.

"I'll bet that stings."

Cwen said nothing, waiting to witness the miracle of her aunt's touch.

Amma's eyes glazed over as she touched her fingertips to the top of the wound. Slowly, she slid her fingers down the length of the slash, the cut disappearing at her magical touch. Cwen had witnessed her aunt's healing powers hundreds of times, yet each time she was in awe of the unique power.

"There now, that should do it." Amma wet the edge of the towel, wiping the last traces of blood away and smiling at her handiwork, for the skin was smooth and intact as if the wound had been a figment of imagination.

Cwen mumbled a thank you.

"Take a shower. Your skin is glistening with sweat," Amma commanded. "I want to talk with you. I'll wait in the bedroom."

I wouldn't be sweating if you didn't keep the temperature so damn high, she thought. Cwen wasn't embarrassed about her nudity. Aunt Amma never seemed to notice whether a person was clothed or not. What Cwen dreaded was the "talk."

Only five minutes passed before Cwen emerged from the bathroom with a towel wrapped around her.

Aunt Amma sat on the bed, perusing her. "You might as well spit it out. I have the Gift, too. I know what you're thinking."

"I'm sick to death of it! The constant teaching and training!"

"Professor Pimbleton assures me that your studies are complete. Vlad also said that your combat skills are at optimum level."

Cwen refused to be placated. She could feel the rush of heat suffuse her face, fueled by immense anger. "For twelve years you've kept me locked in this damn mansion away from the rest of the world! I'll not stand for it any longer!"

"You go outside all of the time."

"Yes, but with Vlad dogging my every move! I'm like a frigging princess locked away in some ivory tower!"

Amma couldn't hold back her smile. "Princesses don't have calluses on their palms from wielding a sword."

Cwen looked at her hand, clenching it into a fist. "I can't take anymore of this! Do you hear me? I need a vacation like a normal person would!"

Amma waved her hand. "Oh, come now, you've had vacations before."

"You call Vlad dragging me up into the High Sierras every summer a vacation? The man gives me a canteen of water, a bow and arrows, a dagger, and pats me on the head and says 'Hide, girl. I'm going to hunt you down.' These excursions last for weeks!"

Amma chuckled. "And you've done well. You've bested Vlad. The hunted turned into the hunter. You even ate your kills raw, not daring to risk a fire to give away your position. I'm so proud of you."

Cwen actually snarled at her aunt. "Why was all this necessary? All I've gotten from you is evasive answers. There's nothing normal about the way I've been raised! I want the truth! Now!"

"It's the Gift. You haven't even reached your full potential yet. You're not like other human beings."

Cwen crossed her arms. "So you've said."

"You've mastered telepathy, communicating your thoughts with another, and reading the minds of people. But you've yet to gain control of psychokinesis; movement of physical objects with the mind, teleportation of objects from one place to another, and . . . other things. Things you've inherited from your mother."

Cwen blew out a breath. "Yes, my mother. Are you really her sister?"

"I've not lied to you about that."

"Then why don't I look like you? You're fair. I'm dark."

Amma didn't let that phase her. "You get your coloring from your father."

"And where are my parents?"

Amma shifted her gaze to the pendant on Cwen's neck. "I don't know. They're missing."

"Now, you're lying. I want the truth!"

Amma stood up, rubbing her arms. "Your parents are on a very important mission. You were just a baby when they left. It was too dangerous to take you along."

Finally, Cwen thought. "A mission for whom? The CIA?"

"They don't work for the government." Amma took hold of the gold pendant around Cwen's neck. "They work for you and me. There are thousands of us with the Gift. If this world were to find out about us, we would be slaughtered."

Cwen was too stunned to speak.

"I promised your mother that I would care for you, protect you, and see that you were capable of defending yourself. And I have fulfilled that promise."

"You sound like I'll be leaving you."

Amma's gaze was on the pendant. "Your mother gave you this. The stone in the center is a green sapphire. Very rare."

"Answer me!"

She looked up at Cwen, dropping the pendant. "One day soon you will be leaving me." At that, Amma left the bedroom.

Cwen watched her go. She had felt Amma's sadness, yet rage still roiled within her. She went to the closet and pulled out some clothes, mumbling to herself while she dressed.

Vlad met Amma in the foyer. He was dressed in a brown turtleneck sweater that didn't quite hide the bulge of the weapon he always carried.

"Cwen's certainly in a snit," she announced.

"She is that."

"How old is she now?"

"Nineteen."

"The time for the bonding grows near." Amma wiped a tear from her eye. "If only she's able to allude the beast that's hunting her."

"We have prepared her well. It's up to Cwen to stay alive until she reaches her mate."

# Chapter 1

*Liambria, Galaxy M100*

Earsplitting screams shattered the raw silence of the infirmary as the woman was seized by another contraction. "It won't be long now," came the surgeon's muffled voice from between the woman's bent knees. Sweat rained down his forehead, but he resisted the urge to swipe it away, refusing to show terror to the imposing figure of the Commander who stood at his back.

The Commander bent slightly at the waist, wanting a good view of the creature that would soon slide from the woman's body. "This is the last of the eggs?" He refrained from lacing a tinge of hope in his voice.

The surgeon only nodded in answer, his eyes on the round pink head about to spill into his waiting hands. A low grunt emitted from the mother as the infant slid from her body. Repulsion almost caused the surgeon to drop the squalling bundle in his hands, yet he held on to give the man at his back a clear look.

A stream of curses poured from the Commander's tight lips as he took in the sight of the deformed, quivering blob of protoplasm the surgeon held. "Kill it!"

The surgeon lifted his eyes to him. "And the mother?"

The Commander's answer was a flaming glare.

"I will silence her," the surgeon said in defeat.

The Commander spun on his heel, heading for the exit of the infirmary, feeling anger roil in his insides as the automatic doors whooshed open. He went straight for the lift, fully intending to blast the Supreme Tetrarch. They could delay no longer. Fresh sperm and ova must be found.

He rushed from the lift as it reached the top of the spiralled tower, barreling into the guard outside the Tetrarch's suite. The guard made a futile attempt to hold the Commander back.

"His Highness is dining," the guard sputtered.

The Commander slowly looked down at the guard's hand wrapped around his forearm, then turned his glare on the man. Looking into those strange orange eyes made the guard shudder, but he felt no shame. No Trexran could withstand the potent gaze of the Commander. Releasing the Commander's arm, he quickly keyed in the code to open the doors of the suite, plastering himself against the wall as the huge man swept past.

The Commander paused at the entrance, hoping the look of the disgust he felt didn't show itself on his face as the doors slid closed behind him. The Supreme Tetrarch was seated at the round table of Liambrian design. At first glance, it appeared to be granite, but was in fact a melding of stone and alloy. With three different cuisines set before him, his leader was quickly shoveling food into his fat face at an alarming rate, surprising the Commander that he didn't choke. The Tetrarch's gluttony could no longer be hidden by the shimmering purple robes of his office; rolls and rolls of flab stretching the loose fabric. The Commander stood at attention while he waited to be acknowledged.

Sweat rained off the Tetrarch's face. The room was stifling. The Commander gazed out the window at the aqua, cloudless sky, the twin suns scorching the air with wavering heat rays. The Liambrians had loved the heat, never installing air-conditioning in any of their buildings.

Within seconds the Tetrarch sat back, emitting a loud belch. A female servant appeared out of nowhere to quickly clear the plates from the table, all the while keeping her eyes downcast, daring not to look at him or the Tetrarch.

After slurping down a glass of water, the Supreme Tetrarch deigned to look at him. "Ah, Maccus. Was it a male or female?" He swiped his face with a napkin.

Maccus gritted his teeth. "It was an abomination! I ordered it slaughtered, Your Highness."

"Most unfortunate." With a slight tilt of his head, he said, "You may address me by my name. After all, I created you." He let out a mirthless laugh, his triple chins jiggling like a Trexran jell worm. "You're like a son to me. And like any doting parent, I sense you have more to say to me."

Maccus let out a sigh, relaxing his rigid stance and rubbing a hand through his black hair, which he wore at non-regulation length for the military. "Bandar, we've exhausted our supply of Liambrian ova and spermatozoa, which is no great loss as they were ruined in the preserving procedures. All implantations have had the same result. Monsters all."

"I've discussed this with the scientists. They've come up with a surer method for the cryogenic process, which will ensure the potency of the germ cells for at least twenty cycles." Bandar sighed. "It's a pity that all the Liambrians we had in captivity died at the precise time your Liambrian mother willed herself to death."

"They're not all dead."

"I know you're referring to the mass exodus." Bandar scowled. "And that rogue, Raynar, breaking free from his cell and escaping with your twin. The two of you were identical in features. I still wonder how he could tell which one of you had been altered by genetic engineering." Bandar inhaled, the rolls of flab around his middle rising and falling with his breath. "I must admit it was a sight to behold when some of the mountains took off in the air. We had no idea this cowardly race was equipped for spaceflight, or had the minds for such subterfuge. Imagine incorporating the terrain with starships."

"Then—"

Bandar crashed a fist on the table. "We've been over this before! Since that time, I've had ships comb the galaxy. The Liambrians are gone!"

Undaunted by Bandar's anger, Maccus plunged ahead. "The Liambrians didn't just disappear into thin air! What they did was leave this galaxy!"

Bandar rose from his chair with effort, pacing a few steps before turning to face Maccus. "This isn't just supposition, is it?"

Maccus shook his head.

"You know this through the telepathy you inherited from your Liambrian parents?"

Maccus nodded.

Bandar rubbed his triple chins. "You know of my dream of creating a master race. All of our DNA manipulations on you while you were in utero proved to me that it could be done. Your strength, intelligence, and courage exceed all the Trexrans, not to mention your psychic and rejuvenating abilities." Bandar strolled around Maccus, who towered above him as if he were a work of art to be admired. "You've sired how many children?"

"Well over a hundred. All ordinary."

"Why this kind of result?"

"I've studied the records from the time when the Liambrians were in captivity. Clearly the child inherits these extrasensory abilities only when both parents carry the DNA."

"Sounds reasonable. Your mother had already conceived by your father when we imprisoned her."

"Not to mention the fact that my mother was a Queen." Maccus couldn't hide the pride in his voice.

"Yes, the double uteruses were most unusual. I wonder how your twin turned out."

"The only way to know is to find the Liambrians."

Bandar regarded him for some time. "Where are they?"
"The obvious place is the galaxy closest to us. The one
we call GRC 200. It's the same as this one, a spiral galaxy.
I'm positive that's where they're hidden."
"Dispatch ships to this galaxy immediately!"
Maccus finally smiled. "I sent a starship there two cycles
ago. Soon we will know if I'm right."
"I should be angry with you. However, you acted wisely.
My goal can be fulfilled." Bandar chuckled. "We don't even
have to bring them back alive. With our new preservation
process, all we need is their gonads."
Maccus hesitated. "True." He would never tell Bandar
what he was thinking. The Trexrans may have conquered
Liambria. However, other than knowing they were cowardly
telepaths, Bandar knew next to nothing about Liambrians.
Maccus knew by his inherited instinct that there was a Queen
among them and he intended to capture her alive and whole.
His soul ached with the need to mate with a female who was
his equal, unlike the dull-witted and inferior Trexran females
who had sired his offspring.

Once he received word of the Queen's location, he would
go and seize her. Then she would be his.

Vlad and Amma were still huddled together in the foyer
when Cwen came flying down the stairs, rushed past them,
and began punching in the security code for the front door.
Amma and Vlad stared in amazement, wondering why she
hadn't escaped before if she knew the code. Vlad ran to stop
her. But it was too late. She was halfway out the door. His
hands were about to grab her when she spun and drop-kicked
him with a violent karate move.
"Cwen, stop! Where are you going?" Amma screamed.
"I'm leaving!" She ran into the night.
Amma clutched the gold choker with the five carat
diamond around her neck with a shaking hand. The fear

radiating from her was like a fierce, solid, tangible presence. She glanced down at Vlad who was writhing and groaning on the floor, holding his groin.

Amma yanked on his arm. "Get up, you fool! Don't let her get away!"

Vlad gasped for breath, twisting and turning in his pain. "I . . . can't . . . female. Give me a minute."

There was no time to waste. Amma bit back her dignity and placed a healing palm on Vlad's groin. In seconds, the color returned to his face.

Vlad popped up like a jack-in-the-box. "God, I trained her well." Admiration was in his voice.

"Don't congratulate yourself yet. Anything could happen to her!"

Sensing the terror in Amma's voice, Vlad pulled up his sleeve and popped the lid of the armband he wore. Activating a switch, he sighed in relief. "Good. She's still wearing the pendant." A low-toned beep sounded from the device. "I've got a good fix on her. It should be easy to track her."

Amma punched him in the shoulder. "Follow her! Now!"

Vlad gave her a jaunty salute and punched another button on the armband. "I'm gone."

With a stirring of the air around him, he disappeared.

Maccus paced his quarters, stealing furtive glances at the intergalactic transmitter, wishing the damn thing would activate. He had sent his second in command, Luca, to the most likely sector of GRC 200 that would have planets that could sustain life. He had given Luca a device he'd constructed to detect the extrasensory perception emanating from the brains of the Liambrians. The tracker had limits, though. Luca would have to be within a light-year of the projected thought-waves. Therefore, he would have to systematically search each solar system.

Maccus himself could identify a Liambrian without the

aid of technology. His brain was sensitized to them. But he had to be in the same room with them. The Trexrans had recorded the resonances of Liambrian brain waves into the computers. Bandar had tested Maccus by having the computer randomly emit the resonances of Trexrans and Liambrians. Maccus could always separate and identify the brain waves of a Liambrian, but distance was a problem. He sure as hell couldn't do it from 56 million light-years away.

But he was ready. As soon as he heard from Luca, he would launch his ship into the stars and race to the next galaxy at ten times the speed of light.

His goal was the same as the Supreme Tetrarch's: Create a race of super beings. But his loyalty stopped there. He would be the father and master of this new life-form and rule the universe instead of that Trexran slug Bandar.

Lofty ambitions, yes. But they could not be attained unless he had a Liambrian Queen.

Cwen didn't know how far she had run in the darkness, but the sense of freedom overwhelmed her. She slowed to a walk, suddenly becoming nervous, this being the first time she was truly alone outside. Vlad had always been with her before. Of its own volition, her hand crept to the pouch on her belt, feeling the security of her Ka-Bar. Vlad had told her never to go anywhere unarmed. Because she was always chilled outside the warm mansion, Cwen wore a heavy wool sweater.

She found herself on Polk Street, gawking like a country bumpkin at the sights before her. The street was brightly lit, lighting the way of the swarm of people seeking pleasures in the night. God, it's just like on television, Cwen thought. But instead of it being two-dimensional, she was seeing everything in 3-D.

Cwen couldn't help staring at the men and women with hair of every color of the rainbow, metal ornaments piercing their noses, ears, eyebrows, lips, and God-knew-what other areas of the body.

Cwen began to walk and gaze at the storefronts. A loud *boom-boom-boom* caught her attention. She supposed it was music. The beat not only assaulted her eardrums, it vibrated through her body as well. Cwen looked at the flashing pink neon sign which proclaimed this establishment as Ted's. She couldn't stop herself from peeking inside the open doorway. The smell of smoke and sweat assaulted her nostrils. Men in black-studded leather gyrated on what she assumed was a dance floor, their bodies writhing and twitching as if they were inflicted with some form of a nerve disorder.

Cwen backed away from the door when one of the dancers shot her an unfriendly look. She wasn't totally ignorant. Men were dancing with men. Obviously this was a gay bar. Reading the thoughts of the man looking at her with disgust, she discovered his unfriendliness wasn't due to her being female. He considered her a geek. She supposed he was right dressed as she was in the black turtleneck sweater, corduroy slacks, and black Easy Spirit Motions. Her ears weren't even pierced. She didn't care. The place served alcohol, which she never drank because Aunt Amma told her it would interfere with the Gift.

She walked on mesmerized by the sights until an enticing aroma wafted through her nose. Cwen stopped and looked up at the sign on the storefront. "Jiggling Java" it read. Ah, this was a place she could go into. Vlad had always brought her cafe lattes when she was cramming for one of Professor Pimbleton's exams. She hoped the five dollars she carried was enough to purchase the delicious beverage.

Soon Cwen took her latte and sat at an empty table, suddenly feeling remorseful at her behavior toward Aunt Amma. As she sipped her brew, her thoughts returned to the past, thinking things hadn't been all bad. Besides the romance novels, Aunt Amma had an extensive library of video discs.

Cwen recalled watching the sci-fi videos over and over again, enthralled by their stories. Aunt Amma had indulged the child in her. Knowing Cwen's love for animals, Amma had seen to it that she had horseback riding lessons. Vlad in tow, of course. Cwen now owned four cats. She suddenly felt guilty and homesick, quickly finishing her latte, and leaving the Jiggling Java.

Cwen quickened her steps in a rush to reach the safety of home.

All of a sudden, someone grabbed her arm and jerked her into a dark alley. A pitiful squeak escaped her before a hand was clamped over her mouth. Cwen found her back pressed up against a solid wall of chest. "Don't make a sound," came a guttural male voice. She looked down and saw the man held what appeared to be a gun.

Closing her mind to fear, she delivered a hard chop to the man's wrist, hearing a satisfying crunch of bone. With a high-frequency pitch, the gun discharged, spewing out not bullets but a bright-blue beam that set the concrete on fire. Cwen had no time to wonder at it, whipping out her Ka-Bar and slashing the man's throat, ignoring him as he crumbled to the ground clutching his neck.

She was about to flee when a high-pitched whine sounded and a blue beam of light shot past her, scorching the cement and halting her flight. Turning slowly, Cwen faced two more men in dark jumpsuits rushing toward her. The tall one held the strange weapon, while the shorter of the two rapidly punched buttons on what looked like, God help her, a device from one of those video discs she'd watched.

Cwen was frozen. She knew there was no way she could survive a blast from the weapon. She couldn't run faster than the speed of light.

As the tall one reached her, he snatched her long braid, jerking her to his chest, pointing the laser gun at her head. She quickly dropped the Ka-Bar. Up close, he was but an inch or two taller than her own five-ten. His glance fell on his fallen comrade, eliciting a growl from him as he jerked harder on Cwen's braid. "Bitch!"

Terrified, Cwen missed the blurred motion of his hand as he slapped her hard. Pinpoints of light spun behind her lids, her nose and torn lip running blood.

"She killed Tran!" the short man said in astonishment.

Her captor squeezed her arm, inflicting intense pain. "Never mind that. What does the tracker say? The cursed device led us to this place." Gripping Cwen's jaw, he scanned her bloody face. "Is she a damn Liambrian?"

The short man fumbled with the buttons on the tracker until it emitted an ear-shattering squeal. "She's Liambrian, all right. But that's impossible."

"Why?"

"All Liambrians are cowards. Not one of them has the courage to defend themselves," he answered.

"They must have evolved." He started dragging Cwen to the back of the alley. "Signal Luca. Find out what we're supposed to do with her."

The short man activated buttons on a wristband, muttering into the device, then listening intently. "Luca ordered that we not kill her. He wants her brought aboard for interrogation."

Aboard? Cwen thought hazily. Aboard what? Who are these guys anyway? What the hell is a Liambrian? All she did know was that she was in serious trouble, these two being more dangerous than any criminals she had seen on the six o'clock news. Reading their thoughts, panic gripped her insides with the realization that if she didn't escape, she was doomed.

A spiralling breeze swirling the litter about the alley halted her captors. With a blast of wind, Vlad materialized out of nowhere, holding one of those weird ray guns. He fired twice, the blue beams dropping the men like rocks. Cwen was too stunned to feel relieved.

Vlad grimaced as he took in the sight of her bloody and pale face. He opened his arms in a gesture of security. It took her a few seconds, then Cwen launched herself into his waiting arms, plastering herself against his chest as he wrapped his arms around her.

"Oh, Vlad! I was so scared! I—I'm sorry I—"

"Later," he hissed. "We've got company."

Cwen turned her head and saw the denizens of Polk Street gawking at them from the alley entrance.

"Hey, are you folks making a movie?" shouted a purple-haired woman with a ring through her nose.

"Great special effects, dude!" yelled a man.

These inhabitants of Polk Street were certainly bizarre, thought Cwen, but she and Vlad must look equally weird with the pile of bodies behind them. She looked up to Vlad. "Please, take me home."

Vlad's look was grim. "As you wish."

He activated the teleporter, giving Cwen no warning. An electrical charge surged through her, making her gasp. The back wall of the alley wavered before her eyes as they suddenly slipped into invisibility.

The mouths of the Polk Street inhabitants dropped open when the man and woman disappeared. "Awesome," the man said.

# Chapter 2

Vlad and Cwen popped into view, startling Amma, who was pacing like a caged animal. Cwen was suction-cupped to Vlad's chest as if they were magnetized, her body quaking in intermittent shivers, eyes squinched shut.

Vlad peeled Cwen from his chest, turning her to face her aunt. Amma gasped loudly at the sight of Cwen's bloody face.

"Lord, what happened?" Amma wailed.

"I . . . I . . . ," was the best that Cwen could manage, still reeling from the shock of being teleported from Polk Street to the foyer in her home.

"She killed," Vlad answered for her.

"Was it them?"

Vlad nodded.

"How many were there?"

"Three males."

Amma clenched her fists at her sides. "You killed them all, didn't you?"

Vlad reddened. "Cwen killed one." He cleared his throat. "I . . . It's been so long since I've fired this damn Ultraviolet Laser weapon. I—"

"So, you just knocked them out?"

"Well, uh, yes."

Amma let out a weary breath. "How long before he gets here?"

"It depends on how much of a hurry he's in."

Amma shot him a scathing look. "You know damn well he'll be flying at top speed!"

"Then I estimate we have a minimum of six hours."

"A . . . Amma, are we expecting company?" Cwen asked.

Vlad and Amma had completely forgotten Cwen was listening to them, unaware that their accents had become tinged with inflections of their native tongue. "It's past time. Cwen has to be told." Vlad shrugged in resignation.

Sighing, Amma went to Cwen, placing comforting hands on her shoulders. "Go upstairs and clean up. When you're done, meet me in the library."

Cwen started up the steps, then stopped. "I . . . I'm sorry, Aunt Amma."

"So am I, child. So am I."

An electronic chirring sounded from the intergalactic transmitter. Finally, Maccus thought, racing to his desk, activating the receive/send switch. "Commander Maccus here."

"Subcommander Luca reporting, sir."

"Be brief."

"We're orbiting a planet named Earth in the GRC 200 galaxy. A scouting party captured a Liambrian female, but she escaped after killing Tran and disabling the other two scouts."

"She killed?"

"Aye, sir. As you suspected, the Liambrians have genetically evolved to incorporate aggression."

It was the Queen! Maccus thought. He was sure of it. "Report on the transmissions monitoring."

"The airwaves are constantly being bombarded with electromagnetic signals. There are hundreds of languages spoken on this planet with several sub-dialects. However, our cerebral translator implantations have been capable of deciphering them."

Maccus grew impatient. "None Liambrian?"

"No, sir. But we've been monitoring a flurry of

transmissions that seem to be encryptic. The translators are ineffective."

"They could be using a scrambled code."

"I suspect so, Commander."

"Luca, transmit your coordinates. I will launch immediately. Dispatch scouting parties to the locations of these transmissions, but take no action against the Liambrians until I arrive."

"Aye, Commander."

"Maccus out."

Wrapped in her bathrobe, Cwen sat in the library, sipping Aunt Amma's revitalizing herbal tea and beginning to feel like herself again after her night of terror. She had showered, washing away the slime of that man's vile touch. Cwen couldn't force the image of her attackers dressed in their tight black jumpsuits, out of her mind. The men's hostility had been a palpable thing. God, she'd actually killed one of them!

Cwen closed her eyes, feeling no remorse for she had read of her imminent doom from her captors' minds. Opening her eyes, she knew that it had been pure survival instinct that had governed her actions.

Who the hell were those guys? she thought. And what was it with Vlad, popping out of nowhere to rescue her, then whisking her back home in the same manner? She still felt a bit light-headed from that bizarre form of travel.

Cwen nearly dropped the steaming mug when Aunt Amma swept into the library, slamming the door behind her. Amma's attire produced another wave of shock. Instead of the usual white blouse, black-tailored skirt, and sensible flat pumps, she was wearing a V-necked jumpsuit made of a dark-grey, shimmering fabric, outlining her sleek form. Thick gold bracelets with a chunk of diamond in the center adorned each wrist, heeled black boots shot her height to an imposing six feet.

Her thick blonde hair hung in a long plait. Amma looked like an avenging amazon from the future.

Her aunt's stance was downright threatening. Amma's face was flushed, fire sparked in her blue eyes as she glared at Cwen.

She flinched as the wave of raw anger radiating off her aunt blasted her. From past experience, Cwen knew that Amma had an incredible temper, but never had it been directed at her. The intensity of her aunt's rage made her stomach roil. Cwen set aside her tea, fully intending to apologize for running away.

Amma held up her hand. "Don't say a word! Running away was the stupidest stunt you could have pulled. Because of you, thousands of lives are affected." Her aunt paced in a circle, her cheeks flaming red. "You haven't got a clue as to what you've done!"

"A . . . Amma, I'm sorry."

"Your apology is useless. It won't help the situation!" Amma shouted, fists raised in the air toward the heavens. Lowering her arms, she looked down, scowling into Cwen's wide-eyed stare. Taking in several calming breaths, Amma strode over to the leather wing chair, sitting down next to Cwen.

Amma sighed, eyes focusing into the distance. "I'm not angry at you. It's this deplorable mess we're in."

Cwen only gazed at her, not daring to say a word. Her aunt's American accent had completely disappeared, replaced by something that had an Asian tonality.

Amma turned in the chair, fully facing Cwen. In an absentminded gesture, she touched Cwen's lip, healing it instantly. "Child, you're ignorant of who and what you are. I've only myself to blame for that."

"You mean the Gift?"

"That and much, much more." Amma looked down, rubbing a thumb across the diamond in one of her bracelets. She'd

HOLD

had her own motives for keeping Cwen ignorant of her true identity. How much do I tell her? she wondered. She hoped her niece was too jittery to ask about the U-V Laser weapon Vlad had used. If she told Cwen the whole truth, the child would immediately have a nervous breakdown. "You're not from here."

Cwen thought about the men in the alley using weapons and devices that surpassed the current technology existing on Earth. "I'm an extraterrestrial."

Amma had a fit of coughing. "Wh—what in the world gave you that idea?"

"Those men in the alley." Cwen cocked her head. "And Vlad. He does have a unique way of getting around."

"There's much you don't know about me either. I'm a scientist. Vlad was using one of my inventions," Amma lied. "You were born on Earth."

"Then I'm Eurasian."

"What?"

"You've been talking with an accent."

"I have?"

"Yes. It sounds Asian," Cwen said.

"Lord, I'm really rattled. I thought I got rid of this damn accent years ago." Amma sat forward, feeling slightly guilty because she had no intention of telling her niece the exact truth. "You're from the future."

Cwen laughed. "You can't be serious."

"Oh, but I am," she said with raised brows. "You don't belong in this time-frame."

Cwen's face paled, but it all could have made sense. This isolation she had endured all her life held a purpose. "You've kept me locked away from society so that I wouldn't inadvertently alter the future."

Amma smiled in relief. All of those sci-fi videos had paid off. "Exactly."

It was Cwen's turn to get agitated. She popped out of the chair, pacing back and forth. "Okay, okay. I can accept this," she lied. This was too much to assimilate. "But I don't understand one thing."

"I'll try to explain anything you want to know as thoroughly and as quickly as I can. We don't have much time."

Cwen nodded. "I understand my extensive education and the sheltered life I've led. What I don't comprehend is why I've been trained for combat."

"So you would be able to protect yourself." Amma sat back, her look turning grim. "You're being stalked by a humanoid beast!"

Cwen halted her pacing. "Those men in the alley?"

"Yes. They were minions of the beast."

Her stomach bottomed out, then shot up to her throat almost gagging her. "He's a male with the Gift, isn't he?"

"Excellent perception. But though you have the Gift, you're untrained. You're no match for him. His ways are governed by greed for power and evil."

Cwen couldn't take it anymore, her knees turning to putty. "What do we do now?"

"We remove you from his path." Amma stood up, walking to a bookcase.

"How?"

Amma didn't answer her. Pushing on a tome of Shakespeare, a whole panel of bookshelves shifted, opening into a room beyond, spilling light into the dim library. "Remove your slippers. The laboratory must be kept static-free."

Cwen obeyed.

"Come along. We must hurry now."

Cwen followed Amma, her jaw dropping when the contents of the room were revealed. It looked like a control room of some kind. Several computer consoles lined the walls, sounding out beeps and blips, their hundreds of lights flashing.

Conventional keyboards were absent, replaced by lighted keypads marked with unrecognizable symbols. Vlad sat at a computer station, dressed in a brown jumpsuit like Amma's, speaking into an undetectable microphone. Cwen couldn't understand a word he said, his speech sounding like gibberish to her.

In a corner stood a tall rectangular metal frame resembling a metal detector she had seen on TV once. What the hell is that? she wondered.

Amma hovered behind Vlad, who by now had ended his conversation with . . . well, whoever.

"Operation Scramble is now in affect," he informed Amma.

"I know the beast is scanning for any unusual transmissions. Do you think he understood our code?"

"Unlikely. Since we just invented it two hours ago."

"I never underestimate that devil." Amma scanned several of the consoles. "What about Self-Destruct?"

"All stations report set, verified, and activated."

"Time?"

"0000 hours." Vlad finally turned to Cwen. "Hello." His accent was so thick she could barely understand him.

"Hi, I think."

Vlad looked her over and saw that her hip-length hair was in a tight braid. "Good. We can't have your hair flying about when you enter the Doorway."

"The Doorway?"

Vlad pointed to the metal detector thingy.

"I'll explain while you get dressed." Amma shoved a pile of leather clothes into Cwen's hands.

Cwen looked at Vlad, her face reddening. "Amma, I'm not wearing anything under this robe."

"Oh, for heaven's sake. Vlad, watch the chronometer and don't you dare take your eyes off of it." Amma turned to Cwen. "There now. Hurry up. The timing is critical."

Cwen pulled off her robe and began to dress quickly. "Child, listen to me and don't ask questions." Amma gathered her thoughts and began speaking rapidly. "Ten years from now, the Earth will go through a great upheaval. A one hundred kilometer asteroid will pass within 1000 kilometers of the Earth, causing extreme gravitational pull on the tectonic plates. The continents will break apart and shift. Land masses will sink into the sea. Oceans will spring up where there were none before. There will be earthquakes, volcanic eruptions, tsunamis, and atmospheric disturbances.

"We'll be sending you to what will become the east coast of the United States, which is now known as New England, consisting of the states: Maine, Vermont, New Hampshire, Rhode Island, Connecticut, and Massachusetts." Amma paused to look at Cwen, who had a puzzled look on her face. "I'll explain your clothing in a moment."

Amma organized her thoughts again. "There will be survivors. Unfortunately, they will deem this event as God's vengeance. They selected to model their new world in the fashion of the Middle Ages, when knights and fair damsels were the rage, with two important differences. Racial strife will be forgotten in favor of survival. And in the time you will be living, women are warriors as well, protecting the castles while the knights wage war." Amma looked at Cwen, who had finished dressing, her face ghost-pale. She thought the child looked fine in her brown leather breeches, boots, and metal-studded leather tunic. Amma turned to Vlad. "She's ready."

Vlad walked over to Cwen, carrying her sword and a lethal-looking dagger. "I know you'd prefer a Ka-Bar, but its design would bring a lot of questions you won't be able to answer." Pain shot through Vlad's chest. His protégé was stunned speechless and immobile. He fastened the belt to her waist, then pushed her to stand in front of the Doorway.

He went to the control console for the device, manipulating the keypad.

Cwen took an unconscious step back when the Doorway began to shimmer with churning blue and violet light. She was suddenly seized with the shakes. A whining noise sounded from the Doorway, rising in intensity until it was almost deafening.

"Two more things, child!" Amma shouted above the noise. "We're sending you to the year 4010! When you arrive, head west until you reach the Castle Acwellen. The people there will shelter you!" Amma nodded to Vlad. "Jump through, Cwen! Now!"

Terror brought her voice back. "I don't want to go!"

"You don't have a choice!" Amma slipped up behind her, giving Cwen a mighty shove.

Cwen's scream echoed for a moment from the swirling vortex.

"God, I hated doing that." Amma tried not to cry, but failed.

"It was time. Maccus, the beast, doesn't have time-travel capabilities," Vlad said with false sympathy, placing a hand on her shoulder. If Amma had told Cwen of her importance, this situation would not have occurred. "I just hope she learned how to speak the King's English of old from all of those romance novels you let her read."

"If not, Sevea will help her."

"I hope so. Otherwise, she won't understand a word her mate says to her," Vlad predicted.

# Chapter 3

*4010A.D.*

Cwen screamed as her body was propelled forward through the kaleidoscope of shifting blue and violet light, arms flailing in a vain attempt to regain her balance. Without warning, her body sailed into sunlight, crashing to the ground like an axed redwood, shutting off her scream.

She panted as a sensation of thousands of needles pricked her skin, jangling the pain receptors of her nerves. She sighed with relief when the pin-prickling agony suddenly ceased. Cwen lay flat on her belly, cursing Aunt Amma and Vlad.

Quickly she flipped over to seek signs of the Doorway. Before her eyes the shimmering blue-violet rectangle was shrinking, then winked out of existence. Damn! That killed any ideas she possessed of jumping back through.

Cwen looked around at her surroundings, which was the clearing in a dense forest. Vlad must have known what he was doing. Otherwise, she might have slammed into a tree instead of landing on the soft bed of the forest floor.

Cwen sat up immediately getting stabbed in the ribs with the hilt of her sword. She adjusted the weapon, wrapping her arms around her knees, trying to come to grips with her circumstances, and focusing on the instructions Aunt Amma had shouted to her. Head west, she'd told her, to this Castle Acwellen. Cwen looked up into the bright azure sky, seeing the sun was straight overhead, marking the time as noon. She would have to wait until the sun began its descent before she could discern which way was west.

Thousands of questions swirled around her brain, but there was no one there to answer them. Had there been an axial shift in the Earth after the upheaval? Was the trajectory of the planet's orbit still the same? Was what she knew as west still west? Cwen cursed at the fact that she didn't even have a compass to aid her.

She sighed, deciding she'd best familiarize herself with the forest and get her bearings. All of Vlad's survival excursions into the High Sierras wouldn't go to waste. Even though he was not with her, Cwen wouldn't shame him by getting herself lost.

First she listened to the sounds around her—birds chirping in the trees, the gurgle of a stream some few paces to her left. The beauty of the forest was an environmentalist's dream: oaks, birches, maples, and other trees she couldn't identify rose majestically into the sky, their thick branches dressed with colorful blossoms. A variety of dark green bushes and other unknown foliage grew in thick clusters on the forest floor. She'd passed from fall into spring, the air crisp free of pollution.

The birds suddenly stopped singing, bringing Cwen to her feet and drawing the sword from its sheath on her left side. She cocked her head, listening intently. There! The unmistakable crack of steps on fallen twigs and branches. Cwen turned toward the noise, assuming a battle stance, sword held at the ready.

Four grungy-looking men emerged from the forest wearing dirty tunics, breeches, and boots. The tallest of them had a dead deer draped over his shoulders. At the sight of her, they halted.

Cwen was downwind from them, almost gagging from the foul stench of unwashed bodies. Didn't they have soap in the 41st century? They all wore swords on their hips. One carried a bow and a quiver of arrows. Beneath the dirt it was hard to distinguish their features. The men all looked alike with dark hair, dark eyes.

The tall one carefully lowered the deer to the ground. "What 'ave we 'ere?"

Cwen said nothing, maintaining her guard. One question was answered though. She now knew what manner of speech was spoken in the year 4010.

"By the look of 'er, she be one of Acwellen's wenches," said the one with the bow and arrows.

The tall one rubbed his mouth in an unmistakable gesture of lust. "Aye. But look at 'er. She's a beauty, ain't she?"

"Put the sword down, woman, afore ye hurt yerself." The man with the bow and arrows began to sidestep, intending to get behind her.

Cwen's eyebrows rose as a string of lewd thoughts rushed into her mind from the men. She had never been able to read Amma and Vlad's thoughts, but the minds of these slimeballs were wide open. They had every intention of raping and killing her. Rage shot up to her brain with lightning speed, tensing her muscles.

The three men in front of her rushed Cwen, drawing their swords just as the other one moved in behind her. Cwen spun quickly, delivering a hard snap-kick to his groin, dropping him to the forest floor.

Before the tall one could react, she completed her spin, bringing down her sword between his neck and shoulder, slicing deep. Blood splattered her as he let out his death howl. Spinning again, she slit the throat of the man with the bow and arrows with her blade, coming full circle to face the other attackers.

The remaining two pressed forward, intending to knock her to the ground. Cwen's left hand shot out, crashing into one of the men's nose. He yelled in pain. She slashed her sword across his belly, ending his screaming. The remaining man's face was pale, but she gave him no time to flee, whipping out her dagger with her left hand and plunging it into his shoulder. The man fell to his knees, whimpering at the sight of the dagger protruding from his shoulder. Cwen gripped the sword hilt with both hands. Her intent was to separate his head from his shoulders.

"Hold!" came a feminine voice laced with authority.

Cwen stayed her hand, turning to look at the source of that command. At the sight of the woman astride the dapple-gray horse, Cwen lowered her sword, her chest heaving with exertion. The woman was all golden, emanating power. As she nudged her steed forward, Cwen stared at her beauty. The woman's hair was bronze, streaked with golden strands lightened by the sun. Her skin was a polished gold tone as if she spent long hours in the sun, her slanted eyes were gold sparked with fury.

As the horse and rider stopped in front of her, Cwen stared beyond the Golden Woman in amazement. There were twelve mounted women behind her, warriors all, wearing outfits similar to Cwen's and armed with swords. How had they come upon her without her hearing them? she wondered. Cwen surveyed their faces in astonishment. The skin tones ranged from the fairest white to the darkest of browns. Amma had been right. There was no racial strife here.

Cwen turned her attention back to the woman of gold, silently working her tongue so she wouldn't blurt out a rapid flurry of 21st century English. "How long have you been here?" she slowly said.

"We witnessed it all."

Cwen now noticed the sword at her side. "Why didn't you come to my aid?"

The Golden Woman smiled, glancing at the bodies on the ground. "You weren't in need of it."

A flush of pride rushed up Cwen's cheeks. She didn't know

why, but this woman's approval of her was important. Tilting her head toward her fallen enemies, she said, "Who are they?"

"Thieves, poachers." The Golden Woman shrugged. "There's no need for anyone to starve here, but there are those who won't work for their food honestly."

"My Lady, please," implored the man with the dagger in his shoulder.

Cwen had forgotten about him. She leaned down, starting to pull the dagger out.

"Leave it!" the Golden Woman shouted. "His life's blood will be gone before he can reach his friends. I want him to tell them the consequences of trespassing on Acwellen land." She looked down at the man. "You may leave, vermin."

"Thank you, my Lady." He scrambled to his feet as if he didn't have a knife imbedded in his shoulder and crashed into the woods.

"'Tis a waste of a good dagger," Cwen muttered.

Golden Woman laughed, the sound musical. "I'll get you another."

Cwen couldn't help but like this woman. She walked to the stream, washing the blood from her hands and sword, drying the blade on the moss growing along the bank. Sheathing the sword, Cwen asked, "What are you called?"

"I am Sevea." She swept a hand behind her. "These are my warriors." The twelve women nodded their heads in greeting.

"I am called—"

"Cwen."

"You know who I am?"

"Aye. You were expected. We will escort you to Castle Acwellen." She turned to the dark-skinned warrior. "Kendra. Her mount."

Kendra released the reins of a large black stallion. Cwen held out her hand and the stallion trotted over to her, his head held high, tail whipping behind him. When he reached her he nuzzled her hand with his nose. God, he was a beautiful animal. The horse was big chested with powerful long legs, solid black except for the white stripe that ran down the center of his head. Cwen stroked his thick neck, his shining hide soft as velvet.

"'Tis true." Sevea smiled down at Cwen. "I was told you have a gift with animals."

"Aye." Cwen passed her hand over his powerful flanks. "Does he have a name?"

"I left that honor to you"

The other women warriors had gathered around horse and woman to witness this wonder, smiles on all of their faces.

Running her hands through the horse's long, thick mane, Cwen announced, "I'll call him Samson."

All of the women laughed. "'Tis fitting," Sevea said.

"You know the tale, then?"

Nods came from all of them. For the first time Cwen looked closely at her new friends—and she did consider them such—noting something unique about them. Although their skin tones varied, all of them had tilted eyes and high angular cheeks, reminding her of the structure of her own face. They all wore their hair as she did, in a single long braid resting against their backs.

Sevea looked up at the sun. "'Tis time to ride for home."

Cwen nodded, mounting Samson in one swift move. Those riding lessons Aunt Amma had paid for came in handy. She walked Samson in a circle, getting a feel for the animal. He pranced for her, showing Cwen he was just as happy with her.

"A moment," Kendra said as she slid off her horse. She walked over to the dead deer, picked it up, and draped it on her horse. After she remounted, she looked at Cwen and said, "Good venison shouldn't be wasted."

Laugher rang through the forest as the women warriors galloped away from the glade.

They rode for what seemed like hours before leaving the forest and resting their mounts at the edge of a large meadow flanked on both sides by rolling hills. Cwen was fascinated by the sight of the green grassland dotted with clusters of wild flowers of every hue swaying in the gentle breeze. The Earth had replenished itself beautifully. This was freedom, Cwen thought as she inhaled deep breaths of the flower-scented air.

"Castle Acwellen." Sevea pointed to a distant large rectangular fortress backed by high grey hills. Twilight was approaching, backlighting the castle with radiant beams of orange, peach, and magenta. Sevea kicked her heels against her horse's flanks, sending it into a gallop.

The others followed. Samson tried to outdistance the other horses as they raced for the castle. Cwen leaned down close to the stallion's neck, laughing as the wind rushed in her face, urging the steed to greater speed.

Samson reached the drawbridge ahead of the others. Cwen reined him in slowly so he wouldn't halt too abruptly and injure himself. She was awed as she gazed at the castle. It was beautiful, constructed of gray stone, tall towers abutted each corner of the rectangular main building. The drawbridge was lowered revealing a mass of people going about their daily duties. Cwen looked up at the gatehouse and saw a woman dressed like the others waving at her. Cwen smiled, returning the greeting.

Sevea drew up beside her. "Welcome home."

Cwen nodded. She followed Sevea into the bailey, where they all dismounted, turning the horses over to the stable boys. Cwen couldn't resist giving Samson a parting pat.

Kendra walked up the castle stairs, opening the large oak door and holding it open for the others. They entered a great hall. It was just as described in all of the romance novels Cwen had read. Sevea watched Cwen as she looked around, mesmerized, taking in every detail. The stone hearth was so huge it could easily roast a whole cow. Long tables with wooden benches ran parallel to the walls. A shorter table, set on a dias, was at a right angle to the other tables. Cwen assumed it was the lord's table for a blue banner with a black wolf stitched in the center hung on the wall above it. Scented rushes lined the floor, and metal cressets were spaced at intervals along the walls, lighting the otherwise darkening room.

"Who's master here?" Cwen didn't know why she was suddenly nervous.

"Lord Ware. Baron of Acwellen," Sevea answered. "I'm his wife." Sevea gave Cwen no time to comment. "Luned, Edris!" she bellowed.

In a few moments two women scurried up to Sevea, bobbing quick curtsies. Neither woman was short and fat as Cwen had visualized. The one that Sevea had indicated as Luned was tall with red hair and freckles sprinkling her cheeks. Her eyes were a sharp green. Edris was shorter with dark-brown eyes and hair. Both wore their hair in a single long braid, which seemed to be the fashion, but each were dressed in grey woolen gowns instead of the leather attire of the warriors.

"See that a bath is brought to the third chamber," Sevea ordered.

"Yes, my lady!" they chorused.

"My husband and his knights are out hunting. You can meet them on the morrow." Sevea smoothed back a loose tendril of Cwen's black hair. "You've had a long and busy day. Rest and food are what you require."

Somehow, Cwen was comforted by Sevea's touch. She followed Sevea up the winding staircase to the second level. Sevea opened a chamber door and motioned her inside.

The room was beautiful but slightly chilled, which explained the need of the fire burning in the hearth. Furnishings were sparse. A big bed on a high wooden frame with white linen and a dark blue cover sat with the head pushed up against the wall, two straight-backed chairs were positioned before the hearth, a chest sat next to a window seat. The window was covered by wooden shutters. A blue carpet covered the stone floor to protect bare feet from its chill. A solid oak table with a basin and pitcher resting on it stood at the right wall. A small table sitting next to the bed held a three-tiered candelabra with lighted tapers, giving the room a soft glow.

Sevea sat on the bed regarding Cwen, who was staring like a wide-eyed child, yet showing signs of fatigue. "Does it please you?"

"'Tis nice. Where do I—"

"The privy is at the end of the hall."

There was a knock at the door and Sevea bid them enter. Several men traipsed into the chamber. Two set a wooden tub near the hearth. Two others immediately poured steaming water into the tub, leaving two buckets on the floor beside it for rinsing. The men left without a word.

Luned and Edris appeared, carrying drying cloths, soap, and a tray of bread, yellow cheese, and steaming tea. They sat the items on the chairs and reached eager hands to Cwen, who backed up, feeling immensely shy.

"Leave us." Sevea stood up. "I'll attend her."

Luned and Edris backed out of the room, not questioning their mistress' order.

Cwen stood where she was, not quite knowing how to tell Sevea she'd rather bathe alone without insulting her.

Sensing her turmoil, Sevea said, "No one has seen you nude."

"Only my aunt . . ."

"'Tis well no male has seen you." Not explaining that comment, Sevea crossed to her, unfastening Cwen's sword belt, letting it fall to the floor. "'Tis the custom here to have assistance while bathing. In the future, I'll be the only one to attend you."

Cwen hesitated a moment, thinking, well, when in Rome . . . She undressed quickly and raced to the tub, stepping in the warm water, her cheeks flaming.

Sevea handed her a ball of rose-scented soap, holding onto her braid so it wouldn't get wet. "You have such beautiful hair. Your body is nicely formed as well. You should not be ashamed of it."

It had to be the quickest bath in history. It wasn't long before Cwen raised up, spilling water over the rim of the tub. Sevea wrapped her in the drying cloth, holding her arm as she stepped from the tub.

"I had word of your size and had clothes made for you." Sevea went to the chest and pulled out a linen shift. When Cwen was dry, she slipped it over her head. Sevea led her to the bed, motioning Cwen to climb in. "Do you want some bread and cheese?"

Cwen shook her head. "My stomach feels weird." She gasped when she realized she had slipped into 21st century speech.

Sevea seemed not to notice, bringing her the cup of tea. "Time travel has that effect. Drink this. It will soothe your stomach." Sevea sat on the bed next to her.

Cwen took a sip of the tea. It was minty tasting. "You know of time travel?"

"I understand all the theories and applications of it." Sevea's speech had shifted to match her own.

It was then Cwen noticed the gold choker and bracelets with diamonds set in the center. "How did you know about my arrival?"

"Your aunt sent a message through the Doorway."

Exhaustion consumed Cwen so swiftly she was unable to ask all of the questions raging in her mind. As she sipped the tea, Sevea began stroking her hair in a maternal fashion.

"Vlad trained you well. I looked upon you with pride as you fought those men in the woods. You didn't hesitate to kill."

Cwen almost dropped the empty cup, speechless. Sevea took the cup from her. "Lay down, child, and rest."

Cwen made herself comfortable, her questioning eyes on Sevea, who continued to stroke her hair. "Who are you, really?"

Sevea smiled. "Haven't you guessed?"

Cwen shook her head.

"I'm your mother."

# Chapter 4

*Earth, October, 2000A.D., San Francisco*

Luca paced the hard walkway the Earthlings called concrete, waiting for the Commander with dread. Maccus was going to be furious, and Luca would be the target for that anger. The Liambrians had escaped them again.

Luca peeked around the corner, gazing at the charred ruins that had once been a square city block. They had triangulated the source of the transmissions to this location. His scouts had confirmed that Liambrians were indeed inside these dwellings. Before the Trexrans had time to glory in their discovery, the entire area had exploded, taking Luca's six scouts with it.

Crowds of Earthlings pressed against the blockades the authorities had set up while they combed the rubble for survivors, but Luca could tell them there would be none.

Luca jumped when the Commander materialized behind him, placing a hand on his shoulder. "Commander, I . . . we . . . " Words failed him as he stared up into the slanted shimmering orange eyes. The fact that Maccus could teleport without the aid of a device always unnerved him.

"They're gone," Maccus stated with calm.

Luca started to ask him how he knew, then remembered the Commander was a strong telepath. He was probably reading traces of the Liambrians' brain waves. "They set off a huge explosion—more of an implosion actually, given the fact that none of the surrounding dwellings were harmed. The Liambrians committed mass suicide again."

Maccus ran his eyes over the destruction. Luca tensed his muscles, waiting for the pain the Commander could inflict with the power of his thoughts alone. One hundred nanoseconds passed and nothing happened. Luca hazarded a glance at the Commander, whose eyes were glazed, focused into nothingness. Luca had witnessed this trance state before. What was Commander Maccus sensing?

"The Liambrians aren't dead." Maccus gazed down at Luca.

"But, but how could they survive this degree of devastation?"

"They weren't here when it happened."

"They weren't?"

"The Liambrians escaped into the future."

Luca was astounded. "You're talking about time travel, aren't you?"

Maccus nodded with a grim smile on his face. "That explains why Bandar could find no trace of them after the mass exodus from Liambria. All they had to do was time-jump a day into the future in space and they would be invisible to the Trexrans."

"Then the Liambrians are lost to us."

Now the anger was in the Commander's eyes as yellow and orange lights seemed to swirl within them. The blast of psychokinetic rage sent Luca staggering back a few paces.

"You blind fool! I'm Liambrian! Or have you forgotten?" the Commander shouted.

Luca vigorously shook his head.

"I see it all now. Exactly how it's done. The technology is so simple."

"You intend to build one of these . . . time-travel devices?" Luca asked, hating to hear the answer.

"Yes. I know where my twin is now—or I should say

approximately *when*. And you're all going to jump through time with me."

Sevea sighed and gazed down at a sleeping Cwen. After Sevea had revealed her identity to her daughter, Cwen had become agitated, spewing out questions and raging at her mother for abandoning her. Sevea had used the Gift to silence the child and put her to sleep. It was a dirty trick, but necessary. How could she possibly tell her that duty came first, forcing her to leave her baby behind in the past?

Sevea watched the wavering light from the candle flames dance across the wall. Cwen had only been in this time-frame for a few hours, which certainly had to be a strain on her nerves. Sevea feared for her child's sanity if she were told too much too soon. She promised herself she would tell Cwen all of it, but slowly. She had the time.

Unable to stop herself, Sevea stroked Cwen's brow. Did the Overlord understand the agony she'd experienced, not being able to hold, feed, and care for her baby? Of course, he didn't, Sevea thought. He was a hard, unfeeling male. The survival of the Liambrians as a whole was his primary purpose.

*Liambria 2, Earth, 4010A.D.*

Vlad stepped out of the Doorway into the chambers of the Overlord, waiting for the pins and needles sensation attacking his body to ease. He swiped the sweat away from his forehead as he gazed at the curved walls of the chamber. The grey walls were actually a melding of alloy and stone, giving them the ability to withstand extreme gravitational stresses. The windows were two feet thick and resilient to extreme heat or cold. The Overlord's long desk was made of slate, supporting the three self-energized computer consoles upon it. The lighting was recessed within the dome-shaped ceiling surrounding a skylight. He had been away so long, he'd almost forgotten what home looked like.

Vlad noticed his Overlord standing at a window with his back to him, gazing into the night. He knew that his leader was aware of his presence, so he waited, observing his master. Vlad was always impressed by the Overlord's height and well-honed body, his blue-black hair tied back into a ponytail that fell to his bare shoulder blades. His neck bore the weight of the gold collar with a large green sapphire in the center, designating his office. Matching bracelets were on his wrists. His posture was that of a warrior about to do battle.

It had been five years since Vlad had seen him. Vlad had returned through the Doorway for the coronation ceremony of the Overlord. It was then he himself had been given the position of second in command.

Slowly the Overlord turned, facing Vlad, his slanted orange eyes appeared to be dancing with flames. Knowing only the English language spoken in this century, he spoke in Liambrian. "Welcome home, Arax."

It took a moment for Vlad to respond to his given name. For so long he had only reacted to his Earth name. "Thank you, Master. But please, call me Vlad." He shrugged. "I'm used to it now."

"Very well." A rare smile appeared. "And I would have you use my name, my friend."

At thirty, Vlad was five Earth years older, yet the male before him looked to be older. He looked haggard, a frown line permanently etched into his forehead. The burden of being Overlord must have weighed heavily on his shoulders.

"How do you fare, Otas?"

"My temper flares quickly these days and the burning inside me intensifies with each breath." Otas motioned Vlad over to the table opposite the desk. He poured him a glass of *Ma-shil-kot*, elixir. Time travel wore on the body. "Sit," he said as he handed the glass to Vlad.

Vlad drank down the white liquid in three gulps, sighing as the drink sent energy into his tired system. And he would need strength for Otas was about to bombard him with questions. He didn't have long to wait.

"Report on Operation Scramble." Otas regretted the harshness of his voice.

"All went smoothly. All Liambrians escaped through the Doorways to their designated time and locations. All records of our false identities in the year 2000A.D. were wiped clean from the Earth's computers. All stations self-destructed at 0000 hours Earth time." All of this was a formality, Vlad thought. Otas' telepathic brain knew all things past and present. It was the future that sometimes became hazy.

"And your mother?"

"Amma will arrive at the estimated time Cwen is safely ensconced in Liambria."

Otas sat down, unable to keep the eagerness out of his voice. "Tell me about my Queen. Does she sense me yet?"

Vlad chuckled. "Cwen has been dreaming about you for months, but she doesn't understand what's happening to her."

"If only I was so ignorant. I burn with the need of the bonding. Knowing she is near is almost more than I can bear."

"You must give her time. Despite your orders, Amma didn't tell Cwen who and what she is. She's still unskilled in the use of the Gift and she doesn't know what it means to be female. Sevea will see to it that her training is complete."

"Yes. I've been in telepathic contact with Sevea. My Queen fights like a warrior and does not hesitate to kill. You have trained her well. I thank you."

"You honor me," Vlad said.

The Overlord turned pensive. "I can feel my Queen, yet I do not know what she looks like. I haven't seen her since she was born. Visualize her for me."

Vlad focused his thoughts on the last image in his mind of Cwen before they sent her through the Doorway garbed in her warrior's clothing. He closed his eyes, holding the visual thought.

The Overlord laid his palm across Vlad's forehead, closing his own eyes. Otas sucked in his breath as his groin grew heavy with need. He removed his hand and opened his eyes. "She is beautiful, and not a trace of evil in her." Otas suddenly scowled. "And she was not attracted to you?"

Vlad's eyes popped open as he fell into fits of laughter. "Not in the least. If anything, she hated me. I drove her hard, never letting up for an instant." Vlad turned serious. "There's no need for jealously. A Queen is beyond my reach. You're the only one who may bond with her. Besides, you forget, she's my cousin."

"I must see her. Touch her. Tonight!"

"Have a care, Otas. Cwen means a great deal to me and she's not ready for the bonding. You could harm her mentally."

"I will be careful." Otas slipped on a black tunic. "Cwen must know that I am no dream." With that, he disappeared.

*Castle Acwellen*

Sevea sensed the Overlord's presence seconds before he materialized. She stood quickly, raced to the foot of the bed, and assumed a protective stance just as Otas appeared.

His imposing figure, draped in black, caused her to place a hand at her throat. His eyes gleamed iridescent orange in the dim chamber. Sevea feared him, but she had to defend Cwen, behaving as the mother she had not been for her daughter's entire life.

"'Tis too soon, Master," she whispered. "Cwen doesn't know the ways of the Gift, or what it is to be female and the Queen."

"Speak our tongue," Otas hissed in Liambrian. "This language holds no words for what I must say to you."

Sevea complied. "She's not ready."

Otas' eyes slid to the sleeping form on the bed, then returned to Sevea. "Amma was remiss in not teaching her the ways of the Gift and being the Queen."

"She felt that it was too much to force on my child. What you intend will—"

"Silence!" He put up a hand. "Listen to me well. Maccus knows we used time travel to escape."

"Impossible! All of the Doorways were destroyed." Sevea couldn't stop the intense fear shooting through her insides like lightning.

"You forget. Maccus is my twin." Otas loosened the strip of leather that bound his hair, shaking the black mass free. "Maccus now understands the technology of time travel. Soon he will complete his own Doorway."

Sevea clenched her fists. "When will the beast arrive?"

"I do not know the exact day, but it will be soon." Otas laid a pouch on the table and removed his tunic. "Cwen will need the protection of my mind."

Sevea knew the pouch contained the jewelry necessary for the bonding. "The power of your mind will destroy her! The binding of your minds will drive her insane!"

Otas ignored her. He walked over to Cwen, placing a hand on her forehead. His Queen was exhausted and deeply asleep. She hadn't heard their hushed voices. "She dreams of me." He turned back to Sevea, his features softening. "Do not fear. I will only perform a partial bonding. I will enter her dreams and make what is subconscious conscious."

"Must you mate with her?"

"You know it is the only way." Otas gently stroked Cwen's cheek, careful not to wake her. "What is her age?"

"Nineteen."

"Good. She has not begun to ovulate. Now is not the time to conceive." Otas reluctancy stopped touching Cwen. "You must begin the instructions on the use of the Gift immediately. She must be able to defend herself against Maccus."

"I'll need the aid of Hebron."

"I will send him to you."

Sevea opened her mouth to say more, then closed it. By the look on the Overlord's face, he knew her thoughts. There was no mercy in his flaming orange eyes.

"Leave us!" commanded the Overlord.

Cwen was immersed in a dream of her phantom lover. She could see his shadowy form, smell the scent of earth, grass, and male. If only he would come closer so she could see his features, touch him.

The dream intensified, and she got her wish. Cwen felt his tangible presence.

"Cwen," came a magnetic deep timbre. "Open your eyes."

In her sleep, Cwen sat up and gazed at the tall form highlighted by the flames from the hearth. Her phantom lover was naked and walking toward her. The sight of his tall muscled form took her breath away as did the erect staff of his manhood. His powerful chest was hairless, but black strands spread from his navel down to a thick triangular mass surrounding his tumescence.

As he sat on the bed next to her, she touched his smooth face. There were no traces of bristles on his square chin. He was more handsome than she could have imagined—blue-black hair hung past his broad shoulders, his skin was bronzed, cheekbones high and angular, the slanted eyes were the color of the sun. Cwen felt the heat burning in those incredible orbs.

The phantom gripped the pendant on her neck, snapping the chain with his powerful hand. His touch was light as he slipped a collar of gold around her neck, fusing the ends solid with his magical touch. "Your mind to my mind," he whispered in some foreign language she didn't understand. He repeated the process of fusing a gold bracelet to her left wrist. "My heart to your heart, " he whispered. Cwen's own heart began to pace rapidly. The sound of his voice alone was arousing. "Your body to my body." Another gold bracelet was fused to her right wrist.

Her phantom lover reached around and unbraided her long, black hair, fluffing it until it hung in a glorious curtain about her. His sun-colored eyes held some emotion she didn't recognize. Dazed, she made no protest when he removed her shift.

He gathered her into his arms, which felt like warm steel. He pressed his lips to hers. On instinct alone, she opened her mouth to let his hot tongue dance with her own. He pulled back, watching her. Cwen felt forlorn as a raging heat burned within her belly.

"Forgive me," he whispered in accented English. "This must be quick."

He pushed her back down, spreading her thighs with his hand. He lowered himself between her open legs. Strong fingers pressed into the secret place that no one had ever touched. Cwen moaned, which he silenced with a kiss. The fingers moved in and out of her, fueling the flames that was the furnace of her need. She felt herself grow hot and moist with the action of his fingers. An emptiness assailed her as those strokes suddenly ceased, leaving her in want for more.

"Bend your knees," he commanded. He gripped her hips, pulling her toward him. His hard and hot shaft pushed part way inside her. "Forgive me," he said again.

He plunged the steel rod into her swiftly, tearing her, shooting a pain from her core to the top of her head. He muffled her scream with his mouth.

He began to move in and out of her, the motion searing, opening their minds to each other. Cwen became aware that he felt what she felt, but he endured the pain with silence.

Flashes from his mind raced across hers, images that were hard to comprehend.

For an instant, power so unfathomable and frightening showed itself to her. She was terrified for she was locked within its embrace. She felt that power surge into the very depths of her mind, producing an intense pain in her head. Again her scream was subdued by his hot mouth. Quickly, his motions speeded up, intensifying their joining. She felt more pain than pleasure.

Soon, Cwen felt the hot bursts of his seed spilling into her. He shuddered with the force of it, letting his full weight fall upon her.

Cwen tried desperately to unlock their joined bodies, but he only raised his head, looking down at her with eyes of fire.

"You are now mine," he hissed.

"Who are you?" Cwen asked, her breath labored.

"Otas."

"What are you?"

"Your husband."

"Is this a dream?"

"I am real."

Cwen struggled fiercely as terror seized her again.

He touched a hand to her thrashing forehead. "*Ja-Da,* sleep," he commanded.

Cwen slipped into darkness.

# Chapter 5

Cwen stirred, fighting her way from the depths of sleep. As her consciousness jockeyed for dominance, the remnants of the dream about her phantom lover occupied her thoughts. Never had the dream been so intense—touch, sensation, and the sight of his face had assailed her. The memory of his strong embrace and their painful mating pushed its way into her waking mind.

Cwen's eyes shot open as she stretched, feeling a burning ache between her thighs. Her hand shook as she brushed hair from her face. Positive she had gone to bed with the mass of black tresses bound, she sat up quickly, a sharp pain stabbing that most tender of places. Gasping, she thought, it's impossible! But the discomfort and her loose hair flowing around her spoke otherwise. As did her nakedness. The linen shift lay crumpled on the floor.

Rising stiffly out of her bed, the red stain upon the linen confirmed her fear. "No!" The man she had coupled with was no phantasm. He had been real! Cwen's mind raced frantically, trying to remember all of the details—the strength of his embrace, the warmth of his scented skin, his deep voice asking for forgiveness as he'd plunged his large manhood within, tearing her maidenhead.

As if to eliminate any further doubts she may harbor, Cwen felt a wetness between her legs—her blood, his seed. She saw the tub of water left from last evening's bath and plunged into it, washing away the evidence of the living nightmare.

Teeth chattering while she dried herself, Cwen fought

for calmness as she noticed the gold bracelets on her wrists and touched the gold collar around her neck. She pulled and tugged, but the jewelry remained in place. Cursing, she dressed quickly in a clean leather tunic and breeches. Looking around the chamber, she was struck with the feeling she was still dreaming, as if she had not stepped through the Doorway into the future. She ran to the shutters and flung them open, feeling a cool morning breeze brush her cheeks. She gazed down at the stone courtyard, then raised her eyes to the distant green grasslands. It was true then.

Who the hell was he? This phantom turned into the living. He had given her his name, swearing to her that he was real. Cwen had to talk with Sevea. She must know who and what Otas was.

Sevea hesitated outside the chamber door. She could feel her daughter's anger and bewilderment. What must Cwen think of her to have let this happen? Sevea would tell her the truth, that it had been the command of the Overlord.

Sevea opened the door and slipped inside, gently closing it. Cwen was at the window, the breeze sending her long, black hair billowing out behind her. Cwen's stance was that of anger. She is truly a Queen, Sevea thought, grimacing as she gazed at the telling stain on the bed linen. Being ignorant, Cwen wouldn't understand what had happened to her body and her mind. Sevea breathed deeply, gathering her courage.

"Cwen?"

"Who is Otas?" Her voice was deceptively soft.

"I'm—"

She whipped around, facing her mother, shouting, "Who is he?"

The psychokinetic blast of anger knocked Sevea to the floor. They had bonded all right, but Otas had given her more than just partial power. Sevea doubted Cwen knew that the

Gift was the force that had knocked her down. She looked into her daughter's eyes. Rage churned in the smoke-green depths. Sevea had to tread lightly. Being untrained, Cwen could unwittingly harm her.

"He's our Overlord." She carefully stood.

"Our what?"

"We don't come from here."

"Not that again! I suppose you're going to tell me I come from another time-frame." Cwen slashed the air with her hand. "I'm tired of half-answers. I want the truth!"

Sevea was prepared for the blast this time, its impact only rocking her on her heels. "I mean we don't come from this planet!" Her own anger was building. "We're not from Earth in any time-frame!"

Confusion replaced rage. "Where do we come from?"

Good. Cwen sounded like a lost child. "From a planet called Liambria, which lies in the galaxy closest to this one."

"A spiral galaxy. We . . . um, Earthlings call it M100."

"Correct." Sevea was impressed by her knowledge.

"Aunt Amma said I was born on Earth."

"True. Your's is the first generation born on Earth, but you are Liambrian."

Cwen paced for a second. "Why did you come here?"

"To escape oppression and possible extinction. Our planet was invaded by a race of beings called Trexrans. They're ruthless scavengers, taking over planets to steal their resources. But the Liambrians became of interest to them because of the Gift."

"Those men in the alley who tried to kidnap me were Trexrans?"

"Yes."

"This explains many things. The advanced technology of the Doorway, the teleportation device Vlad used. But . . . "

"But?" Sevea prompted.

"It doesn't explain what happened to me last night!" The anger was back in Cwen's eyes. "Explain Otas!"

"As I've said he's Overlord of all Liambrians, and your husband."

"My what?"

"You're his Queen."

"This Otas takes my virginity without even introducing himself?" Cwen's fists clenched. "It was more like rape!"

"He had reason to take you as he did."

Cwen was silent.

"Liambrians do more than have sex. It's a bonding of the minds. Otas did what he had to for your protection against the beast."

"I know I'm being hunted, but not *why*."

"Maccus is the beast after you. He wants you as *his* Queen. He's powerful with the Gift. Untrained as you are, you couldn't have protected yourself against him." Sevea sighed. She wondered if Cwen was following her explanation.

"I thought I left this beast in the past."

"Maccus is intelligent. He'll find a way to come into the future." Sevea paused thoughtfully. "Otas gave you a portion of his power when he bonded with you. The jewelry you wear is his mark of ownership."

"He owns me?" Cwen was incredulous, staring at the bracelets on her wrists.

"Mind, body, and heart."

"I don't even know Otas. I feel no love for him."

"Love has little to do with it. You were his from the moment I gave birth to you."

Cwen opened her mouth, then closed it. A red flush rushed up her face, then she ran to the chamber door, jerked it open, and flew out of it.

Sevea chased her down the winding stairs to the great hall. The knights were milling about, but that didn't stop Cwen from barreling through them to the castle door.

Sevea would have followed her, but Lord Ware, her husband, jerked on her arm.

"Who in thunder was that?" he bellowed.

Sevea freed her arm. "My daughter. I must see where she goes."

By the time Sevea reached the courtyard, Cwen was racing across the land astride Samson. She used no bridle or saddle. And she was unarmed. Thank the stars, the bonding hadn't driven her daughter insane. But it had pushed her to blind rage. Sevea bit back her concern. She knew just who to send after Cwen.

Blinded by his rage, Vlad stormed to the Overlord's chambers, fully intending to teleport within. He was about to activate the device when the automatic doors suddenly slid open. The sensors had not been turned off.

Vlad stomped into the suite, finding Otas in the *Chimdae-bang*, bedroom. He was sitting up in his big bed, nude. Before Otas could speak, Vlad slammed his fist into the Overlord's jaw. A lesser male would have been knocked out by the punch.

Otas came to his feet as quick as a pouncing feline. Fire burned in his orange eyes. "Because I call you friend I will give you time to explain."

Vlad knew that Otas could cause him serious injury without even touching him. Showing no fear of the power of the Gift, Vlad raged, "You rutting animal! Why didn't you use Narda to ease your lust?"

Otas crossed his arms over his bare chest.

"Couldn't you wait? I could hear Cwen's screams in my mind. Do you know what it did to me to hear her agony echoing in the night?"

"I not only heard her screams, I felt her pain."

Vlad had trouble finding his voice. "You bonded with her? Without the protection of the Circle of Twelve? You're defenseless while you bond."

"I only partially bonded with her."

"But why? Cwen won't understand. It's too soon." Vlad didn't think he could get any angrier.

Otas reached for his pants lying over the curved back of a chair. "I should have told you this last night," he said as he pulled his pants up. He walked over to the thick window set in the curved wall, shaking his mane of black hair, smoothing it out of his face with his hand. "Maccus will construct a Doorway."

Vlad let loose with a stream of Liambrian curses. "Can you foresee when he'll get here?"

"It will take Maccus time to discover exactly where we are in the future. It could be days or weeks. All I can tell is that it will be soon." He turned his gaze on Vlad. "I had to give Cwen the ability to protect herself."

"The Trexrans raised Maccus. He doesn't fully understand how we bond."

"When he arrives, he'll use the force of his will against her. This is what he believes bonding means."

"You can't know that for certain," Vlad protested.

"I know the workings of my twin's mind."

It always amazed Vlad. No matter the distance of time and space, Otas was always aware of Maccus. Vlad sighed. "How much of your power did you give her?"

The Overlord's face reddened. "For a moment, I lost control. The feel of her . . . never mind. About half."

"Half? Have you lost your mind?"

"I think I have where my Queen is concerned."

"That kind of power from the Gift could be disastrous in the hands of one untrained."

"I've set Sevea and Hebron to the task. It is to be done quickly."

Vlad walked back and forth, thinking furiously. "Before we sent her through the Doorway, Cwen was becoming willful. I predict she won't cooperate with Sevea and Hebron.

We've put Cwen through too many alterations in too short a time."

"What do you suggest?"

"You must go to Cwen. You don't really know her. And...," Vlad hesitated. The Overlord wasn't going to like this.

"And?"

"Apologize."

"Now you are mad," Otas growled.

"Cwen's angry. Can't you feel it?" Vlad watched Otas as he nodded. "Only you can withstand the forces that will be unleashed if Cwen loses control."

Otas raised his brows in understanding. "I can read my Queen's thoughts, but the words are in the tongue of the past. They make no sense." Otas rubbed his chin. "Many emotions rage through her. You are sure it is anger at me I sense?"

"Believe me, Cwen's mad. Do as I've suggested."

Otas nodded. "I will go to her."

"Do it quickly before someone gets killed."

Hair flying behind her, Cwen raced Samson to the end of the meadow, slowing the horse down with a hard tug on his mane. When Samson finally stopped, she slid from his back with a loud groan. Riding the horse had not been the best of ideas. A throbbing pain beat with the rhythm of her heart between her thighs.

A cluster of bolders lay on the edge of the meadow. No way, Cwen thought, settling herself down easily on the soft grass in front of them. She now regretted her complaint to Aunt Amma for a change in her life. Things were now happening so fast her head spun. A husband? And the Overlord of aliens from another planet? The man she had coupled with was a mystery and an enigma. Cwen now remembered the immense power that radiated from his brain, and her scream of terror when she had absorbed its strength.

What the hell was going on? Cwen looked down at the bracelets encircling her wrists. The bands were at least two inches wide set with a large dark green gem in the center. She then remembered the pendent she always wore, reaching to her neck to grasp it. It was gone. When had Otas removed it? she tried to think. The memory was hazy.

Feeling her throat, Cwen found the thick collar around her neck, her fingers rubbing on the gem set there. She was positive these stones were the same as the one in her pendent: green sapphires. If she had a mirror, she knew the smoky-green color of the gems would match her eyes. Besides their beauty, there must be some higher purpose for the stones. But Cwen had no idea what.

Inspecting the bracelets further, she found no catch to release them from her wrists. Indeed, there wasn't even a seam in the metal, as if the ends of the bracelets had been liquified with the flame of a blow torch, yet the heat required to fuse the bracelets would have burned off her hands. She'd felt no heat. How had Otas done it? A shudder passed through her. This was truly magic.

If she wasn't educated, she would think this was black magic. Although she had sensed the unidentifiable power in Otas while their minds and bodies were joined, she'd felt no traces of evil.

Cwen looked up when Samson whinnied. One of Sevea's warriors was riding toward her. She stood up as the woman dismounted and approached her, carrying a sack.

"Sevea sent me to fetch you," the woman said as she reached her.

Cwen recognized her as one of the warrior women in the forest, but there was something more familiar about her. The woman was as tall as she, her braided hair a pale shade of blonde, and her brown eyes held a twinkle of devilment in them. An old memory rushed to the surface of her mind. Could this possibly be her childhood playmate that had vanished when Cwen was seven-years-old? "Sashna?"

"Aye." She smiled. "It took you long enough."

"Sashna!" Cwen ran to her, hugging her tight as if she were a life raft to buoy her in this nightmare sea she had fallen into. "I thought you dead."

"'Twas a rotten trick my parents pulled on the both of us. Forcing me through the Doorway." Sashna stepped back, assessing Cwen. "You've grown quite beautiful."

"And you." She seized on the mention of the Doorway. "Why were you brought here so soon?"

"I was prepared for your arrival."

"You know I'm Sevea's daughter?"

"Aye. We all do. I'm to watch your back."

Cwen frowned. "What do you mean?"

"You're to lead us. Your mother didn't tell you this?"

"No." Confused, Cwen asked, "Lead you to where?"

"We'll be told with the time comes."

Damn, more mysteries. "Do you know of Liambria?"

"Aye. Everyone does. 'Tis a mythical land in the North where the people are faerie."

She doesn't know the truth, Cwen thought. She wasn't going to enlighten her. "I should go back."

"Aye." Sashna held up the sack. "I've brought apples. Your mother said you might be hungry."

"I'll wait until the noonday meal." Cwen gingerly mounted Samson.

Sitting astride, Sashna said, "Do you want to race?"

Cwen shook her head.

Sashna shrugged, kicking her horse's flanks. Cwen gritted her teeth on the long trot back to the castle.

Sevea met them in the courtyard, grabbing Cwen's arm after she'd dismounted. "The baron is furious at your rudeness.

He wishes to speak with you at the noonday meal." Sevea
dragged her to the south tower of the castle. "We'll sneak in
through the kitchen tower."

After many twists and turns and climbing several flights
of stairs, they reached Cwen's chamber.

"Here. Change quickly. The baron doesn't allow females
to come to the table in battle gear." Dressed in a yellow kirtle,
bronzed hair flowing freely down her back, Sevea shoved a
dark-green gown into her hands.

"Why not?"

"It's an insult to the knights. It gives them the impression
that we don't trust them to protect us."

"That's absurd," Cwen said, slipping out of her clothes.
She went to the basin and poured water from the pitcher into
it, washing away the smell of horse and sweat.

"My warriors think so, too, preferring to take their meals
in the north tower." Sevea rushed on. "When you meet the
baron, you must apologize and do it quickly. Don't give him a
chance to yell at you." Sevea helped Cwen into the gown,
settling it around her body. She fastened a thick chain around
her hips, attaching a small dagger for dining.

After brushing out Cwen's hair, Sevea dabbed rose-
scented oil on her neck. "Remember. Be polite. Come, we
must hurry."

Cwen followed her mother into the great hall. The knights
were all seated, displaying the same diversity of skin tones
as the women warriors. And they all wore their hair long in
the Saxon fashion, not sheared as the Normans of old. A thick-
chested man with blond hair, forest-green eyes, and a square-
shaped face sat in a chair behind the table on the dias. He
scowled at her as she approached, making her heart thud in
her chest.

When they reached him, Sevea curtsied. "My lord, my
daughter, Cwen."

Cwen immediately imitated her mother, but she was sure

the gesture wasn't as graceful. "I beg your forgiveness, my lord. My behavior was rude."

Lord Ware set down his goblet of ale. "What made you flee the castle?"

"'Twas anger, my lord."

"With whom were you angry?"

"My husband."

Lord Ware just glared down at her, waiting to hear more. Cwen searched her brain for the storyline from one of the romance novels she'd read. "I was angry because he sent me to my mother while he does his forty days of service to his league, my lord."

"Who has he sworn fealty to?" Lord Ware inquired.

Cwen glanced at Sevea for help.

"Baron Kenrick, my lord," Sevea quickly answered.

Lord Ware grunted. "I've no liking for the man. But your husband must do his duty. Come. Share a trencher with me."

Shit! Cwen thought as she climbed the dias, sitting down gently. Sevea sat on her right. Riding Samson had made the pain down below worse, and the hardness of the chair didn't help.

"Is there something wrong with your seat?" Lord Ware asked.

"No, my lord."

"Then why can you not sit still?"

Cwen's face flamed. "I . . . I had a tumble from my horse," she lied. A tumble in the hay was more like it, she thought.

Lord Ware laughed, a deep raspy sound. "Now you will learn to use a bridle and saddle."

"You saw me?"

"The stable master told me. It amazes me. You're the only one who can ride that devil of a horse."

"You honor me, my lord."

The baron actually smiled, improving on his not exactly handsome face.

A page set a bread trencher in front of them, filled with steaming venison in gravy and potatoes. Cwen gazed down at the meal she was to share with the baron. All she could think about was catching germs from him.

Another servant began to pour wine into her goblet. She placed her hand over it.

"You don't like wine?" the baron asked.

"I've no head for spirits."

The baron glanced at Sevea. "Neither does your mother. Bring water for the ladies, boy." He speared a piece of meat, popping it into his mouth.

Cwen did the same, trying not to think about bacteria.

"What is your husband called?" he asked.

"O—" Sevea kicked her under the table. "Uh, Vlad." She didn't know any other men except Professor Pimbleton and she didn't know his first name.

"'Tis a strange name. Where is he from?" He was looking directly at her so she couldn't turn to her mother for help.

Cwen scrambled through her brain, searching for her favorite authors and titles of their books. She settled on Catherine Coulter's *ROSEHAVEN*. "Rosehaven."

"I've not heard of the place."

Cwen decided the less she said the better and began shoveling food into her mouth. If she didn't think about sharing germs with a stranger, the meal was quite good.

When she was finished, she felt Lord Ware's eyes on her.

"You don't talk much, Cwen."

"I'm just weary, my lord. May I go seek my rest?"

Lord Ware nodded.

Thanking God, Cwen hurried from the hall and raced to her chambers. Sevea followed her shortly.

"Did I make any faux pas?" Cwen asked nervously.

Sevea chuckled. "You did fine."

"Lord Ware isn't what I expected."

"What do you mean?"

"Aunt Amma said I take after my father. I don't look anything like him," Cwen said.

"Lord Ware isn't your father."

# Chapter 6

Cwen sat down heavily on the bed, thinking she couldn't take anymore surprises. She focused her eyes on the floor, refusing to look at Sevea. In less than twenty-four hours her life had been turned topsy-turvy. She'd been told she was from the future, shoved through the Doorway against her will, forced to kill three men in the woods, brought to Castle Acwellen, raped by the Overlord of an alien race, then told that was okay for he was her husband, and she was an alien, too. Now Cwen was told the Lord of the castle was not her father. If Lord Ware was not her paternal parent, who the hell was? She didn't have the nerve to ask.

It all suddenly became too much to bear. Cwen dropped her head in her hands and began to cry with loud tortured sobs. She now yearned to be back in isolation with Aunt Amma, Vlad, and the four cats as her only company.

Sevea sat down beside her, placing an arm across her shoulders. "Don't carry on so, my child."

"I'm not your child!" Cwen had intended to sound vehement, but with the tears in her voice she sounded pathetic.

"You can't deny me. I'm your mother."

"Well, quit calling me a child. I'm a grown woman." She was beginning to get angry, the tears stopping abruptly. Cwen wiped the moisture from her cheeks.

"I apologize. I won't refer to you as a child any longer." Sevea removed her arm from Cwen's shoulders and let go with a loud breath. "We've asked too much of you. You've been bombarded with information we haven't given you time to assimilate. Plus you must be fatigued from your time travel. I owe you explanations and I will give them."

Cwen gazed at Sevea, seeing the glitter of tears in her golden eyes. There was so much she needed to know. Where to start was the problem. Making up her mind, she asked, "If Lord Ware isn't my father, who is?"

"A strong and brilliant Liambrian male. My husband."

"You have two husbands?"

Sevea laughed. "In a sense, yes."

"I think you better start at the beginning."

"When the Liambrians escaped from the Trexrans, I was carrying you. During the flight to Earth, my husband feared for my health and the safety of his child, but we had no choice but to flee the tyranny of the Trexrans."

"Was it the Overlord who ordered the evacuation?" Cwen asked.

"Yes. Several other females were carrying children as well, but he felt the preservation of the race was of primary importance. Which it was."

"Otas has no heart." Cwen thought a moment. "But he carries his age well. I wouldn't have thought he was that old."

Sevea laughed again, deep, musical chuckles that doubled her over. When she regained her breath, she said, "Otas was not Overlord then. He was but six Earth years old. It was his father, Raynar, who was Overlord."

"Oh."

Sevea turned serious, continuing her story. "I gave birth to you one week after we landed. You were born in November of 1980. You were strong and healthy. Raynar was ecstatic because he knew I was carrying a Queen. Your birth ensured that the Liambrians would continue. It was then that you were, um, betrothed to Otas."

Cwen ignored that bit of information. "Then it was Raynar who forced you to abandon me and leave me with Aunt Amma."

"Yes. In past generations Liambrians had no courage. We were cowards. It was Raynar's grandfather who foresaw the eventual takeover of Liambria. It was Raynar's father's generation that inherited the genetic trait of aggression. The males were taught how to fight. The females weren't because they hadn't evolved sufficiently to overcome their fear of battle. My generation was fit for training.

"My Liambrian sisters and I were trained by males for combat, just as you were by Vlad. My combat skills were good enough to catch Raynar's attention, and I was placed in charge of all the females who showed promise as great warriors."

"So far I'm following you," Cwen commented. "But that doesn't explain how you wound up in the future."

"I was getting to that." The memories forced Sevea to stand and pace. "Raynar knew that the Trexrans would eventually find us, so he sent ships to different time-frames. The past. The future."

"So that's how Aunt Amma knew about the Earth's upheaval in 2010."

Sevea nodded. "The scouts eventually discovered this place, which is simply called England now, not New England, by the way."

"What about the real Great Britain?"

"That entire land mass sank into the sea."

Cwen shook her head, thinking of the millions that had died.

The divergence in the conversation did not cause Sevea to lose her place in the storytelling. "There's a difference between learning combat in practice and going into actual battle when lives are at stake. Raynar chose this time-frame over the original Middle Ages because back then women were docile, always needing to be rescued.

"Here, the baronies are always at war with one another, seeking to gain land and power. Raynar chose Castle Acwellen because nineteen years ago Lord Ware's lands were invaded by marauders. He and his knights were away, giving aid to one of his fellow barons. The women warriors weren't as skilled as they should have been, so the castle was taken, and the women raped and slaughtered, including his wife. Only Luned and Edris escaped harm because they were in the woods picking mushrooms.

"When the baron returned, he and his knights rousted the marauders and regained control of his castle. The victory was bittersweet for he had lost his beloved wife, and Castle Acwellen was without women warriors to defend it."

Cwen was enthralled. This was better than reading a novel. "So Raynar sent you here."

"Yes. I was sent through the Doorway with three hundred female warriors. My mission was to separate the weak from the strong. I struck a bargain with Lord Ware. I told him we were from New Devonshire and without a home. I promised to defend his castle in his absence and act as his wife in name only. It took a while, but he agreed to this, as he had two sons and he wasn't in need of an heir."

"Where are his sons now?" Cwen wanted to know.

"They're on a mission to find allies for Lord Ware."

Cwen couldn't keep the anticipation out of her voice. "So what happened with the three hundred warriors?"

"Many failed the test. Some were wounded, others killed. Those that showed cowardice but survived were sent back to 2000 in disgrace." Sevea's voice was hard.

"How many are left?"

"One hundred. The warriors that came to the forest with me to fetch you are the daughters of these first warriors. Liambrians all." Having gotten the story out, Sevea sat down again on the bed.

"How old was I when you left?"

"One month." There was sadness in Sevea's eyes. "You can see why I couldn't take you with me."

Cwen nodded. Then a thought struck her. "What happened to Raynar? Why is Otas now Overlord?"

"Raynar's a broken male. You see, his Queen committed suicide on Liambria after giving birth to Otas. Once Raynar's plans for our future were in motion, he stepped down from Overlord when Otas turned twenty, giving him power over us."

Cwen thought about the aggressive way Otas had taken her virginity. "Is Otas as ruthless as Raynar?"

"I'll tell you only this. Otas is even more powerful than Raynar. Not one of us dare go against him."

God, what kind of man was her husband? Cwen thought. She shivered as she remembered the power emanating from him. She thought to ask more questions.

"Enough," Sevea said. Her daughter would push herself until she keeled over with exhaustion. "You've gone through much these last days. I can feel your tiredness."

"I do feel like I have a bad case of jet lag."

Sevea stroked her hair. "Lie down and rest. I'll wake you for the evening meal." Sevea stood and left the chamber.

Cwen did as bid and stretched out on the bed. She wanted to think about what she had learned today. She still had questions, but her tired body and brain refused to let her organize her thoughts. Cwen closed her eyes. In seconds, she fell asleep.

After the evening meal, Cwen climbed the stairs to her chambers, admiring and feeling the weight of the dagger Sevea had given her. As promised, her mother had gone to the farrier's and picked the best he had to offer. There were scrolled markings on the hilt of the dagger. Cwen was sure it would be accurate if thrown.

She opened the chamber door, felt the warmth of the room, and stepped inside. Luned had started a fire in the hearth and lit the three candles on the beside table. Cwen set the dagger down on the table and pulled the purple kirtle from her body, wearing only the chemise underneath. She picked up the brush, intending to smooth the tangles from her unbound hair so that she could braid it for bed. A soft breeze stirred the air around her, shifting her tresses in its wake. Cwen looked to the window. The shutters were closed. Before she could wonder where the strange wind had come from, she felt that strong palpable presence. She gripped the dagger before turning.

There in front of the hearth stood Otas. He must have teleported from . . . well, wherever to her room. The sight of him sent fear skittering up her spine. How had she not noticed it before? He towered over her, making her feel small and vulnerable. Otas was wearing a black tunic and breeches, his black boots calf-length. Cwen's mouth went dry when she looked at his eyes. They appeared phosphorescent in the dim room, twin circles of vibrant orange.

The tender place between her legs began to throb. If he had come for a repeat of last night's performance, she would refuse. It was not to be borne! Without thinking, Cwen flung the dagger at him, aimed at his throat. Time seemed to stop as the knife turned end over end, racing toward its target. Just as the dagger was mere inches from his neck, its flight was halted. Cwen stifled a scream for the dagger just hovered there in the air, not moving. Otas calmly plucked the knife from the air, setting it on the mantle behind him. Was this just a small taste of his power?

Otas turned back to her. "You are angry, I see."

His words were laced with a heavy Liambrian accent. If she couldn't hurt him with weapons, she could nail him with words. "You're damn right I'm angry! You come in here and rape me without even a 'how do you do,' like I'm some sort of brood mare! You ripped my insides apart! I'm still in pain, you barbarian!"

Otas was shaking his head, his black mane of hair swaying

with the motion. "I do not speak your form of English. The only words I understood were 'rape' and 'pain.'"

Cwen snarled. Her raging speech had had little impact on him. "What you did to me last eve 'twas rape! I gave you no consent!"

"I am Overlord, and you are my Queen! I have no need for consent. I will take you as I wish!"

Anger overrode prudence. Cwen flung herself at him with every intention of scratching his eyes out. Before she could reach him, some unseen force pushed her back, flinging her on the bed. Otas hadn't even moved. What had thrown her back?

Regardless, Cwen rose up and tried to do him physical harm. Back she flew on the bed. Now invisible hands held her down. Good God, Otas was doing this with the power of his mind!

With the gems in his jewelry glowing bright green, he walked to the bed, staring down at her. "Yield!"

Cwen shook her head. The pressure on her body increased, making it hard to breathe.

"Yield!" he said again.

Cwen could no longer take the force of his will. Now she was scared. Reluctantly, she nodded, but the pressure remained.

"Speak it!" Otas commanded.

"I . . . I yield!" The pressure was immediately lifted, and the gems in his jewelry dimmed.

Cwen raised herself on her elbows, not daring to move more than that. She stared up at Otas, amazed he didn't look angry. Indeed, his expression was soft as he stared back at her. If this was what he was like when his mood was mild, what happened when he was angry? She sure didn't want to find out.

"I came to beg forgiveness for the pain I inflicted upon

you." Otas slipped out of his tunic. "But now that I see you and smell your scent, I must touch you."

Cwen stared at his muscled chest, wide-eyed. Psychokinesis aside, any sane woman would be frightened of him because of his size alone. Suddenly there was a loud ripping sound as her chemise was torn from her body by the power of his thoughts. Cwen gasped, trying to hide herself with her hands.

Otas was out of his boots and breeches now, his erect manhood sent fright sizzling to her brain. The jewelry he wore matched hers, but did not cause him to look the least bit effeminate. Cwen contemplated running but knew the attempt would be futile. "M—my lord, you must not! I won't be able to endure the pain!"

Otas didn't answer her. He lay down, easing himself beside her.

Terrified, Cwen tried to scramble away from him, but he pulled her back against his warm body. "Do not fear. I will do you no harm."

Cwen said nothing, thinking, like hell he won't. The throbbing ache from their last encounter was still with her.

"I had reason for taking you as I did." Otas frowned. "There are no words in this tongue to explain it."

"My mother explained."

"And you understand 'twas necessary?"

"Well, sort of."

Otas looked confused.

"I mean, you, uh, joined with me to protect me from Maccus."

"'Tis well you understand." He smiled, showing off gleaming white teeth. His eyes slowly ran down the length of her nakedness. "You are beautiful."

Cwen's face turned flaming red.

As if he sensed her embarrassment, Otas stroked her face. "I gave you no pleasure last eve. Now 'twill be different."

Surprising her, he placed his palm on her mound of dark curls, closing his eyes.

Cwen felt a tingling warmth radiating from his hand. The throbbing pain in her tender folds of womanhood eased, then disappeared altogether. Otas possessed the healing touch like Aunt Amma did. Cwen couldn't help sighing.

At the sound, Otas opened his eyes, staring at her. "The pain is gone?"

Cwen nodded with wonderment in her dark-green eyes. She didn't want to like him, but his compassion for her misery made it so.

Otas traced her features with his thumb. "I held you after your birth. I thought you pretty then. Now that I see you grown, I . . . " His words trailed off when his breath quickened.

Cwen didn't need words to know what was on his mind. She could feel his steel rod pressed against her thigh, growing in heat and length. His strange orange eyes seemed to dim then flare with an internal fire.

Swiftly, Otas covered her mouth in a hot kiss, forcing her mouth open to meet his warm tongue in a tangle of passion. For some time he kissed her so, causing a sizzling bolt of pleasure to surge through her from her woman's core to her head. Cwen moaned with the strength of it.

Otas raised his head, gazing at her lips, puffy and moist from his kisses. "'Tis good. You respond to me." He gave her no time to comment, placing a large hand on her full breast, kneading it, running his thumb over the coral nipple, which immediately hardened, eliciting a grunt of satisfaction from him. Otas bent his head, covering the hard bud with his mouth, suckling her with powerful pulls on her breast. Hazily, Cwen thought it should have hurt, but the pleasurable sensations running through her increased in intensity. Her moans became a litany of desire.

Taking heed of the sounds she was making, Otas sucked harder at her breast, gently nudging her thighs apart with his hand. When Cwen complied, he slid a long, strong finger inside her.

Cwen tensed at the invasion. "No pain," Otas said in a deep whisper. Watching her face, he rapidly moved his finger in and out of her. When the stiffness left her body, she instinctively opened her legs wider, head thrashing from side to side. With his other hand, he searched her petal-soft folds until he found that tiny piece of flesh that was pleasure's center. Gently, he rubbed that nub while continuing the play with his fingers.

"P—please," Cwen begged. What for, she didn't know. She was mindless now, her body in control, her hips shifting from side to side, imploring him for that ultimate penetration.

Finding her hot, moist, and ready, Otas moved himself between her spread thighs, coaxing her to bend her knees. He positioned his shaft just at the opening of her core. Cwen felt him there, shutting her eyes tight, anticipating pain.

"Look at me!" Otas commanded. She couldn't deny him, looking up into his eyes. "You must know it is I who takes you."

With that, he pushed himself full-length inside her, causing her to cry out. Her insides were stretching to accommodate his size. There was a slight pulling sensation that was quickly overridden by intense pleasure. Slowly, he began to slide in and out of her. Each plunge into her depths increased the tension building within her belly. Cwen raised her hips to meet each of his thrusts, pleasuring both of them.

His motions speeded up, his shaft diving deeper and deeper as he lifted her hips to receive his hard strokes. His breathing was labored as was hers. Just when Cwen thought she couldn't take anymore, the pleasurable tension building inside her exploded into intense bliss, sending prisms of light flashing behind her lids, forcing her to cry out his name and dig her nails in his back as she fell through a bottomless vortex.

Distantly, she heard his own shout of pleasure as his body

shuddered with the strength of his release, his seed shooting into her with hot bursts. Then, Otas collapsed on her. They both lay in a stupor, bodies glistening with the sweat of their loving.

When he could breathe steadily, Otas raised his weight off of her onto his elbows, keeping their bodies locked.

"I didn't know it would be like this between us," Cwen whispered, gazing into his eyes, which had lost their flame.

"Nor I."

"We didn't . . . bond this time?"

"Nay. We mated." Otas' look turned serious. "I gave you more *Kang-Yak*, power, than I should. You must be trained in the use of it. You do not understand the danger."

Cwen had a pretty good idea after being thrown around by the power of his mind. "Who is to teach me?"

"I've set the task to Sevea and Hebron." Otas kissed her forehead. "You must obey them in all things."

"I'll only do so on one condition."

Otas looked confused again, not understanding the syntax of 21st century English.

Cwen tried again. "I must strike a bargain with you."

Otas stared at her some seconds, then nodded.

"I have questions. They must be answered. Then I will obey."

"'Tis fair. We have asked much of you." Otas freed himself from her body and stood, picking up his clothes. He was motionless as he stared down at Cwen, her glorious black hair flowing around her. She probably didn't realize her legs were still spread, he thought, giving him a good view of where he'd just been. "You please me, my Queen."

Cwen didn't know how to respond to that. Instead she blurted, "Must you leave?"

"There is much to be done."

"Godspeed." Cwen suddenly felt an emptiness, trying to delay him further. "Where do you go?"

"Liambria." With that, he popped out of view with a slight stirring of the air where he'd been.

Liambria? she thought. Then Cwen was suddenly hit with a realization. He had not been wearing one of the devices Vlad had used on his arm. Indeed, he'd been completely naked. Did Otas possess the power of teleportation with his mind alone?

# Chapter 7

$S$evea climbed the winding stairs, carrying a tray laden with bread, salted pork, cheese, and tea. Cwen must have been really exhausted, she thought. It was past midmorning and her daughter had yet to emerge from her chambers. Balancing the tray on one arm, Sevea knocked lightly on the door. No answer.

With a mother's concern driving her, Sevea eased the door open quietly and went inside. At the sight of Cwen, she almost dropped the tray. Tangled in the bed covers, most of her daughter's naked body was exposed and her hair was draped over her face. Having been in a similar position in the past herself, Sevea knew the aftermath of a night of passion when she saw it.

Sevea closed the door with her foot then set the tray on the table in the corner. She went to the bed and surveyed Cwen, who slept like the dead. Spotting a bit of white linen on the floor, Sevea picked it up, gasping as she recognized the garment as a shredded chemise. It was clear the underclothing had been ripped from Cwen's body. Dark visions of what must have occurred last eve shot through her mind, bringing with it an uncontrollable rage.

"Cwen!"

Her daughter stirred minutely, sighed, then snuggled deeper into the feather mattress. Using the power of the Gift, Sevea shouted, "Cwen!" Blasting her daughter's mind as well as her ears.

Cwen shot out of bed, freeing her sword with one swift

move, and prepared to do battle with whatever danger threatened her.

If her fear and anger hadn't been so great, Sevea would have admired Cwen's warrior instincts. Both hands held the sword hilt with readiness to strike, her green eyes were wide and alert searching for the enemy, her legs spread apart for balance, and her hair flowing wild about her falling to her hips.

"Did Otas rape you?" Sevea shouted.

Oblivious to her nudity, Cwen's eyes shot to her mother. "There's no danger?"

"There is if what I suspect is true!"

Cwen became aware that she stood before her mother in naked glory. She lowered the sword, holding it casually in her right hand. "It wasn't rape."

Sevea held up the torn chemise. "Explain this then."

Cwen looked at her mother unable to explain what she didn't understand herself.

"Otas ripped this from you, didn't he?"

Cwen's cheeks heated. "Not with his hands."

Sevea gasped, holding her hand over her heart. Had the Overlord abused his powers of the Gift and forced Cwen to mate with him? Overlord, or no, Sevea was enraged. The first bonding had been of necessity, but this was not to be tolerated. "I don't care if he used his hands or his mind. Answer me!"

"He tore it from me without using his hands," Cwen admitted. "But that was after I attacked him."

"You attacked Otas?" Sevea was astonished even though she had been contemplating doing that very thing herself. She had not realized her daughter was so bold. "I think you better explain."

Cwen sighed, sliding her sword back into the scabbard. Her mother wasn't going to let this go. "I was angry that he had taken me that first time without my consent. So I . . . threw my dagger at him."

Sevea was speechless for a moment.

"The dagger you gave me has good balance," Cwen stated matter-of-factly.

Sevea's knees weakened, forcing her to sit down on the bed. Cwen didn't realize how much danger she would have been in if the Overlord had lost his temper. He'd obviously controlled his raw power, for her daughter stood before her whole and alive. "What did the Overlord do?"

Cwen hesitated, searching her mind for the right words to describe what her husband had done. "He used psychokinetic power to stop the knife, then tossed me on the bed with that same power and subdued me until I yielded to him." There! She hoped that that was enough. Cwen couldn't talk to her mother about the intimacies of their mating.

"And then?"

Cwen couldn't help slipping into 21st century euphemisms. "He took one look at me and got turned on. That's when he stripped me. And then we . . . made love."

"You didn't refuse him?"

Cwen cocked a brow. "He told me as his Queen I couldn't refuse."

"So you just submitted to him?"

"Not exactly."

Sevea tilted her head in question.

"After he begged for my forgiveness and healed my sore, uh, place, I couldn't resist him." She blushed from her neck to the top of her head.

Sevea was astounded again. "Otas showed compassion?"

Cwen nodded.

Sevea began to laugh, understanding who was responsible for this compassion. It had to be her nephew, Vlad/Arax. As the Overlord's second in command and friend, he was the only one who would dare tell Otas he had been wrong. Vlad had protected Cwen since she was a child, which made his mind attuned to hers. He must have heard Cwen's screams in the night just as she had.

"Why do you laugh?"

Controlling herself, Sevea answered, "It's too complicated to explain."

Suddenly, Cwen became embarrassed by her undressed state and went to the chest, pulling out a kirtle and chemise and quickly putting them on.

"So he pleasured you this time," Sevea said knowingly.

Cwen remained silent, picking up the brush on the table and pulling it through her tangled locks.

Sevea regarded her, noticing that Cwen's hands shook as she worked her hair. Sevea rose and went to her daughter, turning Cwen to face her. Cwen's mind and eyes held the burden of worry. "What troubles you?"

"Does the Overlord wish children?"

"Of course. It's your duty as his Queen."

"It's impossible." Cwen went to the window and opened the shutters, staring out across the fields. "I'm barren."

Vlad stood to the side in the Overlord's chamber, watching Otas gaze out the window with his back to him. As usual when he was in his chambers, Otas was shirtless, his black ponytail resting against his back. Judging by the marks left on his shoulder blades, Cwen had forgiven him. Vlad supposed it was male pride that prevented Otas from using his self-healing power to eliminate the scratches.

The doors slid apart to allow Hebron entrance. As always, Otas remained as he was, his back facing someone he'd summoned. It was a method of intimidation Vlad knew, for none could break through the barriers of the Overlord's mind and read his thoughts.

Hebron stood at attention, waiting for the Overlord to address him. Hebron looked fatigued, shadows underlining his green eyes, his black hair a bit mussed even though the length of it was secured with a leather strip.

"Report on the installation of the Inter-Dimensional Leap unit," Otas ordered.

"The installation is complete. All testing proved successful. Raynar will launch at sunrise to begin the search for a habitable planet." Hebron's words were stiff.

"Excellent. I've another task to assign you." Otas then turned to face Hebron. "There are only five of us who know I have bonded with my Queen, you among them."

"Yes, Master."

"My Queen is untrained in the use of the *Kang-Yak*, power, I have given her. I'm sending you to Castle Acwellen to aid Sevea in her training."

"Yes, Master," Hebron responded.

"My Queen has many questions. You must answer them all if you are to gain her cooperation. Sevea expects you tomorrow evening."

"Understood." Hebron hesitated. "Does she know who I am?"

Otas shook his head. "I left that honor to you."

Hebron nodded his head. "I thank you, Master."

"Dismissed."

Hebron left, looking a bit less tired than when he'd entered.

Vlad looked over to Otas, who was shaking his head in puzzlement. "Is there something wrong?"

"I sensed much anger in him. I don't understand why."

Vlad rolled his eyes. For someone as controlled and intelligent as Otas was, he could be completely obtuse at times. "It's the scratches on your back."

"What?"

"The marks Cwen left on you while you were, um, joining." Vlad shook his head. "You shouldn't have let Hebron see them."

"Why should my mating with my Queen anger him? It is my right."

"True." Vlad slapped him on the shoulder. "You don't understand because you've never been a father."

Sevea stood still and watched Cwen, stunned speechless by what her daughter had just said. Cwen was barren? Filled with a great foreboding, Sevea slowly sat on the bed. What her daughter had revealed boded ill for the Liambrians. The continuance of the race was at risk. A barren Queen meant extinction. "How do you know you're barren?"

Cwen turned from the window, her hand rubbing her abdomen in an unconscious gesture. "I've never bled."

It took Sevea a minute to understand. Shaking her head, she said, "That doesn't mean you're barren."

"You forget I've studied anatomy, biology, and physiology!" Cwen couldn't keep her voice from rising. "An absence of menses means no ovulation, which equates to no babies!"

Sevea was so relieved she fought to keep her face expressionless when she felt like laughing. "You've only studied the physiology of Earthlings."

"So?"

"So you don't know anything about Liambrian reproduction."

"Liambrians are humanoid, aren't we?"

"Yes. But we're not homo sapiens." Sevea could not hold back the smile any longer. "Liambrian females don't begin to ovulate until they reach twenty."

"We don't?" Cwen's face was a portrait of confusion. "What you're saying is that in a little over one month I'll start my menses."

God, help me, Sevea thought. It was time for lesson number one. "There's no blood after ovulation. If conception doesn't occur, then the uterine lining is reabsorbed."

Cwen let out a stream of curses. "Damn, Aunt Amma! All

of these years I thought something was wrong with me. I begged her to take me to a physician." Cwen stomped around in a circle. "Amma knew of my torment. Why did she let me suffer?"

"An Earthling physician would have discovered that you have two wombs. This anomaly isn't unusual in Earth females, but when such an oddity is discovered a variety of tests are performed. Anatomically, you're designed differently than Earth females. You would have been marked as a freak of nature bringing knowledge of your existence to the medical and scientific fields."

Cwen looked at her mother with a clarity of understanding. "They would have found out I was an alien."

"Correct. And what would the Earthlings have done?"

Cwen thought about that. "Earthlings have a bizarre habit of dissecting anything they don't understand." She shuddered at the thought.

"Exactly."

"How will I know if I've ovulated?"

"Your hormones will rage inside you, making you . . . somewhat disagreeable." Sevea only told her half of the truth.

"What you describe sounds a lot like PMS."

"That's as good a name for it as any." Sevea hoped Cwen would ask no more questions for they were treading on dangerous ground. Her daughter wasn't ready to hear that it was her anatomy that made her the Queen. That through genetics Cwen was destined to lead a complicated and often dangerous life. Sevea didn't want her daughter to hate her for giving birth to her. Hesitantly, she said, "Did I explain it well enough?"

"Yes. Now I understand some of Amma's motives for keeping me isolated." Cwen flushed suddenly. "I do have a question about Liambrian sex."

Guarded, Sevea said, "Ask."

"After Otas showed up that first night, you told me that Liambrians bonded when they had sex." It was a struggle to get the question out. "Last night, Otas and I just . . . uh, did it. Weren't we supposed to do some of this bonding stuff?" Sevea sighed to herself. "Liambrians don't always bond during mating. Sometimes, we're just driven by our passions, lust, if you will."

Cwen thought about that, then blurted, "Am I really Otas' wife? I mean, he's not just using me?"

Sevea gasped at the question. "It would be sacrilege for any Liambrian male to bond with a female and not claim her as his wife. The bonding is our form of marriage and it's for life. There isn't even a word for divorce in Liambrian."

Cwen looked dubious.

"The Overlord was there at your birth. He was present to lay claim to his Queen. Otas was only six, but he was capable of touching your mind and imprinting his essence on your subconscious. This was done so that when the time came to bond, you would know him."

Cwen thought about the scent of earth, grass, and male that had always accompanied her dreams about the phantom lover. "I recognized him."

"You no longer doubt me that Otas is your husband?"

Cwen shook her head and went to the tray on the table, snatching a piece of cheese and munching on it. When she was done, she said, "Otas and I made a bargain."

Sevea raised a quizzical brow.

"You and this Hebron must answer all of my questions before I cooperate and submit to the Gift Training."

Sevea spewed out curses in Liambrian. Had the Overlord lost his mind? She and Hebron couldn't possibly tell Cwen everything. She would run for the hills screaming like a maniac all the way if she were given full knowledge.

Cwen observed Sevea. Obviously her mother didn't like this bargain, but Cwen didn't care. She'd been pushed this way and that, blindly following orders. Well, no more! "Who's Hebron?"

Rage brought Sevea to her feet, staring at her daughter with sparks of anger in her eyes. "I'm forbidden to tell you."

"Not good enough."

Sevea stalked over to Cwen. Before she could stop herself, she slapped Cwen hard. "How dare you get insolent with me!"

Cwen looked at her mother with shock, holding her cheek. Aunt Amma had never hit her. Sevea looked as if she would kill her. Cwen suddenly had no desire to lock horns with her mother. "I apologize."

"Don't ever speak to me in that manner again!" Sevea was shaking inside with fear, but refused to let her daughter see it. She had been right to seek the aid of Hebron for the Training. For what Cwen did not know was that she had the ability to strike her mother dead with the power that Otas had given her.

# Chapter 8

Vlad watched the confusion shift across Otas' face, remembering how the Overlord had been raised. Raynar had concentrated all of his efforts on training his son to be the perfect Overlord withholding his fatherly affection, which had produced the emotionless male that was Otas.

Vlad had earned the position of second in command because of genetics. His role as Otas' friend and confidante through his compassion for the miserable and lonely child Otas had been.

When they were children, Vlad would often find the younger male curled into a tight ball, hiding in one of the crawlways of the engine room of the starship, tears streaming down his cheeks. Otas had hidden when he cried, for Raynar had forbidden him to do so, telling him it showed weakness and that vulnerability was a thing an Overlord dare not show.

The first time Vlad had come upon him in his hiding place Otas had proclaimed that his father didn't love him. After much time, Vlad finally convinced him that the duties and responsibilities of being the Overlord had made Raynar so cold. It was a lie, of course, but it worked. That was when the strong bond between them had been formed. From then on, Otas would seek out Vlad when his emotions got the better of him.

No one understood Otas as Vlad did. His friend had been raised in much the same manner as Cwen, isolated from the world. As the Liambrians were docked on an alien planet,

Otas was never allowed to mingle with Earthlings. Most of his life was spent on board the starship. All of the combat training, instructions for use of the Gift, and preparation for being Overlord had taken place there. Hence, the reason Otas didn't speak 21st century English.

After the Mind-Touch ceremony at the time of Cwen's birth, Otas and Vlad had been whisked to the future to Liambria 2, where they remained close companions until Vlad reached manhood. Vlad had been eighteen when he was sent back through the Doorway to train and protect Cwen. But he didn't object to the separation from Otas. Indeed, it had been an honor to protect his friend's Queen.

Vlad's thoughts returned to the present as he continued to watch Otas. Nothing had changed between them. Twelve Earth years separation had had no effect on their bond of friendship.

Finally, Otas' expression changed from confusion to decision. "I've thought it through. I still see no reason for Hebron's anger over my coupling with my Queen."

"You forget, even though he made trips into the past, Hebron hasn't seen his daughter since her birth. Cwen's now a grown female married to his Overlord. She doesn't even know who he is. The emotion behind his anger is a father's jealousy," Vlad explained.

Otas walked over to the couch, which resembled a black, wood-framed futon in design, and sat down. "He has known all along that Cwen and I would bond. His feelings are illogical."

"Maybe. But they're there just the same." Vlad joined him on the futon, changing the subject. "So Cwen has forgiven you?"

"She didn't say the words, but by the way she responded to my touch, I'd say she has."

"And language wasn't a problem?"

"It was initially." Otas smiled in remembrance. "At the

first sight of me, her rage was great. She threw her dagger at me."

Vlad couldn't help laughing. Cwen had the habit of trying to do a person physical harm when she was angry. "And you used the Gift to subdue her."

"Yes. But that didn't stop her mouth. My Queen spit words at me that made no sense. It sounded like English, but I swear I understood but two words of it. *Rape* and *pain*."

Vlad stiffened. "You did apologize, didn't you?"

"Of course. I may not speak her language, but I can read the feelings in her mind." Otas actually blushed. "I took pity on my Queen and healed her before the mating."

Maybe there was hope for Otas yet. He'd shown compassion to Cwen, something he'd never given anyone. "There may be one problem with the language barrier. Did you say the word *mating* to her?"

"That is what we were doing."

"To Cwen mating is something animals do. Next time, tell her you're making love."

"There is no love. She is simply my Queen."

"Cwen's a romantic. You need to use softer words with her."

Otas crossed his arms. "I am no poet. That is something females do. You insult me."

Vlad was exasperated. Otas was as dense as a black hole. "Then I predict more arguments in the future."

"I can be reasonable."

"How so?"

"I made a bargain with my Queen. Sevea and Hebron must answer all of her questions before she will obey them in the Gift Training."

"Is that what you meant when you told Hebron that Cwen had questions?"

Otas nodded.

"Are you mad? Don't you realize what you've done?" Vlad shouted.

"I gained her cooperation."

"Not so." Vlad sat forward. "Cwen's inquisitive and intelligent. She won't stop asking questions until she knows everything. And when she finds out what her destiny is to be she'll do more than throw daggers at you." Vlad jumped up and began to pace. "You never should have given her so much of your power. Cwen has no control. She won't be able to contain her temper. When she gets angry, she'll unknowingly strike out with the Gift."

"I can handle her. My power is greater than hers. She won't be able to harm me," Otas stated with satisfaction.

"What about everyone else? Even with their combined strength, Sevea and Hebron can't defend themselves against the power of Cwen's Gift." Vlad opened his hands in supplication. "You've put them in danger."

Otas shot up off the futon with the realization of what he'd done. He'd become so besotted with mating with her he'd lost his reason. As Overlord he must always maintain control. "I've made a grave mistake."

"I'll say." Vlad watched Otas unlace his hair, clawing his hands through it as if it made him think better, his eyes a vibrant orange, glittering with rage. Vlad hoped that anger was not directed at him, but to the Overlord himself.

"We must resort to subterfuge." Otas lowered his arms and clenched his fists. "I'll instruct Hebron and Sevea not to tell my Queen the whole truth. She is ignorant of what it means to be Liambrian. Therefore, they will only partially teach her the ways of the Gift."

Vlad sighed in relief. "And the power of *Cho-rok Bul*, the Green Flame?"

"Only I will instruct her in its existence and use." Otas nodded to Vlad. "I thank you, my friend. I lost control. I've been a fool."

"Not a fool. Just a male who's beginning to feel love."

Otas shook his head. "It must go no further. As Overlord

the survival of the Liambrian race is my primary responsibility. I will not show such weakness again."

Otas stared out the window at the mountains beyond, their peaks still capped with the glistening white of snow. Spring had only just arrived, leaving a chill in the air at this altitude. His own mountain fortress was environmentally controlled: Liambrians were used to the heat of the home planet's twin suns, keeping the temperature a comfortable 80 degrees.

After arriving at the conclusion that he'd acted unwisely with his Queen, he'd sent Vlad in search of Hebron. Otas frowned as he thought of his foolish actions, letting his lust for his Queen get the better of him. And physical attraction was all it had been, Otas tried to convince himself. He didn't even know Cwen, what made her laugh, what her interests were, what she thought about the circumstances she found herself in. Vlad had unknowingly pointed out Otas' ignorance to him. One thing he was sure of, his Queen could be manipulative—a trait useful as the wife of the Overlord, but not to be used against him. He would have to make it clear where Cwen stood with him.

The swoosh of the automatic doors to his chambers alerted him of Hebron's arrival. He waited until Hebron stood behind him before turning to face the father of his Queen. Looking upon Hebron, he was struck by the strong resemblance Cwen bore to him. Until now, he'd only regarded Hebron as a male under his command, not as a father. His recent talk with Vlad had brought that knowledge to the forefront of his mind.

His Queen's flowing hair was the same black color with a hint of magenta highlights. Her smoke-green eyes were a match to Hebron's slanted ones, the high cheekbones tilted upward at the same sharp angle. Cwen had even inherited the shape of his mouth, but on her the full lower lip was sensual, beckoning to be kissed.

Otas was seized with alarm at the direction his thoughts were taking, feeling a surge of anger at his weakness, which was reflected in his orange eyes.

Hebron instinctively flinched at the sight of the liquid fire in the Overlord's eyes, knowing he was defenseless if his Master chose to blast him with the full force of his rage.

"I owe you an apology," Otas said.

Hebron didn't react for a second, not believing what the Overlord had just said. Cautious, he remained silent.

Otas was as unbelieving as Hebron. Never before had he shown mercy. "I owe you an apology," he repeated.

Hebron gazed downward. The look in the Overlord's eyes was in conflict with his words. "I don't understand."

"As the father of my Queen, I failed to show you courtesy. I should have informed you of my intention to bond with your daughter."

Surprise showed in Hebron's eyes. Then, as was custom, he nodded in acceptance.

Otas let out a breath, clasping his hands behind his back. "I must alter my order to you regarding my Queen's training."

Hebron stopped himself before he asked why. No one questioned the Overlord's motives. "I await your command."

"I don't want all of Cwen's questions answered. My Queen is not to gain knowledge of everything that concerns her."

"That will make it difficult to gain her cooperation. Sevea and I have been in constant telepathic communication. My wife was forced to strike her when Cwen became insolent. My daughter wanted to know who I was. I'd forbidden my wife to tell her. My daughter didn't accept Sevea's answer. Fortunately, Cwen is ignorant of what powers she's capable of wielding. Sevea wasn't harmed." Hebron began to pace, forming his words carefully in his mind. "I predict that in time Cwen won't be so easily controlled. We'll be forced to submit to her will and answer any question she puts to us."

"Vlad tells me Cwen in unable to break through the Mind-Shields of Liambrians. She only knows the thoughts of Earthlings." Otas moved to his desk, sitting down. His height alone intimidated his people. He wanted Hebron comfortable with the discussion. "Answer all of her questions. However, make them simple answers, or half-truths. Lie if you must."

"And the Gift? How much are we to teach her?"

"Only that which she will need to protect herself from Maccus."

"And *Cho-rok Bul*, the Green Flame?"

"Say nothing. I will instruct her when she has earned the right to learn of its existence."

Hebron became worried. "But that aspect of the Gift may come upon her unexpectedly. Someone may get killed."

"If the victim is humanoid, I'll be able to sense his fear and pain before death occurs. Plus, I will be aware when my Queen activates it. I will teleport to the location and stop her." Otas folded his arms on the desk.

"Which brings me to another point. Cwen has seen you disappear from view without the aid of the teleportation device. What do—"

Otas' eyes became intense. "How do you know this?"

"You forget, Master. I'm her father. Therefore I'm attuned to her mind. I sensed her surprise when you left after you . . . coupled."

Otas grimaced. What had Hebron thought of him the night of the bonding? He had most likely sensed her agony. "Tell her that only I have this ability."

"I also sensed question in Cwen before you left. Where did you say you were going?"

Somehow the tables had turned on Otas. He, the Overlord, was now under scrutiny by his father-in-law. "Liambria."

"And where am I to say that is?"

Otas cursed before he could stop himself. "The truth. In the north."

"And what Liambria is?"

"My fortress." Otas stood, not liking the feeling of being criticized. He'd had enough of that as a child. It was time for intimidation again. Before Hebron could speak his mind, Otas said, "My Queen will wonder why she does not live with me. You are to tell her that my duties require me to be away for long periods of time. It is safer for her to stay at Castle Acwellen." Otas turned his back on Hebron, staring out the window. "Do not explain that there are several tests she must pass before I complete the bonding and give her full power."

"That's wise," Hebron said with condescension.

Otas faced Hebron, his orange eyes swimming with ire. Hebron may be the father of his Queen, but it was time he remembered who was Overlord. "*Chung-bun-han*, Enough!"

The psychokinetic blast landed Hebron on his behind and fear caused him to scoot back several feet from Otas.

"Listen to me well, Hebron." Otas stood over the male on the floor. "You may tell my Queen of the evolutionary processes and genetics of Liambrians. But under no circumstances do you inform her that Maccus is my twin!"

Nodding, Hebron sputtered, "Y—yes, Master." He then scrambled to his feet.

"One final thing," Otas said with satisfaction, feeling in control again. "Cwen is not to know that we will leave this planet when Raynar finds us a suitable home!"

Hebron took that as a dismissal and turned to leave.

"Hebron!"

His feet wanted to continue walking, but Hebron stopped. "Yes, Master?"

"My Queen is not to call me 'My Lord.' It offends me. Teach her how to address me in Liambrian. From now on she is to call me *Sa-Jang*." Otas waited until he could smell the fear as well as sense it radiating off Hebron. "Now, you're dismissed."

*Earth's Orbit, October, 2000A.D.*

Maccus looked upon the six crewmen Luca had picked for the first scouting party to venture through the Time-Jump unit. Luca himself was doing a poor job of hiding his nervousness from the crew. With a nod of his head and a glare from his orange eyes, Maccus signaled Luca to tell the men of their mission while he set the controls for the unit. Luca quickly explained to the men that they were to simply step into the future through the metal frame Commander Maccus had constructed. They were to do nothing but observe and record what they would see on the recording device. The Commander would reopen the time-window in thirty minutes, and all they had to do was step back onto the bridge.

The Time-Jump device began to whine loudly, causing the scouts to take a step back.

"Stand ready," Maccus ordered as the blue and violet light began to swirl within the frame.

The men were terrified of the mysterious mission, but they had no choice. It was do as commanded, or die by the strange powers of the Commander.

"Now!" Maccus said.

The men jumped into the time unit without hesitation. Immediately their screams echoed from the vortex as the window through time closed.

"Bring them back! Bring them back!" Luca shouted.

Maccus stood calmly and walked to the metal frame. "We'll have to wait the full thirty minutes. The Time-Jump unit can't be reset." Maccus looked down at Luca. "You're sure these are the weakest men under my command?"

"Yes. But that doesn't mean they deserve to die in this crazy experiment of yours!"

Orange and gold flames swirled in Maccus' eyes. "Would you rather I'd sent you first?"

Luca shut his mouth and shook his head, trying to keep his thoughts that Commander Maccus was insane from forming in his mind.

The thirty minutes seemed like an eternity when the time-window finally opened up. One screaming crewman fell through the frame. His hair and clothes had been burnt off, yet he held on tenaciously to the recording device as the pin-prickling pain added to his agony.

Without a word, Maccus grabbed the recording device and took it to the bridge computer.

Luca kneeled down and took the injured crewman in his arms. "What in the ten Trexran Hells happened?"

"Volcano . . . lava . . . earthquakes . . ." The man died in Luca's embrace.

Luca glared at Commander Maccus' back while he studied the disc from the recorder. Six men dead, and for what? A mad chase after the Liambrians.

"Interesting." Maccus turned to Luca. "A massive asteroid will cause an upheaval on this planet."

"What time-frame did you send them to?"

It took Maccus a long time to answer him. "Ten years from now."

"Then surely the Liambrians died in this catastrophe."

"No." The Commander's eyes held a glazed look. "They've gone farther into the future. And I intend to find them."

"But it may take centuries for this upheaval to abate."

Maccus turned his blazing gaze on Luca. "Even if we have to search a millennium, I will not give up my quest for the Liambrians!"

Trexran curses spilled from Luca as he stared at the dead man in his arms.

Cwen sat with her legs curled beneath her on the window seat, gazing at the coming twilight. The fields had faded to a soft gray with just a tinge of green. She'd been sitting there, reflecting on her life since Sevea had silently left the chamber. Cwen imagined she could still feel the sting of the blow her mother had landed her, raising her hand to rub her sore cheek.

Cwen had no doubts that Sevea could have flattened her if she was of mind. She had much to learn about being a daughter, she thought. Aunt Amma had been more like a general in her behavior toward Cwen, which left her clueless as to what was expected of her. She could only draw upon the teaching in the Bible to honor thy father and thy mother. Getting flippant obviously didn't come under the heading of honor, judging by Sevea's reaction.

Cwen blew out her breath in resignation. Instinctively, she knew her life would continue to be a trial of endurance with the challenge of adapting to new knowledge of who she really was and what that entailed. The largest adjustment would be that as wife of the Overlord. By her actions the previous evening, Cwen was resigned to this business of "mating" as Otas called it, but deep down she somehow understood that it was more than the act of giving into passion. She didn't know exactly what influence her marriage to Otas had on the Liambrian race. However, after setting off Sevea's temper she was afraid to ask another question. It wasn't the pain of being hit that she feared, but the combined look of anger and hurt that had been in her mother's eyes. Feeling like a recalcitrant child, Cwen had remained in her room, not daring to cross her mother's path.

A knock sounded at the door, and Sevea swept in before Cwen could bid her to enter. Her mother was wearing her warrior's gear, sword and dagger hanging from her belt. Sevea's bronze-colored hair was bound in the long braid of a female fighter. Cwen couldn't meet her eyes, not knowing what to say to her mother.

"I was told that you didn't finish the food on the tray this morning and that you failed to come down for the noonday meal." Sevea regarded Cwen, who showed no signs of having heard her. "Look at me!"

Cwen looked to her, saying nothing.

"You've not eaten. Are you ill?" Sevea knew this couldn't be so because Liambrian immune systems fought off diseases tenaciously.

Silence still.

"Is there something wrong with your tongue?"

Cwen caught the annoyance in her mother's voice, deciding it was best to answer lest there be a repeat of the morning's performance. "I'm not ill."

Sevea noted the chill in the room and reached over Cwen to close the shutters. "Then why haven't you eaten?" she asked, striking flint to the candles.

"I've been thinking." Before Sevea could misinterpret her answer as insolent she added, "It's a bad habit I have. Since I was a child, when I'm trying to work something out in my mind, I have no appetite. It used to drive Vlad crazy."

Sevea took off her sword belt, laying it on the chest. "What worries you?"

"I'm afraid I don't know how to behave as a daughter. I have no point of reference. Professor Pimbleton didn't teach me about relationships." Cwen looked down. "I'm sorry if I offended you."

Sevea said nothing, walked to the hearth, and began building a fire. In no time, she had a good blaze going. Sighing, she sat in one of the chairs. "Join me. You have to be chilled."

Cwen was more than chilled. Her feet and hands were as ice. She did as she was bid, settling on the opposite chair, holding her hands to the heat of the flames.

"I don't know how to act as a mother, either," Sevea admitted.

Cwen looked at her with surprise.

"I know I'm to give love and discipline to my child, but how much of each I'm still learning. I shouldn't have struck you."

"I pushed you to it."

"Perhaps." Sevea gazed at the flames, choosing her next words with care. "You weren't given time to learn what a daughter is, nor was I allowed to act as mother to you. You're the result of your upbringing."

"Am I a bad person?"

Sevea laughed mirthlessly. "No. Just an ignorant one." Hebron had communicated with her telepathically on the Overlord's new command regarding Cwen's Training. "You're allowed to ask questions, but there will be times when Hebron and I just can't answer them."

"You're referring to Otas, aren't you?"

"Mostly. None of us knows the motives of the Overlord. And none dare question his actions." Sevea paused. "But you do have the right to know what I expect of you."

Cwen waited for her to say more.

"You probably want to know why you're not living with the Overlord."

Cwen shrugged. "Otas told me he has much to do. I've just arrived here and I assume I must learn what it means to be Liambrian before I can act as the proper wife to him."

Sevea relaxed inwardly. That was one dangerous hump she didn't have to hurdle. "True. You may ask me questions if you wish."

Cwen was cautious. "That day I fled the castle you sent Sashna after me. My old friend said some things I don't understand."

"Such as?"

"Sashna said she was to watch my back, and I was to lead them. Lead them to where?"

Careful, Sevea thought to herself. "I'm in command of all the female warriors. In time you will be in command of their daughters. Twelve of them were with me when we met you in the woods."

"All I've ever done was take orders. I don't know how to give them," Cwen protested.

"You've inherited my ability to lead, and your fighting skills surpass any of those you'll lead. That alone earns you the right to command."

"And being Otas' Queen?"

"That is right by inheritance."

Cwen pondered that for a moment, then thought of something that had been nagging her from that first day. "You said that all of the warriors are Liambrians. I noticed that while there are similarities in the features of the warriors, the skin tones range from fair to dark. Were there different ethnic groups on Liambria?"

"Not ethnic in the sense that Earthlings see it. Skin color isn't an issue with Liambrians. It has to do with evolution. Where the first Liambrians were living on the planet. Those that lived closer to the equator developed brown skin to protect them from the rays of the twin suns. Those on the poles of the planet became fair."

"It's much the same as Earth," Cwen observed.

"Evolutionarily, yes. But not sociologically. Only one language was spoken on Liambria. As technological advances enabled world travel, fair-skinned bonded with dark-skinned, producing the wide range of skin tones you see today."

"You're talking about genetics. Do all Liambrians have the Gift?"

Safe ground, Sevea thought. "Of course, that's what makes us who we are. There are different degrees of it, but all have the Gift. Hebron will teach you more of this."

Cwen steered clear of any questions regarding Hebron. "Sashna mentioned the Doorway. But she doesn't know she's Liambrian, does she?"

Sevea stiffened, for she was about to lie. "No, she doesn't. How do you know of her ignorance?"

"She thinks Liambria is a mythical place in the north where the people are faerie." Cwen cocked her head, gazing at her mother. "When Otas left last eve, he told me he was going to Liambria. Why the deception?"

"Believe it or not, you're more advanced than the daughters. Not only were you mentally prepared through education, but Amma had a motive for plying you with all of those science fiction video discs. The concept of being an alien was easy for you to accept. When the time is right, the daughters will be told of their true identities."

Cwen couldn't believe what little knowledge she had was more than the others possessed. "Does Otas really live in Liambria?"

Alarm bells went off in Sevea's head. "He does. His, uh, fortress is there."

Cwen was silent some seconds. "How does he get from there to here without using a teleportation device?"

"Only the Overlord has the ability to go where he will with the power of his mind."

Cwen grunted as she thought that her husband was indeed powerful. "Will I ever see his home?"

"When the Overlord deems it's time." Cwen was being cooperative, so Sevea figured it was time to teach her a few things. "You must never tell anyone that you're the Overlord's Queen. Including you, only five of us know you have bonded with him."

"It's because of the beast, isn't it?"

"Yes. It's for your own protection." Sevea rose and went to the chest, digging through it until she came up with a pen and spiralled notebook. "Lord Ware must never see this. It's illogical, but the Earthlings in this century have no use for paper and pen. All communication between the baronies is done by messenger."

Cwen nodded.

"I must teach you the proper way to address the Overlord."

Cwen raised her eyebrows in question as Sevea scratched something on the notebook.

"Never call him by his name. It lacks respect." Sevea showed her what she had written. "The Liambrian alphabet doesn't have Arabic letters. We use symbols. This is as close as I can come to it using the English alphabet. It's phonetic."

Cwen looked as what was written there, frowning. *Sa-Jang.*

"Try saying it."

"Say-Jang."

Sevea flinched. "The A is pronounced with an *ah* sound. Saw-Jawng."

Cwen worked her mouth, trying to get it out. "Saw . . . Jawng."

Sevea pursed her lips. "Almost. Even though it's hyphenated, say it faster, like one word."

"SawJawng."

Sevea smiled. Her daughter was a quick study. "One more time."

"*Sa-Jang.*"

"Perfect! The Overlord will be pleased."

Cwen had a thought. "What do I call you? Surely, Sevea isn't proper."

Sevea's golden eyes sparkled. "I'm afraid the Liambrian word is somewhat difficult to pronounce."

"I've always dreamed of meeting you. May I address you in English?"

Sevea smiled with affection as she nodded. "I'll have Edris bring you your supper. Would you like a bath, also?"

"Yes, mother."

Sevea giggled with delight as she headed for the door.

"Mother?"

Sevea turned to look at her.

"What does *Sa-Jang* mean?"

"Master."

# Chapter 9

Master? She was to call him Master? Cwen still couldn't get over it. She sat on the blue carpet in front of the hearth wrapped in a blanket, shivering as she tried to dry her wet locks. During her bath, Sevea had assured her that all Liambrians called him *Sa-Jang*, that none dared not address the Overlord so. But as his Queen, didn't that give her some leeway? Spring had receded for the night, bringing with it a coldness comparable to an Arctic windblast. The stone walls of the castle might have been made of blocks of ice for all the good it did to have the hearth going. The flames seemed useless in her freezing chamber. Her thick hair was never going to dry. She'd give anything for a 1800 watt hair dryer, not that she'd have an electrical socket to plug it into.

The air around Cwen stirred, chilling her even more because she knew that the disturbance announced the arrival of her husband. Cwen turned around and saw Otas standing a few feet behind her, a deep frown on his face as he gazed down at her. At the sight of his imposing figure, calling him Master didn't seem like such a bad idea after all.

"*Sa-Jang*," she said as she started to rise.

Otas motioned her to stay where she was. Although he was pleased she had addressed him as *Sa-Jang*, it didn't erase the frown from his face. The chamber was freezing, and Liambrians liked warmth whether they were raised on Earth or not. His wife's hair was thick like his, tending to hold moisture, which meant there was no way it was going to dry this night. He wasn't worried about her catching what Earthlings called a cold for Liambrians were made of sterner stuff. What concerned him was her comfort.

Cwen was unnerved by his silence. She was sure she had pronounced *Sa-Jang* correctly. So what had caused the flame of anger in his orange eyes? Cwen hadn't ever been able to read the thoughts of Aunt Amma or Vlad. Nor her mother's, now that she thought about it. It was as if she were Superman, but now she had lost her powers. Liambrians must have some form of invisible barrier surrounding their brains preventing her access. She was positive her husband's barrier would be thickest of all.

As she watched him, the dark sapphires in his gold collar and bracelets began to glow with a moss-green light in the dim room. Cwen held her breath, knowing he was activating his power. She had no idea what he was about to do and didn't have the courage to ask. Cwen just hoped that whatever it was wouldn't hurt, as she braced herself unconsciously.

A few seconds had passed when the gems lost their glow. Otas' frown disappeared with the deactivation of the stones. Cwen had no idea what had just happened. Fright had kept her eyes locked on her husband.

"Look before you," he said with his heavy accent.

Cwen jumped at the sound of his deep voice, hesitantly looking down. On the floor in front of her were two items: a rectangular-shaped box made of some unidentifiable metal, and something that looked like, God help her, a hair dryer. Cwen picked up the hair dryer thingy, noting it had no power cord, but on the handle was a button with a strange symbol that could only be a switch.

Otas sat down next to Cwen, smiling at the perplexed look on her face. "'Tis cold in here. Your hair will remain wet." He positioned the rectangular box a few feet from her, pressing a button on the top. The thing made no noise, but a blessed warmth radiated from it.

"Wh—where . . . I mean, how did—"

"Dry your hair," Otas instructed, nodding to the object in her hand.

Cautiously, Cwen depressed the button and a blast of hot air flowed from the cylindrical opening of the thing. It too, made no noise. Encouraged, Cwen let the blanket fall from her shoulders, revealing the linen shift she wore. She picked up her brush and began to dry her hair enthusiastically. It only took five minutes for her hip-length hair to lose its wetness. Even with the suped-up models of the 21st century, it had usually taken her five times as long to dry her mass of hair.

With her hair no longer wet and the warmth radiating from the space-aged heater, she felt quite comfortable. "Thank you, *Sa-Jang.*"

"'Tis my duty to see to my Queen's comfort." He couldn't help grasping a handful of her hair, running his fingers through it. The black tresses had natural waves to its soft strands shining with magenta highlights. As he stroked her hair, Otas looked into her eyes. "It pleases me the way you say '*Sa-Jang*'"

Cwen blushed. "I was told 'tis what all Liambrians call you."

"'Tis true." Otas removed his black tunic, stretched out his legs and leaned on an elbow, propping his head up. "But the way you speak it sounds like a song." Otas began to stroke her bare arm.

Electric shocks from his touch set her body to tingling. With a shaking finger, Cwen pointed to the heater. "How is the thing powered?"

Otas' strokes moved to her throat, touching the sensitive skin there. "Your words make no sense to me. You will have to speak to Hebron. He understands your tongue."

Exasperated, she tried another question. "From where did you get them?"

His hand moved to the soft skin above her breasts. He smiled as she shuddered in reaction. "From my chambers."

Cwen wanted to know how he'd teleported the items to her room. She opened her mouth, but the shimmering light in his orange eyes stopped her from speaking.

"I will answer no more questions." He cupped her breast in his hand, feeling the weight of it. "I wish to mate." Otas grimaced. "'Tis not the right word, but I know no other."

At this point, Cwen didn't care what he called it. His hand on her breast was making her melt inside. She couldn't keep her eyes off his muscled chest, wanting to run her hands across the smooth skin. "May I touch you, *Sa-Jang?*"

"'Twould please me." Otas freed her arms from the shift, gaining full access to her breasts.

Gasping at the sensation of his thumb running across her nipple, she responded in kind, smoothing her hands over his chest. Cwen wondered if his brown nipples were as sensitive as hers, rubbing the hard pebble of one between her fingers. The low grunt that escaped him assured her that they were.

Suddenly she wanted to run her hands through his mane of black hair, freeing it from the leather thong. Cwen became emboldened, raking her hand through his hair and working his nipple at a fast pace. She ignited a fire in his orange eyes, which churned with golden flames. Her own insides began to burn.

With a low growl, Otas stood, quickly removing his boots and breeches. His manhood sprang forth, growing in its tumescence. Cwen's breath caught at the sight. She couldn't believe her body capable of receiving such a huge rod.

She had no more time to wonder at the miracle of mating for Otas was down on his knees, swiftly pulling the shift down her body and over her feet until she lay naked before him. He straddled her on all fours, capturing her mouth in a blazing kiss. Otas pushed his flaming tongue deep into her mouth, forcing a moan of pleasure to emerge from her throat.

He kept their mouths locked so long she became breathless. When he raised his head to stare into her smoke-green eyes, she was panting with passion. Encouraged, he kissed a path down her neck to her chest, taking a hand and kneading her right breast. At the same time his warm mouth closed over her other breast, devouring it with strong suckling pulls. Losing control, Cwen began to emit cries of pleasure as her hands grasped his head and her back arched to receive the tantalizing sensations his mouth was providing.

His mouth left her breast, kissing a pathway down over her belly. Shock hit her when those hot lips buried themselves in her mound of tangled curls. This action hadn't been in the romance novels Aunt Amma had selected for her. "N— nay, *Sa-Jang*! 'Tis not proper."

"All a husband does to his wife is proper."

He pushed her thighs apart with his knees, locking his mouth to her womanhood. His hot tongue delved into the soft petals of flesh, seeking to taste her female nectar. Another growl escaped him as his tongue found her sensitive bud causing her hips to lift in reaction. Cwen let out a cry as his strong finger pushed its way inside her. He worked her that way, tongue teasing, finger sliding in and out, until she could bear no more.

"*Sa-Jang*, please!" Cwen begged.

He rose above her again on his hands and knees, his groin heavy with the need to enter her. "Touch me." His voice was deep and husky.

Cwen's eyes were glazed with passion, telling him words no longer had any meaning to her. He took her hand and curled her fingers around his hot shaft. Instinct took over as Cwen ran her hand up and down the length of him. He was hard as steel, yet the skin was like velvet.

Otas could bear no more. "Guide me inside you."

Cwen opened her legs wider, placing him at the entrance of her woman's core. With deliberate slowness, he pushed himself within. She moaned as she felt her insides stretching to receive him and stretching more when he had fully lodged himself in her simmering sheath.

He grasped her hips and held firm while he moved in and out of her with speed, his plunges not exactly gentle. Cwen couldn't help crying out every time he thrust himself fully within her, the pleasure from that friction taking her beyond ecstasy, the build up of tension in her belly reaching the flash point.

Sensing she was near release, Otas pounded her harder and harder, his own body drenched in sweat, begging for surrender.

"*Sa-Jang!*" she screamed as she was thrown through a kaleidoscope of colors, her body weightless and shuddering with pleasure. Her mind shut down with the impact of her orgasm, flinging her into a soundless darkness.

What sounded like an animal howling spilled from Otas as his seed burst forth, seeming to go on forever, leaving him locked in ecstasy.

When Otas opened his eyes, he had no idea how much time had passed. He was sitting back on his heels, his Queen still joined to him. Her body lay limp, her head turned to the side with a curtain of black hair covering her face. He reached down and moved her hair aside, seeing that her eyes were closed. He shook her gently, but she didn't respond. Fear shot through him at the thought he'd killed her, but the rise and fall of her chest assured him she lived. He'd heard of this unconsciousness after pleasure, but had never witnessed it.

Otas remained still, waiting for his Queen to come around. Finally, her eyes opened, blinking several times as if she didn't know where she was. She turned her head to look into his eyes. Her green eyes were clear but showed confusion.

"*Sa-Jang?*" she whispered. "What happened?"

He had no English words for it. "You suffered *Ju-Gum.*"

Cwen stilled looked confused.

"Did I cause you pain?"

Cwen shook her head, becoming aware of her position. Otas was still inside her, her thighs resting on his strong ones, her feet touching the floor behind him. She started to rise.

"Do not move!" Otas growled.

Cwen obeyed out of fear. The look in his eyes was terrifying.

"I came to you for a purpose."

Cwen thought it best to stay silent.

Otas ran his eyes over her body, pleased by her good muscle tone. There was no fat on her anywhere. The body of a warrior. Her large breasts were made to suckle his children, her pelvis designed to bear them. He stared down to where their bodies connected, then looked back into her eyes.

"I know your body," Otas stated. "But I know you not."

Cwen became alarmed as she felt him begin to grow inside her.

"With our bodies joined thus, your mind is open to me." Otas reached down, placing his palm on her forehead. "Reveal yourself to me."

Cwen suddenly found she had no will. Her life with Aunt Amma and Vlad flashed like rapid-fire snapshots. Killing the Trexran in the alley. The trip through the Doorway. Her growing relationship with her mother. Her marriage to Otas. All of her feelings stored for her entire life spilled out of her mind in a rush of thoughts.

She looked into Otas' eyes, which were flicking back and forth as he read her mind. The pressure on her brain produced a throbbing pain that was growing in intensity. Filled with terror, she screamed, "Cease, *Sa-Jang*! You hurt me!"

Otas stared into her eyes, understanding dawning in his mind. Her life had been much as his was. The loneliness, the uncertainty, the lack of parental love, all of it. Yet he had an advantage. He'd known all along what his destiny was. His Queen knew nothing, but she continued on each day no matter what surprises were in store for her.

"'Tis enough." Otas stopped sucking her thoughts from her mind. He kept his hand on her forehead long enough to end the pain his probe had caused.

Cwen let out the breath she'd been holding when the pain ceased. "What did you learn?"

"You still please me, my Queen." Otas began to stroke her body in a lazy fashion, as if he had all night.

Cwen felt his hardness increasing within her. "S—*Sa-Jang*, you do not leave?"

The orange flames glittered in his eyes. "I stay the night."

Sevea bounded up the stairs, her mind preoccupied with intentions of getting Cwen out of the castle. Her daughter had been cooped up in her chamber for a whole day and Samson was giving the stable master fits by kicking in the slats of his stall. The horse needed a good run. And so did his mistress.

Sevea pushed open the chamber door without knocking and was brought up short. Before her stood the Overlord, rage flashing in his orange eyes, his naked body prepared to do battle. He held no sword, of course, but he had no need of one. Sevea forced her eyes to his face, not wanting to see the weapon he had between his legs. Sevea wondered if Cwen felt as small as she did when faced with the Overlord's height. She began to speak, but Otas shook his head.

*She sleeps*, Otas said in Liambrian with his mind, glancing at the bed where Cwen lay.

*Forgive me, Sa-Jang.* Sevea easily switched to telepathic communication. *I didn't sense your presence.*

*Why is there no bolt on my Queen's door?*

Sevea flinched. The Overlord was hopping mad. Any excuse she gave would sound ludicrous and intensify that anger. *I will see to it immediately.*

Otas did not respond. He just stared at Sevea intently.

Dressed in leather battle gear, Sevea found herself sweating. The cause was more than the Overlord's intimidating

presence. The room was hot. She gazed over to the hearth
and saw the heater and hair dyer. *There will be trouble if the
Earthlings see evidence of our technology.*

*You are resourceful. Hide them. I will not have my Queen freeze!*
Sevea nodded, feeling uncomfortable. She knew she was
intruding, but Sevea didn't know how to make a graceful exit.
It didn't take a genius to realize the Overlord was immensely
annoyed.

*Why did you come?* Otas asked impatiently.

*Um, Cwen hasn't been outside for two days. I thought we should
take a ride.* God, she sounded so ridiculous.

Otas frowned. *When I am finished here, I will send her to you.*

Keeping her eyes on his face, Sevea nodded as she backed
to the door. There was nothing else she could say. The Overlord had no intention of leaving any time soon, and she wasn't
about to tell him anything different.

After the door had closed, Otas opened the shutters, letting in air and light, then returned to the bed. It was way too
short for him, but at the moment he didn't care. Cwen had
her back to him as he eased himself against her. Seeking the
warmth of his body, she turned in her sleep to face him, her
breasts pushed up against his chest.

Otas gritted his teeth, feeling the heaviness grow in his
groin. What was it about his Queen that made him lose control over his body? He knew that she didn't love him for he
had read it in her thoughts during the Mind-Probe. Her
thoughts had been in the words of 21st century English, but
he had no trouble interpreting her feelings. He'd had every
intention of telling her he would strike no more bargains with
her, but his insatiable lust had killed that notion.

Otas stroked her hair, rubbing his other hand down the
silky skin of her back. The feel of her only made him grow
harder, causing a low growl to escape him, which woke her.

Cwen turned part way on her back as he looked down at
her, the smoke-green eyes alert. A soft blush suffused her

cheeks as her mouth opened then closed without making a sound.

"Why do you not speak?" His voice was deep, but the timbre soft.

"I've never seen you in the light."

"And?"

"You're most beautiful."

He couldn't help it. He laughed deep, rumbling chuckles. Cwen smiled in response. Suddenly, he stopped, touching a hand to her face. "I have never seen you smile."

"It doesn't please you?"

"It pleases me." He lowered his head until their lips were almost touching. "It drives me to do this." He gave her one of his soul-searing kisses.

Cwen laced her fingers in his thick hair, kissing him just as hard as he did her. He growled in his throat, flinging the covers back. His large hand ran over her body with speed igniting her desire.

Before she knew what was happening he parted her legs, sliding his manhood into her. Her quiet cry stopped his movements. She had to be sore for he had taken her three times in the night, plunging into her forcefully each time. He looked down at her. She held her lower lip between her teeth. "Do you wish me to stop?"

Cwen shook her head.

"I will be gentle and quick."

And he was, bringing the act to fruition in a matter of minutes. He was able to keep his eyes open during the ecstasy he felt, watching her face as she found her release, crying out, "*Sa-Jang*." The sound of his name coming from her lips sent a feeling shooting through him that he could not identify.

He raised up on his elbows, holding her face with his hands, their bodies still attached.

Cwen couldn't stop staring at his eyes. The shifting patterns of orange and gold were mesmerizing. She knew he would talk with her now while their bodies were joined. Cwen didn't understand why he did this. Judging by all of the romance novels she'd read, Otas' actions were unusual.

"Why do you stare?" he asked.

"'Tis your eyes. They're like the sun. Twin stars."

At last he understood something she said to him. "And yours are like the green sapphires in the jewelry you wear. You are as a shining gem." Otas astounded himself. He never thought he'd be able to be poetic.

They had been staring at each other for some time when Otas remembered Sevea. "Your mother wishes you to join her riding."

"I must go." She said it, but she didn't move.

"Not yet." His gaze turned intense. "I have a question."

Cwen waited.

"Why do you let me take you?"

"You said 'tis my duty as your Queen."

Otas studied her face. "'Tis the only reason?"

"By your order, *Sa-Jang*."

Apparently, that wasn't what he wanted to hear. The light in his orange eyes dimmed, then flared like a super nova. He moved off her in one swift motion, snatched up his clothes, and popped out of view without a word spoken.

Cwen sat up, staring at the spot he'd been in when he disappeared. Puzzled, she thought, what did I do?

# Chapter 10

Cwen sat on the bed, braiding her hair, trying to figure out what in the blazes had happened. Otas had asked her a question and she had answered it honestly. Why he was angered, she didn't know.

Cwen got out of bed, her gaze falling to the heater and hair dryer Otas had teleported to her chambers. The Earthlings of this time-frame would surely freak if they saw them. Switching the heater off, she was amazed that it cooled immediately. She gingerly laid the heater flat and pushed it and the hair dryer way under the bed. She'd be damned if she was going to give them back to him, having no intention of freezing again after a bath.

When she stood up, she suddenly remembered her mother was waiting for her and quickly washed and dressed in battle gear. If they were to venture outside, they would obviously need to be armed. Fumbling with the buckle of her sword belt, Cwen left her chamber.

She found Sevea sitting alone at the high table in the great hall, chin in hand, a frown on her face and a platter of meat pies at her elbow.

"I'm sorry I took so long," Cwen said.

Sevea's face flamed red. "And I'm sorry I didn't knock on your door."

Cwen was confused for a second, then the realization of what Otas had been wearing, or rather not wearing, dawned in her mind. "You saw Otas?"

Sevea nodded gravely. "It's a sight I never wish to see again."

Cwen knew exactly what she meant. Otas was intimidating enough with his clothes on, without them he was downright frightening. Cwen pictured the scene of her mother confronting her husband in her room and burst out laughing.

"This is nothing to laugh about. He's the Overlord, for God's sake." Sevea tried to sound indignant, which only made her daughter laugh harder, forcing her to lose her own dignity and join Cwen. Sevea burst forth with musical chuckles.

Cwen collapsed in the chair beside her mother, holding her sides, tears streaming down her face. She couldn't remember ever having laughed like this.

Sevea was the first to regain control. "Doesn't his size terrify you?"

Cwen's giggles turned into coughs. When she could breathe again, she asked, "Are you talking about all of him, or—"

"I didn't dare look there! I wouldn't be able to face him again."

Cwen quieted, turning solemn.

"You're afraid of him."

"He scares me."

"Is that why you let him touch you?"

"I only do so because he says I must." Cwen stared at her mother a second. "You said the same thing."

Sevea's look turned grim. Her daughter only submitted to the Overlord because they had told her she had to. She could feel Cwen's confusion, but there was no repulsion there. It was time to have a serious talk about feminine matters. "Why don't you eat? We'll get the horses and go where we can speak more privately."

After her night spent with Otas, Cwen was ravenous, downing three meat pies in a matter of minutes.

When she had finished, Sevea leaned over, whispering in

her ear. "The Earthlings must not see the heater and hair dryer Otas gave you."

"I hid them way under the bed," Cwen whispered back.

Sevea sighed and nodded in relief.

The horses were saddled when they reached the stables. Samson was so glad to see Cwen he couldn't hold still, causing his mistress to mount him when he was on the move. They galloped the horses away from the castle, heading north, Sevea leading the way. The air had not lost its chill of the previous evening. Cwen was glad for the warmth the leather tunic and breeches provided.

When they reached a glade between a dense copse of green maples, Sevea reined in her dapple-gray.

"You mate with the Overlord because we commanded you to, yet you enjoy it, don't you?" Sevea continued the conversation as if there'd been no interruption.

Cwen patted Samson's neck a while before she looked at her mother. "He makes me feel things I didn't know were possible. Our, uh, mating was so intense it caused me to faint last eve."

Sevea cocked her head. "You suffered *Ju-Gum?*"

"Otas said I did. Whatever it means."

"It means that the Overlord is not only a skilled lover, but he so immerses himself in the joining that he delivers extreme pleasure to you." Sevea watched her daughter's reddening face. "Whether he knows it or not, Otas has love for you."

"I don't want his love. Nor do I wish to feel this pleasure. I try not to, but my body takes over my mind." Cwen shook her head, puzzlement on her face. "I don't understand it. I have no love for him. How can I? I don't even know him."

"What you have is *koi*, sexual attraction for him." Sevea frowned. "*Koi* is much more complicated than mere attraction. It's a sexual desire and ambiance that will increase over time."

"How do I get rid of this *koi*?"

"What's done can't be undone." Sevea stared off into the distance. "During the Mind-Touch ceremony at your birth, the Overlord implanted his essence into your mind so that when it became time for you to bond, you would seek no other."

Cwen cursed profusely, blazing her mother's ears. "For my entire life I've never been given any choices!"

"Would you have another male touch you as Otas does?"

Cwen thought about the intimacy of the act. "No," she admitted. "Mother, tell me. Do you love my father?"

"Of course." Sevea was surprised by the question.

"But did you love him at first?"

By the stars, her daughter was like one of the castle dogs, working a bone until there was nothing left of it. "No."

"Then why did you bond with him?"

"I, too, had no choice. My husband was chosen for me by Raynar because of genetics."

"Genetics?"

"Your father and I carried the right genes, DNA and RNA helixes, to produce a Queen. You."

Cwen was shocked. "I'm a product of genetic engineering?"

"You weren't formed in a test tube. Your conception was natural." Sevea looked to the sky. Dark-gray clouds were upon the horizon, racing for them swiftly. Sevea looked back at Cwen. "We should head back. It will rain soon."

"I want to know more of my conception," Cwen protested.

"You'll have to await Hebron. He arrives tonight. He'll teach you all about Liambrian genetics."

*Liambria 2*

Vlad fought for his very life as Otas rained blow after blow on his sword. Otas had the power to kill with his thoughts alone, Vlad thought. So why was he trying to decapitate him with a sword? They battled thus across the large floor of the war room, until Vlad had had enough. Vlad incorporated martial arts into his sword defense, kicking Otas powerfully in the stomach, doubling the Overlord over long enough to disarm him. Otas' sword went sailing end over end, crashing into the wall.

If they hadn't been alone, Vlad never would have disgraced the Overlord with disarmament. But he was tiring and bleeding from several nicks on his arms and shoulders for they wore no safety padding.

Otas recovered quickly, a look of murder showing in his eyes as he took a step toward Vlad.

Vlad spread his legs apart, gripping the sword hilt with both hands. "Cease, Otas! Or by *Ha-nu-nim*, God, I'll make your Queen a widow!"

At the mention of his Queen, Otas stopped, yellow and orange lights shifting in his eyes, confusion racing across his face. "I lost control, didn't I?"

Cautious, Vlad still held the sword. "You've been acting like a Liambrian *mow* that's gotten drenched with his fangs and claws bared." He continued to watch Otas, the confusion on the Overlord's face holding. Vlad had seen that look before when Otas lost control of his emotions. Rage had been the route masking any other feelings that ruled his mind. Vlad slowly lowered the sword, knowing it was useless trying to read his friend's mind. "What troubles you?"

The Overlord inhaled deeply. "Cwen."

Vlad was patient. It would take time for Otas to form his emotions into words.

Otas didn't pace. He stood motionless until his mouth

was capable of speaking the thoughts in his head. "While I was joined with my Queen I asked her why she allowed me to mate with her."

"And?"

Otas frowned. "Her answer was that I command it, but I could read the fear within her."

"Cwen mates with you out of fear?"

Otas nodded.

"Yet she isn't cold to your touch."

Otas shook his head. "She is the opposite. Her responses to me are as fire. My Queen suffered *Ju-Gum* last eve."

Vlad's eyes widened. "I'm impressed. I didn't know you had it in you." He observed Otas for a moment. "You're confused because Cwen's feelings are in conflict with her actions?"

"Yes. I did a Mind-Probe on her, trying to gain understanding."

"What did you learn?"

"Only that she has much courage. My Queen is completely ignorant of what it means to be my wife, yet she blindly enters each new day." Otas rubbed the back of his neck. "I feel she expects something more of me, but I do not know what it is."

Vlad thought over what he'd heard so far. "I understand Cwen. Right now she feels no better than Narda. Like chattel you use to ease your lust."

"They are different. I did not bond with Narda."

"But Cwen doesn't fully comprehend what bonding means. She knows she's wed to you, but nothing more." Vlad chose his words carefully. "You must make your Queen aware that you have love for her."

Otas shot him a glare. "I cannot give her what I don't possess."

"You're wrong, my friend. No matter how small, it takes love to bring a female to *Ju-Gum*."

Otas absorbed that for a time. "How do I show her this . . . this love?"

"I'm sure Cwen doesn't know that your Mind-Probe was an intimate act between you. You must explain these things to her."

"How?"

"With patience." Vlad had a brainstorm. "Cwen always read Earthling romance novels. I never understood why. Since she was my charge, I needed to know her mind as well."

"What are these novels?"

"*Chaeks*, books, that tell stories." Vlad shrugged. "When Cwen slept, I had nothing better to do, so I copied one of the novels and fed it into the computer in the laboratory and translated it into Liambrian. I still have the disc. I thought you might have need of it."

"Are you telling me to read it?" Otas was incredulous.

"Why not?" Vlad smiled. "It'll tell you what your Queen thinks love is, and you can educate her on what Liambrians call love. It will give you a point of reference."

Otas spat out the worst of Liambrian curses. "Bring me the disc."

"Only after you've healed my wounds. I'm bleeding like a stuck *dong-mul*." Vlad studied his friend as he applied his healing touch. Otas by nature was a speed-reader. He could have the book finished in an hour. If he didn't slow down at the love scenes, that is.

The weather had turned foul. Lightning flared, thunder crashed, a deluge drenched the soil around the castle. Cwen awaited her mother in her chambers, fussing with her hair, straightening imaginary wrinkles from the dark-green kirtle she wore. Because Hebron was expected, Sevea insisted that Cwen look her best.

A soft tap sounded at the door, and Sevea entered. "Hebron is here." She looked radiant dressed in the bronze-colored gown that matched her hair. There was an expression on her mother's face that could only be called wistful.

"Who did you tell Lord Ware he is?"

Blushing like a schoolgirl, Sevea said, "My cousin." She surveyed Cwen, smiling with approval. "We should go down. The evening meal is about to begin."

As they walked down the winding stairs, Cwen thought, just what I need. Another trainer. She wondered if he would be as merciless as Vlad had been.

At the entrance to the great hall, Cwen stopped, gazing at the tall Liambrian speaking with Lord Ware. He wore his long black hair in a ponytail, a dark-green tunic covered his torso, black breeches and black boots completed the outfit. A sword and dagger were strapped to his hips, which seemed to be the subject of the conversation with Lord Ware.

"You say you aren't a knight, yet you bear arms," Lord Ware was saying. "Are you good with a sword?"

The tall Liambrian nodded. "'Twould be foolish to carry the thing and not know how to use it."

Sevea swept up to the men purposely interrupting their conversation. She motioned to Cwen, who came forward. "Hebron, I wish you to meet my daughter, Cwen." A shy smile appeared on Sevea's face. "Cwen, my cousin, Hebron."

Hebron turned his head to look down at Cwen, startling her with the intensity in his dark-green eyes. She swore to herself she'd never met this man before, yet somehow he felt familiar. As was the custom, Cwen curtsied to him.

In a gallant gesture, Hebron took her hand and kissed the knuckles. His eyes held humor as he said, "I hear you are quite the warrior."

It was the same with this man as it had been with her mother. His approval of her fighting skills was important. "I was trained well."

"I know." Hebron continued to stare until Lord Ware summoned them to the high table.

OLD

Cwen was seated next to Hebron, who would share a trencher with her. It was odd, but she wasn't concerned about catching germs from Hebron. Cwen felt she should start some kind of conversation with him, but before she could speak Hebron shook his head.

*We will talk later*, Hebron said with his mind.

Cwen's own mind heard him loud and clear, astonishing her for she hadn't spoken with anyone in this manner since she'd gone through the Doorway.

The meal was a quiet affair with the exception of the thoughts of Lord Ware. He didn't believe the handsome man at Cwen's side was his pretend wife's cousin because Sevea couldn't keep her eyes off Hebron. It made Cwen suspicious as well. Try as she might, Cwen couldn't read the thoughts of Sevea and Hebron.

At the end of the meal, Sevea stood, addressing Lord Ware. "Please excuse us, my lord. Hebron, Cwen, and I have important family matters to discuss."

Lord Ware only nodded, not exactly looking pleased.

Sevea led them to a chamber above stairs, which was lighted with candles and fire from the hearth. Two settees were set against the right wall, five chairs circled the hearth, the stone floor was covered with a thick burgundy carpet. Two shuttered windows would give the room plenty of light during the day.

Hebron moved to the fireplace, warming his hands and glancing at Sevea. "Leave us."

Her mother hesitated for a second, then left without a word.

While Hebron had his back to her, Cwen observed him. Instinctively she knew he wasn't as powerful as Otas, but his mere presence was intimidating. It was so silent she could hear the downpour raging outside the castle. While she waited for Hebron to move or speak, she wondered just what kind of Gift Training was she supposed to receive from this man?

Seeming to sense her thoughts, Hebron turned to face her, his dark-green eyes inquiring.

Cwen stared back at him, noting the gold collar and bracelets that marked him as a Liambrian. The gems in his jewelry appeared to be emeralds like Vlad's. Before she could stop her mouth, she said, "I suppose you're my teacher."

Hebron laughed, surprising her. "More like a Gift Master."

The man had a beautiful smile, causing her to relax. "You know all about me, don't you?"

"While you were growing up with your Aunt Amma, I made several trips through the Doorway to check on your progress. I know of your fondness for sci-fi videos and romance novels."

Cwen jumped at the pause in his recounting and blurted, "But I never saw you."

"You weren't suppose to."

Cwen cocked her head. "Why were you checking on me?"

Hebron shrugged. "It was my duty."

Another mystery, Cwen thought.

"The mystery will be solved in a moment," Hebron said, reading her mind. "At this time, I'm now your Trainer of the Gift." He paused as he read the confusion on Cwen's face. "I understand you have a propensity for asking questions."

"I made a bargain with the Overlord. All my life I've done as I was told, never knowing why. Much has happened since I stepped through the Doorway. But I still know next to nothing, except that I'm a Liambrian Queen married to the Overlord. I won't go a step further until I learn what in blazes is going on."

"First lesson. You're not a Liambrian Queen. You're *The Queen*."

Cwen opened her mouth, then closed it at the penetrating look in Hebron's eyes.

"I've modified the bargain you made with the Overlord.

For every question that you ask of me, you must learn some aspect of the Gift."

Cwen couldn't help but snarl. It would take her forever to find out anything.

"Save your displeasure for someone who fears it. It has no effect on me." Hebron was lying of course, but she didn't know that. "Also, in the mornings before the lessons, you and I will practice combat. Otas doesn't want you growing soft and fat."

Cwen gasped loudly. *Why the nerve of that—*

"You may now ask a question." Hebron cut off her thoughts. "Choose carefully. I will only answer one question this night. The Training begins tomorrow."

Cwen was steaming, unaware that the gems in her jewelry had begun to glow. Hebron kept the fear from his face, awaiting her question.

Cwen sensed that Hebron wasn't as ruthless as Otas, but he wasn't a pushover either. She didn't quite know what to make of him. In her perplexity, the stones dimmed, making Hebron sigh with relief inwardly.

Safe ground, Cwen thought to herself. Stay on safe ground. "I know you're not my mother's cousin. Who are you, really?"

"I'm your *Aboji.*"

Cwen started to spit out, "My what—" but stopped herself in time for it was another question. "I don't understand."

Hebron stared at her some seconds, looking her over from her face to her slippered toes. "I'm your father."

Thunder crashed as Cwen stood agape. She knew her mouth hung open, but she was helpless to close it as she stared upon Hebron. This man before her was her father? she thought, then realized it must be so. No wonder he looked familiar to her. The smoke-green eyes were the same as hers, as was the thick black hair and the facial structure. There was no denying it.

Conflicting emotions sped through her so quickly she was unable to latch on to a single one—feelings of rage, abandonment, and longing for parental love. Hebron opened his arms to Cwen, forcing her to choose which emotion was strongest.

She raced into his spread arms, bursting into tears as he hugged her to his chest. "A—all of my life I've felt so lonely. Why didn't you come to me during your trips through the Doorway?"

Hebron ignored his own order that she ask but one question. "It was forbidden by the Overlord."

"It was cruel." Cwen swiped at the tears on her cheeks. "I needed you."

Hebron looked down into his daughter's eyes, tears glistened in his own. "And I you. But your mother and I had duties to perform for the good of all Liambrians." He took her face in his hands, his expression begging for forgiveness. "You were never out of my heart or my mind. There were times I didn't think I would ever hold you so."

Cwen could not stop herself from crying as she listened to his deep voice. It wasn't the low timbre of Otas', but the throaty sound of his own pain kept her tears flowing.

Hebron rubbed the tears from her cheeks with his thumbs. "I've had love for you since your mother carried you in her belly. Nothing has changed. Do you understand, *Tanim*, daughter?"

Cwen managed to nod.

Hebron kissed her forehead. "I could hold you thus all night, but there's one other who also needs the strength of my arms." He dropped his hands to his sides.

"Mother?"

"Yes. Sevea and I have been apart for some time."

Cwen became concerned. The look Lord Ware had worn

at the evening meal could only be interpreted as jealousy. "What about Lord Ware?"

"He's of no concern." Hebron shrugged again. "If he intrudes upon us, I'll use the Gift against him."

Cwen started to ask him how he would do this.

"Enough." Hebron nodded his head to the door. "Go to your chambers. Otas awaits you."

Cwen purposely delayed leaving. "What am I to call you?"

"Father." Hebron didn't like the look of fear that had crossed his daughter's face at the mention of Otas, but he didn't have the power to intervene on Cwen's behalf. "Go now. You mustn't keep the Overlord waiting."

Cwen nodded, but made no move toward the door.

Hebron thought he'd have to escort her there, but finally she turned and left the chamber, her feet dragging.

Otas sat in Cwen's chamber in total darkness. He had no need of the candles for he could see in the night. Besides, it made him think better. He'd read the disc Vlad had given him twice through, wondering how Earthlings had continued their species when their mating was without depth. There was passion, yes, but no melding of the minds. Earthlings engaged in time-consuming mental processing and analysis of their relationships. They were unable to simply accept the differences between male and female. Mutual consent appeared to be a big issue. Something that he hadn't given Cwen. No wonder his Queen had misconceptions about their joining. Reading about fictional coupling was entirely different than engaging in the real act, especially if the participants were Liambrian. He'd asked Vlad to teach him the proper words in Cwen's form of English so that he could speak with her.

Light spilled from the hallway, alerting him to his Queen's arrival. Otas heard her gasp at the darkness of the room. With the power of his mind, he set the candles to flame, which caused his wife to jump.

Cwen cautiously entered the room, bolted the door behind her, and found it warmed by the heater. She spotted her husband sitting in one of the chairs before the cold hearth. She moved slowly and stood before him.

"*Sa-Jang*," she said quietly, unsure of his mood for his pupils were so large only a slim ring of orange showed in his eyes. Perhaps he still held the anger within him from the morning.

"I have not come to bed you." Otas was irritated by the relief that appeared on his Queen's face. "Sit. I would talk with you."

"Why didn't you tell me Hebron was my father?" she asked as she sat next to him.

"'Twas his right to tell you. Not mine." He kept his eyes forward because if he looked at her, Otas would lose control of his body.

Cwen accepted that, waiting for him to get on with his "talk."

"I would not have you mate . . . make love with me out of fear."

"What of your command that I do so?"

"I will no longer ask it of you." Otas couldn't help looking at her. Even with her eyes red-rimmed from crying, his Queen looked beautiful in the green gown with her glorious hair flowing about her. He fought the tightening in his loins. "I do not wish your hate."

"'Tis too late." She looked at him to gauge his reaction. Otas' pupils had constricted to pinpoints of black.

"You hate me because I drove you to *Ju-Gum*?" Her mind was so open it was easy to read her feelings.

"It's only because of this *koi* you put in my mind that I respond to you. I wasn't given a choice."

"Nor I."

Cwen rose her eyebrows. "How can this be?"

"There is only one Queen. I had *koi* for you before your birth."

"You're a man. How can you have *koi?*"

Anger sparked in his eyes. "I am not a 'man.' I am a Liambrian male. You insult me." Otas tried to cool his growing temper. "In Liambrians, both *sungs*, genders, have *koi*. The need I have for you cannot be stopped."

Feeling like she needed to be higher than he, Cwen stood, looking down at him, feeling a rage grow within her. "It must cease! I won't give in to this *koi* again!"

The gems in his Queen's jewelry began to glow. He stood quickly as he sensed what portion of the Gift she was about to unknowingly activate.

Cwen felt the anger grow inside, causing a great pressure in the front of her brain. She wanted to beat the pulp out of Otas for implanting lust into her mind. What felt like an electrical surge rushed up to her brain, the gold collar and bracelets becoming warm against her skin. Without warning, the powerful current seemed to shoot out of her forehead, aimed directly at her husband.

When the psychokinetic blast hit him, his hair and clothing rippled as if he stood in a wind tunnel, yet his body remained unmoving. Cwen suddenly realized she was causing the effect, but was unable to stop it, fear squeezing her insides as a millstone crushed wheat.

The stones in Otas' jewelry began to flare hotly as she looked on with horror. With his hair flapping around him, his orange eyes took on a green fluorescence. All at once she felt her own psychokinetic energy turned back on herself, forcing Cwen to her knees with the strength of it. Cwen gasped as a pain rivaling a hammer blow struck her head, making her grip the sides as if it would fall from her shoulders. Somehow, he shut off the power blasting from her brain.

Cwen didn't know if seconds or minutes had passed when

the pain ceased. Hazarding a glance at Otas, his hair and clothes were now still, but the look on his face was frightening.

"You have no control!" His voice was deceptively soft as the green sapphires lost their light. "If 'twas not me, but another, he would have been killed!"

She sat back on her heels, saying, "Forgive me, *Sa-Jang*. I don't understand what happened."

His eyes vibrant with different shades of orange, Otas said, "'Twas your anger that caused the release of *Kang-Yak*, power. You have no understanding how dangerous the Gift is." He couldn't help slipping into Liambrian, clawing his hands through his hair. Until this moment, he hadn't accepted how much of an error he'd made by giving his Queen so much power. Lowering his hands, he glared down at his wife. "It will gain you nothing to turn your anger on me! By *Ha-nu-nim*, never do so again!"

Shaken, yet still bold, she shot back, "I won't if I don't have to bear your touch!"

"*Koi* or no, I will not touch you unless you wish it!"

"I'll never wish it!"

"You lie!" Otas growled. "I feel it in you now!"

Cwen gritted her teeth, feeling her insides burn with need. Somehow their mind-battle had turned into excitement. "Leave me!"

"When you wish my touch, I will know and return, *Katai*, wife." With that, Otas vanished.

# Chapter 11

Hebron's breathing was harsh as he lay trapped in Sevea's embrace. Her breaths were as labored as his. They lay in his chamber on the third floor, where they'd spent the night loving each other instead of sleeping. When he regained his breath, Hebron rose up on his elbows, keeping his body tightly joined to his wife's, gazing down into her golden eyes.

Sevea looked upon her husband, his eyes more smoke than green, expressing his uneasiness better than spoken words. She knew him as well as she knew herself, asking, "What troubles you?"

"Our daughter." Hebron stared at his wife for some seconds. "Cwen's emotions are in great turmoil. Can't you feel it?"

Sevea closed her eyes, using her mind to sense their daughter. She read many uncontrolled emotions flowing from Cwen: rage, confusion, doubt, fear, and rising sexual need, which her daughter was trying to suppress. When Sevea opened her eyes, she said, "Cwen can't take anymore pressure."

Hebron nodded in agreement. "I predict she'll break if I force the Training on her now. Yet I can't go against the Overlord's orders."

"Cwen has only been here a few days, and all we've done is force her to be the Overlord's Queen. We haven't given her time to assimilate all of this new information." Sevea ran her hands through Hebron's black hair. "What do you suggest?"

"Cwen's emotions must be dealt with first. She mustn't lose her mind as Otas' mother did." Dark-green was now replacing the smoke in his eyes. "I'll take her to *Hyu-shik* and be the father I was never given a chance to be."

"How long do you intend to be gone?"

"Three, perhaps four days." He frowned. "Will there be a problem explaining our absence to this Lord Ware?"

"He's easily controlled. I'll take care of it."

Hebron kissed Sevea's forehead. "I don't wish to leave you, but our daughter's sanity is at stake." Reluctantly, he moved off his wife. "I must gather provisions for the journey."

"I'll assist you."

Hebron's eyes darkened again. "You'll tell Otas where we've gone?"

"You know I must." Sevea shrugged. "He'll know anyway. He's always aware of his Queen's whereabouts."

Cwen sat on her bed waiting for Hebron, dressed in battle gear, sword and dagger strapped to her hips. She tried to keep her hands from shaking in her lap, but was unsuccessful for she was really scared. The power she had unleashed on Otas last eve had been terrifying. Cwen still didn't know how she'd done it. Until then, she'd only half-believed she was an extraterrestrial. Now there was no possibility of denial. She was afraid of her very thoughts, trying to keep them focused on what her father would teach her today. Cwen was in no mood to practice battle, but her father had ordered it, giving her no room to disobey.

She jumped when the knock sounded at her chamber door. Hesitantly, she rose and opened it. Her father stood before her dressed in a white tunic, black breeches, and boots, carrying two packs with leather straps that must have been the 41st century version of backpacks. She looked at him questioningly as he entered the room and bolted the door.

Hebron looked upon his daughter feeling a pain squeeze

his heart. Now that he stood before her, the inner turmoil that he'd sensed from a distance was worse than he'd thought. Untrained as she was, Cwen's mind was wide open, giving anyone with the ability to read it full knowledge of her fears and feelings.

He noticed that she was dressed for battle as he had commanded. Setting down the packs, he moved to her, unfastening the sword belt. "I'm countermanding my own order. We won't fight today."

Cwen only looked at him in query.

"You need a vacation from all of this." Hebron swept his arm in a wide arc.

"Otas will be angry."

"Let me worry about the Overlord." He slipped the straps of one of the packs on her shoulders.

She looked at her sword and dagger he'd thrown on the bed. "Vlad said I should never go out unarmed."

Hebron looked at his daughter with pain in his eyes. All she knew how to do was follow orders. She had no independent thought. He doubted she really had a sense of self. "I'm your father and I'm armed. I'll protect you," he said as he slipped the other pack on.

Not knowing what to say, Cwen blurted, "Do you have a horse in the stables?"

"Horses can't carry us to where we go." He opened his arms to Cwen.

Unquestioning, she moved into them, hugging his waist. "Where are we going?"

"*Hyu-shik*." With that, Hebron activated the teleporter, and they vanished from the room.

*Liambria 2*

Vlad listened intently as Otas recounted the events of the previous evening. As he'd predicted, his cousin had lost control and unleashed the power she was ill-prepared to handle. Vlad sat on the futon in the Overlord's chambers, watching Otas pace in a rare moment of agitation.

"My wife has no concept of how powerful the blast was she sent against me." Otas stopped pacing long enough to claw his hands through his hair and stare at Vlad, the orange and gold colors in his eyes shifting rapidly. "And she didn't even cry out at the pain I caused when I shut off the flow of psychokinetic force."

"I warned you. My cousin has knowledge about many things, but in some ways she's no more than a petulant child. What you witnessed was a tantrum." Vlad stared up at Otas, his look serious. "We're just lucky it was you that received the force of her anger. Otherwise, we'd have a dead person on our hands."

"That's another thing." Otas paced again. "I don't deserve this hate she has for me because of our mating. She doesn't understand that *koi* is just there. We are both susceptible to it."

"Even though she read all of those Earthling romance novels, I don't think Cwen consciously realizes she's female and that desire is only one of the aspects of being so."

"True. And I don't think that—" Otas suddenly stood motionless, his eyes looking like dual solar flares.

Vlad jumped up at the sight of his friend. "What's wrong?"

"Hebron!" Otas let loose with a barrage of curses. "He's taken my Queen to Hyu-shik! Does he try to keep her from me?"

Vlad let out the breath he'd been holding. By the look on Otas' face, he'd thought something was seriously wrong. "You're reacting with your emotions, not logic. Hebron's only following your instructions."

"I didn't tell him to take her so far away!"

"I'm sure Hebron has his reasons. Castle Acwellen isn't

exactly the perfect place for Gift Training. The Earthlings wouldn't understand it. Hebron only seeks privacy."

Otas looked calmer, but the fire in his eyes still burned. "Perhaps."

"I don't know why you worry. You have the ability to go where you will," Vlad reminded him.

"And if she loses control? I would not have the death of her own father on my hands."

"If she activates again, and Hebron is in pain, you'll know it. You can teleport there before serious damage is done."

Otas didn't look convinced. "I hope you're right, my friend."

*Hyu-shik*

When they materialized at this place called Hyu-shik, Cwen had her eyes closed, her face buried in her father's chest. She still found this form of travel unsettling. The first thing she noticed was the warmth of the air and the gentle breeze held no chill.

"Open your eyes," Hebron said, looking down at her.

Cwen did as bid, staggering a little as the wave of light-headedness hit her. Hebron steadied her. Cwen gasped at the things surrounding her: palm trees swayed gently in the wind, gold, red, and pink hibiscus flowers perfumed the air, ferns that stood taller than she were a rich dark-green, a clear pool of water rippled with the waves caused by the waterfall that cascaded into it. At the sight of it, Cwen now heard the gurgling roar the waterfall made. She'd seen pictures and read of tropical paradises, of course, but she'd never been to one.

"Where are we?" she asked as she slipped the heavy back-pack from her shoulders.

Relieving himself of his own burden, he answered, "An uninhabited island in the south Atlantic. There are animals here, but no humanoids."

"We must be thousands of miles away from Castle Acwellen," she said in astonishment. "I didn't know we could teleport such long distances."

"Range doesn't matter with the teleporter. What counts is that you know where you're going."

"Have the right coordinates, you mean."

Hebron smiled. His daughter may be reaching the breaking point, but she wasn't stupid. "Correct." He pointed to a cluster of dark-green foliage that formed a natural canopy against the elements about twenty yards away. "We'll set up camp there." He picked up his pack and moved to the site.

Following her father with her own pack, Cwen realized it was more than just warm, it was hot. The temperature had to be close to ninety degrees, she thought. By the time she covered the short distance to where Hebron stood, she was sweating profusely, her leather battle gear sticking to her skin. She dropped her pack next to Hebron's, wiping the sweat from her forehead.

Hebron pulled the tunic over his head, revealing a smooth, well-muscled chest. "Vlad taught you to swim, didn't he?"

"Yes," Cwen answered suspiciously. Vlad had made sure she could swim all right. But he'd done it by making her hold her dagger between her teeth, loaded down with the weight of a pack on her back. Did her father have similar ideas?

"Remove your clothes. There's nothing like a swim to refresh oneself."

Cwen only stood there, face reddening.

Hebron looked at his daughter, raising his eyebrows. "Why do you hesitate?"

"I—I don't have a swimsuit."

"You're wearing a chemise, aren't you?"

Cwen only nodded.

It took Hebron a moment to understand what was wrong with his daughter. "By *Ha-nu-nim*, I'm your father. I'm not some crazed male out to harm you." He was out of his boots and breeches, wearing the Liambrian version of undershorts. Hebron started to pull off the shimmering garment, but thought better of it. He'd shock his daughter's sensibilities if she saw him in the raw. He stood, folding his arms, waiting for Cwen to disrobe.

Cwen quickly removed the battle gear, her face flaming. Consciously, she knew Hebron was her father, but she had no control over her embarrassment. With speed, she raced back to the pool and dived into it in one smooth motion.

The water was cool, but not teeth-chattering cold. Cwen could see the bottom of the pool through the clear blue water. Assorted fish skittered out of her path as she swam for the surface. She turned on her back, floating in lazy circles, feeling tension seep from her body. Distantly, she heard the splash as her father dived into the water.

Without warning, Hebron surfaced next to her, grabbing her waist and tickling her. Cwen couldn't hold back the giggles. She didn't know herself she was ticklish. She splashed him with water, gasping out, "Stop, father! You'll drown me!" Her words just made him tickle her more.

Hebron smiled at her laughter, which sounded like tinkling bells. He doubted she'd ever laughed with abandon before. "I knew you would be ticklish, for I am, too. Like father, like daughter."

It was a mistake to tell her. Cwen attacked back, forcing deep, throaty chuckles to emerge from Hebron. They played like children in the pool for an hour until Hebron said, "We've had no breakfast. I don't know about you, but I'm hungry."

Laughing still, Cwen responded, "I'm ravenous."

They swam back to shore, emerging from the pool into the hot air. Hebron kept his face expressionless as he gazed upon Cwen. The wet chemise hid nothing of her well-formed body from his view. No wonder the Overlord couldn't keep his hands off his daughter. She was a sight to behold. The fact that she had sprung from his loins sent pride rushing through him. "Come." Hebron took her hand, leading her back to the campsite.

Hebron dug into one of the packs, pulling out a folded square of gray shimmering fabric. Opening it to its full size, he spread it upon the ground in the sun. "Sit."

Before she sat on the blanket, Cwen brushed the black granules from her feet. "Is this stuff sand?"

"Yes," Hebron answered as he laid out bread and cheese accompanied by water in a metal container.

"Why's it black? I thought sand was beige or lighter."

Hebron sat on the blanket slicing off pieces of cheese. "This island was formed after the upheaval. It's still growing. The sand is mostly lava that's been ground down by the water." He munched thoughtfully on bread and cheese. "There's an active volcano on the opposite side of the island."

Cwen stopped chewing. "Are we in danger?"

"Not at the moment. We predict an eruption will occur in a year or so."

Cwen stretched out on the blanket when she'd finished eating, emitting a sound of contentment. "I love this heat."

"All Liambrians like warmth. Our home planet has two suns." Hebron lay on his back, placing his hands under his head.

Looking upon her father, she thought his body as well-toned as Vlad's. Indeed, she could not tell her father's age, although he had to be older than Vlad. As she gazed at his bronzed form, Cwen realized she was beginning to love her father. It didn't matter that she'd only known him but a few hours. He was strong-natured, she had no doubt, but he'd showed compassion for her feelings. Something that she'd lacked while growing up.

"Why did you bring me here, father?"

Hebron turned his head to her, his smoke-green eyes darkening with anger. "You're showing signs of immense stress. I won't have you broken."

"Was I acting weird?" Cwen flinched at the word she'd chosen.

"Not yet." Hebron had no difficulty understanding her manner of speech. "It was in your mind. I could read your emotional turmoil there."

"Are my thoughts so open?"

"Yes. And they shouldn't be. Only Otas should be able to read your mind, no other."

At the mention of the Overlord, a mixture of fear and confusion raced across Cwen's face, causing Hebron to turn on his side and prop his head on his hand. "Tell me your feelings about Otas."

"He'll get angry."

Hebron grasped her chin, forcing her to look into his eyes. "*Tanim*, I'm not a tattletale. Stress comes from having no emotional release for things that trouble you. Talking is the best cure for confused feelings."

Cwen stared at her father, surprised at the tears that shined in his eyes. Yes, she needed to talk about Otas, but where to begin. After a moment, she decided it was best to work backward, starting with the events of last evening. Looking down, she confessed, "I'm afraid I did find a path for emotional release. Last night, I was angry with Otas and I . . . "

Hebron stiffened, knowing what his daughter was going to say, asking her anyway. "You what?"

"I—I blasted him with the Gift. I don't know how I did it. It just happened," she said in a rush.

"*Kom-un Chi-ok*, Black Hell!" Hebron cursed. "What did Otas do?"

"Somehow he shut off the power, but he was so angry he was yelling at me in Liambrian. The only thing I understood was that I would have killed someone else." Cwen's hands began to shake. "Is this true?"

"Only the Overlord can withstand the psychokinetic power you unleashed on him. If it had been someone else, human or Liambrian, they would have been slammed into the wall, their bones crushed."

Cwen gasped, covering her mouth with her hands. What if it had been Sevea or Hebron?

"You're not completely at fault. It's all of us. Otas included." Hebron pulled his daughter to him, placing her back against his chest. "How can we expect you to control something you don't understand?" He felt his daughter shaking, placing a hand on her forehead to soothe her nerves. When the shivering stopped, he asked, "Do you believe you're Liambrian?"

Cwen thought it over. "I'm not one hundred percent convinced I'm an alien, but I've only to look into the Overlord's eyes to know he's not an Earthling. No human has eyes that churn with colors of orange and gold, and that shine with an inner light."

"Only Otas has such eyes," he lied, thinking of Maccus. "It's what marks him as Overlord." Hebron continued to soothe his daughter's temples. "I'd planned on not teaching you anything today, but what happened last night can't be repeated."

"I'll do whatever you say."

"Do it because you wish it, not because I command it!" There was a definite edge to his voice.

"I don't want to hurt anyone by accident."

"I must explain something to you first." His voice softened as he rubbed his palm across her forehead. "The Liambrian brain has psychic receptors, here in the frontal lobes. If the Earthlings were to do a CAT Scan on one of us, they would think there were multiple tumors in our brains. The number of these receptors varies depending on the amount of the Gift one possesses. Otas has the most. You next. Are you with me so far?"

"Yes."

"What you did last eve was activate the psychokinetic

receptors with rage. It's dangerous to do so because with anger there's no control. You must be conscious of how much or how little power you unleash. I'll teach you to control the activation of these receptors."

"How?" Cwen wanted to know.

"Because we need to expedite the process, I'm going to put you to sleep."

Cwen turned on her back to look at her father. "You mean hypnosis?"

Hebron shook his head. "It's much more complicated than that. Do you trust me?" At her nod he sat up, crossing his legs. "Lay your head in my lap."

Cwen was scared, but she did as he'd asked.

Hebron placed a hand on either side of her head. "Sleep," he said softly.

Unable to stop herself, Cwen resisted. Hebron increased the power of the Gift, making her head tingle. "Sleep," he said again.

She tried to hold on to consciousness, but her father's power was too strong. Soon thought ceased, and she slipped into the void of darkness.

# Chapter 12

Cwen was in a dream state, asleep, yet awake. She found herself miniaturized, walking within her brain. She continued to move forward past the brown pituitary gland, fascinated by the blue veins and red arteries that fed oxygen to the gray matter of her brain. The neurons were silver ribbons crisscrossing in their message paths to complete the electrical synapses of her brain's functions.

Just up ahead were the frontal lobes. Hebron's voice guided her to the set of psychokinetic receptors, which were round and pink in color, a pair situated anteriorly in each lobe. Following her father's instructions, she could now feel the receptors in her head. Suddenly it seemed easy to activate them. *On*, she said with her mind. The pink receptors began to glow with a neon brilliance, producing a definitive pressure in her forehead. Cwen waited several minutes getting the feel of this new sensation before thinking, *Off*. The receptors dimmed, eliminating the pressure she'd felt.

From somewhere far away, Cwen could hear Hebron calling to her. *Awaken* reverberated in her mind. Cwen opened her eyes, blinking at the stark blue sky. The sun had descended to a late afternoon position. Her head still lay in her father's lap, his hands holding her forehead firmly.

"Cwen?"

"I'm awake," she said, sitting up to face him. "How much time has passed?"

"Three hours."

Cwen cocked her head, staring at her father.

Hebron stood. "Now, let's see if my Mind-Touch was successful." He pointed to a large rock about ten feet away. "Move it."

Cwen focused her eyes on the rock, squinting as she tried to activate the receptors. When she felt a tingling pressure in her forehead, Cwen concentrated harder, causing the rock to slide several feet to the left.

"Good, good." Hebron patted her head. "Now, destroy it."

Cwen looked up a him, aghast.

"Do it," Hebron said sternly.

Cwen quickly stared at the rock, feeling the pressure in her head again. This exercise was harder. She was concentrating so hard her head began to ache, but the rock remained unharmed. Getting exasperated, the word *destroy* popped into her mind. At that exact instant, the rock exploded into thousands of tiny pieces, scaring the life out of her. Cwen couldn't help holding a hand over her heart.

"Excellent." Hebron stared at his daughter, pleased by the fright that showed on her face. "Now you appreciate how powerful the Gift is. You must remember not to use it out of anger, or you won't have control. Using it for defense purposes is acceptable."

Cwen nodded that she understood, shivering not only because the temperature had dropped several degrees, but also at the thought of turning that power on someone. It seemed terrifying.

Hebron knew what she was thinking, but said nothing, letting her ponder the seriousness of the Gift. He pulled on his breeches and dug into the pack for more food, also pulling out a shimmering, white garment. Handing it to Cwen, he said, "The nights turn cool. Put this on."

Cwen put on the white garment, feeling warmer immediately even though it was sleeveless and fell just above her knees. There were ties at the waist, which she cinched and secured with a tight knot.

"That's called a *wanpisu*. It's what all Liambrian females wear." He handed her a hunk of cheese and bread. "Sit and eat. We missed lunch."

They sat together, eating their meal in silence. The bond between them was growing stronger as if they'd never been apart. Cwen couldn't read her father's thoughts, but she knew he must feel as she did. Cwen became self-conscious when she felt her father's dark-green eyes on her.

"Why do you hate Otas, *Tanim*?"

Her father was certainly blunt. "I'm not sure I understand it myself."

Hebron studied her for some seconds. "You dislike the *koi* you have for him."

Cwen sighed. "Don't I have any secrets from you?"

"No, but that can be corrected." Hebron stretched out on his side, hoping that his relaxed posture would help her to speak her mind. "Explain to me why you resent the pleasure passion brings you."

"Because it wasn't my doing. Otas implanted the feeling in my mind. If he hadn't done so, I wouldn't respond to him."

"You're wrong there. The Mind-Touch ceremony at your birth was just a formality. You're genetically programmed to respond only to Otas. The mere implantation of *koi* doesn't bring about *Ju-Gum*."

Cwen's face heated. Did he know everything that passed between the Overlord and herself? His next statement answered the question for her.

"Even now, I can feel you burn for the Overlord's touch." Hebron took hold of her braid, rubbing its thickness between his fingers. "Your confusion comes from not knowing what it means to be female."

"I do. I learned from the romance novels I read."

Hebron grunted. "What passes between Earthlings as

mating is shallow. One-dimensional, if you will. When you couple with Otas, not only are your bodies thrown into the task, but your minds as well."

Cwen suppressed her embarrassment at speaking about such things with her father. "Is that why he, uh, stays joined with me after the act and speaks to me?"

"Yes. To roll off a female and fall asleep after mating is sacrilege to Liambrians. Haven't you felt that your minds were communing while you're joined with the Overlord?"

Remembering the Mind-Probe Otas had done on her, she answered, "Yes. But besides being his Queen, he doesn't really know me."

"Nor you him."

"Do you know Otas very well?"

Hebron shook his head. "None know the workings of the Overlord's mind but Vlad."

"Vlad? He's here in this time-frame?"

Hebron cursed silently. Of course, his daughter didn't know about Vlad, for no one had told her. "Yes. Vlad's second in command to the Overlord and his only friend."

Now it all made sense. It was why Vlad had been so merciless. Cwen remained silent thinking this over.

"No wonder you're confused about what passes between male and female." Hebron was reading her mind again. "Your Aunt Amma never explained it to you, and the only males you knew would never pursue you sexually. There's no disgrace in the feelings of *koi* you have for Otas."

"Or the way I respond to him?"

"No." Hebron tilted his head. "The pleasure he gives to you is remarkable. I didn't know he had it in him. I thought him cold."

"If I'm the only one he would bond with, how did he get this experience he obviously has?"

Hebron swore at himself. He'd walked into that one.

"Before a Liambrian male bonds, he's able to have relations with a female of his choosing."

Cwen couldn't stop the jealousy rising inside her. "Who is she?"

"I won't answer that. It's up to Otas to tell you if he wishes." With that, Hebron pulled another square of Liambrian fabric from one of the packs. Night had fallen while they'd been talking. Stretching out, he motioned Cwen to join him. "The Mind-Touch process wears one out. It's time for bed."

Cwen snuggled next to her father under the cover, her mind still working on the things that they'd discussed. "Father?"

"Yes," Hebron said with a yawn.

"You said I was genetically programmed to respond to Otas."

"It's true."

Cwen was persistent. "I want to know what you mean."

Hebron wrapped his arm around her waist, squeezing gently. "Go to sleep. We'll discuss genetics tomorrow."

In minutes her father snored lightly. Cwen fumed at the thought of Otas in another female's arms. She thought she'd remain awake, but Hebron's snores were hypnotic. Soon she slept.

Cwen dreamed deeply, her raging lust focused on Otas. Her hands felt the warmth of his smooth-muscled chest as she ran her palms across him, igniting his desire as well as her own. She could feel his hot manhood pressing against her. Moaning in her sleep, she began to position herself to accept him.

Instead of the pleasure Cwen had been anticipating, she felt an annoying yet painless nudge in her side that shattered the dream into a thousand fragments. Blinking at the brightness of the blue sky, she saw Hebron standing over her, kicking her with his foot.

"Wake up, *Tanim!*" he shouted, blasting her ears and her mind.

Gasping, Cwen sat up quickly, seeking the security of her absent sword. "Are we in danger?"

"You are if you don't get up!" Hebron scowled down at his daughter. "The morning is half gone."

Cwen untangled herself from the blanket, standing on none too steady feet. "I thought we were on vacation."

Hebron growled at her. He shoved a cloth and soap in her hands as well as what looked like a jet-propelled toothbrush. "Go wash. I would teach you something else this day."

Still groggy from sleep, Cwen stared dumbly at the high-tech toothbrush, asking, "This is for my teeth?"

Hebron plopped a glob of white cream on the bristles. "Of course. Do you think Liambrians are barbarians who scrub their teeth with a stick?"

Goodness, her father was grouchy. Daring not to anger him, she said nothing, going to the pool and quickly finishing her ablutions. When she returned to the campsite, Hebron took the items she'd just used from her and shoved a chunk of cheese and a slice of bread in her hands.

"Sit down and eat. I'm anxious to begin."

As she chewed, Cwen watched her father. He stood over her bare-chested, legs spread, hands on hips. She didn't have to read his mind to know he was angry with her. What did I do? she thought. It was hard, but she forced the wad of cheese down her throat, and boldly asked, "Are you always this way in the mornings?"

"I am when I get no sleep because my daughter's mind broadcasts her thoughts of *koi* and joining with Otas!"

Cwen blushed from her chest to the top of her head. "You know of my dream?"

"By *Ha-nu-nim*, I wish I didn't!" Hebron grasped his long hair and secured it with a leather thong. "I accept that you're married to the Overlord, but I don't want to know what passes between the two of you in your bed!" He closed his eyes trying to force the images from his mind. "You must learn to keep your thoughts to yourself!"

"You intend to teach me how to shield my thoughts?"

"If I have the time!" Hebron looked to the sky, then back at Cwen. "If I heard your siren's song, you can be sure that Otas did!"

"But he's thousands of miles away."

"Don't you know anything? Distance means nothing to the Overlord. His mind is aware of all Liambrians, especially his Queen. With the thoughts you were projecting, it wouldn't matter if you were on another planet! Believe me. Otas will come. I just don't know when."

Cwen became so nervous she couldn't finish her breakfast. She remembered her husband's threat that he would know when she wanted his touch. She'd been betrayed by her own subconscious. "Teach me quick!"

"What I would teach you will only give *me* peace of mind. You can't shield your thoughts from Otas."

Frantic, Cwen tried to think of a way out of this. Even though Otas could read her mind, there was no way in hell she'd admit to the amount of desire she held for him. Staring at her father in his anger, she thought he looked extremely powerful. Surely, he would protect her from the Overlord. Cwen opened her mouth.

"Don't you dare ask me to do what you're thinking! No Liambrian in his right mind would go against Otas!" In his rage, Hebron's eyes were dark with no traces of green. "The Overlord will be angry that I brought you here as it is. Would you have me turned to dust?"

Defeated, Cwen shook her head.

Hebron gazed down at his daughter who, by all appearances, was resigned to her fate. But her emotions were raging inside her head. He felt great remorse for his anger.

He'd brought Cwen to Hyu-shik to alleviate her mounting stress and instead he'd just added to it.

Studying her thoughts for some moments, Hebron discovered her primary source of agitation was the marriage to the Overlord. For whatever reason, her Aunt Amma failed to instruct Cwen in matters of the heart. There had been the romance novels, of course, but none of the novels he'd read had storylines as complicated as the reality of his daughter's life. Hebron's daughter was of high intelligence. Feeling enlightened, he came to the conclusion that what Cwen lacked was pertinent information. Knowledge would hopefully enable her to come to grips with her raging emotions.

Hebron took in several calming breaths. "I beg your forgiveness for my anger. I had reason to become upset, but you don't understand why. I would explain if you let me."

Cwen looked up at him, her smoke-green eyes free of tears. "I'm listening."

Encouraged, Hebron sat down next to Cwen, running his hand along her long braid. "It's not only me who shouldn't know your thoughts, but all Liambrians. You've only partially bonded with Otas. When the bonding is complete, you'll have knowledge of the Overlord that none should know. Especially—"

"Maccus?"

Hebron nodded gravely. "As his Queen, you must protect Otas as he does you. Given the chance, Maccus would destroy the Overlord."

"Why?"

"One reason is you. In his twisted mind, Maccus believes you should be his. The other is pure hatred for Otas."

"What has my husband done to Maccus to earn such hatred?"

"The mere fact that he was born," Hebron answered.

"It makes no sense."

"I know, but I'm not permitted to tell you more than that."

There it was again. That order that forbade her knowledge. Cwen looked at Hebron with exasperation. "What do you know of Otas besides him being the Overlord? As a man, I mean."

Shaking his head, Hebron said, "Never refer to your husband as a 'man', or call him so to his face. The word *man* is a definition of Earthlings, who are far below us on the evolutionary scale. Your husband is a Liambrian *male*. And you're not a woman, but a Liambrian *female*."

"I've already gained the Overlord's anger by calling him a man. It seems so petty."

"That's because you don't comprehend male pride. I would be insulted, also."

"We're digressing," Cwen stated. "Tell me what you know of Otas."

Hebron let go of her braid, placing his arm on her shoulders. "What I tell you is mostly supposition, for none know the Overlord as Vlad does. And never does he disclose information about his confidential talks with him."

"What you think will be adequate."

Hebron stared at the waterfall, putting his thoughts in order. He must form his words carefully, giving his daughter information yet not revealing too much. "Otas was raised much as you were. In isolation. He was six-years-old when we arrived on Earth, but never was he allowed to mix with the Earthlings, not even when we jumped through time to the future."

"That explains why he doesn't understand my English."

"What little English Otas knows, he learned in the last five years since he became Overlord."

Cwen absorbed that. "Exactly how old is he?"

"Twenty-five years. Not much older than you."

Cwen just blinked, waiting to hear more.

"His father, Raynar, was unkind to him. We all witnessed it. The result was that Otas became cold and, as far as any of us can tell, emotionless." Hebron looked into Cwen's eyes. "Though he would never admit it, I believe him to be lonely. That's why you're so important to him."

"Are you saying he comes to me not only because of lust, but because of need?"

Hebron hesitated, getting nervous, for he was sure the Overlord was monitoring them. But he plunged ahead. "That's what I think."

When she thought about her husband, Cwen couldn't imagine him needing anyone or anything. The hidden message in what Hebron was saying suddenly dawned on her. "You're also saying that I respond to him the way I do for the same reason."

"Yes." Hebron squeezed her to him. "I know how you were raised. To protect yourself from hurt you formed a barrier around your heart. Your distress about your marriage is because Otas tore down that invisible wall. You feel vulnerable, adrift, don't you?"

She didn't want to admit it, but she answered, "Yes."

"Give it time. You've only been here a matter of days. Soon you will come to terms with your feelings." Hebron positioned himself behind Cwen, folding his legs. He placed his palms on her forehead. "The time grows late. I must teach you how to shield your thoughts."

"What do I do?" Her father's hands on her head felt comforting.

"First I must explain the anatomy of the Liambrian brain. You remember where the subarachnoid space is in Earthlings?"

Cwen nodded. "It's between the bones of the skull and the brain."

"In Liambrians, there's a membrane that lies between the cranium and the subarachnoid space riddled with electrical neuron pathways. This membrane is what shields your thoughts from others once activated."

Cwen looked confused for a second. "How do I . . . uh, turn it on?"

"You must think of what you wish to do. Try it."

Cwen furrowed her brow, concentrating for all she was worth.

Hebron grunted. "I can still hear your thoughts." He thought a moment. "When we teach Liambrian children how to do this, we sometimes advise them to use a word to trigger the action."

Like a mantra for meditation, Cwen thought, trying to think of something that would have meaning to her. Suddenly, visions of sci-fi videos flitted across her mind. *Shields up*, she said with her mind. Immediately, a sound like white noise buzzed in her head.

"Ah," Hebron said in relief, not hearing the cacophony of his daughter's mind. "As a test, shut it off."

Cwen thought about that for a second. *Lower shields!* The white noise disappeared.

Hebron frowned at the racket her thoughts were making. "Good. Now, activate it again."

*Shields up!* Cwen thought. Again the white noise.

*Blessed peace*, Hebron said to himself. "Whatever word you used to lower your Mind-Shield, don't ever think it. If you don't, your thoughts will always remain hidden."

It was going to take some time to get used to the white noise sound, she thought. "All right."

Hebron lowered his hands, but he didn't move away from Cwen. At the moment he was thinking about the good night's sleep he was going to have.

"Father?"

"Hmm?"

"What are you going to do when Otas gets here?"

Hebron was silent. He hadn't figured that out yet.

# Chapter 13

Cwen lay beside her father, wearing a clean chemise and letting the afternoon sun's heat dry her hair after her bath in the pool. They both lay silent, absorbed in their own thoughts. The white noise buzzing in her head was quieter now, which she was thankful for because she was sure the sound would drive her nuts.

At the moment, thoughts of her husband preoccupied her mind. What Hebron said about Otas being lonely explained many things. Not only did he seek her out because of sexual need, but for companionship as well. If he possessed such an empty feeling—one that Cwen was familiar with—she felt she could accept him better for it made him seem less threatening. It had to be a great burden for him to oversee an entire race of beings and be privy to their thoughts as well, yet stand alone with his emotions. It sounded like a great deal of hard, lonely work to Cwen.

These reflections brought to mind questions of her own role as the Overlord's Queen. Hebron had told her she was *The Queen*, which implied that there were duties she was to perform, but she had no idea what that entailed. Cwen glanced at her father, who lay on his back wearing only the Liambrian boxer shorts. He was so still, she wasn't certain if he was awake.

"Father?" she whispered, turning on her side.

"There's no need to whisper. I wasn't asleep." Hebron turned his gaze on his daughter, seeing the worry in her smoke-green eyes. "What troubles you?"

"Exactly what is it about me that makes me the Overlord's Queen?"

Hebron turned to face her, propping his head on his hand. "I'd intended to let you rest for the remainder of the day. What you ask me is rather complicated."

"Not knowing will give me no rest."

"Very well." Hebron turned inward, gathering his thoughts, trying to condense what should have taken Cwen years to learn into a few paragraphs. "Let me start with the evolutionary process of Liambrians."

"Okay." Cwen sat up, folding her legs.

"Genetic advancements are controlled entirely by the Overlord. He has the ability to see within Liambrians, detecting the minute DNA and RNA helixes, and what traits lie in the genes. Prior to Raynar's grandfather, Liambrians had no traits of aggression. We were pretty much cowards."

Looking at her father's powerful chest and arms, Cwen found this hard to believe. "Mother told me some of this."

"I know. What you don't understand is how the evolutionary change came about. It directly involves the Overlord and the Queen." Hebron watched his daughter's face for signs of perplexity. There were none. "The Liambrian race is a collective mind. When the Overlord senses it's time for an evolutionary leap, there's a special mating process he performs with his Queen that alters the current genetic patterns into new ones. Once this event has occurred, the reproductive cells of all Liambrians alter to the new form."

Nodding, Cwen said, "That's how Raynar's grandfather incorporated aggression into Liambrians."

"Correct." Hebron knew that his daughter didn't fully understand the impact of what he was saying. "Your mother explained some of your anatomy."

"She told me Liambrian females have two wombs."

"You misunderstood her." Hebron closed his eyes for a second. When he opened them, he said, "You're the only

Liambrian female with double wombs. No other has this configuration."

"Does that mean I'm destined to bear twins?"

"Not necessarily," he lied, holding to his promise to Otas regarding Maccus. "That much is left to random chance. The fertilization of the ovum in Liambrians is pretty much the same as in humans. What's different is that this special joining, called *Bal-Dar*, ensures the continuance of Liambrians."

The color drained from Cwen's face. "Are you telling me that if I don't do this . . . this *Bal-Dar*, the Liambrians will be sterile?"

"That's right."

Cwen shot off the blanket, ran to the pool, and stared at the waterfall. Now she understood why Earthlings drank alcohol and smoked cigarettes when they were stressed. Cwen felt she could certainly use one or both.

If she didn't let Otas touch her, she would be responsible for the extinction of an entire race of beings. Something told her that mere submission would not be enough, she would have to be an active participant in the process. She wanted to rage at God, but now that she knew she was Liambrian it would do no good to curse the god of Earthlings.

Reluctantly, she returned to Hebron, who now sat facing her. Reaching him, she said, "I think you better explain this *Bal-Dar*."

"I'm afraid I can't. Only the Overlord knows what goes on during the process of *Bal-Dar*. We're only allowed to know of its existence." Hebron patted the blanket, indicating for her to sit. When she had, he continued, "But I can explain what anatomical parts are involved besides the obvious ones."

Cwen shot her father an irritated look.

Undaunted, Hebron explained, "The Overlord has an extra organ called the *Gew-Seen*. This is where the genes are altered. And you only have one large ovary, called *Lun-Chow*. Somehow during *Bal-Dar*, the *Gew-Seen* effects your *Lun-Chow*, altering the genes to match his." Hebron watched his daughter's face. There was no confusion, but a look of defeat etched her features. "I'm afraid that's all I know. You'll have to ask Otas the rest."

Cwen sighed loudly. "There will be a problem there because of the language barrier."

"Once you have fully bonded, the Overlord will speak your tongue."

Cwen gazed at her father. "How is it that you, mother, Aunt Amma, and Vlad have no trouble with my form of English?"

"We were bombarded with constant lessons on language discs. While we were awake. While we slept. Our missions were to start immediately and there was no time to waste on us fumbling with a foreign tongue."

"Why doesn't Otas do this?"

"Frankly, he doesn't have the time. You've no idea how much of his brain capacity is in constant use. He doesn't even totally shutdown when he sleeps."

Cwen didn't want to, but she suddenly felt sorry for her husband. Otas ruled a race of beings, yet from her observations of Hebron, they all feared him. Did any of them love him as their ruler? As a person?

Hebron watched his daughter. He'd hit her with an incredibly heavy burden, yet her Mind-Shield held, containing her thoughts. Hebron couldn't tell what she was thinking and feeling. "Do you wish to ask me more questions?"

"I think I've learned enough this day to last me a lifetime." Cwen stretched out on the blanket. "Rest sounds like a good idea. God knows when I'll be able to do it again."

Cwen closed her eyes, thinking there was no way she could sleep after listening to Hebron, but minutes later she slept deeply.

The feel of the blanket covering her woke Cwen. She looked

around her and saw that the sun had gone down, bringing with it the night chill. Hebron stroked her hair.

"I'm sorry I woke you. You were sleeping so soundly, I'd intended to let you remain so for the night."

"It's okay," she said, yawning. "Actually, I'm hungry. What do we have to eat?"

"The cheese is gone, which is just as well. It wouldn't have lasted much longer in this climate." Hebron set food in front of her. "I hope you don't mind dried meat, bread, and some fruit I picked while you slept."

Shaking her head, Cwen dug into the food. The dried meat and bread disappeared without comment, but when she tasted the fruit, she exclaimed, "Mangos! I love these."

Hebron sat next to her. "I'm surprised that you know what they are. Your Aunt Amma never had a taste for the exotic."

"It wasn't my aunt that introduced me to mangos. It was Vlad. Not only did he see to my combat training, he controlled what food I ate. It was always low-fat, high protein, and complex carbohydrates. Fruit was a big part of Vlad's no nonsense diet." Cwen smiled at the memory. "There were only a few fruits that he brought home that I didn't like. Mangos were my favorite. It was one of the few indulgences he let me have."

Hebron smiled as he watched his daughter polish off the mango, licking her fingers in ecstasy when she'd finished. Hebron handed her the *wanpisu*. "Put this on before the night turns colder."

Cwen quickly slipped on the Liambrian dress, sitting back down. The previous evening they'd gone to bed before this degree of blackness was upon them. She'd started to comment on how dark it was when a stack of wood fashioned for a campfire burst into flame. Startled, she looked at Hebron, who hadn't moved. "How did you do that?"

Hebron tapped his forehead. "Would you like me to teach you how?"

"I think I've had enough learning in the last two days. I just want to relax." Cwen ran her hand through her loose hair. She'd fallen asleep without braiding it. There were probably millions of tangles in it. "I should have brought a brush."

Hebron dug through one of the packs, pulling out just the very thing. "Here. Sit before me. I'll fix your hair."

Cwen scooted in front of her father, feeling her love for him increasing. It was as if Hebron was trying to make up for all of the physical contact between father and daughter that had been denied them. Cwen sighed as Hebron smoothed the snarls from her hair with a gentle touch.

"Otas didn't come." She hadn't meant to voice her thoughts.

The brush stopped. "You sound disappointed."

Cwen lowered her head for a second, then raised it. "After what you've told me, I believe I may have misjudged him."

"Perhaps." The brush started its soothing rhythm again. "In time you'll know your husband better than any of us. But this I can tell you now. Otas would never knowingly hurt his Queen. Emotionally or physically."

"I think you're right. He's a sensitive man . . . uh, male. He was upset when I told him I hated him."

The brush suddenly got caught on a tangle, causing his daughter to flinch. Hebron knew it must have hurt, but he didn't care right now. "How could you say such a thing to your husband?"

"At the time I meant it."

"And now?" Hebron tossed aside the ten strands he had pulled out.

"I want to talk to him. Explain why I said it."

"You really didn't answer me."

"I don't hate him."

Hebron grunted. "It's not just *koi* making you say that?"

"No. I must see him."

Hebron started to braid her hair in silence. His daughter would get her wish. He'd had telepathic word from the Overlord. Otas would come with the sunrise.

Minutes before sunrise, Hebron stood on the rocks above the waterfall wearing the white tunic and backpack. This was the appointed place he was to await Otas. He could see his daughter sleeping down below. He'd wanted to tell her about the Overlord's arrival, but Otas had forbidden him to.

Hebron had a clear view on his left of the sun as it cleared the horizon on the ocean in its ascent. With it came the stirring of air that announced the Overlord's arrival. Hebron turned to face him, or rather, look up at him. His daughter suddenly seemed too small for this giant of a male. As always, the Overlord was dressed in black with the addition of a sword and dagger strapped to his hips. He carried a pack of his own.

"*Sa-Jang,*" Hebron said in greeting.

The Overlord's eyes swam with shifting orange and golden light, displaying an emotion that Hebron didn't recognize. It wasn't anger, but Hebron became uncomfortable.

"Have I displeased you, *Sa-Jang?*"

The Overlord shook his head. "Just the opposite."

Though their voices were similar in deepness, Otas' voice sounded lower, reminding Hebron who was master. Hebron hesitated in speaking, afraid he would awaken his daughter.

Reading his mind, Otas said, "She sleeps deeply. She won't hear us. Besides, the falls cover our voices."

"What have I done to gain your pleasure?"

"I have been monitoring all that was said and done by you. My Queen still needs practice, but you have taught her what usually takes years in two days."

"You honor me." That strange look was still in the Overlord's eyes. Hebron didn't know how to react to it.

Otas was aware of his father-in-law's discomfort, saying, "Did you have to tell her I was lonely?"

Hebron stopped his amusing thoughts before the Overlord could read them. "I told the truth, didn't I?"

Otas reluctancy nodded. "I would not have her pity."

Daringly, Hebron smiled. "It's not pity she feels for you. But a sameness that will eventually bring you closer."

Otas only grunted.

"I've discovered a few things about my daughter myself. Her stress and anger come from ignorance." At the Overlord's scathing look, Hebron held up his hand. "I'm not saying she should be told everything at once. Otherwise, she would go the way of your mother, Taki. For every command or action she's told to make, a simple explanation will gain her cooperation. It doesn't have to be the full truth."

Otas absorbed this for a few minutes. "I will heed your advice."

"I thank you, *Sa-Jang*." Hebron rolled up his sleeve to gain access to the teleporter. "One more thing."

"Yes?"

"After being with me for this time, I predict your size will become of interest to her."

"Are you saying she will be afraid of me?"

"My daughter has great curiosity. She'll want to know just how tall you are." Hebron himself was getting a stiff neck from looking up at him.

"I don't know how to say it in her tongue."

"You're about *six-eleven*."

"Six-eleven," Otas repeated. "The numbers make no sense."

"Trust me. She will understand." With that, Hebron popped out of view.

Otas lowered his pack and sat on the rocks by the falls, watching his Queen sleep and listening to her *koi* driven dreams of him. He couldn't help it. One of his rare smiles appeared.

Cwen lay still with her eyes closed, listening to the birdsong echoing around her. She really must have been uptight not to have heard them before. She stretched lazily, thinking of the vivid dreams she'd had of Otas. Never had they been this intense before. Her sexual desire was out of control, all right. She even imagined she could smell the scent of earth, grass, and male.

The distant splash told her that her father was up, diving into the pool. Pulling back the blanket, she thought, I don't blame him. It was still early morning, but the temperature was nearing the eighties.

She went to the bushes to relieve herself, then brushed her teeth with the space-aged toothbrush Hebron had left out for her. She stared down at the plate of food he had set out in surprise. There was fresh bread, cheese, and mango. Hadn't he said the cheese was gone? With her stomach growling, she decided she didn't care and ate with abandon.

The *wanpisu* became too warm as the temperature continued to rise. She removed it, leaving on the chemise, and sat back down watching the swimming figure in the pool. Cwen decided she would go swimming after her breakfast had digested.

It was strange, but the scent of earth, grass, and male continued to assault her nostrils even though she was awake. Following her nose, she sighted the pile of clothes tucked under the canopy of foliage with her. She gasped at the sight of the black boots. They were way too big for Hebron. Just when that realization hit her, a dark shadow fell over her.

Even before Cwen turned she knew who stood behind her. She couldn't help sucking in her breath at the sight of Otas, who stood in front of her in naked glory, his wet hair slicked back, beads of water running off his body. There was an intensity in his orange eyes that made her jittery.

"Wh—where's my father?" Cwen grimaced. She sounded like a lost child.

Twisting the water from his long hair, Otas answered, "Hebron has gone to Castle Acwellen."

She knew it was a stupid question, but she asked it anyway. "Why have you come?"

"I answer your call to mate."

The colors in his eyes shifted so rapidly it made her dizzy. Flushing, she looked him over. He truly was beautiful to look upon—the smooth-muscled chest, the tight abdomen rippling with good muscle tone, the strong long legs, the black triangle of curls that surrounded his large erection, the bronze hue of his skin.

There had already been a flame of passion in her belly from her dreams. The sight of him ignited it into a raging inferno. Cwen didn't know what possessed her, but she suddenly wanted to taste him. Rising slowly to her knees, she firmly gripped his manhood, running her hand along its length. Even though he'd just come from the water he was hot. Cwen looked up at his face with questioning eyes.

"Do what you will," he said in a none too steady voice.

Feeling brazen, Cwen locked her lips around the tip of his shaft. His whole body shuddered in reaction. She added her warm tongue to the play, stroking him with its softness, kneading him with her hand. Her own desire increased as she worked him, causing his whole body to spasm. She speeded up her actions of arousal.

Otas pulled on her thick braid, forcing her mouth from him. "Cease, *Katai*! I would come inside you." He got on his knees and quickly unlaced her chemise. He had her naked in seconds, pushing her back none to gently. He only gave her one long, searing kiss for his need was great.

Locking his mouth on one of her breasts, he sucked hard, eliciting a cry from her. Forcefully he parted her thighs and drove a finger deep within her. Back and forth the finger slid while his mouth pulled powerfully at her breast. In no time she was as crazed as he.

"S—*Sa-Jang*!" she yelled with the force of her release.

He felt her contractions with his finger, but he was not finished yet. He waited a few beats until her body settled and her breathing slowed, laying himself full-length upon her. He grasped her face, shouting at her, "Look at me!"

Cwen opened her eyes, gasping at the sight of his. They were as bright as the sun.

"Say you wish me to take you!"

"*Sa-Jang*, please!" She wasn't afraid. She was in need.

"Speak it!"

She couldn't take the sight of his intense eyes anymore. Closing her eyes, she shouted back, "Take me, *Sa-Jang*!"

With a grunt of satisfaction, he raised one of her knees and drove himself deeply in her sheath. The sensation was like lightning for them both. He yelled. She screamed. Otas pounded her like there was no tomorrow until both of them lost command of their brains, their bodies in total control.

His name became a litany flowing from her mouth until her insides seemed to implode, then erupt into hot colored prisms sending her into darkness.

Otas' brain completely shut down with the force of his release. It felt as if the very life flowed from him as his seed shot forth into her dark depths. His roar of pleasure sent the birds skittering from the trees.

Again, there was that time-lapse when he opened his eyes. At first he didn't know where he was, but he felt his Queen still joined to him. Looking around, he identified his surroundings as Hyu-shik. He was sitting back on his heels again, having no idea how he'd gotten into that position. Thank *Ha-nu-nim* he'd left Vlad in command, for he had known nothing for several minutes.

He looked down at his Queen, who was unconscious again. It didn't surprise him because he'd suffered his own form of *Ju-Gum*. Gently, he stroked her face until she opened her eyes.

Looking at him, she asked, "*Ju-Gum* again?"

"I, too, suffered *Ju-Gum*."

"Isn't it dangerous for you? This unconsciousness?"

He nodded. "Do not fear. Vlad is in command." He gazed at a point above her head for a few seconds, then returned his eyes to her. "All is well."

Cwen was joined to him, yet she felt a need to touch him, running her hand across his chest. "My dreams brought you to me?"

"You do not know the strength of your *koi*."

Recapping what had just happened between them in her mind, she said, "I begin to understand."

He smiled down at her, lazily stroking a breast. "When we are alone like this, you may call me *Shunjin*. You have earned the right." His eyes were solid orange, having lost the firestorm.

"What does it mean?"

He lowered his head, trying to hide his blush, but she saw it anyway. Raising his head, he answered, "Husband."

# Chapter 14

Cwen lay on her back, thighs resting on Otas', his shaft still within her. She stared into his orange eyes as she contemplated what he'd just told her to call him. *Shunjin*. Somehow that word was more intimate than his given name, and its meaning of husband sent a strange tingling through her belly. She wanted to speak to him in Liambrian, but her tongue wasn't capable of forming the syllables.

Rubbing the back of her hand across his hairless chest, she said, "Husband."

He smiled down at her. Even though she had spoken in English, the word sounded like music coming from her lips. He smoothed his hand across her taut belly, struggling for the right words to explain what they were doing. "*Katai*, I would explain what we do now."

Cwen had an idea from what Hebron had told her, but it seemed important to him to tell her of this ritual after coupling. "I await your words."

"After Liambrians . . . make love, we remain together so that our minds are . . . joined like our bodies. The custom is called *Saeng-Gan*."

Cwen kept her face serious, not permitting herself to smile. Otas was obviously having a hard time pronouncing the new words he'd learned for the occasion. She would never let him know that his Liambrian accent was so thick that she barely understood what he was saying. Nodding, she said, "I understand."

He visibly relaxed. "If you wish it, my . . . thoughts are open to you."

Cwen found that she could read his mind. However, the words of his thoughts were in Liambrian. Before she could stop herself, Cwen laughed.

A pained expression crossed his face. "My . . . thoughts amuse you, *Katai*?"

She shook her head vigorously. "Nay. Your mind speaks Liambrian. I don't understand the words."

He stared at her some seconds knowing what she meant, for her mind spoke in 21st century English. "My . . . feelings are there. You can . . . read them, can you not?"

Cwen discovered that she could. What she read in his mind astonished her. Her husband was beginning to love her, yet resented it. He felt it made him weak. Now she was sure that telling Otas that she hated him had hurt her husband deeply. "I don't hate you." Cwen tapped her forehead, indicating that he should read her mind as well.

His eyes glittered with gold as he read her feelings. What she called hate was resentment for the lust she could not control. She felt it drew strength from her, making her vulnerable. Love had not blossomed yet, but she cared for him deeply, though cautiously. "We are the same, *Katai*."

He placed his hands on her thighs, running his palms along the length of them. Until that moment she'd had no idea how sensitive they were, feeling that burning grow in her belly.

Cwen felt bereft when he slid himself from her, rising to his feet. He held down a hand to her, nodding toward the pool. There was no hesitancy in her as she clasped his hand and raced to the cool water with him. They both split the water with clean dives.

They were both strong swimmers, complimenting each other on their skill. As she floated on her back, he swam up from beneath her, grasping her waist. The look in his eyes told her he had no intention of tickling her as her father had done. A different sort of play was on his mind.

Moving towards the rocks at the edge of the falls where the water was shallow, he pushed her back up against a cool boulder. Lifting her hips, he said, "Open yourself to me."

What was it about him that made her turn to clay to be molded? She opened her thighs at his command. Before she knew what was happening, he slid himself within, forcing a moan of pleasure from her.

He held himself still as he watched the passion smolder in her smoke-green eyes. Giving her a half smile, he said, "It would not do for us to suffer *Ju-Gum* in the water. This must be quick."

And it was.

Cwen lay on her side, watching Otas sleep, or a least she thought he was asleep. They were stretched out on the blanket, nude. The hot sun had dried their hair some time before. He was on his back, his magnificent chest rising and falling in slow breaths. Cwen was glad that his eyes were closed for she couldn't help running her own up and down the length of him.

At a fast glance his bronzed skin looked like the work of a good tanning oil, but now she could see there were no areas of lighter skin left by clothing. His skin tone was natural as was hers. A thought occurred to her as she looked at the smooth skin stretched across the muscles on his chest. None of the Liambrian males she'd seen had beards or hairy chests. Hebron hadn't shaved once while he was with her.

Her hand rose, but she resisted the urge to touch his smooth skin.

"You may touch me."

Cwen jumped at the sound of his voice. "I thought you asleep."

He turned his head to look at her, his eyes churning with the orange and golden lights. "Only partly."

"What were you doing?"

He frowned in exasperation. "I was *Dut-da*, monitoring."

Hebron had explained to her that the Overlord never truly slept, his mind constantly working. "I understand. Is everything all right?"

His look became confused.

Cwen ran her hand across his chest to soothe him. Trying different words she said, "All is well?"

"Yes." He looked at Cwen, giving her one of his rare smiles. "Your touch pleases me."

Cwen was mesmerized by the sight of him in the light of day. His incredible eyes were ringed with long black lashes, his blue-black hair looked even darker in the bright sun. Her gaze ran the length of him. "How tall are you?"

"Your words make no sense."

"How, um, *long* are you?"

Still the confused look.

Cwen sat up, touching a hand to his head, then reaching way down to touch his foot. "What is the length?"

"I understand now. Six-eleven."

Cwen's mouth dropped open. His accent had been thick, but she could have sworn he said "six-eleven." "Six-eleven?"

He nodded. Her father had been right. She was curious about him.

She also wanted to know how long a certain part of him was, but even if she had the words she thought the answer would scare her. Her hand moved to his belly, causing his muscles to twitch. "Where is *Gew-Seen?*"

He took her hand and moved it below his navel. Flattening her palm, he pushed on it.

She could feel a definite hard round bulge. "And *Lun-Chow?*"

He rose on his elbow, pushing Cwen on her back. His large hand spanned her pelvis. "*Lun-Chow* cannot be felt. It lies deep somewhere here."

Cwen couldn't help it. Fright shot through her, causing Otas to gaze down at her. "You fear *Bal-Dar*," he stated.

"I don't know what to do."

"*Bal-Dar* is done by me."

"Does it hurt?"

He had the confused look again.

Cwen tried to keep the fear from her face and voice, but failed. "Will there be pain?"

Gold and orange swam in his eyes as he considered lying to her. But she had a right to know what to expect. Keeping his hand on her abdomen, he placed hers over his *Gew-Seen*. "There will be pain. For us both."

*Earth's Orbit, November, 2000A.D.*

Maccus sat at the control console of the Time-Jump unit, watching the chronometer countdown the nanoseconds before he activated the window through time. He was expecting Luca to return with a progress report on the whereabouts of the Liambrians.

The Commander had lost many scouting parties that had traveled into the future due to the upcoming upheaval the Earth was going to experience. A sneer crossed his face at the thought of the ignorance of the Earthlings. In ten Earth years what they knew as the high-tech civilization they lived in would be turned to dust. He had no intention of warning them. Each to his own fate.

Since communication devices didn't work through the Time-Jump unit, he and Luca had passed written messages back and forth through time with the aid of a metal cylinder that was simply pushed through the time-window at preset intervals.

By all indications, the Liambrians had fled into the future to the year 4010, where the Earthlings had forsaken technology in favor of a simpler time in their history that they called the Middle Ages.

At the moment, ship's stores was making costumes to fit the period as well as weapons. Maccus shook his head. Swords and daggers of all things. He looked around the bridge of the ship at his crew. None of them would be able to defend themselves with such archaic weapons. However, he had no intention of leaving the U-V Laser weapons behind in the past. It would give them an advantage in the time-frame they were to conquer.

His men began to look like shaggy Trexran canines as he'd forbidden any of them to shear their hair so that they would blend in better with the inhabitants of the year 4010. His own long hair would fit in nicely with the period. They'd all been down to the planet for lessons in horseback riding as this was the mode of travel where they were going. It was imperative that they look and act like they belonged in the time-frame. The cerebral translator implants would take care of any difficulties with language.

Maccus smiled. The Earthlings were complacent and smug in their belief that their planet was well-protected. His ship had been in orbit for over a month and none of their tracking devices had been able to break through the dampening field surrounding his ship. The Trexrans were virtually invisible to the inhabitants of the planet.

If his goal of finding the Liambrian Queen was not of primary importance, Maccus might consider conquering the backward planet, as it was rich in natural resources. But he no longer had sufficient manpower to do the deed. He'd sent the other Trexran ship back to Liambria, manned by all of the males who were married and had families back home. His present crew now consisted of unattached men.

The chronometer sounded a loud beep that broke into Maccus' thoughts. Activating the keypad on the Time-Jump unit, the blue-violet shimmering light appeared within the metal frame. In a few seconds Luca stepped through to the bridge.

Luca dropped all of the items he'd been carrying as the prickling sensation assaulted him. He bent low, hugging himself until the feeling eased.

"Can nothing be done about this pain?" Luca snarled at Maccus.

Deactivating the Time-Jump unit, Maccus stood, smiling down at Luca. "The ability to bear pain will make you stronger."

Trexran curses flowed from Luca as he gathered the items he'd dropped. He handed the Commander the recording device. "This contains all that we saw in this place the Earthlings now call England. We detected many Liambrian females at a location called Castle Acwellen. No males were found."

"How odd," Maccus said as he removed the disc from the recording unit and popped it into the bridge computer. Images from the disc flashed across the screen. All of the females wore strange outfits and rode horses. Swords and daggers hung from their hips. By their facial structures alone, the Commander could identify them as Liambrian. "Some of these females are young, which indicates the males are there in the future with them." He turned to Luca. "You detected no Liambrian ships?"

"No, sir. But that doesn't mean they're not there. The Liambrians have similar dampening fields around their starships as we do."

"True." Maccus frowned at the screen. There was no way he could tell from the recorded images if the Queen was among them. He would need to be near her to sense the sexual ambiance that marked her as Queen.

"What's the plan now?" Luca knew the answer, but asked anyway.

"Why, we're all going to the future, of course."

"There's a flaw to this plan."

Maccus raised a quizzical brow.

"Someone will have to remain behind to operate the Time-Jump unit. Otherwise, we won't be able to come back."

"I have no intention of returning to this time-frame."

"But what about the Supreme Tetrarch?" Luca sputtered.

"That Trexran slug is now on his own. His dream of creating a master race is now mine."

Luca started to argue that it was mutiny, then changed his mind. The Commander's eyes were shifting with orange and yellow light, letting him know that Maccus was about to lose his temper. "I await your orders," Luca said instead.

Maccus pulled him over to a new computer console. Luca didn't recognize any of the indicator lights or the script on the keypad. He looked at the Commander in puzzlement.

"We've been busy while you've been away." Maccus swept his arm toward the computer. "I've modified the engines. This entire starship is now a Time-Jump unit."

Luca could only stare at him, speechless.

"I've calculated the approximate time the Liambrians arrived in the future. We'll arrive several days after them." Maccus paced a few steps. "The way I understand it these castles are called baronies. Small seats of power. We'll conquer one of these castles close to this Acwellen."

"You expect us to do this with swords?"

Maccus chuckled, shaking his head. "We'll use our weapons, of course. My plan is to make it look as if the damage was done with swords."

Otas lay still with his hand spanning his Queen's pelvis, waiting for her reaction to what he'd just told her. With smoke-green eyes focused on her hand covering his *Gew-Seen*, his wife's face was expressionless, her mind racing with thoughts he was unable to read. He wanted to speak to her, offer reassurance, but he knew she needed time to assimilate what he'd said.

Finally, she looked into his eyes. "*Bal-Dar* must be done. If there is pain, so be it." She rubbed her hand across his abdomen, palpating his *Gew-Seen*. "'Tis my duty as your Queen."

If only his mother, Taki, had been so brave. "Your courage pleases me, *Katai*." He slid his hand up her body until he reached her face. Otas had come this far. He must tell her the whole truth about the second half of the bonding. It would be the most difficult of all, giving his Queen full power. Otas gripped her chin, forcing her gaze to his.

His eyes swam with golden light, leaving little orange in their depths. By the expression on his face, he was worried. "What troubles you, husband?"

"It is the *Kyol-hon*." He struggled with the right words to explain what he must. "I only gave you . . . half-strength."

Understanding dawned in her mind. He was trying to tell her about the bonding. Cwen nodded so that he would continue.

"When I complete *Kyol-hon* it will be more difficult for you. It will cause you great pain and . . . " Exasperation crossed his features. He had no English words for it. "The *Kang-Yak*, power, will send you into the dark."

Cwen's eyes widened with apprehension before she could stop herself. God, were there anymore awful surprises in store for her as the wife of the Overlord?

His wife's eyes were dark with no traces of green. "'Tis only fair that I tell you these things. Raynar told my mother nothing. She became mad." He stroked her cheek with his thumb. "I would not have your hate."

Cwen let out her breath. She was scared, but she didn't hate him. He had no more choice in these matters than she did. The pained look on his face squeezed her heart. "I don't hate you." To show him that she meant it, she kissed him hard.

Otas ended the kiss abruptly. "I would . . . make love with

you, but I cannot." He rose, pulling her with him. "I must return you to Castle Acwellen and go to Liambria. Vlad calls."

She was disappointed that the vacation was over, but she said, "I understand."

He hugged her to him, stroking her back. "*Na Sa-rang Tang-sin.*"

She pulled back. Otas' eyes were vibrant with fire. "I don't understand your words."

He knew she didn't. He would never admit he'd just told his wife that he loved her.

# Chapter 15

*Castle Acwellen*

Sevea and Hebron stood at attention when Otas and his Queen materialized within the locked chamber. Cwen held tightly to his neck while his arms circled her waist. She didn't acknowledge her parents. Her eyes were only for Otas.

"Leave us for a moment." Otas didn't even gaze upon them. "I would say farewell to my Queen."

Hebron and Sevea glanced at each other before doing as the Overlord bid.

Now aware that she was alone with her husband, Cwen asked, "Why did you send them away?"

With eyes shimmering, he answered, "I would kiss you now. To do so in front of your parents would show weakness."

Cwen opened her mouth to tell him that was absurd, but his warm mouth locked to hers, shutting off the words. The kiss was of such intensity her knees weakened, forcing her to hold tightly to him. He kissed her as if it was for the last time.

All too soon he ended it before passion overwhelmed him. Holding her face in his hands, he gazed into her green eyes. "I do not wish to leave you."

"Then stay." She was breathless with desire.

His mane of black hair shifted with the shake of his head. "I cannot."

She didn't know why, but suddenly she was seized with a sense of loss. "When will you come to me again?"

He backed away from her, the shifting gold and orange

lights in his eyes expressing an emotion she couldn't read. "I know not." That said, Otas dematerialized.

Something was wrong. Radically wrong. Cwen clasped her hands over her mouth as she tried to smother the sobs that escaped her.

Hearing their daughter's anguish, Hebron and Sevea rushed into the chamber. Their daughter just stood there, crying out her heart. Hebron moved to her, hugging her to his chest.

Tears rolled down her cheeks as she looked up at Hebron. "Why does he leave me?"

Hebron looked to his wife. "She must be told," Sevea said.

The behavior of Otas and her parents was beginning to scare her. Bracing herself for bad news, Cwen stopped crying, wiping away the tears. "Told what?"

Unsure of how she would react, Hebron held his daughter tighter. "Maccus comes."

*Liambria 2*

Otas materialized silently in his *Chim-dae-bang*. He wasn't ready to face Vlad yet. Lowering the pack to the bed, he tried to shake off the passion raging through him. He must suppress these urges for his Queen before he could assume his role as Overlord. Sweat dotted his forehead as he fought the tightness in his loins. He pulled the tunic over his head, tossing it to the floor as he went into the bathroom. As quietly as he could, Otas swiped his chest and forehead with a cloth dampened with cold water.

Tying his hair back into a ponytail with a leather thong, he let the emotions of anger override desire. It was the only way he could deal with the situation that was about to be thrust upon him.

Otas walked to the doorway of the bedroom, gazing at

Vlad who sat at the Overlord's slate desk, manipulating the keypads on the computers. Vlad's expression was intense.

With the silence only a trained warrior could accomplish, Otas walked up the desk. "Report."

Vlad looked up in relief. "Thank *Ha-nu-nim* you're back."

To maintain control Otas showed no signs of friendliness on his face. "Report," he repeated.

Attuned to his friend's moods, Vlad did as asked. "I've been monitoring an energy surge over the southern hemisphere. A power surge of this size could only come from a dampened spaceship. I've communicated with all Liambrian ships in orbit and they report no sightings."

"It is Maccus."

Vlad now noticed the look on Otas' face. His orange eyes flamed like twin suns. "You're certain?"

"Need I remind you Maccus is my twin?"

Vlad rose swiftly, putting distance between himself and the Overlord. He could feel the intensity of the anger flowing off him. Vlad wanted room to maneuver if that rage was released. Cautiously, he said, "I know you're always aware of Maccus." Otas only looked at him. Encouraged, Vlad continued. "By all indications, that's a Trexran ship I'm monitoring. They possess dampening fields just as ours do."

Otas moved to the desk, gazing down at the computer screens. "Maccus turned his whole ship into a Doorway."

Sidestepping to the opposite side of the desk, Vlad asked, "Why does he wait? I've been tracking that power surge for hours."

"He plays a game with us." He locked his eyes on Vlad. "We will let him make the first move."

"And what of your Queen? Shouldn't you bring Cwen here?"

"As you are aware, she must pass certain tests before I complete *Kyol-hon.*"

Vlad was exasperated. "Who said anything about bonding? I meant for safety."

Otas slammed his fist on the desk, sending a crack skittering along the surface. "My Queen remains at Castle Acwellen!"

"Why are you doing this?"

He was silent.

Angry himself now, Vlad observed the Overlord for some seconds. "You do more than test her courage. You question her loyalty."

Still the silence.

"Do you truly believe Cwen will choose Maccus over you?"

"My Queen does not love me." The fire in his eyes burned brighter. "My twin may be more to her liking."

"You judge my cousin unfairly!" Vlad's rage made his head pound.

"Do I?"

It took everything Vlad had not to hit the Overlord. "You're truly mad if you think Cwen would willingly go to Maccus!"

Cwen didn't faint, but her legs could no longer support her. She sagged in her father's arms. Hebron immediately lifted her and placed her on the bed. His daughter's face had gone ghost-pale.

"M—Maccus is here, now?" Cwen stuttered.

"Not yet. But he will come," Hebron answered.

"That's what Otas meant when he said Vlad calls. It also explains why he was acting so strange when he left."

Hebron and Sevea said nothing.

A thought occurred to Cwen that caused a slow burn of anger to rise within her. "If Otas knows it's me that Maccus is after, why didn't he take me with him?"

"We don't know," answered Hebron. "Otas' thoughts are closed to us."

"Why does this Maccus want me? No one has told me this."

Hebron hesitated in answering. Sevea touched his shoulder. "Our daughter has a right to know," she said.

Hebron sighed. "Maccus intends to use you to build a master race that possesses the Gift."

Cwen was incredulous. "He's a Trexran. From what I read in the minds of the ones that attacked me in the past they're quite ordinary. His plan makes no sense."

Hebron coughed. "Maccus is Liambrian."

"What?" Cwen shot off the bed in a rage. "Why didn't you tell me?"

Sevea tried to answer. "We—"

"No. Don't tell me." Cwen cut her off before Sevea could finish. "You were forbidden to tell me."

"*Tanim*—" Hebron tried.

Cwen paced in agitation. "Maccus intends to perform *Bal-Dar* with me, doesn't he?"

"He can't do *Bal-Dar*," Hebron answered.

Cwen turned on her father, cheeks red. "Why not?"

"He has no *Gew-Seen*. Only the Overlord possesses this organ."

"Then I don't understand—"

"He plans to kidnap you and force himself upon you." Hebron hated the bluntness of his words.

"Rape?" Cwen suddenly felt sick again, sitting down heavily on the bed. She looked to her parents. The strain on their faces was immense. "There's something you're not telling me."

Sevea nodded to Hebron, who said, "Maccus was genetically altered by the Trexrans while in utero. Their engineering produced the beast that Maccus is." Hebron rushed on before his daughter could interrupt. "From what Otas tells us, this master race can't be created with the use of Trexran females. Maccus needs you to carry out his plan."

"But you told me that Maccus can't perform *Bal-Dar*. Without it, the Liambrians would be sterile. His plan won't work."

Hebron didn't want to tell her the worst of it, but he had to. "Maccus is capable of impregnating you." He ignored the look of shock on Cwen's face. "Remember I told you that we're a collective mind. If you conceive by Maccus, the germ cells of all Liambrians will alter to this new matrix. The result would be children born with the flawed Gift and nature of the beast."

"Then he'll need more than me. He requires all of the Liambrians to carry out his vile scheme."

"Maccus doesn't fully understand Liambrian evolution. But he's intelligent." Hebron looked to Sevea. "In time he'll figure this out. Then, *Ha-nu-nim* help us."


Vlad thought he would never express what he was about to say to the Overlord. "Otas, you're a fool."

He only glared at him.

"You love your Queen and she loves you, although she doesn't realize it yet! Otherwise, you wouldn't have suffered *Ju-Gum* on Hyu-shik! You were unconscious a full ten minutes!"

Otas' face reddened. "You know of my time-lapse?"

"You forget who you're speaking to. Next to you and Cwen, I possess the most number of psychic receptors. My range isn't as great as yours, but I can monitor Liambrians as you can. It's what makes me second in command. Your thoughts are closed to me, but I'm aware of your emotions and when you're unconscious."

The Overlord turned his Mind-Shield up to full capacity, preventing Vlad from reading his confused feelings. "I haven't forgotten who you are."

"Then alter your plans! Bring Cwen here now and protect her!"

"The Queen remains where she is."

Vlad's face reddened with outrage. He didn't miss the fact that Otas hadn't referred to Cwen as *his* Queen. "Then I predict that when Cwen meets up with Maccus, what love she holds for you now will turn to hate!" With that, Vlad spun on his heel and left the Overlord's chambers.

Otas stood where he was, wondering if he had just lost his only friend.

Cwen slowly stood, rubbing her hands across her face. Gazing at her parents, she said, "Leave me alone for a while. I need to think."

Sevea placed a hand on her shoulder. "Cwen, we—"

"Leave her be," Hebron interrupted, pulling on Sevea's arm. The chamber door closed softly behind them.

Cwen walked to the open shutters. The sun was still ascending toward noon. It had been afternoon when she and Otas had left Hyu-shik. She hadn't accounted for the time difference between here and the island.

What a hell of a homecoming this turned out to be, she thought. Her husband had virtually abandoned her to imminent danger. Otas had known of the maniacal beast, Maccus, yet he'd left her to fend for herself. Why?

Cwen folded her arms and leaned on the stone windowsill, looking out on the green grasslands and pondering her circumstances. The intimate interlude on Hyu-shik with Otas had indicated that he regarded her in every way as his Queen. Why else would he explain to her the difficulties of *Bal-Dar* and *Kyol-hon*? Perhaps leaving her at Castle Acwellen had not been abandonment, but a test to see how she would handle the situation. Judging by the fact that she was trained for combat, her role as Queen of the Liambrians was not to be a passive one. The safety and continuance of the species was of paramount importance.

Her jaw set into grim determination. The first order of

business was to make sure she avoided being captured by this Maccus. It was the only way to protect the Liambrians.

The sun had set by the time Hebron and Sevea arrived outside Cwen's chamber. Both of them listened intently with their minds, trying to get a sense of their daughter's mood. They sensed nothing.

"Now I'm sorry I taught her how to use her Mind-Shield," Hebron whispered to his wife.

Balancing a tray laden with roast beef, potatoes, peas, and tea, Sevea said, "We must go inside. Our daughter must be frightened by these new events."

Just as Hebron raised his fist to knock on the door it swung open. His daughter stood before him not looking the least bit frightened. Indeed, she had the look of a warrior Queen about to engage in battle.

"Good. You're both here," Cwen said as she stepped back to allow them entrance. "I was about to summon you."

Sevea crossed to the table in the corner and set the tray upon it. "I've brought your supper. You forget to eat while you think."

"Sit by me while I eat. I have questions." It was an order.

Hebron dragged the chairs from the hearth, sitting Cwen in one and his wife in the other. He stood behind Sevea, saying, "Ask."

Cwen speared a potato with her dagger. "If I'm to stay out of the hands of Maccus, I need information."

Hebron stared at her with wonder. The crying, uncertain female she had been earlier was gone. Her green eyes were pure smoke, indicating contained aggression. He realized he wasn't talking to his daughter, but to Otas' Queen. "What do you want to know?"

"Start with the Trexran takeover of Liambria. I would know everything about the enemy."

Nodding, Hebron paced a few steps, gathering his

thoughts. His daughter's room was brightly lit with several candles he observed, thinking they were in for a long session of brainstorming. He cleared his throat and began, "To give you full understanding of just what occurred, I have to tell you of Raynar's Queen, Taki."

Swallowing a bite of roast beef, Cwen said, "Otas told me his mother went mad during *Kyol-hon* and *Bal-Dar.*"

Nodding, Hebron continued, "Taki was more than mad. She was also devious and evil. There was a problem with the integration of aggression in our evolutionary process. A small portion of Liambrians used their new inheritance for the good of all. However, a larger group became self-serving. The Liambrian race was split into opposing factions. Taki held great hatred for Raynar. She never accepted her fate as Queen."

"So Raynar forced *Kyol-hon* and *Bal-Dar* on her," Cwen surmised.

"Correct. Raynar had no choice. There was but one Queen, and it was time for an evolutionary leap." Hebron paced with his hands behind his back. "Taki used the power she gained from the bonding against the Overlord. Through the use of the collective mind, she amassed thousands of followers who refused to learn combat skills and heed the orders of the Overlord.

"The planet was in political chaos when the Trexrans arrived. Having foreknowledge of this event, the Overlord had gathered all that were loyal to him in a hidden valley on Liambria. Ten years before the arrival of the Trexrans, these loyal Liambrians had begun to build starships to make our escape. Your mother, your aunt, and I were among those behind the Overlord. We trained hard for combat and honed our skills of the Gift." Hebron stopped speaking, gazing at Cwen. "In case you haven't guessed it, all of the Liambrians here on Earth are part of a massive military operation."

Cwen thought about Aunt Amma's and Vlad's behavior

the night she was shoved through the Doorway. "Certain things are beginning to make sense. I've many questions, but I'll wait until you've finished."

Hebron nodded to his daughter. "The Trexrans took over Liambria without firing their weapons. Taki and her group essentially just handed the planet to them. Taki made friends with the leader of the Trexrans, the Supreme Tetrarch, which terrified Raynar because his Queen carried Otas. Taki didn't know where Raynar and the rest of us were hidden, but she betrayed the Overlord by telling the Trexrans everything she knew about Liambrians.

"The Tetrarch became fascinated with the Gift and the possibility of creating a master race. He turned against Taki and her followers, taking them all into captivity. As they were cowards, they gave no resistance. The Trexrans began genetic experiments on the Liambrians." Hebron couldn't help it. Anger began to lace his words. "These conception experiments were not done naturally. The males and females had their reproductive organs surgically removed." Hebron couldn't go on, walking to the hearth and staring at the cold ashes within it.

Cwen now wished she hadn't eaten. She suddenly felt sick. "This is how Maccus was formed?"

Sevea looked to her husband. He wouldn't be able to speak until he controlled his rage. "Not quite," she answered. "His mother had already conceived."

Cwen was afraid of the answer, but she asked the question anyway. "And Otas? Was he subjected to genetic manipulation while inside his mother?"

"Thank *Ha-nu-nim* he wasn't. They let him be to use as a comparison study against Maccus." Sevea badly wanted to tell Cwen that Maccus was Otas' twin, but she could not.

Cwen sighed loudly with relief. "How did Raynar get Otas away from the Trexrans?"

"Fortunately, Taki was ignorant of just what powers

Raynar possessed as Overlord. A Liambrian male is aware of his child from the moment of conception. When the time grew near for Otas' birth, Raynar allowed himself to be captured." Sevea couldn't help rubbing the diamonds in her bracelets in agitation. The retelling of that horrible time was difficult. "Within an hour of Otas' birth, Raynar escaped from his cell and rescued his son. Before teleporting from the Trexran stronghold, he killed many Trexrans."

"How?"

Sevea looked to Hebron, who shook his head slightly. She dare not tell Cwen of the Green Flame. "With, uh, psychokinesis."

Cwen pondered that for a moment. "But that's not when you escaped from the planet. You said Otas was six-years-old when you arrived on Earth."

"No, it wasn't. It took us five years to complete the number of ships we would need to carry all of the loyal Liambrians to safety."

"How many escaped?" Cwen asked.

"Just under two-hundred-thousand."

"What happened to the rest?"

"When Taki willed herself to die, the collective mind followed her into death."

"A waste of lives," Cwen said, then she had a thought. "How may starships left the planet?"

"We needed ten starships to carry our people and all of the animals we'd gathered."

"Are you telling me each ship holds twenty-thousand?" Cwen was incredulous.

"Liambrian starships are roughly ten kilometers in diameter."

"How could you possibly hide ships of that size and so many people from the Trexrans?"

Hebron moved to his daughter, his anger now contained. "We had dampening fields around the entire area where we were hidden. The Trexrans thought us ignorant of such advanced technology. We were undetectable to them."

"I understand now."

He was proud of her, running his hand along her braid. She was handling this new knowledge quite well.

"Where are all of these starships now?"

"Here. In the future. Some are in orbit. Some docked on the planet."

"That means that the ships are Doorways also."

"Very good. That's how we evaded the Trexrans."

Cwen stood and walked in a circle, hands on hips. She was thinking furiously. "So what has happened is that Maccus built a Doorway. Am I right?"

"Only partially. We've had telepathic word from Otas. Maccus turned his entire ship into a Doorway. He's in orbit around the planet," Hebron said.

Cwen paled, but she controlled her fear. "How could he know where we went?"

"Maccus is powerful with the Gift. He most likely read our psychic traces left behind when the Liambrians fled the year 2000A.D."

Cwen stood still, staring at her parents. "Is he as powerful as Otas?"

"No," Hebron answered. "But since you haven't fully bonded with the Overlord, he's stronger than you."

"There's something else I don't understand." Cwen frowned. "This Maccus has never even seen me. And now that I know how to use my Mind-Shield, how will he know I'm the Queen?"

Hebron stalled. Sevea touched his arm and said, "She must know."

"By your *koi*," Hebron said flatly.

"What?"

"Yours is the *koi* of a Queen. Maccus is capable of sensing it."

# Chapter 16

$V$lad stood at a window in his quarters, sipping a glass of *Ma-shil-kot*. He'd had to take a shower because he had been so hot with rage. He wore only his underwear, his long brown hair still dripping water.

The glass hovered in front of his lips as he sensed Otas outside his door. He knew his friend was worried about their argument. Otherwise, he would step forward and activate the door sensors.

Vlad sighed. *Enter, Otas,* he said with his mind.

After the whoosh of the doors had subsided, Vlad turned to face the Overlord. Otas' eyes were pure gold, indicating his degree of worry. He hadn't even bothered to put on a shirt as he usually did when he left his chambers. Vlad decided to let him speak first.

"I would not lose you as friend. I would explain my reasoning if you let me." Otas' speech was halted.

"I understand more than you know." Vlad moved to the round table and sat, motioning for Otas to do likewise. "I've protected Cwen for so long it seems I'm unable to stop."

Otas sat, saying nothing.

"You're reacting to what your father taught you about females, aren't you?"

"My mother was genetically flawed. She was evil."

"But you're not. *Bal-Dar* corrected any bad traits you could have inherited from her."

"The way I look is a bad enough trait." Otas looked down. "Except for my eyes, I've the look of my mother, which earned me my father's hate. Every time he looked upon me he saw Taki."

Vlad couldn't help feeling pain for his friend. Otas sounded like the lonely child who had hidden in the crawlways of the starship. "I can assure you Cwen's nothing like Taki. I doubt if she even knows how to be devious. She would never betray you to Maccus."

"If only I was so certain."

"You're experiencing the doubt of a male in love." That brought the orange back into the Overlord's eyes. Vlad held up a hand. "You forget. We touched minds as children. I know your feelings as if they were my own. Admit you love your Queen."

"I wish it were not so, but I can't help but love her."

Vlad smiled. "There. That wasn't so hard, was it?"

"It was more difficult than you know."

Vlad chuckled for a few seconds, then turned serious. "If you came to explain why you left Cwen at Castle Acwellen, I already know the reason."

"This is the hardest test she must pass."

"I know." Vlad downed the glass of *Ma-shil-kot*. "She must find her way to you, leading the daughters of Sevea's warriors all the way. As your Queen she must be able to command."

Otas added, "And the daughters must earn the right to leave this planet with us."

Vlad knew of the terrible burden the Overlord faced. Raynar's *Bal-Dar* hadn't been completely successful. There were still many Liambrians that were cowards or tinged with evil. By the use of his powers the Overlord had already atrophied the psychic receptors and wiped the memories clean of ten thousand Liambrians. They had been sent through the Doorways to different time-frames after the Earth's upheaval, left behind to fend for themselves. Vlad let out a heavy sigh.

"I know what you're thinking." Otas interrupted his thoughts. "Sometimes I feel no better than a Trexran. What

I do to those who are flawed is no better than genetic engineering."

Vlad shook his head. "There can't be a recurrence of what happened on Liambria. The race must operate as a whole, or there will be no survival for any of us."

Otas made no comment, the gold and orange lights swimming in his eyes again.

"Cwen won't choose Maccus over you."

"How can you be so certain?"

"Cwen recognized you when you partially bonded with her, didn't she?"

"Yes."

"Maccus only looks like you. What you are inside is as different as light and dark. Cwen will be able to tell you apart," Vlad assured him.

"It's the biggest test of all."

"And she will pass it."

Otas turned pensive.

"I predict that Maccus will be angered by her lack of acceptance. You know she isn't as strong as he with the Gift. He'll use it against her."

A firestorm raged in the Overlord's eyes. "If it comes to that, I'll intervene."

"That's all I wanted to hear you say, my friend."

The composure Cwen had maintained all evening slipped off her like oil. She spit out every foul word that came to mind, blazing her parents' ears. When she ran out of curse words, she shouted at her father, "Don't tell me I'll have every Liambrian male on the planet sniffing at my skirts!"

Hebron's face was bright red. Where had his daughter learned such language? "No, thank *Ha-nu-nim*. Only Maccus can sense your *koi*."

"Like Otas is able to?"

Hebron cleared his throat. "His range isn't as great."

Cwen stared at her father askance. "Just how did Maccus gain this ability?"

Hebron hoped she hadn't figured out how to read Liambrian minds. What he was about to tell her was a blatant lie. "He, um, Maccus developed this acute sense through the genetic engineering he was subjected to."

Cwen said nothing, her eyes so full of smoke they were black. She paced a few steps, saying, "I'll just have to deal with it." Thinking clearly again, she stood in front of her parents. "I realize we're all well-trained in combat, but just how are we to defend ourselves against the Trexrans with only the use of swords? They are no match for those ray gun things they carry."

"The weapons are called Ultraviolet Lasers," Sevea answered. "We can disarm them with the Gift before the Trexrans have a chance to fire their weapons."

Cwen looked doubtful.

"What your mother says is true," Hebron broke in. "With the use of psychokinesis we can whip the U-V lasers right out of their hands."

"The Trexrans rely so heavily on their weapons they aren't good in-close fighters. Our warriors can easily defeat them," Sevea added.

"Then I'd best practice my skills of the Gift. But I can't do it inside the castle," Cwen said.

"You can't be thinking of going outside!" Sevea's voice was laced with worry.

"It's the only way. The Earthlings would never understand what it is I'm doing. In fact, they'd probably think I was a witch."

"I'm afraid she's right," Hebron agreed.

Cwen looked to Sevea. "You said all of your warriors know I'm the Queen, didn't you?"

"The mothers know, but the daughters don't."

"We don't know when Maccus will move on us. Until

then, I'll practice combat with father each morning and the Gift in the afternoon. I need you to lend me twenty of your best warriors. And I mean not just good with swords, but experienced with the use of the Gift. They will go with us to the woods."

"I'm not sure I like it, but I'll do as you say," Sevea said.

Hebron placed a hand on Sevea's shoulder. "Our daughter's plan is sound. We must give her every advantage if she's to face Maccus."

Sevea said nothing, staring into Hebron's eyes. Her golden ones were filled with anxiety.

Vlad smiled inwardly as he watched Otas relax now that they were friends again. No matter what he did Otas would never lose him as friend, but Vlad wouldn't tell him that. Otas could be so stubborn that it was often useful to shake him up sometimes.

"By the way, Narda has been asking for you. She wants to see you on the Agro-deck." Vlad watched the Overlord try not to blush and not succeed.

"I know. There's probably a bug on one of the cabbages."

Vlad shot him an irritated look. "You know as well as I do what she wants. You."

"I have no more need of her."

"I should hope not." Vlad watched Otas rise. "What are you going to tell her?"

"I haven't figured that out yet."

"I have one suggestion." Vlad's look was serious.

"What's that?"

"Put on a shirt. Otherwise she won't be able to keep her hands off you."

Otas growled as he turned to leave, Vlad's laughter ringing in his ears.

Narda couldn't contain her excitement as she fluffed out her

hip-length blonde hair. Otas had sent word that he was coming. She knew she looked fine in her red *wanpisu*, tugging on
the bodice to give him a good view of her ample bosom. It
had been an honor when he'd fused the gold jewelry to her
neck and wrists marking her as the one in charge of the Agro-
deck. The rubies in her jewelry gleamed in the artificial
sunlight as she thought of the greater honor of giving his
body to her.

None of the males she coupled with could make her body
sing like Otas did. He'd only been a young male of sixteen
when Raynar had sent her to him with the instructions to
teach his son about mating. It wasn't long before the student
surpassed the teacher. What Otas did to a female was guided
by pure instinct and his ability to read the mind of the one he
was pleasuring, bringing her to fulfillment. He had yet to bring
Narda to *Ju-Gum*, but that was only because he held some
portion of himself back during the act. He'd talked with her
after coupling, but not with the intimacy of *Saeng-Gan*. Never
had they shared minds.

Tonight would be different. Otas hadn't come to her in
over thirty sunrises. His blood must be as fire, she thought.
She turned when she heard the automatic doors swoosh open.

Narda was unable to keep the anticipation out of her blue
eyes as she looked upon him. As always he was in black, his
thick hair bound in a ponytail. Bowing her head, she said, *Sa-
Jang*."

Otas found he could say nothing as he stared at Narda.
She was pretty, yes. But how had he ever thought her beautiful? Narda was eight years older than he, still young by
Liambrian standards. After being with his Queen, this female
with lust on her mind before him looked homely and used.

Narda became nervous at his silence. His eyes swam with
different shades of orange, displaying his irritation. "Have I
angered you, *Sa-Jang*?"

He looked out over the Agro-deck which spanned the

entire circumference of the fortress. Nothing looked amiss. "Why have you summoned me?"

Narda couldn't help flinching at his cold tone of voice. But she was undaunted. Soon she would have him purring like a Liambrian *mow*. "I wanted to give you a report on how well the crops are doing. All of the Earthling fruits and vegetables are compatible with our soil. Even the tropical fruits you had us bring from Hyu-shik grow well."

He had passed from irritation to anger. "What you say to me could have waited until morning! I read lust in your mind!"

Daringly, she moved towards Otas, intending to hug his neck. But he stopped her with the force of his will.

"*Sa-Jang*, I want to mate with you."

"I do not wish it."

Narda gasped. It couldn't be possible! Had she lost her appeal? She had bragged about her liaisons with the Overlord to the other females. Now they would laugh at her. "Have you found another to slake your desire?"

"You know I use no other females here!" His eyes had become an inferno.

Narda was afraid of his anger, but she couldn't possibly lose her position as the Overlord's paramour. "It's the Queen, isn't it?"

"All know there is no Queen at Liambria!"

Narda couldn't stop the tears forming in her eyes. "Th—then why don't you want me?"

Otas' stomach tightened inside. He didn't want to hurt her, but he must. "You appeal to me no more."

What came out of Narda's mouth was a cross between a gasp and a sob.

He softened his voice. "You have done well with the Agro-deck." He then turned and left.

Anger began to replace hurt in Narda. His rejection of her couldn't possibly be due to her loss of desirability. Someone had turned him against her. She didn't know how, but she would find the one responsible. *Ha-nu-nim* help whoever it was. Narda fully intended to wreck havoc with their life.

*Earth's Orbit, 4010A.D.*

Maccus studied the screen in his quarters, perusing the images Luca and his scouts had just brought to him of the band of Liambrian females in the woods. What captured his interest was the lone male among them and the female who tenaciously battled him with her sword.

He was aware of Luca standing behind him awaiting his orders, but he was enthralled. The black-haired female was fascinating to watch. Not once did she flinch or hesitate to fend off the violent blows the male rained on her. Her courage exceeded what was expected of a Liambrian and her beauty was beyond belief.

"Who is she?" Maccus asked Luca.

"Unknown, Commander." Luca braced himself for the inevitable anger. When nanoseconds passed and nothing bad happened to his person, he volunteered what little information he possessed. "All I know is that for the past five mornings the male and female come with the group of Liambrian females on horses to this spot in the woods."

"Does she lead them or follow behind?"

"She leads with the male at her side."

Although Luca couldn't see it, Maccus actually smiled. He couldn't sense what the Liambrians called "*koi*" from the recording, but by her combat ability and his own precognition he was sure it was the Queen. "You have the coordinates to this area?"

"Aye, Commander."

Finally, he turned to face Luca, his orange eyes reflecting his excitement. "Tomorrow morning I want a group of your men to surround the area. Use the teleporters and be quiet about it."

Luca nodded. "Do you wish us to kill them?"

Orange and yellow lights began to churn in Maccus' eyes. "All but the black-haired one fighting the male."

"Do you want us to bring her to you?"

Maccus just stared beyond Luca, thinking. Maybe this was going to be easier than he'd thought. Conquering the castle that bordered the Acwellen land was more bother than he wanted. Snatching the Queen from the woods was a much simpler plan.

"Commander?"

Maccus focused his eyes on Luca, shaking his head. "I will capture her myself."

The sun would rise in another hour, which gave Cwen little time to prepare. In the dark she lit a candle on the beside table, but her aching body refused to move more than that. Groaning, she flopped back down in the bed.

Cwen had thought Vlad was merciless. Rubbing her sore sword arm, her mind compared Hebron to Attila The Hun. Her whole body ached with tortured muscles used to fend off her father's sword swings and martial arts attacks. Even the roots of her hair hurt, which she supposed was understandable as her brain throbbed with a steady beat.

Her father had been just as tenacious with the Gift practice. He refused to speak out loud with her, forcing her to use telepathy for communication with him and Sevea's warriors. Hebron had battered her brain constantly by trying to force his will on her. Cwen's Mind-Shield strengthened because of the bombardment. He had said this punishment was to ensure that Maccus couldn't read her mind. He'd also taught her how to resist the psychokinetic forces sent against her. The ultimate test had been when he'd ordered her to lift a fallen tree using psychokinesis yesterday. She had done it, raising trunk, roots, and all two feet from the ground. But her poor head had been pounding ever since.

*Cwen, it's past time to rise*, Hebron said with his mind.

She knew her parents stood outside the chamber door. Cwen didn't have the strength to get up and open the door. Head throbbing, she answered, *The door is unbolted.* She hoped Hebron took the hint and entered on his own.

The candle flame flickered as Sevea and Hebron entered and stood by the bed. *You shouldn't have left the door unlocked*, Hebron scolded with his mind.

*I was too tired to remember.*

*Fatigue is no excuse for—*

"Can't we use our tongues?" Cwen rubbed her temples. "Telepathy pains me."

Sevea took a good look at Cwen's pale face, then scowled at her husband. "You push her too hard. She's in no shape to practice combat." Sevea placed a hand on her daughter's forehead, closing her eyes. When she opened them, she glared at Hebron. "Cwen's in agony."

"Then heal her," Hebron hissed. "Maccus won't care what kind of physical condition she's in. Pain or no, he'll take her."

Sevea couldn't argue with him for she knew he was right. With her hand still resting on Cwen's head, Sevea sent healing energy through out her. When she could sense no more pain within her daughter, she removed her hand.

Cwen sat up, wide-eyed, flexing her sword arm. All of the pain was gone. She felt as whole and hearty as she had on Hyu-shik. "You're like Aunt Amma."

Sevea chuckled softly. "In healing, yes. But in other ways, no."

Cwen wanted to ask her what she meant, but Hebron spoke up before she could.

"Get dressed. The others await us."

Hebron left the chamber, giving Cwen no time to argue.

Sighing, Cwen got out of bed.

Leading Sevea's warriors to the clearing in the woods, Hebron observed his daughter. During the ride from the castle, Cwen had been unusually quiet. For the last five days they had used telepathy for communication in case they were being spied upon by Trexrans. Using his mind, Hebron asked, *Why are you so silent?*

Patting Samson's neck, she glanced at her father. *I was thinking about Otas' mother. I can't believe she chose death over caring for her son. Do all Liambrians have the ability to will themselves to death?*

*We do, but it's rare that any do so. Liambrians love life. Natural death occurs soon enough.*

Cwen kept her gaze on her father, pondering what he'd just said. *Just what is the life span of Liambrians? You don't look very old to me.*

Hebron smiled. *That's because I'm still a male in his prime. The life span of Liambrians is approximately two hundred years.*

Cwen's mouth dropped open. *You're serious?*

*I wouldn't lie to you about this.*

*How old are you?*

*Forty-five.* Hebron kept himself from laughing out loud at the expression on his daughter's face. *I know to an Earthling I would be middle-aged.*

*And mother?*

*She's forty.*

Cwen was quiet again as they reached the glade in the woods, thinking no wonder Aunt Amma had seemed so ageless. She and Hebron reined in their horses as Odelia, second in command to Sevea, directed the others to form a protective circle around the Queen and her father.

Cwen was about to dismount when the lack of morning birdsong came to her attention. *Stay mounted!* she directed everyone.

*What do you sense?*

Cwen raised her hand to her father for silence. She needed all of her brain's senses to listen for danger. It wasn't long before she heard the unmistakable crack of a twig being stepped on. *We're surrounded by Trexrans!* she said to all.

Hebron cocked his head and listened with his mind. *You're right. I can read their thoughts. They intend to kill all but you!*

Grasping her sword hilt, Cwen shouted, "Odelia! Trexrans are all around us! Disarm them and slice off the teleportation armbands! Leave none living!"

Cwen had barely given the order when the Trexrans moved in on them, crashing through the forest foliage, weapons aimed to kill. As one, the psychokinetic force of the Liambrians sent the weapons sailing in the air before a shot was fired. Chaos ensued. Swords drawn, the warriors attacked the confused Trexrans. Odelia spun her horse toward a Trexran who had intentions of fleeing by teleportation. Instead of aiming for such a small target as the teleporter armband, Odelia simply sliced off his entire arm, oblivious to his howls of shock and pain.

All of Sevea's warriors took Odelia's lead, dispatching any Trexran they could reach. Cwen tried to join in the fray, but Hebron pulled on Samson's reins.

"No, *Tanim!* Where there are Trexrans, there's Maccus! Ride for the castle!" Hebron whacked the flat of his sword on Samson's rump, sending the horse into a fast gallop. "I'll catch up with you when all of the enemy are dead!" he shouted after her.

Cwen barely had time to duck a low branch as Samson barreled through the dense forest. She tightened her grip on the reins and squeezed her knees against the horse's sides. If she tumbled off Samson at this speed, she would be badly injured.

Even though the horse was doing all the work, Cwen's breathing was as labored as Samson's. On he raced through the woods, splashing through streams and jumping obstacles without losing his stride. Cwen was bent low, stuck to Samson like iron to a magnet.

Just as horse and rider crashed into another clearing, something large and heavy launched itself from the trees, knocking Cwen off Samson. The force of the momentum sent them tumbling over and over on the forest floor. When they finally came to a stop, Cwen was pressed into the ground on her belly from the heavy weight on her back. The fall had knocked the wind from her, leaving her gasping for breath, her vision blurred.

For a split second the weight lifted as a strong hand flipped her over onto her back. With the pressure on her body again, Cwen shook her head to clear her blurred vision. Blinking several times, she couldn't believe what she was seeing. The bulk upon her was Otas.

# Chapter 17

Otas sat behind his desk while Vlad stood at attention in front of him. This morning their behavior was not that of friends, but as the Overlord addressing his second in command. "How many ships have been outfitted with the Inter-Dimensional Leap units?"

"Counting Raynar's ship, four."

Otas stood and went to the window behind his desk. "Six more starships to go." He turned to face Vlad. "This process is taking too long. We must be able to launch all ships the moment we get word from Raynar. Is there no way to expedite the installations?"

Vlad shook his head. "These new units are more intricate than the Doorway mechanisms. We don't dare rush, or mistakes will be made. All ships in the fleet must have fully functional Dimensional-Leap processors. Otherwise, when it comes time to jump dimensions, we may inadvertently leave twenty-thousand Liambrians behind due to technical failure."

"You're right, of course." Otas ran a hand through his unbound hair. "It's just that I'm concerned about Maccus. The sooner we're beyond his reach, the better."

"Agreed. I've no liking for this waiting game we play."

"Nor I—" Otas started to say more, then went rigid and stood stone-still. The colors in his eyes shifted the full spectrum of red-orange to yellow. His gaze focused on a point only he could see.

At first, Vlad was unconcerned for he'd witnessed this trance state of Otas' before. The Overlord was deep in

*Dut-da*. But when the pupils of his eyes constricted to such a minute size that they were invisible, alarm bells went off inside Vlad's head. "Otas?"

No response.

Vlad knew it was useless trying to reach the Overlord while he was in this state, so he activated his own psychic receptors. In a microsecond he sensed Cwen's confusion. *Maccus*! *Dut-da* or no, he must wake Otas from his trance. Desperate, Vlad did the only thing he thought would work. He punched Otas in the jaw.

His head only moved slightly from the impact of the blow. Vlad started shaking him, yelling at the top of his voice, "Otas, wake up! You must teleport to Cwen now!"

Otas only stood where he was.

Gasping for air, Cwen stared into the orange eyes in the face that hovered above hers. Had Otas lost his mind? she wondered. He could have injured her severely, knocking her off Samson's back the way he had. Thank God the forest floor was soft with soil and rotting vegetation.

Orange and gold began to shift in his eyes as he slowly smiled. The smile turned into a leer. Something's not right here, Cwen thought. Otas had never looked at her that way. Then it hit her. She wasn't smelling earth, grass, and male. The scent wafting through her nose was that of spice and rubber, of all things. Fright and awareness made her stomach flip-flop. Quickly she scanned the face above her—same eyes, same thick black hair, same face, same everything, but this was not her husband. *My God, Maccus*!

"You're not *Sa-Jang*," she said stupidly.

Maccus sat up abruptly, straddling her hips, throwing back his head with laughter.

Now Cwen was positive this wasn't her husband. Laughter was something Otas did rarely. Knowing she was in serious trouble, Cwen swung her arm, intending to knock him off her with a karate chop.

Maccus moved like lightning, gripping her wrist before she connected with his neck. "So, my brother calls himself Master."

Cwen said nothing, silently cursing every Liambrian she knew for not telling her Maccus was Otas' twin.

Maccus gripped her chin. "You're more beautiful than I expected. It wouldn't do to have an ugly Queen. And you *are* the Queen, aren't you?"

Cwen didn't answer. His accent was guttural like the Trexrans in the alley, but he spoke her form of English well.

"Don't speak if you wish. I know you're the Queen by your *koi*." Maccus looked her over. "I'll enjoy taking you, but it will be more sensual if I knew your name. What are you called?"

"Guess." Cwen didn't know why she became flippant. After all, this was the beast.

Anger flared in his orange eyes as he squeezed her chin painfully. In a reflex action, Cwen strengthened her Mind-Shield as he tried to probe her mind. She could feel the rage begin to build within him because he couldn't break through her barrier. His face became a twisted mask of evil as he increased the force of his will. Cwen bit her lip as she concentrated on blocking her thoughts. She could feel a definitive bowing in her Mind-Shield. As her head began to pound, she realized she wouldn't be able to stand the pressure much longer. Her Mind-Shield would shatter and reveal everything about her and what she knew about the Liambrians. She couldn't allow it to happen!

In desperation, Cwen activated her psychokinetic receptors, thinking if she could move a tree, surely she could move Maccus. Holding nothing back, she blasted him with the full force of her power.

The impact of her energy flung Maccus from her, sending

him sliding several feet away from her. Cwen rose with speed, drawing her sword. Out of the corner of her eye, she noticed Samson standing at the edge of the clearing. Her faithful horse had not run away after losing his mistress. If only she could get to him.

Maccus jumped to his feet quickly. There was no mistaking the anger raging in his eyes. Astonished, Cwen found that she could read his thoughts. Maccus had every intention of raping her on the spot! Terror sent her sprinting toward Samson.

"If you want to play rough, so will I!" Maccus shouted.

Before she could reach the horse, Maccus' psychokinetic wave sent her tumbling to the ground. The next blast knocked the sword from her grip. Sweat poured from her body as she thought, I can't let him take me! Maccus came closer and closer. Nothing had prepared her for a battle such as this. Forcing her body to resist the power of his mind that tried to pin her to the ground, Cwen rose to a sitting position.

As fast as she could, Cwen whipped out her dagger and flung it at Maccus. Her aim was true. The knife imbedded itself into his neck with a sickening thunk.

Maccus didn't even break his stride as he pulled the dagger free. There wasn't even any blood in the hole left by the weapon.

At the sight of this, Cwen finally screamed.

Maccus laughed maniacally at her terror, increasing the pressure to hold her down. When he stood over her, he ripped the leather battle gear from her body with the force of his mind.

Down to her chemise now, Cwen began to emit little sobs. She belonged to Otas. She couldn't allow this male to rape her, but she was powerless to stop him.

Keeping her pinned with his will, Maccus dropped to his knees and straddled her. He pulled the black tunic from his body, baring his well-muscled chest and strong arms.

Crying in earnest now, Cwen couldn't believe this was happening. Maccus looked like her husband, but his soul was the darkest of blacks.

Suddenly Samson charged Maccus, rising on his hind legs to strike him with his front hooves. Maccus turned his attention from Cwen and shot his power at the horse. Samson rolled over and over in the dirt.

In the split second Maccus was distracted, Cwen tried to gouge his eyes with her nails. Her purpose was to blind him. She missed her target by a millimeter, raking long, bloodless farrows in his cheek. Apparently, he wasn't impervious to pain. Maccus backhanded her so hard she lost consciousness for a few seconds.

When Cwen wakened from her stupor, Maccus was gazing down at her. "It's useless to fight me. I intend to make you mine!" With that, he began to knead her breasts painfully.

Nausea gripped her stomach with the realization that Maccus would carry out his threat.

Vlad was frantic. Maccus was about to rape Cwen, and Otas just stood like a statue. There was only one thing to do. He was no match for Maccus, but he had to attempt to save Cwen. He flipped the lid on the teleporter armband. Just as he was about to activate it a strong hand clasped his shoulder. He looked up at Otas, whose eyes were still doing that red, orange, and yellow dance, but the pupils were now visible.

Without a word, Otas disappeared.

Suddenly, twin beams of bright blue light shot past Cwen's head, striking Maccus in the chest. He flopped forward onto Cwen. Free of the psychokinetic force that had held her down, Cwen wiggled out from under him, sobbing all the while. Looking behind her, she saw Hebron and Odelia riding toward her, holding U-V Laser weapons.

When they reached her they dismounted quickly. Standing on shaky legs, Cwen stumbled into her father's arms.

Hebron grasped her shoulders. "Did he hurt you, *Tanim?*"

Cwen knew what her father was asking, but she couldn't speak yet. She shook her head.

"*Tanim?*" came weakly from Maccus. "Of course, he's your father."

Hebron zapped Maccus again with the U-V Laser until he moved no more.

Cwen looked down at Maccus and was immediately disappointed. He still breathed. She looked around the glade and spotted her sword. Disengaging herself from Hebron, she went to retrieve it. With purposeful strides and sword in hand, she stalked back to Maccus. Hebron and Odelia were shouting something at her, but she ignored them. Nothing would stop her from chopping off this beast's head! Cwen raised her sword.

Just as Cwen was about to deliver the death stroke, Otas materialized behind her, gripping her wrists. "Stop, *Katai!*"

As she turned and stared into her husband's face, rage overrode the fear she had experienced. Cwen knew Otas wouldn't understand her, but she yelled at him anyway. "Where the hell have you been? This, this dirtbag almost raped me! Why in God's name didn't you tell me he was your twin? I'll never forgive you for this! Never!" She inhaled. "Why don't you let me kill the bastard?"

Otas only looked at her. His eyes were frightening with the colors shifting from red to orange to yellow.

Hebron intended to have his say. Yelling in Liambrian, he said, "Answer her! Maccus would have done *Kang-Gan* on my daughter if we hadn't stopped him!"

"Quiet!" Otas growled.

Hebron shut up, but Cwen started to open her mouth to say more. A look from Otas silenced her.

"Odelia, are all the Trexrans dead?" Otas asked in Liambrian.

"No, *Sa-Jang*. One escaped."

The Overlord cursed. "Gather all of their weapons. We may have need of them in the future."

Cwen became even angrier because she couldn't understand a word they were saying. Otas still held her wrists in a grip that was almost painful.

"Hebron, have Sevea teleport to Liambria. She will need to sit in for her sister, Amma, on the Circle of Twelve."

"You intend to complete *Kyol-hon*, now?" Hebron made no attempts to hide his anger.

"My Queen passed the test. I will finish *Kyol-hon*," Otas said simply.

It was the one word Cwen understood. "The hell you will! I'm not going anywhere with you!" Cwen began to struggle, trying to free her wrists from his hold. "I hate you! Do you hear me? I hate you, *Sa-Jang*!"

The Overlord touched his fingers to her forehead. "*Ja-Da*, sleep."

Cwen slipped into the dark of slumber.

### *Liambria 2*

Fighting her way from the depths of deep sleep, Cwen sighed as she stretched her body. Her first thought was of how comfortable the bed felt, cradling her form in its supportive softness. As she became more conscious, Cwen realized she was nude, the blanket covering her body was cool against her skin, which felt clean as if she'd just bathed. She raised a hand to her unbound hair. It had been washed as well. Cwen had no memory of bathing. Confused, her eyes popped open. Above her was a curved skylight revealing the night stars.

Panic seized her as the memories of her fight with Maccus flooded her mind. Cwen sat up, gasping. Where the hell am I? she wondered. The walls of the room were curved and appeared to be made of polished granite. Dimmer lights were recessed in the arced ceiling. This was unlike any architecture she'd ever seen.

She gazed down at the bed she was in. It was huge, the cover made of shimmering blue fabric. Suddenly she sensed someone in the room with her, pulling the blanket tight around her breasts. "Who's there?"

"It's okay, Cwen. It's only me," came a voice from the shadows.

She recognized that voice. How could she not? She had listened to it for twelve years. "Vlad?"

"Yes." He stepped from the shadows and sat in the curved-back chair beside the bed.

At first she was glad to see him, then she remembered that at the moment she hated all Liambrians. "Where am I?" she asked in a cold voice.

"Liambria. You're in the *Chim-dae-bang* of the Overlord's chambers."

Cwen looked past Vlad at the closed door. "Where is he?" she whispered.

"There's no need to whisper. He's in the other room. Deep within mediation." Vlad shrugged. "Besides, the room is soundproof."

"What of my thoughts?"

"When he's in that state, he hears nothing but his own mind."

Cwen gave Vlad a scathing look. "He's preparing for *Kyol-hon*, isn't he?"

Vlad's answer was a nod.

"It won't happen. He has a lot of explaining to do before I let him touch me again."

"He anticipated this." Vlad held up lengths of rope. "I was supposed to bind you to the bed. But I couldn't."

"You disobeyed Otas for me? Why?"

Vlad rubbed a hand over his face. "Listen, Cwen. Aren't

you wondering why a male is in here with you while you're unclothed?"

"I just assumed it was some kind of protection thing. You're second in command, aren't you?"

"Yes, but I'm also a relative."

Cwen's eyebrows shot up.

"Amma is my mother."

Cwen stared at Vlad. The memories of her life with Aunt Amma and Vlad rose to the surface. It all made sense now. Even though he was second in command, Vlad had always deferred to Amma. A son minding his mother. "We're cousins."

"Right. Only a male relative is allowed to live with and protect the Overlord's Queen."

"Intimacy is forbidden between blood relatives?"

"Correct. There's no such word as incest in Liambrian."

"But you care enough about me not to have tied me up. You risk Otas' anger."

"I've protected you most of your life. I do so now." Vlad inhaled deeply. "Right now I'm protecting you from yourself."

"Because I refuse *Kyol-hon*?"

"You know it will happen anyway. Forced *Kyol-hon* is what drove Otas' mother insane." Vlad looked at her with caring in his brown eyes. "I don't wish the same for you."

Cwen pondered his words. "There's much to be explained before I willingly submit to him."

"The Overlord will explain everything after you've bonded."

Cwen shot him a dubious look.

"You'll gain knowledge from the bonding itself. Also, Otas will be able to speak your tongue."

"You're asking me to forgive him."

"You must. For the good of our people. Your parents told you what happened on Liambria. If the same thing occurs again, our race won't survive."

Cwen knew what he said was true. There were no other options. "I'll go through with it. But there's much I need to know from you."

"You're referring to Otas. His actions mystify you. I'll tell you only this. The Overlord is completely insecure when it comes to matters of the heart."

Cwen said nothing as she absorbed this information.

Vlad stood. "One final thing. When Otas comes to you, he won't speak. He's deep in his mind." With that, Vlad moved to the door, passing through after it whooshed open.

Cwen was deep in thought herself as the door silently slid closed.

# Chapter 18

Cwen's thoughts ceased when her bladder vied for attention. Looking around the room, she cursed herself for not asking Vlad where the bathroom was. Finally, she spotted a concave, rectangular panel of metal that could only be a door. Quickly, she walked to it, then stopped. There was no doorknob. How was she to open it? Moving closer to see if she could find some kind of latch, she jumped when the panel slid back, revealing the lighted bathroom. Obviously it was an automatic door, but she couldn't detect the sensors that had to be there.

Forgetting about the damn door, she went to the toilet, which appeared to be made of stainless steel. There was a problem when she finished her business. The thing had no tank. Therefore, there was no visible handle. How the hell do I flush it? she thought. Cwen began searching for the flushing mechanism.

She was so intent on her purpose that she didn't hear Otas as he moved to stand in the doorway. He watched her for some seconds, then stood behind her and touched a hand to her back. She emitted a squeak as she spun to face him. The sight of his eyes almost made her scream, but she controlled her quivering vocal chords. The colors of red, orange, gold, and yellow no longer shifted in his eyes. The hues were sectioned off like wedges in a pie. There was no trace of his pupils.

Remembering what Vlad had told her about Otas not speaking, Cwen refrained from asking him where the flushing mechanism was. Sensing what she searched for, the Overlord pointed to the floor. Cwen looked down and saw a round button with a white symbol on it. She stepped on it. There was an immediate whoosh as the toilet's contents were sucked down by what sounded like a high-powered vacuum.

Getting the hang of this space-aged restroom, Cwen moved to the metallic sink. There was a spigot, but no knobs. She searched for and found the keypad like buttons. One was marked with a red symbol, the other was marked with blue. Deciding on warm, she depressed both and quickly washed her hands. The towel rack was the only thing that looked familiar to her, she thought as she dried her hands.

Cwen became jittery when she faced Otas again. She had been so intent on the mystery of the toilet she hadn't noticed that her husband was as naked as she. She experienced a bizarre feeling that this wasn't Otas, but Maccus. She moved forward and buried her nose in his chest. He smelled of earth, grass, and male. She sighed with relief. She was safe. If she didn't think about *Kyol-hon*, that is.

Without a word, he pulled her from the bathroom and led her to the bed, which had the cover turned down. She couldn't help it. Fright shot through her, turning her knees to putty. Before she sagged to the floor, Otas lifted her in his arms and gently laid her on the bed.

His gaze was locked to hers for what seemed like an eternity, his strange eyes making her feel trapped. When he knelt on the bed and straddled her hips, Cwen shivered involuntarily. Fleetingly, she realized she was more frightened now than she had been while in the hands of Maccus. Otas' speechlessness unnerved her.

He began to run his hands through her long black hair, his eyes never leaving hers. Instinctively she knew that if she shut her own eyes to block out the weirdness of his she would insult him. Cwen forced her lids to remain open.

Otas stroked her face with his large hands, moving

downward to massage her neck and shoulders. His touch began to have a relaxing effect on her. When her shivering stopped, he slid his hands down the length of her body. With slow strokes, his hands passed over her breasts, waist, and abdomen. He added more pressure with each touch causing her body to tingle with arousal.

Cwen felt her nipples harden and her insides come alive. In the back of her mind she was aware that this was ritualistic foreplay, for Otas hadn't even kissed her. The inside of her belly began to burn with desire as his caresses increased in both pressure and speed. Soon her breaths came in soft pants.

At the sound, Otas lay on his side, keeping a hand smoothing down her body. With the other hand he nudged her thighs apart. She gasped as he slid two fingers within her, prodding her with a sensual motion. Her hips lifted off the bed as he added a third finger to the play, stretching her, preparing her to receive him.

The entire time his eyes never left hers. Through her passion, Cwen could feel the tingling in her head as their minds were linked. She became aware of Otas' heated arousal as well as her own.

Eyes unwavering, he laid upon her, spreading her legs wider with one of his own. His fingers were quickly replaced by his hard manhood. He pushed himself within, inch by slow inch. Cwen cried out at the sensation of sizzling steel stretching her insides. Once he was wedged fully inside her, pelvis to pelvis, he began a slow circular rhythm with his hips. The sensation was like none she'd felt before. Moaning, Cwen's body rapidly moved toward release.

Keeping up the arousing motion, Otas gripped Cwen's face, forcing her to look into his eyes. She was powerless to stop the oncoming orgasm. It came with such force she screamed as her body went rigid, the intense pleasure shooting to the top of her head, her inner sheath contracting around her husband's rod. All the while their gazes were locked.

Cwen didn't lose consciousness, but she wished she had. Her breath came in hitches as the colored wedges in his eyes began to spin. The Mind-Link strengthened as he continued the circular motion of his hips, arousing her again.

Even though her body was singing with the tantalizing sensations Otas was producing, Cwen became intensely aware of her husband's mind. With the colored lights spinning in his eyes, he began to feed her his thoughts—who he was, what he was, what he felt. Cwen felt pressure in her brain, which increased as the thoughts came faster and faster in rapid-fire images. She desperately wanted to close her eyes, but he had total control over her brain.

Cwen's breath came in gasps as she learned what her husband was. The power he wielded was so dangerous, so immense, so alien. Her head began to throb. Because they were of one mind, she knew what was happening. He was preparing her psychic receptors to receive his power. Little cries escaped her as fright scurried through her. There was no way her mind could absorb Otas' power!

His hips moving at a faster pace, Otas gripped her face more firmly. Cwen screamed at the sight of his eyes. The colors in his eyes spun so rapidly they blended into pure white. At that exact moment, Otas' power surged into her mind. Cwen screamed again as the pressure in her brain increased to such intensity she thought her head would explode. On and on the power flowed from him to her, Cwen screaming all the while.

She couldn't take anymore, but Otas' power continued to surge forth. She dug her nails into his shoulders as waves of pain shot from her forehead all the way down her neck. She emitted a combined scream and cry as her neck spasmed in reaction to the agony she was experiencing.

Somehow, through her pain Cwen could hear Otas yelling. This hurt him as much as it did her. That was the last thought she had. In a final burst of agony, she fell into an abyss of blackness.

Otas knew his wife was unconscious, but he continued on, pouring into her the last portion of his power. With that done, he allowed his own sexual release. He screamed with the power of his orgasm, his seed shooting forth so long it drained him.

Otas fought to stay conscious. He had to check on his wife. Her arms were flung to the side, her breaths shallow. Her eyes were still open, but he knew she saw nothing.

Satisfied that he hadn't killed her, he rolled to the side and let darkness take him.

The door to the *Chim-dae-bang* slid open. Vlad stood in the doorway. He was drenched in sweat. It was his duty to guard the Overlord during *Kyol-hon*. The room may have been soundproof, but that didn't stop him from hearing their screams in his mind. It was something Vlad would never forget.

As was his duty, he checked the pulses in their necks. The beats were steady. *It is done*, he said to the Circle of Twelve with his mind.

Returning to the bed from the bathroom with a basin of cold water, Vlad wiped the sweat from their bodies. With her eyes open the way they were, Cwen looked dead. A shiver passed through Vlad as he gently closed the lids. He covered them both with the blue blanket. They would remain thus for the rest of the night.

He left the room, leaving the door open. He stretched out on the futon. He would guard them for the night. Until Otas regained his senses, Vlad was in command.

Vlad's last thought before sleep claimed him was that he was glad Otas was Overlord and not him. He would never be able to subject his Queen to *Kyol-hon*.

*Earth's Orbit*

Luca shuddered inwardly while sweat made his uniform stick to his skin. He'd been standing in front of the Commander for six hours while he was telling his version of the disaster that had occurred on the planet over and over again. It wasn't the retelling of events that had Luca upset, it was the grisly visage of the Commander. Maccus' eyes were doing a mad dance of colors—red to orange, orange to yellow, then back again. The bloodless gaping hole in the Commander's neck didn't help, as well as the gouges that ran from the corner of his left eye to his chin.

It had always been rumored that Maccus couldn't be killed. Luca hadn't believed it until now. He was so weary Luca couldn't help shifting his position. The action brought that terrible gaze to him.

"Tell it to me again, Luca," Maccus ordered from his command chair on the bridge.

"Commander, please. I've nothing more to add and . . . I'm really tired."

That brought a glare from Maccus and a psychokinetic pressure that sent Luca to his knees. "Have a care, Luca. I'm not exactly pleased that you live while the rest of my men are dead!"

"If I had been dead, I wouldn't have been able to save you and teleport you back to the ship."

"You fool," Maccus snarled. "I was in no danger. The Liambrians know I can't be killed. Tell me what I wish to know!"

Luca stood on wavering legs and began the tale again. "Just as you ordered, we materialized in the woods and surrounded the Liambrians. I swear we made no sound, but she knew we were there."

"She?"

"The black-haired one you ordered us not to kill."

"The Queen," Maccus mused.

"Yes. She gave the command to attack. The next thing I knew was that the U-V Lasers were somehow ripped from our grasps. She knew about the teleporters. Those crazy females started hacking off the arms of my men before they could activate the teleporters. And—"

"How is it you escaped?" Maccus wanted to know.

"You know I'm a quick thinker, Commander. The men were wasting valuable time trying to set the coordinates back to the ship. Then this virago came barreling down on me and I simply set the teleporter to send me a kilometer away. Fortunately, it was in the location where I found you."

Maccus grunted. "So you witnessed what passed between the Queen and I."

"Yes," Luca answered cautiously.

"I didn't know you were such a voyeur, Luca."

"It wasn't that. That female has some kind of power I don't understand. I was afraid she would harm you."

"As you saw, I'm more powerful than she is." Maccus rubbed his chin. "Skip the part where the male and female stunned me with the U-V Lasers. What happened while I was unconscious?"

"Well . . . the Queen, as you call her, tried to decapitate you with a sword. I fully intended to run to your rescue when out of nowhere this male materialized." Luca ran a hand through his matted hair. "I swear, Commander, he was your spitting image. He stopped the Queen from harming you. Why, I don't know."

Maccus had no intention of telling Luca the reason. "He's my twin."

"Your twin, sir?"

"You heard me. Who do you think we've been chasing across the galaxies and time?"

"I thought it was just the Liambrian female you were after."

"The Queen is of paramount importance to my plans. But let's just say I have unfinished business with my twin." Maccus stood from the command chair. "I'll be in my quarters formulating a new plan to capture the Queen."

Luca was glad to see him go. He couldn't stare at that gaping hole in the Commander's neck another nanosecond. Nor the raspy whistling sound of Maccus' voice caused by the wound. It was also said the Commander could heal himself. Luca hoped it was so.

Maccus stared at the injuries the Queen had inflicted upon him in the mirror in his quarters. He wasn't impervious to pain, the wounds hurt like blazes. But he'd let his crew see them before he healed himself. Judging by the terror of him he'd read in Luca's mind, the wounds had had the desired effect. Mutiny was not a thing he had time to deal with at present.

While the injuries closed with the activation of his self-healing powers, Maccus thought of the Queen. She was magnificent, unlike his flawed mother. He'd never met Taki, but the Supreme Tetrarch delighted in telling him what a sniveling coward she had been. Not so was the black-haired female. Even though she'd cried when he was about to rape her, she'd fought him until she could fight no more. Maccus believed her tears were more of frustration than fear. And the strength of her will was impressive. He had bombarded her with the full force of his power, yet her thoughts had remained hidden from him.

Maccus smoothed a hand over his healed cheek. Magnificent, he thought again. Since she had referred to his twin as *Sa-Jang* rather than husband, he assumed no bonding had taken place between the Queen and the Overlord. He still didn't know the black-haired one's name, but if his plan succeeded, he would learn all there was to know about his Queen.

# Chapter 19

Cwen was awake, but she was afraid to open her eyes. Her head felt strange. Perhaps *strange* wasn't an appropriate word for what she was feeling. *Bizarre* was more like it. All of the psychic receptors in her brain were pulsing steadily as if they were being bombarded with surges of electricity. She guessed it was morning because she could see light behind her closed lids. Cwen was scared that brightness shooting through her pupils would bring on the terrible pain again.

God, she couldn't just lie here like this all day. She had much to say to Otas. The anger she'd suppressed last night rose to the surface, giving her courage. Slowly, Cwen raised her lids, gazing upward. At first her vision was blurred, but the morning light brought no pain. Several minutes passed before her sight cleared and she could make out the curved skylight above the bed, the sky beyond a bright blue.

Okay, Cwen, she told herself, try sitting up. She did and was immediately hit with a wave of light-headedness. Breathing slowly, Cwen waited until the dizziness passed. Gazing across the bed, she saw that Otas wasn't in it. But she felt his presence. Turning her head, she found him sitting in the chair by the bed, shirtless, barefooted, black pants covering his lower body, his left ankle resting on his right knee. His black hair was unbound and wet as if he'd just taken a shower. His eyes were back to what was normal for him, gold and orange swimming in their depths. Cwen cursed inwardly. Obviously, he felt better than she did, looking whole and hearty.

Flashes from the *Kyol-hon* of the immense power her husband possessed raced across her mind. Even with everything that had happened in the last twelve days, deep down she hadn't fully accepted being a Liambrian. The male sitting next to the bed definitely was not of this Earth. He was an . . . alien.

Cwen felt that addressing him as *Sa-Jang* was not sufficient. He was so much more than a mere Master. But she had no other words to call him. "*Sa-Jang*," she said.

"Husband."

Cwen stared at him stupidly.

"We are alone, *Katai*."

Indeed they were. Cwen was in her husband's *Chim-dae-bang*, sitting in his big bed. Nodding and immediately regretting the action for it made her dizzy, she whispered, "Husband."

Even though he knew, Otas asked, "How do you feel?"

Cwen thought about that for a second. Trying to come up with an answer in 41st century English made her head ache. So she stuck with the language she'd spoken all her life. She didn't care if he understood her or not. "Weird."

"I know the feeling. I felt the same way when my father passed me his power when I became Overlord. Weird is the only way to describe it."

Cwen's mouth dropped open. It had been laced with a heavy Liambrian accent, but he'd spoken in perfect 21st century English.

Reading her thoughts, he said, "Don't be so surprised. Your father and Vlad told you I would speak your tongue after *Kyol-hon*." He could see the sweat shining on her skin. "Would you like a bath?"

Feeling grungy, she answered, "A quick shower ought to do it." She slid her legs over the side of the bed.

He knew she wouldn't be able to stand long enough for a

shower, but he didn't argue with her. Otas stood up, waiting to catch his wife before she hit the floor.

Trying to ignore her spinning head, Cwen got to her feet and immediately pitched forward into his arms.

He lifted her in his strong arms. "You are going to have a bath. You can't even stand for a second." He carried her to the bathroom, lowering her feet to the floor while he supported her with his arm. He punched the buttons on the wall, and the tub began to fill with tepid water. He could feel how hot his wife was, a cool washing would help her.

When it was filled, he lowered her into the tub. He twisted her long hair into a knot and secured it to the top of her head with a clip he'd had in his pocket. Grabbing a sponge and a bar of soap, Otas began to scrub Cwen.

"I can bathe myself."

"No, you can't." He smiled at her reddening cheeks. "Besides, who do you think bathed you last night?"

"You?"

The smile disappeared and was replaced by a frown. "You had cuts and bruises everywhere. I healed them all." His eyes sparked with anger. "It's amazing no bones were broken from the way Maccus knocked you off your horse."

Cwen became angry herself. If he knew what was going on between her and Maccus, why hadn't he come sooner? She opened her mouth to ask just that.

"Later," he hissed. "We'll talk after we get you settled."

The bath done, he quickly dried her off and carried her back to the *Chim-dae-bang*. He slipped a dark-green *wanpisu* over her head, settling it around her body. This one was shorter than the one she'd worn on Hyu-shik, falling to mid-thigh. It was also made of a lighter weight fabric. Cwen climbed back on the bed at his urging. He propped a pillow behind her back.

On the bedside table sat a pitcher and a tall blue glass. Otas poured a white liquid into the glass and handed it to her.

"You need nourishment, but right now solid food will make you nauseous. This is *Ma-shil-kot*. It contains all of the nutrients your body needs." He frowned again. "You may not like the taste."

Cwen took a sip and was surprised. "I've had this before. Vlad used to give it to me all of the time. I thought it was a protein powder drink." She chugged the liquid down.

He poured her another. "Drink as much as you want. *Kyol-hon* drains the body."

While she was drinking the second glass, Cwen found that Otas' thoughts were open to her. His mind spoke in a jumble of Liambrian and English. She sensed a powerful emotion running through him which was reflected in his eyes. Cwen concentrated harder, trying to identify what he was feeling. She almost choked on the drink when she realized Otas was jealous of Vlad.

"Why are you jealous? Vlad and I are cousins."

His cheeks flamed. "I had not intended for you to read my mind."

"Answer my question," she said, then thought about who her husband was. "Please."

A pained look crossed his face. "Under normal circumstances, the Overlord and the Queen grow up in close proximity to each other. We were separated by time and distance. I envy him the years he spent with you while you were growing up." He lowered his head. "Vlad watched you turn from child to grown female. He knows you better than I."

Cwen finished the *Ma-shil-kot*. "I have the same problem. Vlad knows you better than I do, also."

He lifted his head. "You are wise, *Katai*. I hadn't looked at it that way."

Cwen blushed at his praise.

"Do you want more?" He nodded toward the empty glass.

She shook her head. "I'm full now, thank you." And she did feel a bit stronger. Wonderful stuff, this *Ma-shil-kot*.

Otas took the glass from her, setting it on the table. He sat back in the chair and stared at her, his expression serious. He said nothing for several minutes.

Cwen got fidgety. "Why don't you say something?"

He passed a hand through his black hair. "I have much to say to you, but I don't quite know where to begin."

Cwen saw that his eyes had gone pure gold, indicating his degree of worry. She couldn't go all soft now. She was still angry with him. "Why don't you start with Maccus? Why didn't you tell me he was your twin?"

His wife's eyes were solid smoke with no green in their depths. "I didn't give you credit for having strength of will, or loyalty."

"It's called trust."

"I'm sorry I didn't trust you." Otas exhaled heavily. "I was brought up to believe that all females were deceitful."

"I know the tale of Taki and Raynar." Cwen studied him a while, probing his mind. What she discovered angered her further. "You were testing me, weren't you?"

He was silent.

"Did you really think I would choose Maccus over you?"

He could feel her rage building. He thought it best to answer. "I wasn't certain. I know you hold no love for me."

Cwen sighed. Vlad was right. Otas was totally insecure where females were concerned. "I've only known you twelve days. But already I care for you. Can't you tell by my sexual desire?"

That got a smile out of him. "Your *koi* drives me to distraction."

She smiled in return. "How do I know? I may love you now, but not know it. I was never taught about female feelings. Always it was the combat training, the lessons." She shrugged.

"We've all done you a disservice. You should have been

told from the start who and what you are. I was. It didn't make life easier, but knowledge kept me going."

"As Earthlings say, it's never too late to learn." Cwen became pensive. "Tell me all about Maccus."

"Maccus should never have been born. You understand how identical twins are formed?"

"Of course. After conception the zygote splits in half. The sections contain all of the chromosomes to form two complete individuals."

Nodding, Otas continued. "This event is unprecedented in Liambrians, especially in the formation of an Overlord. This mishap occurred because of the faulty *Bal-Dar* between my parents. Twins are common, but are formed from two different eggs. The Earthling description is fraternal twins, I think."

Cwen nodded. She was fascinated that he'd learned this vocabulary from her during the bonding.

He moved to the bed, feeling a need to sit closer to her. "Once the Trexrans had my mother in captivity, they began their experiments. Her double womb made her perfect for a case study. Maccus was implanted in the one on the left, me in the right. Thank *Ha-nu-nim* they selected me as the control for comparison to their genetic manipulations.

"Their tampering produced the differences between Maccus and myself. Fortunately he has no *Gew-Seen* and his power of the Gift is weaker than mine. But he has one attribute I don't possess."

He paused so long, Cwen became nervous. She placed her hand on his bare shoulder, noting the scratches left by her nails. "Husband?"

He was aware of where her hand rested, knowing she saw the marks on his shoulder. Closing his eyes, he activated his self-healing powers.

Cwen snatched her hand back as if she touched fire when the scratches disappeared. "You can heal yourself?"

His answer was a nod. "Now that *Kyol-hon* is complete, you'll have the same ability in time." He fell silent again. He didn't know how to tell her the worst of it regarding Maccus.

Cwen could only read part of her husband's thoughts. He was agitated and the source was Maccus. She grasped his chin so that he would look at her. His eyes were still gold. "If Maccus is such a threat, why did you stop me from killing him?"

"Because he's a replicater."

"A what?"

"The Trexrans took the gene I possess for self-healing one step further in Maccus."

"I still don't understand."

"You know what a flatworm is, don't you?"

"Yes." Cwen was totally confused.

"We had a similar creature on Liambria. What happens when you slice one in half?"

"Each half grows into a complete new flatworm."

Otas just stared at her, knowing she didn't quite understand the impact of what he was saying.

At her husband's silence, Cwen pondered flatworms and Maccus over and over again in her mind. Then it hit her. "A—are you saying that if—" She couldn't even get the words out.

"If you had cut off his head, there would have been two Maccuses to deal with."

Cwen's face paled. "That's what my father and Odelia were shouting at me."

"Yes."

"Now I understand why they only knocked him out with the U-V Lasers. If they had blasted him to atoms, there would have been—"

"Billions of him," Otas finished for her.

Thinking of the bloodless hole in Maccus' throat left by her dagger, she concluded, "He can't be killed."

"Not in any way we've discovered yet."

Cwen became frightened. "Can he kill you?"

"The strength of my Gift prevents that. Maccus can never get close enough to me to slice off my head. That's the only way he can kill me."

He looked at Cwen's pale face. Fatigue showed in her eyes, but she would keep talking if he let her. She needed rest after *Kyol-hon*. So did he, for that matter.

Being diplomatic, he said, "I grow tired. I need to rest." He stretched out on the bed, opening his arms to Cwen. She curled against him, her back to his chest. He placed an arm across her waist. "*Katai?*"

"Yes?"

"I am curious. I know you were really angry with me. Why did you let me perform *Kyol-hon?*"

"I wasn't in the mood to go nuts," she answered saucily. Then more serious, "For the good of our people."

He was silent for some seconds while pride gripped his heart. "I wouldn't have let Maccus rape you."

"I know that now."

"*Na Sa-rang Tang-sin*, I love you," he whispered, then sleep claimed him.

A thought struck Cwen as she listened to Otas' even breathing. He understood her language, but she didn't understand his. She was too tired to ponder it for long, the sleep of one fatigued shut off her thoughts.

Otas stood in his office, gazing down at his mother-in-law, who still wore the white robe of the Circle of Twelve. Because hers had been the biggest sacrifice of all Liambrians—having been ripped away from her baby with her breasts still full of milk and sent on a mission far into the future—he regretted what he was about to say to her. He decided it was best to let her speak first. "*Mal-ha-da*, speak," he commanded.

It took Sevea all she possessed not to let her voice quaver with tears. "*Sa-Jang*, before I take my leave of you, I want to see my daughter."

"She sleeps." He shook his head. "And she is no longer your daughter, but your Queen and my wife. Cwen is now my responsibility."

The tears fell before Sevea could stop them. "M—my time with her was so short. We were just beginning to know each other." Sevea swiped angrily at her wet cheeks. To cry in front of the Overlord showed weakness.

In a rare moment of compassion, Otas moved to Sevea and placed his hands on her shoulders. He stared into her golden eyes for some seconds. When she tried to duck her head and hide her shame, he lifted her chin. "Your tears do not offend me. It tells me what I've already read in your mind and heart. Despite your separation, you hold great love for your daughter." He actually smiled down at her. "You please me."

Sevea was shocked by his caring manner. "I—I mean . . . " Words failed her.

"Did you think me heartless?"

Sevea couldn't lie for he would know it. "Well, yes."

Otas chuckled deeply as he swiped tears from her cheeks with his thumb. "Let it be our secret. It would not do for all Liambrians to know I can show mercy."

Sevea smiled at his words.

Otas dropped his hands. "My Queen inherited your courage and tenacity in battle. For this I thank you."

Sevea nodded in acceptance.

"I don't know where she gets her temper from, though."

Musical giggles escaped Sevea. "That part of her is Hebron." She had never been this comfortable with the Overlord before. Perhaps Otas absorbed some parts of Cwen during the bonding.

Otas grunted. Cwen would wake soon. Although he was

enjoying this exchange with Sevea, he must be there when his wife awakened. "I will return my wife to Castle Acwellen when she has recovered."

"I understand."

Otas' eyes took on a serious guise. "I don't think you do. During *Kyol-hon* I gave my wife full power and knowledge. When you see her again, she will be . . . different."

Sevea pondered this for a few seconds. "She'll be like you."

"Correct."

There was nothing more to say. Sevea turned and left the Overlord's chambers.

Otas sat on the bed, watching his wife toss and turn in her sleep and flail her arms. Part of him wanted to stop what was happening to her brain but logic prevented him from interfering. She must become accustomed to the forces of the Gift.

Cwen sat up abruptly, eyes wide, a scream on her lips. "Th—the voices!" She gripped her head in agony. Somehow through the cacophony in her mind, she noticed Otas sitting next to her. "Thousands of voices talking in my mind! Make them stop, *Sa-Jang*! Make them stop!"

"I cannot."

"You bastard!" she cursed. "What have you done to me?" Cwen wanted to yell at him some more, but screams came out of her mouth instead. She couldn't take all of this noise in her brain.

Otas gripped her wrists and shouted, "Listen to me, *Katai*! Only you can stop the voices in your head!"

She could barely hear him through the racket in her mind. "How?"

"Think it!"

"What?"

"Simply command your brain to quit listening to the voices!"

Cwen thought Otas mad, but she did as he said. *Stop*! she said with her mind. There was instant silence. Cwen tried to slow her breathing. She had been hyperventilating from fright. When her breathing became steady, she glared at her husband. "What the hell was that?"

"*Dut-da*."

Cwen frowned. Where had she heard that word before? Then she remembered. *Dut-da* had been what Otas said he was doing on Hyn-shik. "You mean I was listening to—"

"The thoughts and emotions of every Liambrian on the planet, with the exception of myself and Maccus."

"Jesus!" Cwen looked at Otas with new respect. "You do this all of the time?"

"Yes."

"How can you stand it?"

"Over time you get used to it."

Cwen thought furiously for some minutes, staring at the handsome visage that was her husband, this . . . this creature from another planet. "Why did it come upon me so suddenly?"

"It's the way I performed *Kyol-hon*."

As if that explained it, Cwen thought. "I don't understand."

Otas stood and paced for a few seconds. "Even though I understand your tongue, it's hard for me to put into words."

Cwen crossed her arms. "Try."

He smiled at her flippancy. "All right." He clasped his hands behind his back. "You know my mother went insane during *Kyol-hon*."

"Yes."

"It could have been prevented if my father had more control and less anger." He searched his mind for words in English to explain what he meant. "Think of your brain as a computer."

Cwen wanted to tell him to get real, but said instead, "Go on."

"Think of your brain as a hard drive. During *Kyol-hon*, I downloaded all of the knowledge and power that I possess." He looked to her to see if she was still with him.

"So far, I'm following you."

"What I did was program your brain to activate different aspects of the Gift at timed intervals. Slowly, so to speak. If all of your psychic receptors had activated at once . . . ," he shook his head at the thought. "That way lies madness."

"Thanks, I think."

Otas gave her a quick smile. "You're welcome." He sat on the bed next to her and ran a hand through her hair. "Are you okay?"

"I think so."

"That doesn't sound convincing."

"I—it's just that this is all hard to believe. Me sitting here with you." She gazed into his vibrant eyes. "The fact that you're an alien from a planet that lies in the next galaxy." Cwen shook her head at the enormity of it all.

"You forget. You're an alien as well."

"I know. I know." She inhaled slowly. "That's the hardest part to believe."

He made no comment. Otas lay down and pulled her against his bare chest, rubbing a hand down her back. At times, silence was best.

Cwen felt soothed by his close presence. The thoughts of all the Liambrians on Earth had been disconcerting. She hadn't understood the language of the thoughts, but the emotions she'd read had been tangible. They had run the gamut of joy to intense hatred. The memory of a powerful emotion caused her to stiffen.

"*Sa-Jang!*"

He knew what she was thinking and feeling, but he encouraged her to speak. "Easy." He held her tighter. "Tell me what's on your mind."

"During *Dut-da*, I sensed intense evil. Many of your . . . I mean, our people hate you."

"I am aware of them."

"But won't the same thing happen here as it did on Liambria?"

"No." He was silent some seconds. "They will be dealt with."

She turned on her back to see his face. "How?"

He remained quiet, his eyes shifting from red to orange to gold.

Cwen found that she had the answer within her own mind. She gasped as she received a visual image of her husband shrinking and deactivating the psychic receptors of those flawed, then wiping their memories clean. These hapless Liambrians were then tossed through the Doorways like garbage. Cwen tried to move away from Otas for suddenly he scared her to death.

He held her in place with ease. "You must accept all that I am, *Katai*."

All at once her mind became a well of confusion. Which twin should she be more frightened of? Maccus, the beast? Or Otas, the Overlord?

# Chapter 20

Maccus belched loudly after downing his third cup of Trexran ale. The brew was powerful, but it didn't take away his anger and frustration. It was now midnight. He'd been here in his quarters since leaving the bridge, running the details of the failed attack on the Liambrians over and over again in his mind. The damn Queen, he thought. She'd disarmed his men by using psychokinesis. A fact occurred to him causing Maccus to sit up straighter. The black-haired female he had subdued in the glade had weaker power than his. She didn't have the strength to do the deed. So what in ten Trexran hells had happened?

Maccus choked on his drink when the answer hit him. A collective mind! Not just the Queen, but all of the Liambrians had used psychokinesis against the Trexrans. This new breed was nothing like his mother's cowardly people. These Liambrians killed mercilessly and thoroughly. How had they evolved so quickly?

Maccus pondered that for some time, then decided that *how* was irrelevant. A collective mind, he thought again. Maccus now realized he needed more than just the Queen. He required all of the Liambrians to achieve his goal of creating a master race. Much of it was already done for him, but by adding his genes into the matrix . . . the possibilities were endless.

One problem stood in his way. Maccus frowned. These were the people his twin ruled. "*Sa-Jang*" the Queen had called him. The only solution was to kill his brother. Maccus shrugged. It was something he'd wanted to do from the moment the Supreme Tetrarch had told him of the existence of his twin and that his own father had abandoned him and left him in the hands of the inferior Trexrans. Maccus clenched his fist. He'd been tossed aside like refuse.

A calmness came over Maccus. He would have the Queen, all of the Liambrians, and a very dead twin. Maccus poured more ale into the cup and began formulating his plans.

Good God, my husband is a monster, Cwen thought. Before she could stop her mind, an image of Otas wielding an ax over the neck of a defenseless Liambrian with his head in the block formed in her mind. She gasped at her runaway imagination.

Evidently, Otas had read her thoughts as well. He roughly pushed her away and sat up, his eyes looking like twin flamethrowers. He shot off the bed and stalked to the window. With his back to her his stance was rigid, fists balled at his sides.

Looking at his bare broad back with the length of his ponytail resting against his shoulder blades, Cwen didn't know what to do or say. His mind was completely shut off to her, but she knew that she had hurt him. "Husband?"

He remained as he was and silent.

Cwen wanted to go to him, but she was afraid of what he might do to her in his anger.

A low snarl escaped him as he spun to face her. "You think me a monster?" Otas began to shake with the strength of his emotions. "Do you actually think I would do you harm?"

Cwen gulped at the sound of his voice. He wasn't shouting, but he may as well have been for the power of his tone rendered her speechless.

"Well, do you?" This time he shouted.

Even with the distance between them, Cwen could see the flames raging in his eyes. She wanted to shake her head, but she found herself frozen under the intense gaze of her husband.

Otas stared at her that way for some minutes. "I am no executioner," he finally said, cursing at himself inwardly for his voice had cracked with emotion. Of their own volition the tears began to fall.

At the sight of this huge male that was her husband crying, Cwen felt no bigger than an ant. She rose from the bed, her intention to go to him and give whatever comfort she could.

Otas held up his hand. "Stay away!"

"Husband," Cwen implored.

"*Tat-da Wi-e*, shut up!" Otas spun back to the window resting his forearm on the glass, and let the sobs flow free.

Cwen didn't understand the words, but there was no mistaking their meaning. She stood still, mouth closed, feeling like ten kinds of an idiot for having reduced her powerful husband to this emotional display. The sound of his throaty sobs was heartbreaking and gut-wrenching.

Crying still, Otas moved from the window and went into the bathroom. The door swooshed shut behind him.

As time passed Cwen became concerned. She could read nothing from her husband's mind. She hoped to God he wasn't suicidal.

Finally he emerged from the bathroom, in control of himself again. He sat on the side of the bed, looking at his wife. She stood where he'd left her, pale-faced, not knowing what to do. "Sit, *Katai*." He patted the bed.

Cautiously, she did so, not getting too close to him.

Otas pulled her to him. "Touch me."

She placed a soothing hand on his shoulder, kissing the bulging bicep there. "I'm sorry my runaway thoughts caused you to cry."

"The cause was not just you. It has been a long time in

coming." He looked to her with eyes that were now calm. "I gain no pleasure from what I do."

"I never thought that."

He just stared at her some seconds. "I know. It's just one of the burdens I must bear as Overlord. It's the logical thing to do, yet it pains me."

"That was very apparent." Cwen thought a moment. "Is there no other way to separate the good from the evil?"

"A mere separation is useless. We learned that from what happened on Liambria. Raynar, my father, did not have this power to strip those flawed of the Gift and empty their minds so that they could not betray the loyal Liambrians." He looked at her beseechingly. "All that is left of my race is on this planet. If I didn't do what I must, the Liambrians would not survive. Do you comprehend what I'm saying?"

"Yes." Cwen stroked his face, then ran her hand down his ponytail. "How is it that you have this ability while your father didn't?"

He smiled mirthlessly. "Even though the *Bal-Dar* between my parents was forced, they succeeded in the creation of me."

"So Raynar programmed your attributes into the genetic matrix during *Bal-Dar*."

"Correct."

Cwen suddenly had a terrible thought. "Do I have to do this . . . this . . . "

"It's called *Chi-u-da*." The revulsion on his wife's face was unmistakable. "And no, you cannot do the deed. Only I possess this power. I am *Ku Chi-u-gae*, the Eraser."

"Thank God."

"But you do play a role in who is selected for *Chi-u-da*."

Her heart sank to her knees. "How so?"

"By *Dut-da*. There are times when you must perform this task for me. Earlier you were able to sense the thoughts and

.D

emotions of the flawed Liambrians. I can't be everywhere all of the time. None must be overlooked."

"Great," she said without enthusiasm.

He chuckled, stroking a hand through her hair. Their gazes locked for some seconds. "You're feeling stronger, aren't you?"

"I wasn't thinking that. How did you know?"

"By your *koi*. It's interfering with my thoughts."

"Shit."

He looked confused. "Why are you talking about feces?"

Cwen sighed. Otas may speak English, but he didn't have the hang of cursing. "Forget I said anything."

"If we're to engage in love play, we need nourishment first. I'm hungry. Aren't you?"

"I'm starving."

"Good. What do you want? Fish, fowl, or meat?" Otas asked as he stood, pulling on a black shirt.

"I'm hungry enough to eat all three."

He smiled. "I'll go order something prepared."

Before he could pass through the threshold, she said, "Husband."

He turned to look at her. "Yes?"

"I'm sorry if my thoughts upset you. I'll try to keep them to myself."

"It will do you no good. I know what's on your mind before you even think it."

"Then why can't I read your thoughts whenever I wish?"

"Because I am Overlord."

That answer made sense, for no one should be able to read Otas' mind. "And how is it you speak English but I don't understand Liambrian?"

"Why, it is because I'm a male." With that, he left the chamber.

Cwen cursed quietly, hoping he couldn't hear her.

While Otas was gone, Cwen inspected his *Chim-dae-bang*. Running her hand along the curved wall by the big window, she discovered that the structure was not granite. It had the feel of metal, not stone.

Gazing about the room, she was intrigued by this place Otas called home. Although the bed was large, it took up very little space. The room was enormous, but had little furniture. The black-framed bed, bedside table, and curved-backed chair were all that was sitting on the wall-to-wall black carpet. Despite the grayness of the metallic walls, the room was amazingly bright, almost cheerful, but not quite. Objects for ornamentation were absent. There was no evidence of items Otas used for recreation. Odd, she thought, no closets. Where were his clothes?

Cwen sighed and moved to the portal her husband had passed through. With a whoosh the panel slid open. Well, at least I'm not a prisoner, she thought.

The sound of computer blips and bleeps brought her gaze to the slate desk behind which sat Vlad. Delight etched her features. Running to him, she said, "Vlad!" Her intention was to hug him.

Vlad rose quickly and backed away from her. "*Yo-Wang*," he said with a fist pressed to his chest, then stood at attention.

Cwen was puzzled by his behavior. "Is there something wrong?"

"No, *Yo-Wang*." His brown eyes were focused above her head. "Is there something you wish to command of me?"

"Command?" she sputtered. "Goddamn it, Vlad. We're cousins! I won't let you treat me like I have some disease!"

"I only do you honor. You are wife of the Overlord." It pained him to treat her so formally, but he had no choice. "To act otherwise is forbidden."

Cwen suddenly felt like the lonely child she had once been.

"Return to the *Chim-dae-bang*, *Katai*," Otas said from behind her.

Cwen hadn't heard him enter. "But—"

"Leave us."

She turned to look at Otas. The sternness on his face stopped her from arguing. Feeling like she had just committed some major mistake, she returned to the bedroom. After the door had slid closed, she pressed her ear to the panel, but she could hear nothing. Sighing, she sat in the chair broodingly.

"The food will arrive shortly," Otas said as he entered.

The pain of loss she was feeling kept Cwen silent.

He knelt in front of her, lifting her chin so that she couldn't avoid his eyes. "Your pain grieves me."

"I seriously doubt that."

"You are wrong about me." He let out a breath. "Vlad only gives you the respect that is your due as my wife. It's protocol." He touched her cheek. "I have lived with the coldness of it all of my life. I didn't think of how it would effect you."

"Is everyone going to treat me that way?" she asked in a quavering voice.

"Yes."

"Mother and father?"

"They too. I'm sorry. They are no longer your parents, but subjects under your command."

The loneliness that cloaked itself around her was suffocating. "Then I have no one."

"You have me."

The look she gave him was scathing. "At least you have Vlad as your friend and confidante. Sometimes a female needs feminine companionship."

"I remind you that Vlad is also my second in command." He gave a smile that made him look mischievous. "I've selected a second for you. She will be everything to you that Vlad is to me."

A spark of hope shot through Cwen. "Who is she? Where is she?"

"I cannot tell you."

"Then how the hell am I to recognize her?"

"When the time is right, you will know." Otas listened with his mind for a second. "Our dinner is here."

"I'm not hungry anymore."

"You lie. I can feel how famished you are. It's making me weak." He stood, pulling her with him.

"Wait." Cwen held back. "What does *Yo-Wang* mean?"

"Queen," he answered as he dragged her to the outer chamber.

The aromas wafting up her nose made Cwen's mouth water. Vlad was setting out the food on the round, black table in the corner. She refused to look at him as she sat. Apparently it didn't bother Vlad for when he was finished he left the Overlord's chamber without a word.

All of Cwen's attention was focused on the feast before her. If she didn't know better, she would think she was in a Chinese restaurant, not that she'd ever been to one. Vlad had always ordered takeout. "This food looks Asian."

Otas chuckled as he sat down. "Liambrian cooking styles are very similar. Please eat. I can take your hunger no more."

Cwen didn't need encouragement. She plucked a breaded morsel from a plate and popped it in her mouth. The consistency and flavor was similar to shrimp, but that wasn't what it was. "Delicious," she mumbled after she'd swallowed. "What is it?"

"*Sae-u*. It's a small but tasty sea creature."

Neither one of them spoke as they attacked their dinner with vigor. It wasn't long before they had consumed all of the dishes set before them.

Cwen sighed with satisfaction as she sipped from a glass of water. As promised, there had been a fish, a fowl, and a meat cuisine served with what looked like blue rice, but was not rice. The spices were unusual and tasty. The vegetables crisp and flavorful.

.D

Cwen finally looked up at Otas. The expression on his face was intense. "Is something wrong?"

"No," he answered with a shake of his head, his eyes shone with a molten heat.

"Then why are you looking at me that way?"

"When our food has digested, I intend to drive you to *Ju-Gum*."

First there was darkness devoid of thought. Then consciousness. Otas slowly opened his eyes; the black bars of the headboard coming into focus. He shook his head to clear his muddled thoughts. Again he found himself sitting back on his heels, his shaft buried deep within his wife who lay beneath him, unconscious. His intentions had been to push his wife to *Ju-Gum*, but her fiery passion and responses to him had sent him into the dark as well. Silently, he cursed. Vlad had been in command since the bonding as he was now. If Otas kept losing control of his mind while mating, Vlad would have to spend a great deal of time commanding the Liambrians.

Otas stared down at his nude wife, deciding to let her come around on her own. He resisted the urge to push the curtain of hair aside that covered her face and stroke her until she awakened. Instead, his eyes ran over her magnificent body. Again he was pleased by what he saw. The body of a warrior. But soon that warrior would bear his child.

Cwen's loud sigh brought his attention back to her face. Her thick lashes fluttered a few times before her eyes opened. She looked directly at him, but said nothing. There was no need to speak, for their minds were as linked as their bodies. They were deep within *Saeng-Gan*.

Otas didn't touch her, keeping his mind focused on her thoughts. If he did so, he would become aroused rapidly and right now he didn't have the strength to go through *Ju-Gum* again. His brows rose at the direction his wife's mind was taking.

"It does not please me that you think of Maccus during *Saeng-Gan*."

Cwen smoothed a hand across his chest to calm him. "I'm just wondering why I couldn't sense him during *Dut-da*. Since you're Overlord, I understand why I couldn't sense you."

"You forget. Maccus is my twin."

Cwen frowned. "I'm not likely to ever forget that fact."

"What I'm saying is that even though he isn't as powerful as I am, he does share some of the attributes I possess. I'm always aware of him, but I can't always read his thoughts."

"I could read his mind loud and clear when he tried to . . ."

"Rape you?"

Cwen nodded.

"In his excitement Maccus was projecting his thoughts. I doubt that he was aware he was doing so." Otas felt Cwen shudder beneath him. He knew what she was thinking. "Don't worry. Now that you have my full power, Maccus won't be able to pin you down with the Gift."

She pondered that for some seconds. "You say that you've given me your power. Laying here the way we are, I can feel your strength. Your power hasn't diminished."

"I explained it too simply." Otas closed his eyes in thought. When he opened them, he said, "The power that you have has always been yours, but it lay dormant until a catalyst could initialize it. The amount of the Gift that I have is the only force that could have activated your psychic receptors. I'm the key, so to speak."

"So between the two of us—"

"We possess great power of the Gift."

Power that she didn't comprehend, Cwen thought. "And all of this new knowledge that I have, it was there all along?"

"That is different. The knowledge that you now have was given to you by me during *Kyol-hon*."

"But I still know next to nothing."

Otas chuckled at her frustration. "That's because I programmed the knowledge to be released slowly. At preset intervals. Full knowledge would have—"

"I know. Driven me insane." Cwen grew weary of such serious talk. "Tell me, what do you do for fun?"

"Fun? I do not understand."

"You know, like when children play. Adults need recreation, too."

A pained expression crossed his face. "I never played as a child."

"Never?"

"Not once. It was forbidden by my father."

Cwen felt sorry for him. At least she'd had the video discs and romance novels to entertain her. Some parts of the Overlord were still that lost and lonely child. "If we ever get out of this mess we're in, I'll teach you how to have fun."

"I would not have your pity," Otas growled.

"You don't. I'm thinking of myself as well. All of this formality of being the Queen will soon bore me to death."

A fire lit in Otas' eyes. He took one of her breasts in each hand, kneading them sensually. A look of shock showed on her face as she felt his erection grow. "Until we find some other way, this will have to do as fun."

Passion overtook Cwen before she could comment.

# Chapter 21

Cwen opened her eyes to the light of sunrise filtering through the skylight above the bed. Otas lay on his stomach, black hair hiding his face, an arm draped across his wife's middle. Cwen stared at him awhile, trying to determine if he truly slept or was in *Dut-da*. Gingerly, she lifted his arm and slid out of bed. Gently, she laid the deadweight of his arm back on the bed. Otas didn't move. He's truly out, she thought. Their night of love play had exhausted him. But not her. For some reason she felt invigorated as she walked to the large concave window.

Peach-colored rays from the rising sun highlighted the five snow-capped mountain peaks in the distance. The sight of the snow made Cwen wonder at what altitude her husband's fortress lay. Husband, she thought as she hazarded a glance back at Otas, who still hadn't moved. Cwen shook her head at the wonder of it all. To find oneself an alien and married to the Overlord of that race of extraterrestrials surpassed the imagination of a proficient screenwriter.

But it was all real. Cwen raised her wrists to look at the gold bracelets encircled there. The green sapphires sparkled with the morning light while she contemplated the male that was her husband. Something that Hebron had said to her on Hyu-shik came to mind. She must never reveal what she knew of the Overlord, which at this point wasn't much. But Cwen now understood that Otas was a male of deep emotions. He could be easily hurt.

*Ku Yo-Wang*, Vlad had called her. The Queen. The full

impact of who and what she was was just beginning to sink in. Cwen didn't quite know exactly how she felt about being the wife of the Overlord. She liked him a lot, she admitted to herself. The way she behaved while they made love proved that. But this so called protocol Vlad had subjected her to was painful. She didn't want people bowing and scraping to her. In her mind, she was just Cwen, a young female who didn't fully understand what was going on around her, but met each day as a new challenge to be overcome. Of one thing she was certain. She was a damn good warrior. Unconsciously, she rubbed the gem in one of her bracelets as she allowed her thoughts to run free.

Otas made no sound as he stared at the nude profile of his Queen. The mass of black hair falling to her hips enhanced the beauty of her body. Her breasts were high and full, but the rest of her was well-muscled and lean. It amazed him that she was his. His wife was more than he had expected—highly intelligent, adaptable, beautiful, and completely unpredictable, which delighted him. No, he thought, his days would not be boring.

Using his warrior's skills, he silently slid from the bed and slinked up behind her, placing his hands on her shoulders. At his touch she said nothing and leaned back into his nude body. There was no need of words, for with their minds linked he knew what she was thinking. Otas kissed the top of her head.

They stood that way for several minutes until she said, "You were truly asleep, weren't you?"

"Yes. Vlad woke me."

The timbre of his voice reverberated down the length of her spine, causing a strange tingling in her belly. It wasn't lust. It was something unknown to her. Ignoring this strange feeling, Cwen stated, "You weren't in *Dut-da*." She turned her head slightly and rubbed her cheek against his chest. "I thought you never really sleep."

"Ordinarily, I don't." The feel of her cheek rubbing

against his breast made it hard for him to think. "My brain needed to recover from *Kyol-hon*. It takes a great deal of effort."

"I believe it." There was humor in her voice. "Have you recovered?"

"Completely." He rubbed her shoulders as he watched her hand working her bracelet. "Did I put them on too tight?"

"No. I find them a comfort when I'm thinking." She turned to face him. "Events have happened so quickly. I've never had the opportunity to ask you just how did you fuse the jewelry?"

"It's an aspect of the Gift that makes me able to blend metal." He touched a hand to the wall. "Our architects have the same ability. This wall is a melding of alloy and an ore we call *tol*. It's extremely strong and resilient. It can't be shattered."

"Interesting." Her eyes were focused on his gold collar with the green sapphire in the center. "My father told me that this is a military operation. These gems in our jewelry signify our rank, don't they?"

"Correct."

"Hebron, Vlad, and Sevea's warriors wear emeralds. What does that mean?" She didn't need to ask about their's for they were the highest rank.

"They are warrior class. Vlad has the highest rank of all."

"Sevea is a warrior, but she wears diamonds."

"Sevea is more than a mere warrior. The degree of her Gift allows her to sit on the Circle of Twelve." By the confusion on his wife's face he knew she didn't fully understand. "The combined strength of twelve Liambrians fitted with diamonds equals my full power. If for any reason I become incapacitated, there will always be a ruling government."

Knowledge she didn't realize she had popped into her mind. "They're assembled during *Kyol-hon* and *Bal-Dar*, aren't they?"

He nodded. "During those times, I'm unable to protect myself and oversee my people. Vlad takes over the task of *Dut-da*."

Cwen had had enough lessons for the morning. "This is all very intriguing, but I would like to see the rest of your fortress."

"I'm sorry, but it is not yet time."

A flush of anger reddened her cheeks. "You expect me to spend days or weeks only in this room?"

"No." His orange eyes were unreadable. "I'm sending you back to Castle Acwellen in a few minutes."

"What?"

"You heard me, *Katai*."

"You bring me here for the bonding, yet you intend to send me away? Doesn't a wife belong with her husband?"

"Under normal circumstances, yes. But these are hard times. Maccus is still out there." He pointed to the sky. "There are still many things to be done before the Liambrians can be safe."

"Shit!" came out of her mouth before she could stop it.

"Feces again, *Katai*? I don't understand."

"I'm angry, you idiot!"

Otas scanned her mind. Indeed she was. "What I will tell you will quell that anger."

Cwen lifted her chin stubbornly. "Talk."

"I have a task for you to perform. Sevea told you that you're in command of the daughters of her warriors."

"Yes," she said cautiously.

"You are to bring them here."

"You mean teleport them here?"

"No. By horseback. You're to lead and command them. It should take you three weeks adding in factors for contingencies."

Cwen snarled. "First of all, I don't even know where *here* is! Second, all I've ever done was take orders, not give them!"

"You did well commanding Sevea's warriors to attack the Trexrans."

"That's because I was scared shitless, you fool!"

"You were constipated?"

"Oh, just forget it!" She stomped away from him.

"*Katai*," he said calmly. "Come back here."

Reluctantly, she did.

Otas placed his hands on her shoulders. "Trust yourself. The ability to command is inherent in you. Besides, you absorbed some of my command abilities during *Kyol-hon*."

"If you say so." Cwen sighed. "Why do you want me to do this?"

"The daughters have no idea as to their true identities. I'm using you as an example. They must prove themselves before I accept them as worthy Liambrians."

"All right. I'll do it, not that I have a choice. How many are there?"

"Not counting you, thirty."

Cwen stopped the curses before they spilled out. "And just how do I find you?"

"Our minds are linked. You may not know my thoughts, but you can always find me."

Cwen folded her arms. "Terrific."

Even though she stood rigid as stone, he cupped her face and kissed her. "I'll send you back now."

"Wait. I have a question."

"Yes?"

"You can teleport yourself and other things without the aid of a device, right?"

He nodded.

"Can Maccus?"

"Yes."

"Can I?"

"Not yet."

"Hmm," was all she said. "OK, I'm ready now."

Otas frowned. "I have a question, too."

Cwen slapped her thigh in exasperation. "Ask."

"How did you know it was Maccus and not me that knocked you off your horse?"

"He stinks," she stated flatly.

He couldn't help but smile as he sent her to Castle Acwellen.

### Castle Acwellen

When Cwen materialized in her chamber, she found her parents standing at attention before her. Neither of them said anything, their faces expressionless. Which was fortunate because she had appeared before them naked as a jaybird. Even with the warmth of the heater radiating behind her, Cwen's body broke out in goosebumps.

*I had your parents warm your room. It's eighty degrees inside Liambria. I knew you would be cold.*

Cwen's eyes widened at the sound of Otas' voice in her head. It was as if he stood right next to her.

*Don't be so shocked.* Kyol-hon *has permanently linked our minds.*

*Why don't they say something?* she asked telepathically.

*They're waiting for you to acknowledge them.*

*I suppose calling them mother and father is out.*

*Correct. Use their names.*

Great, Cwen thought to herself. She was just getting the hang of being a daughter. Now she was to treat her parents as underlings.

*They expect it.*

Cwen sighed. *When do I start this journey back to you?*

*Soon. I will summon you.*

*All right.*

*Katai?*

*Yes?*

*Na Sa-rang Tang-sin.* That said, Otas broke the telepathic communication.

Whatever, she thought. Cwen stared at her parents, feeling awkward as hell. She found she could read their minds with ease. A payoff from *Kyol-hon*, she guessed. They weren't any happier about this role reversal than she was, but they accepted it for they were used to Liambrian protocol. Cwen sighed as she thought, I guess I should get the ball rolling.

"Sevea. Hebron," she said.

"*Yo-Wang*," they each said with fists over their hearts.

Oh, please, Cwen thought with irritation. She noticed the pitcher and basin sitting on the table in the corner and went to it. While she washed quickly, Sevea hovered behind her.

"I had the water warmed, *Yo-Wang*."

Cwen looked at her mother. Sevea wore battle gear, her bronze hair pulled back into a tight braid. It was ludicrous having this amazon be subservient to her own daughter. Despite her thoughts, Cwen said, "Thank you."

Cwen went to the chest and pulled out a chemise. After she had put it on, she reached for the brown leather battle wear.

"If I may, *Yo-Wang*?" Hebron said.

Cwen looked to her father, who held up a black metal-studded tunic and matching pants and boots. She raised a brow in question.

"As Queen your color is dark-green, but in this century that color leather is not to be found. We thought the Overlord's color would be appropriate."

"That was thoughtful of you, fath . . . Hebron," Cwen said as she took the outfit from him and dressed with speed.

Like magic, Sevea produced a tray of meat pies. "Otas told us you hadn't eaten."

Cwen said nothing as she munched on a pie. Scanning her parents' thoughts she discovered they knew of her mission for the Overlord. I might as well get on with it and think like a Queen. After washing down a pie with water, she asked Sevea, "What do your warriors call you?"

"When the Earthlings aren't around, *Hom-Yong*."

"What does it mean?"

"Captain."

"Hmm," was all Cwen said as she snatched another pie and bit into it. After she'd swallowed, she asked, "Sevea, which of the daughters knows the land best?"

"That would be Sashna."

"Have her meet me in the stables." Then a thought struck her. Did she still have a horse? The last she saw of Samson was when Maccus attacked him. Her poor steed had been rolling in the dirt. "Hebron, what of Samson?"

He knew what her concern was. "He's fine. He sprained his foreleg in the battle with Maccus, but my wife healed him. He's fit for riding."

Thank God, Cwen said to herself. "Saddle him for me. I'll be down in a few minutes."

Her parents took that as a dismissal and left the chamber.

Cwen cursed silently as she brushed out her hair and plaited it into a thick braid. After strapping on her sword and dagger, she left the chamber.

Sashna awaited her astride a large bay stallion, holding Samson's reins. At the sight of his mistress, the horse broke free and trotted over to Cwen. He butted his big head against her chest, almost knocking her over.

"I'm glad to see you, too," Cwen said with laughter as she stroked Samson's neck. The horse quivered with excitement as she mounted him. She turned to Sashna. "Take me to high ground in the north. I would see the lay of the land."

"As you command." Sashna sent her bay into a gallop.

Cwen followed, realizing she hadn't even said hello to her old friend.

Two hours ride took them to the crest of high hills. Using

her mind, she sensed the location of Otas. Cwen could see the mountains of Liambria far in the distance. "What lies between here and those mountains?"

With sunlight glinting off her pale blonde hair, Sashna answered, "There are long fields, but most of the land is dense forests. There are many safe streams for water to drink."

"What of danger?"

"There are wild boars aplenty, and thieves who rob and murder careless travelers."

Cwen thought about that for some time. "Are there any castles along this route?"

"Nay. We'll be on our own, *Yo-Wang.*"

Cwen muttered curses under her breath, then the realization of what Sashna had just called her hit her. "What did you call me?"

Sashna gave her an impish smile. Her brown eyes sparked with devilment. "*Yo-Wang.* You are the Queen, aren't you?"

Cwen could only stare at her childhood friend. Was this possible? Cwen scanned Sashna's mind. What she read there astonished her. "You know everything, don't you?"

Sashna's giggles were her only answer.

"Why didn't you tell me what you knew when you came to me in the meadow?"

Sashna turned serious. "I was forbidden to. Besides, you weren't ready to hear it."

Cwen shook her head. "And that hokey story about Liambria being a land where the people are faerie." Cwen cocked her head in remembrance. "You also told me you were to watch my back. What does that mean?"

"You're still the same as when you were young. You have to have all of the facts before you believe anything." Sashna reached over and clasped her hand. "By order of the Overlord, I'm your second in command."

Cwen looked down at their joined hands. "My husband

said I would recognize you as friend and confidante, but I didn't"

"That's because you thought yourself alone."

"And you were sent through the Doorway so long ago to—"

"Prepare for your arrival. I know I'm an extraterrestrial, specifically a Liambrian. I've been trained in combat and the use of the Gift. I know of the Trexrans. I speak Liambrian as well as 21st and 41st century English."

"Well, you're ahead of me there. I don't understand Liambrian." Cwen looked to her neck and wrists. "You wear no jewelry."

"I have it. I was told not to wear it until the time came. I was the Overlord's big secret."

Only one of them, Cwen thought. "What's your rank?"

"Warrior class. I wear emeralds."

Cwen was ecstatic, but somehow she knew they didn't have a lot of time to revel in their reformed friendship. "These daughters. What kind of warriors are they?"

"Many are good, but some . . . " Sashna shrugged.

"And they know nothing about being Liambrian?"

Sashna nodded.

"Great." Cwen squeezed Sashna's hand, then let go. "Tomorrow morning assemble them in the list. I'll test them in battle." Cwen nudged Samson into a slow walk.

Coming along beside her, Sashna said, "This husband of yours, Otas."

"Yes?"

"What's he really like? I only met him the one time when he gave me my jewelry. I found him . . . scary."

Cwen thought about that from everyone's perspective including hers. "Believe me. He *is* scary."

# Chapter 22

Maccus sighed with satisfaction as he inspected the device strapped to his wrist. For every problem there was a technological solution. Even though his head had ached from the amount of Trexran ale he'd consumed, he'd stayed up all night constructing the amplifier. He could sense the Queen's *koi* with his mind, but his range was limited. The amplifier would enable him to home in on her from ten kilometers distance.

Maccus had no doubt that his twin would come seeking the Queen once he had her in captivity. It was the perfect plan. Maccus would have the Queen. And he intended to kill his brother in front of her.

His laughter echoed in his quarters long after he'd teleported to the surface.

Cwen rode in silence at Sashna's side. She was deep in thought, going over the list of supplies they would need for the journey to the Overlord.

Sashna cleared her throat loudly, causing Cwen to look at her. "You've said nothing for the last hour. I become bored with my own thoughts, *Yo-Wang*."

Cwen sighed. "Do me a favor. When we're alone, call me by my name."

"But that wouldn't be proper to—"

Cwen shot her an irritated look.

"Okay." Sashna lifted her shoulders. "What were you thinking just now . . . Cwen?"

"Just making preparations for the journey." She jerked her chin forward. "How far are we from the castle?"

"A little more than a kilometer."

Cwen didn't comment, thinking Sashna had a good sense of distance in the wilderness. She had been trained well.

As the horses entered a clearing in the forest a thin beam of blue light shot across their path and exploded the trunk of an oak. Sashna's horse reared, spilling his rider to the ground. She landed with a loud thud. She squeezed her knees against Samson's sides, staying seated.

Cwen didn't turn to check on Sashna for with her mind she knew she was all right. Her attention was on the foliage. She scanned the area for Trexrans, but sensed nothing.

Without warning, Maccus materialized in front of her with a U-V Laser weapon aimed at her chest. His smile was maniacal.

Using the Gift, Cwen snatched the weapon from his hand. It sailed swiftly into her own grip. She aimed the laser, but didn't fire.

Maccus' look was one of disbelief. "The last time we met, you were weaker."

Cwen slammed him back up against a tree with her mind, pinning him there. "As you see I'm much stronger now."

Maccus nodded, though it was difficult with the pressure on him.

"What do you want, Maccus?"

"Besides you, I wish to know the location of *Sa-Jang*," he answered arrogantly.

Cwen laughed. It was a terrible sound. "I'll never tell you where my husband is."

Maccus was enraged but he could do nothing. The force the Queen used on him was greater than his own power. His twin had already taken what Maccus considered his. Had he impregnated her? Maccus couldn't tell. "Husband?"

Cwen said nothing, sliding the lever on the U-V Laser with her thumb.

Sweat broke out on Maccus' forehead. If she blasted him to atoms, his cells would replicate into millions of duplications of himself. The prospect was unacceptable. His desire was to be the only Master of this new race. Trying to buy time, Maccus said, "This is no way to treat a fellow Liambrian."

"You're a Trexran abomination."

"My mother was a Liambrian Queen!" There was actually a sniveling in his voice.

"Taki was flawed and a coward."

"How dare you speak of—"

Cwen fired the laser weapon. Maccus stayed where he was until she released him with her mind. Then he fell forward on his face.

Cwen jumped down from Samson and ran to Sashna, whose face showed shock and confusion. "You're not hurt. Hurry. We have to get out of here."

"That was Maccus? He looks just like—"

"He's Otas' twin. I'll fill you in when we reach the castle." Cwen heaved her up and pushed her to her horse. "Hurry. I only stunned him. He won't be out long."

Cwen mounted Samson with a leap. Sashna followed suit. They headed for the castle at full gallop.


Cwen and Sashna galloped the horses right into the stable, scattering the workers there. "Leave us!" Cwen shouted.

When they were alone, they dismounted. "What the devil is going on?" Sashna asked.

Cwen held up her hand. *Sa-Jang!* she said with her mind. *I heard all.*

*Maccus is up to something.*

*Agreed. Be ready to ride when I give the signal.*

*I will be.*

*Katai?*

*Yes?*

*Na Sa-rang Tang-sin.* Then he was gone from her mind.

There it was again. Cwen still didn't know what the hell he'd just said, but she couldn't worry about that now. Sashna was just about hopping up and down with excitement, anticipation, and fear.

While they unsaddled the horses and rubbed them down, Cwen explained all that she knew about Maccus.

"And you weren't even scared," Sashna commented in awe.

"The hell I wasn't!"

Sashna looked at the U-V Laser weapon Cwen was tucking into her breeches. "Where did you learn to use that thing?"

"I guess from Otas' mind during *Kyol-hon.*"

"Your use of the Gift is impressive."

"Thanks. But your performance was not."

Sashna looked crestfallen.

Cwen clasped her shoulder. "You must be prepared for anything, my friend. I need you."

"Yes, *Yo-Wang.*"

"Cwen," she reminded her.

That brought a small smile from Sashna.

"What does *Na Sa-rang Tang-sin* mean?"

"I love you."

Cwen's brows shot up. "You're certain?"

Sashna nodded vigorously. "*Na* is I. *Sa-rang* is love. *Tang-sin* is you."

"I'll be damned," was all Cwen said.

When Cwen entered the great hall, it was packed with smelly knights. Holding her breath, she tried barrelling through them to get to her chambers. A bulky knight stepped in her way, bringing her up short.

"Women are forbidden to be garbed for battle in the great hall," he informed her.

He was a head taller than she, but after being with Otas this knight looked puny. "Out of my way, you brute!"

"Be you deaf, woman!" He shoved her in the shoulder.

Cwen whipped out her sword and pressed the point of the blade at his throat. "Never touch me, you beast!" Her voice was low. "'Tis my chambers I seek."

A loud guffaw erupted from the high table. "I see you have recovered, Cwen," Lord Ware observed.

She didn't know what he was talking about. A quick scan of his mind told her that he'd thought her abed with fever these last days. "Completely, my lord." Cwen kept the blade at the knight's throat.

"'Tis . . . 'tis the daughter of Sevea?" the knight stuttered.

"Aye."

"You could have warned me."

"You have been away a long time, Brun." Lord Ware chuckled some more. "Sometimes 'tis best to let a man learn things on his own." He looked down to Cwen. "Don't skewer him. He's one of my best knights."

Cwen sheathed her sword. "Goodnight, my lord." She rapidly headed for the stairs, laughter ringing out behind her.

When she reached her chamber, Cwen found her parents within.

"*Yo-Wang*," they greeted her.

Cwen removed her sword belt and slammed it on the chest. "Can we dispense with this damn formality?"

"The Overlord will be displeased," Sevea said.

Cwen spun on her. "He will not! I have a lot of thinking to do and I can't be fumbling around with Liambrian proto-col!" She couldn't believe she'd just shouted at her mother.

Hebron laughed. "Our daughter is right. Otas knows her mind. He won't be angry."

Cwen relaxed slightly, looking to Sevea. "I need you to start gathering provisions for three weeks immediately."

"I've already started. You have dried meat for two weeks,

cheese, thirty-one water skins, and bread is being baked day and night."

"Thanks." Cwen smiled at her. "What of weapons?"

Hebron handed her a dagger. "Including you, each has a sword and two daggers. I'll have the bows and arrows you need ready in the morning."

Cwen only nodded. Her mind was working rapidly, trying to find details she might have overlooked.

"Cwen?" Sevea said.

She looked at her.

"They're not as well-trained in combat as you are."

"I know. I intend to fight each one in the morning to test their skills."

Sevea turned and headed for the chamber door.

"Where are you going?"

"If you intend to do battle with thirty warriors, you'll need a big dinner."

Hebron began to laugh. Cwen joined him, but it only slightly relieved the tension running through her.

As she had ordered, the daughters were assembled when Cwen arrived. All but Sashna took an unconscious step backward at the sight of the black-garbed Cwen. She frowned as she scanned their minds. They were all terrified, but for Sashna. Cwen motioned Sashna to come to her. When she did, they turned their backs on the frightened females.

"What ails them? she whispered.

"Why, you, *Yo-Wang*."

She scowled. "Cwen," she hissed. "Maybe wearing Otas' color of black isn't such a good idea."

"The color does make you look formidable, but that's not the reason for their fear."

Cwen looked at her with impatience.

"You forget, twelve of us saw you kill three men in the woods with the aid of no one. The rest have heard the tale."

"This is the reason for their terror?"

"Yes."

Cwen looked her up and down. "And you? Are you terrified?"

"Of what?"

"Me. I intend to fight with you first."

That got a reaction from Sashna. "But why? The Overlord has already named me as your second in command."

Cwen jerked her head toward the daughters. "They don't know that. You must prove to them your worth."

Sashna cursed under her breath. "Just don't cut off a limb."

"Join the others," Cwen commanded.

Once Sashna had reached the group, she followed and stood before them. Cwen waited several minutes before speaking, making eye contact with each of the daughters. "You have been told that I command you."

Hesitant nods from all.

"By order of Sevea, we're to embark on a dangerous journey. But I 'twould test your mettle first. Each of you must fight with me." The fear level rose several notches. Cwen walked up to Sashna. "You're to be first." Cwen moved to the center of the list.

When Sashna came within striking distance, Cwen swiftly drew her sword and attacked. Sashna whipped out her own blade and deflected the blow that would have decapitated her. Cwen threw everything she knew into the assault, raining blows on Sashna's sword before her friend could recover from the last bone-shattering clang of swords.

On the battle went until Cwen was satisfied that she couldn't disarm Sashna. "Hold!" she shouted, though she was panting with exertion.

Sashna held still, but she didn't lower her sword. Her breathing was as labored as Cwen's.

Cwen sheathed her sword to convince her friend that the combat was over. "I name you second in command." She turned to face the daughters. By their expressions, the terror remained. "You'll follow the orders of Sashna as if they were my own."

It was slow in coming, but finally they said in unison, "Aye, my lady."

Cwen searched their faces and settled on the dark-skinned countenance of Kendra. She remembered her from the day she'd first arrived in this time-frame. She pointed to her, "You're next."

So the morning passed with Cwen battling each of the daughters. None were equal to Sashna, but twelve stood out as very good warriors, eight fair, and the remaining nine pathetic.

"You must be ready to ride at any moment. Prepare yourselves." Cwen looked them over a final time. Four of the daughters were in tears. She'd tried not to, but she had nicked a few with her blade. "Sashna, I would speak with you. The rest of you are dismissed."

"What are we to call you, my lady?" Kendra piped up.

Cwen thought about that for some seconds. The use of the Liambrian word, *Hom-Yong*, for captain would only confuse them. "Cwen," she answered simply.

The daughters dispersed, rubbing aching muscles. Cwen sympathized with them. Her own muscles were screaming with the torture she had put them through, but she stood erect, not daring to show weakness to those under her command.

When they were alone, Cwen asked Sashna, "What do you think?"

"We can depend on Kendra, Lora, Ting, Raslen, Nelda, Tavya, Edina, Annis, Bernia, Diera, Maida, and Gudren."

"Agreed." Cwen rubbed her sword arm unconsciously. "What I'm worried about are those last nine. They'll fold for sure during combat, if not outright flee." Cwen shook her head. "The Overlord will never accept them as true Liambrians."

"Perhaps." Sashna thought for several minutes. "Has it occurred to you that all Liambrians aren't warriors?"

"Explain."

"The way I understand it there are Liambrians in every field. Healers, architects, engineers, chefs, farmers, scientists, and the like. Their contributions are just as valuable as the warriors'."

"I hadn't looked at it that way." Cwen became pensive. "Their skills are important, which means we'll have to protect them if danger occurs."

"This is going to be a long journey. I'm tired already."

"Me too." Cwen turned to head back to the castle. "I have some thinking to do. I'll talk more with you later."

When Cwen reached her chamber, she found she was too weary to think about anything. She flopped on the bed, wearing her black battle gear and sword belt. She was asleep in seconds.

The knights bantered loudly during the evening meal within the great hall. The roaring guffaws of Lord Ware could be heard above the din. Sevea and Hebron were not among them.

The large oak door banged open, bringing with it a cold wind and the battered and bleeding sons of Lord Ware. The noise immediately stopped. The two sons stumbled up to the high table and fell to their knees before their father. Both of them breathed with shuddering breaths.

"Ale!" Lord Ware shouted. "Bring ale for my sons!" He rounded the high table, stepped from the dias, and knelt before his sons. "Cadmon, Galeron, what the devil has happened?"

Cadmon, the older of the two, quaffed a full tankard of ale before he spoke. "Baron Kendric is dead. His castle has fallen to marauders."

"And his knights?"

"All dead, father."

Lord Ware frowned. Kendric's castle lay six hours hard ride to the south. Were these marauders on their way to Acwellen? "Who beat you?"

"He calls himself Lord Maccus." Cadmon shuddered at the memory. "He's a giant, father! Never have I seen such a one."

His son stood two heads taller than he and was no weakling. An ill feeling fell over Lord Ware as he asked, "Why were you beaten?"

Cadmon held out his tankard for more ale. It was filled quickly. After downing half of it, he answered, "He wanted us to bring him one of Sevea's wenches. He threatened to do the same to Castle Acwellen if we didn't."

Lord Ware's brows knitted downward. "Did he describe her?"

Cadmon nodded, inhaling slowly. "'Tis a woman with hair of midnight and eyes the color of moss. She wears black leather." Cadmon gingerly touched his bleeding brow. "I tried to tell him there was not such a one here, but Lord Maccus would have none of it."

"'Tis Cwen he seeks," Brun spoke up.

"I know no Cwen."

"'Tis the daughter of my wife," Lord Ware informed him. "She came while you were away."

"We must give her to this Maccus, lest Castle Acwellen fall," Brun said.

Lord Ware pondered this for some time. Sevea would hate him, but he would do what he must to retain what was his. "Bring Cwen before me," he ordered Brun.

With a nod, Brun said, "I saw her take the stairs at the noonday meal. I've not seen her come down."

Brun headed for the winding staircase with five knights behind him.

*Wake up, Katai!*

Cwen sat bolt upright in the dark chamber. She had been deeply asleep, but she was more than alert now. *Sa-Jang?*

*You're in great danger. Come to me now!*

Cwen jumped off the bed and slammed into someone. A hand clamped itself over her mouth before she could scream.

"It's me, *Tanim*," Hebron whispered. "Hold tight."

Hebron and Cwen dematerialized just as the door to her chamber crashed in.

Brun and the five knights came thundering back down the stairs. "She's gone!" Brun shouted.

Lord Ware cursed. Now that he thought of it, he hadn't seen Sevea since morning. "Has anyone seen my wife or her women?"

None answered.

Lord Ware's expression was murderous. "Cadmon, where did you leave Lord Maccus?"

"He and his men were gathered outside Kendric's castle." He gripped his father's arm. "They ride to Acwellen!"

Lord Ware rose. "Then we meet them in the field!"

"You can't leave the castle defenseless!" Brun protested.

"Do you wish to be trapped inside these walls like cowering women?"

"Nay, my lord."

"Then to arms!" Lord Ware shouted.

Cwen and Hebron materialized in a huge candlelit room. Sevea and several of her warriors stood at attention. "*Yo-Wang*," they all said.

Cwen quickly looked around her and was amazed. Liambrian technology was everywhere. Self-energizing computers sounded out their electronic bleeps, the frame of a Doorway stood several feet to her left.

D

"Where are we?" Cwen asked her father.

"In an underground room of the north tower. The Earthlings never come down here."

"What the hell is going on?"

"Sevea will explain. I must return to Liambria immediately."

Cwen was frightened and needed the comfort of her father's arms, but she knew she couldn't show weakness in front of the Liambrians gathered.

Hebron held a fist to his chest in salute. Cwen copied her father. He nodded, then popped out of view.

Before Cwen could ask a question, Sevea shoved a tankard of *Ma-shil-kot* into her hands. "Drink quickly, *Yo-Wang*. You'll need it for strength."

Cwen took the drink and chugged it down.

"Listen carefully." Sevea's expression was intense. "The Overlord read in Maccus' mind his scheme to take over Baron Kendric's castle. His intention was to use this as a jumping off place to conquer Acwellen and seize you. Maccus is on his way here now."

Cwen wished she hadn't drunk the *Ma-shil-kot*. Her stomach was doing flip-flops.

"Otas let you sleep while we put our escape plan in motion," Sevea continued. "Sashna and all the daughters await you twenty kilometers to the north. We'll send you through the Doorway to join them. The time that you will arrive there will be three hours from now. That should give you a sufficient head start."

"The Trexrans will be following us?"

"We can't be certain of what Maccus will do. We dare not take any chances." Sevea smiled, which relieved some of the tension around them. "Besides, my scouts told me that the Trexrans come by horseback and they're terrible riders."

"What of Lord Ware and the knights?"

"They ride to meet Maccus in battle."

"They go to their deaths," Cwen stated with certainty.

"We can't interfere in what's to be." Sevea inhaled. "We've sent those serving the castle to a nearby village. When we leave, Acwellen will be empty."

Cwen experienced another sense of loss. She scanned her mother's mind, picking up images of Liambrian technology. But she couldn't identify the location. "Where do you go?"

"To my next assignment." Sevea looked to her with caring in her eyes. "We'll meet again, *Yo-Wang*."

It was small, but Cwen had a ray of hope.

"Now I wish you to meet someone you must take with you." Sevea signaled to Odelia, who stepped forward with a Liambrian child before her. "This is Jena."

Cwen tilted her head in question. The young one was the spitting image of Odelia. Auburn hair pulled back into a long plait, eyes the color of cinnamon, and wearing brown battle gear. "I'm to take a child with me?"

"*Yo-Wang*, if I may?" Odelia said.

Cwen nodded to her.

"My daughter is twelve and knows she's Liambrian. She doesn't know how to use a sword, but she'd good with the bow." Odelia smiled. "Jena rides like you. Her steed is not a palfrey, but a gelding." Odelia's eyes teared. "I cannot take her where I go. I ask that you protect her and deliver her safely to Liambria."

Great, Cwen thought, although no emotion showed on her face. They were going into unknown danger with nine useless warriors, and now she must look after a child. "I'll protect her with my life." Cwen held out her hand to Jena, who took it immediately.

"I thank you, *Yo-Wang*." Odelia placed her fist on her chest and backed up.

Sevea held up two hooded cloaks. "The nights turn cold.

These garments have linings made of Liambrian fabric. They will keep you warm and dry when it rains."

Cwen and Jena put on the cloaks. Cwen's was black with a dark-green lining while Jena's was brown with blue on the inside.

Odelia sat at the Doorway station. "It's time."

Keeping her voice steady, Cwen said, "Thank you for everything, Sevea."

"Until we meet again." Sevea held her fist to her heart.

The loud whine of the Doorway forced Cwen to shout, "What of the equipment, Sevea?" She was thinking of all of the Liambrian technology located in this tower. Maccus must not be able to track them.

"There's a Liambrian starship in orbit above us. We'll teleport the equipment there. When Maccus arrives, Castle Acwellen will contain nothing but rats."

Satisfied, Cwen pulled Jena with her through the shimmering, blue-violet Doorway.

Cwen and Jena stepped from the Doorway into the middle of dense bushes. Cwen gritted her teeth so she wouldn't make a sound as the pin-prickling sensation assaulted her nerves. "The pain will stop in a minute, Jena."

"I know. I've been through the Doorway before."

Cwen cocked a brow. "You speak my form of English well."

"Of course."

Tough kid, Cwen thought. Her senses located the daughters. Jena followed her as she made her way to the waiting females.

"Cwen," Sashna greeted her, then noticed the young one. "Who's this?"

"Jena. She's under my protection."

"This is who that big white gelding is for?" Sashna asked in surprise.

"His name is Kan," Jena informed her.

There was a full moon. In its light, Cwen could see the line of mounted warriors waiting for them. She was pleased by the way Sashna had set up the formation. Cwen would ride in the lead. Behind her, Sashna and Kendra would ride with Jena between them. The rest of the column had the best warriors interspersed with those weaker.

After they'd mounted, Cwen took a deep breath. Well, here goes nothing, she thought. Cwen was doing this for a husband whose power and authority strained the senses.

*Katai, I await you.*

*I'll do my damndest to bring everyone to you safely, Sa-Jang.*

*If you're in serious trouble, I'll intervene.*

*Let's just hope that doesn't happen.*

*Katai?*

*Yes?*

*Na Sa-rang Tang-sin.*

Cwen smiled as she gave the signal to ride.

D

# Chapter 23

*The Road to Liambria*

After they had ridden for an hour in the moonlit night, Kendra said, "Cwen?"

"Yes?"

"Where do we go?"

Cwen considered lying, then decided the truth was best. "Liambria."

"Liambria 'tis a myth," Kendra replied with a laugh. She thought Cwen was joking.

"'Tis real."

Kendra straightened in the saddle as she thought about that for a few seconds. "Why do we travel to a place where the people are faerie?"

"Because, Kendra, we're faeries."

Kendra opened her mouth to tell Cwen she was mad, then closed it. Their leader may have thoughts that were fanciful, but she could fight like the devil. Kendra was sore in places she didn't think were possible from her combat with Cwen. Besides, Kendra shrugged inwardly, Cwen thought enough of her fighting skills to place her in a position to watch her back along with Sashna. Kendra vowed that Cwen wouldn't regret her choice.

The column rode on in silence, which Cwen was thankful for. Ever since Otas had awakened her, she had been running on pure adrenaline. All of her actions up to this point had been instinctive.

Now that Cwen was assured that Maccus was well behind them, she allowed her brain to do a bit of *Dut-da* on those following behind. Her warriors were too fatigued to be frightened by this abrupt journey. Even the horses beneath them were weary. Cwen gazed back at Jena, whose head kept nodding in an attempt to sleep then jerked back upright in false wakefulness.

Cwen looked up at the position of the full moon. From its location she guessed it to be around three in the morning. She signalled Sashna to join her. When she did, they trotted their horses several paces ahead of the others.

"This is a bad way to start a long journey," Cwen said quietly. "I can't tell whose more tired. The daughters or the horses."

"Both." Sashna's eyes looked black in the moonlight. "We left Castle Acwellen shortly after you exhausted everyone in battle. We rode hard to reach the meeting place where Sevea told us to await you."

Cwen's brows lifted in surprise. "Why didn't anyone awaken me?"

"Sevea had orders from the Overlord to let you rest."

"Is he mad?" Cwen said angrily. "How am I to command them if he would coddle me?"

"He doesn't." Sashna chuckled. "Otas knows as well as I do that you won't truly rest until we reach Liambria."

"Perhaps." Cwen gazed back down the line. "If these females don't get some sleep, I'll have to carry them to Liambria."

"Agreed." A strange look appeared on Sashna's face, her eyes staring into nothingness. "There's a glade not far from here. It should make a suitable campsite."

"How do you know that?"

"I see and know things." Sashna shrugged. "Before they happen. While they happen. Sometimes after. It's my strongest portion of the Gift."

"Precognition," Cwen said more to herself than to Sashna. Otas' choice for her second in command seemed very wise. "Pass the word down the line that we'll rest soon. I won't have low morale become a problem."

Sashna nodded with a smile and went to do Cwen's bidding.

As Sashna had predicted the clearing was perfect. There was room to tether the horses, fallen logs to rest their backs against, and the dense forest surrounding the glade kept the cold wind at bay.

There had been some grumbling when Cwen had ordered that no fires were to be built. The daughters all wore brown cloaks like Jena's. She had assured them that the garments were made from the hands of the Liambrian faeries and would keep them warm. Kendra had tried to stifle her giggles all the way to her post to guard the horses.

Since she was rested Cwen kept watch over the sleeping forms in the clearing. Lora, Ting, Raslen, and Nelda silently walked the perimeter. In three hours, they would awaken their reliefs and catch some sleep themselves. Sashna would relieve Cwen at the appointed time.

With her back resting against a log and a knee propped up, Cwen watched the small figure of Jena approach.

"Can't you sleep?" she whispered when Jena reached her.

"I—I'm cold."

Cwen quickly scanned Jena's mind. The child was as warm as she. Jena missed her mother. Cwen opened her cloak. "Sit by me. I'll warm you."

Jena didn't hesitate, snuggling up to Cwen like a kitten as she wrapped the folds of the cloak around them.

A soft sigh escaped Jena.

"Better?"

Jena was silent some seconds. "Are you really the Queen?"

"That's what everyone keeps telling me." Cwen realized

she was talking to a child and shouldn't joke in such a manner. "I'm truly the Queen."

"You aren't like I expected. You're nice."

Cwen looked down into the innocent cinnamon eyes. "Didn't you think I would be?"

Jena shook her head. "I thought you would be like the Overlord."

It was Cwen's turn to be surprised. "You've met him?"

"Twice."

Cwen tried to learn the reason for her husband's interest in this young female by probing her mind. Jena knew nothing useful. "My husband scares you."

"H—he doesn't smile like you do. And he's so . . . big."

Cwen fought to keep from laughing. Otas had scared the daylights out of her too when they'd first met. In fact, sometimes he still did. "Jena, you know the Overlord cares about all of us, don't you?"

"That's what my mother said."

"It's true." Cwen hugged her close. "Hush, now. You need to sleep."

Jena didn't argue. She rested her head at the side of Cwen's breast. Mere seconds passed before she slept.

Cwen shook her head in wonder. The last thing she had expected to do on this journey was play mother to someone else's child.

### *Earth's Orbit, Liambria*

Sevea viewed herself in the mirror in her quarters, thinking it was amazing the burgundy *Yang-bok*, jumpsuit, still fit her perfectly. All of those years spent on Earth hadn't produced a flabby and fat body. How she looked was not the important thing on her mind at the moment however.

It had been close to twenty years since she had commanded this starship. She'd done a damn good job of it even though she was pregnant with Cwen; racing from galaxy M100 to the Milky Way, praying to *Ha-nu-nim* the Trexrans wouldn't catch up with them. But alas, two thousand years later, they had.

Sevea inhaled deeply as she left her quarters. As she walked the short distance to the bridge, she noticed that the floors, ceiling, and walls were in impeccable shape. The Liambrians that had commanded the ship in her absence had taken excellent care of it. Only an hour earlier Sevea and her one hundred warriors had assumed command of this vessel, relegating those that had piloted the starship to lesser positions.

Sevea shook her head at the irony of it all. Her daughter was traveling in the most archaic manner to Liambria, while her mother had arrived in less than sixty minutes. Even with her new abilities gained from the bonding, Cwen still hadn't guessed what her own mother truly was. The captain of a starship.

Sevea paused before activating the automatic sensors to the bridge doors. The *Yang-bok* was so lightweight compared to the leather battle gear she felt almost naked. Not to mention the absence of the weight of her sword belt. Her wedge-soled black boots designed for spaceflight even felt strange.

Sevea inhaled as she thought, This is no different than what I have been doing. I've always been in command. Thinking thus, she stepped forward. The bridge doors opened with a swoosh. She stepped within.

Odelia, who had been sitting in the command chair and was wearing a grey *Yang-bok* quickly rose to her feet. "*Hom-Yong wi-e ku Ta-ri*, Captain on the bridge!" At her words, the bridge crew jumped to their feet and stood at attention, awaiting Sevea's orders.

Sevea herself stood speechless as she took in the sight of the bridge. It looked familiar, but after being at Castle Acwellen for so long it appeared . . . alien. She recalled the oval shape of the bridge as well as all of the duty stations—navigation, helm, communications, the viewer screen, tactical, engineering, ship's monitoring, all of it.

Sevea just stood where she was, staring around her. Odelia, who was the second in command, signaled her with a raise of her auburn brows. The look told Sevea that the crew was awaiting her orders.

Sevea shook herself, then said rather gruffly, "Report."

Odelia fought to keep herself from smiling. "We're in stationary orbit over Liambria. The Overlord sent a coded message that all starships are to land immediately. It seems Maccus' ship is heading toward the equator. Even though we have our dampening field activated, the Trexrans will be able to track our power surge."

Sevea nodded. "It will be just as it was on the planet Liambria. With all starships docked with the engines off and the dampening fields in place, we'll be invisible to the Trexrans."

"Correct," Odelia agreed. "Otas also ordered that communications be limited to Liambria *Myong-Yong*, Command, only for docking instructions." Odelia moved to the helm station and sat. "He also wishes to see you in his chambers after we've landed."

"So noted," Sevea said as she sat in the command chair. The rest of the crew did likewise, assuming their positions at their stations. Sevea looked at the ends of the armrests on her chair, which contained miniature viewing screens of all stations on the bridge. "Josha, hail Myong-Yong on a scrambled frequency."

"Aye, *Hom-Yong*."

In seconds the hail was answered on the bridge speakers. "This is Liambria Myong-Yong. Identify," said a male voice.

"This is *Liambria Five* requesting docking procedures," Sevea replied.

"*Hom-Yong* Sevea, you are to dock between *Liambria Four*

and *Liambria Three*. The Overlord has ordered that transmissions be limited to avoid detection by the Trexrans. You'll have to land manually. If you have difficulty, we'll advise. Myong-Yong out."

Oh, this is good, Sevea thought. She hadn't manually landed this starship since their arrival on Earth. Gazing at the tense faces of her crew, it occurred to her that they hadn't either. The Earthlings had a saying that once you learn how to ride a bicycle you never forgot. She hoped that was true.

Sevea looked at the screen on the armrest that showed the ship's trajectory in relation to Myong-Yong. "Helm, starboard thrusters at 23.57 degrees."

Odelia was so intent on what she was doing, she forgot to say, Aye, *Hom-Yong*. Sevea forgave her the oversight for she was scared herself. "Begin descent, one quarter sub-light speed."

Not one person spoke as the starship dropped through the Earth's stratosphere. There was very little vibration from the forces assaulting the vessel. Sevea smiled to herself. Her ship had always given a smooth ride.

"Helm, port thrusters thirty-seven mark three degrees," Sevea ordered.

As *Liambria Five* entered the atmosphere, the vibrations increased, causing the ship to shudder and the crew to sweat.

"Helm, starboard thrusters ten mark eight degrees." Sevea viewed the position of the ship again. They were right on target for Myong-Yong. "Helm, retro-thrusters."

Everyone was quiet as the ship slowed its descent. *Liambria Five* slid neatly between *Liambria Four* and *Liambria Three*, touching the ground with a definitive thunk. The crew sighed with relief with their mouths and their minds.

Sevea herself wanted to jump up and down with glee, but as Captain that would be undignified. "Well done, everyone." That brought smiles to the tense faces.

Sevea stood. "*Chung-Yong*," she said to Odelia. "You have control." That said, Sevea left the bridge.

*Liambria 2*

Hebron had his nose pressed to the window in the Overlord's chambers. Sweat poured from his forehead like rain. Otas stood behind him with one of his rare smiles on his face. He was glad Hebron had his back to him.

When Hebron turned to him, Otas' expression turned somber. "I told you she could do it, Hebron. Did you not believe me?"

Hebron's knees were wobbly from watching his wife land that massive starship. "It's not that I doubted you, *Sa-Jang*. It's just that Sevea hasn't piloted that vessel since we arrived on Earth."

Even though their behavior was formal, Otas thought his father-in-law needed some praise. "You have a remarkable wife, Hebron. And you yourself are the smartest Liambrian under my command with the exception of Vlad." He stared at him some seconds. "I thank you for my Queen. She has inherited the best qualities from you both."

Hebron was shocked by the Overlord's words, but he nodded his head in acceptance.

With a stirring of the air, Sevea materialized within the Overlord's chambers. When he looked to her, she said, "You wished to see me, *Sa-Jang?*"

He nodded, but what he wanted to do was twirl her in the air. He was proud of the way she'd handled the huge starship. Otas now understood how Cwen felt about this damned Liambrian protocol. He really liked his in-laws, yet as Overlord he couldn't display that affection. "I am pleased at the way you and your crew handled *Liambria Five*."

Sevea nodded in acceptance of his praise.

Otas still had the urge to hug her, so he placed his hands behind his back. "I am aware that my Queen got safely away. What concerns me is the possibility that Maccus will be able

D

to read the psychic traces left behind by your warriors when you abandoned Castle Acwellen."

"I, too, thought of this. During Operation Scramble in the past, the Liambrians were in a panic, leaving psychic patterns of their thoughts. So while we worked to teleport the equipment to the ship, I ordered my warriors to sing a song over and over again."

Otas quirked a brow in question.

Sevea couldn't help letting a giggle escape. "We sang, 'Hi ho, hi ho, it's off to work we go.'" She whistled the tune.

"The words are nonsense," he said in amazement.

"Exactly."

Hebron had no control over his laughter. When he could speak, he said, "The song is from a famous Earthling fairy tale. It's not meant to have meaning. When Maccus arrives at Castle Acwellen, this is all he will sense telepathically. I believe his reaction will be much more dramatic than yours."

Otas thought about that for a few seconds. Control was the only thing that kept him from laughing. "So, Sevea. There is no Liambrian technology left at Acwellen?"

"There's nothing left at all."

"Explain."

"Not only did we take our equipment, we took the animals, too. The castle dogs, cattle, goats." Sevea shrugged. "And all of the horses. They're good breeding stock and will mix well with our *mals*. Maccus will find nothing but vermin."

Otas did smile this time. "And my Queen has no idea that you are in command of *Liambria Five*?"

"Even with the knowledge that she's Liambrian, Cwen doesn't fully comprehend the reality of spaceflight."

"I agree." Otas thought for some seconds. "Yours was the last starship to land. All ships will remained docked until we get word from Raynar."

"What of the Inter-Dimensional Leap processors?" Sevea asked.

"That is why I brought Hebron here. Counting yours, there are still four ships that need the units installed. With Hebron's supervision, the task should be completed before my Queen arrives." Otas turned pensive, orange and gold shifted in his eyes. "Cwen will only have a matter of days to become accustomed to the idea that we will leave this planet."

*Castle Acwellen*

Maccus' mood was foul as he drank a fourth tankard of the weak brew the Earthlings called ale. His backside ached abominably from the jostling ride on those hairy beasts. They'd met this Lord Ware and his army ten kilometers from the castle. Even though the knights outnumbered his men by one hundred, their show of strength was pitiful. Maccus had no time for such ridiculousness, so with the exception of Lord Ware they'd blasted all of the Earthlings to atoms.

Since there was no longer a need to keep up the pretense that they belonged in this century, the Trexrans had abandoned those miserable beasts and teleported the rest of the distance to the castle. And it was all for nothing.

Maccus slammed the tankard down. Acwellen had been abandoned, but that didn't trouble Maccus for he would be able to read the psychic traces left behind by the Liambrians. He'd forced Lord Ware to show him where these so called warriors had lived.

The thought of the empty North tower angered him further. There had been psychic traces left by the Liambrians, but they made no sense. Using the amplifier on his wrist, Maccus was unable to detect the *koi* of the Queen. She was not within a ten kilometer radius of the castle. Where had she gone?

Maccus downed the rest of the ale. He'd been in contact with his ship, which was now in orbit above Acwellen. His men could detect no power surges that would indicate a

.D

dampened Liambrian vessel. There were a few transmissions detected. However, they'd ended so quickly his men couldn't triangulate the source.

Hi ho, hi ho, it's off to work we go, played itself over and over again in Maccus's mind. Nonsense. Pure nonsense. The word *work* didn't help. Did it mean the Liambrians had fled to the future again? Or the past? When and where was work?

# Chapter 24

The fifth day of travel brought them closer to Liambria. With each step of Samson's hooves, Cwen could sense Otas more strongly. So far they had gone their way unmolested by marauders. Cwen prayed their good luck held for she and the daughters would reach Liambria ahead of the three week estimate, which is why she let them eat their fill of the two weeks rations they'd brought. Including Cwen, the daughters had big appetites.

Cwen constantly did a *Dut-da* on Jena to see how the young one was holding up. What she learned gripped her heart. The child worshiped her and tried in every way to emulate Cwen.

Sashna trotted up alongside her, breaking her silent musings.

A silent signal passed between them before they galloped their horses some distance ahead of the others.

"Is your lack of sleep catching up with you?" Sashna asked.

"Why do you think that?"

"You've been very quiet for the last two days." Sashna scratched her shoulder. "I just assumed it was fatigue."

"I was thinking about Maccus." Cwen didn't look at her, keeping her eyes focused ahead, seeking any signs of movement. "I don't understand why he just didn't attack Acwellen directly. Why go to the trouble of taking over Kendric's castle?"

"I asked my mother the same thing in our last moments

D

together. Maccus may look like Otas, but..." Sashna gave a little shudder.

"But?"

"He can't sense Liambrians from a distance. Maccus had no way of knowing just how many of us were at Acwellen until he was told after beating Lord Ware's son."

"So he figured the odds were acceptable. That's why he advanced on Acwellen."

"Correct. He may be weaker than the Overlord, but he's stronger with the Gift than any of us." Sashna glanced at Cwen. "Except you, that is. How he intended to capture you is a mystery."

Cwen thought about the U-V Laser she still carried tucked in her breeches. "Maccus probably intended to zap me with his ray gun."

Even though what Cwen said had a humorous ring to it, neither of them laughed, falling silent.

Cwen cursed herself for not remembering the first rule of traversing unknown territory. Don't talk, listen. The birds had stopped singing, and no animals skittered through the brush. She turned Samson about and shouted at Sashna, "We're about to be attacked!"

Cwen was horrified as they galloped back to the column of daughters. Several men wielding swords broke from the trees and attacked the unsuspecting females. The stronger warriors returned the attack, while the weaker sat frozen on their steeds, screaming.

Cwen yelled in rage as she saw that Jena was unprotected for Kendra was engaged in battle with a man on her right. A grungy brute swung his sword toward Jena. Samson reached the man in time. Cwen lobbed off his head with a single stroke of her blade.

Cwen jerked on the reins and halted Samson, then quickly slid from his back. She raced back to Kendra and sliced the tendons in the back of the man's knees who fought her. Before he could sink to the ground, he lost his head as well.

"Kendra, protect Jena!"

Cwen didn't wait for an answer as she joined the melee. God, how many were there? Thirty? Forty? Cwen didn't ponder the question as she slashed her blade this way and that, dispatching anything that remotely looked like a man.

Sashna stayed astride, wreaking havoc from her horse, as did the other warriors.

Cwen continued to scream maniacally as she fought three at once. She was aware that a fourth moved up behind her. There was little time to spare in killing the three in front of her. Cwen's blade was a blur as one lost both arms, another his head, a third yelled in horror as his innards spilled to the ground. She spun to attack the man moving up behind her. There was a sickening thunk and a gurgle as an arrow point protruded from the man's neck. Cwen looked up in surprise at the source. Jena was quickly notching another arrow into her bow.

Cwen fought on for what seemed like hours, but was only a matter of minutes, until the clang of swords stopped and the yells of battle ceased. Cwen still gripped her sword as she looked around her. The only ones living were the daughters. Cwen did a quick count. Thirty. Someone was missing.

She cursed herself again for not remembering the weaker warriors' names. "Sashna, who's missing?"

Sashna's breathing was as harsh as Cwen's. "Zeda."

"She fled!" Ting volunteered.

"Ting, Raslen, find her!" Cwen ordered.

While they were gone, Cwen walked over to Jena, who was of a mind to keep an arrow notched. "Thank you, little one."

Jena gave her a shy smile. "And thank you." She nodded to the headless man on the ground beside her.

Cwen assessed the rest of the warriors. By the grace of

God there were only minor nicks and cuts. She moved the group some distance away from the corpses as they were already collecting flies.

Cwen was becoming anxious when Ting and Raslen finally returned with Zeda, who was slumped over her horse's neck. When they reached her, Zeda slid to the ground. Cwen gently turned her over and gasped. The slash in her tunic wet with blood indicated a belly wound.

Shit! Cwen thought to herself. What the hell am I supposed to do now?

*Heal her, Katai. You have it within you.*

Cwen looked up at the daughters gathered around her and Zeda. Of course they hadn't heard Otas. Zeda's moan brought her attention back to the matter at hand. Cwen slowly lifted the leather tunic, trying to keep the concern off her face as she gazed at the deep gash on Zeda's abdomen.

Zeda opened her eyes and looked at Cwen. "F— forgive . . . me." That said, she passed out.

Out of nowhere, rage built up in Cwen. "Don't you dare die on me, Zeda!" She placed her hands over the wound, the bracelets and gold collar becoming warm. The green sapphires glowed as Cwen felt some kind of radiant energy flow from her arms to her hands. Before her eyes the wound began to close, then disappeared all together. The green sapphires lost their radiance. Cwen couldn't believe what she had just done, rubbing Zeda's belly as if she had imagined the wound.

Cwen became aware of the silence around her. She could hear the soft rustle of the leaves in the breeze. She looked up at the daughters. Sashna included, they all wore looks of astonishment.

"'Twas not a jest," Kendra finally said. "You are a faerie."

Cwen gazed into her dark eyes. "Nay, Kendra. We're all faeries."

It was late afternoon that found Cwen sitting on a log in a clearing that Sashna's uncanny ability had found for them. She'd decided that the daughters had had enough for one day. So did she for that matter. What other aspects of the Gift had she gained from the *Kyol-hon* with Otas? Cwen was afraid to find out.

She'd healed all the minor wounds of the rest of the daughters, who didn't quite know what to make of her. They'd all washed the blood from themselves in the stream that ran along the glade. Cwen kept her eyes on Jena. The young one felt she hadn't drawn her bow fast enough during the battle, so she kept shooting arrows into the trunk of an oak at the edge of the glade.

Cwen shuddered at the memory of almost losing Jena and breaking the promise to Odelia to protect her daughter with her life. Cwen had no intention of letting Jena out of her sight again.

She was so intent on watching Jena, she didn't hear Sashna sit down beside her.

"*Yo-Wang*, I beg your forgiveness."

"I told you to call me Cwen," she replied irritably.

"If I hadn't distracted you with my yammering, you would have known we were in danger sooner."

For only a split second, Cwen looked at her, then back to Jena. "The fault wasn't yours, but mine. I should have known better. I was trained for combat and survival under any conditions."

"But if I hadn't—"

Cwen sighed. "Sashna, give it a rest. What's done is done. It can't be changed."

"Well, I learned a valuable lesson today."

"Vlad will be glad to hear it."

"Who's Vlad?"

Cwen raised her eyebrows as she watched another of

D

Jena's arrows thunk into the tree. "I'm surprised you don't know. He's to Otas what you're to me."

"The Overlord has a friend?"

Cwen laughed mirthlessly. "Yes. And a second in command. Vlad arrived in the past after you disappeared. Until recently, he was my Trainer in combat and survival. I don't want to know what he thinks about my performance today."

"Do you have any idea how many men you killed today?"

Cwen snorted. "The only one I'm aware of is the one that almost killed Jena."

"Ah, that's why you went berserk."

Cwen couldn't help looking at her.

"We all talked it over. The count was twenty."

"You're joking."

"Can't you read the daughters' minds?"

Turning her eyes back on Jena, Cwen did a quick *Dut-da* on the daughters. They were more terrified of her fighting ability than the miracle of healing Zeda. "Well, I'll be damned."

Sashna chuckled.

"You were right."

"About what?"

"All of the daughters weren't meant to be warriors." Cwen leaned her elbows on her knees. "Zeda is a good cook and enjoys it. I read it in her mind when I touched her."

"She does cook well. Zeda made all of the meals served in the north tower."

Cwen grunted. "Zeda doesn't think twice about slaughtering a lamb or chopping off the head of a chicken. But in battle . . . "

Sashna stood abruptly, saying, "Oh, my God!"

Cwen jumped up. "What? What?"

"Jena's in danger!"

At first Cwen didn't know what she was talking about, then she heard it. The unmistakable snorts of a wild boar on the rampage sounded from the rustling bushes in its path. "Jena! Run!" Cwen screamed as she bolted for the young one, Sashna behind her.

Jena ignored her and calmly notched an arrow.

Cwen panicked as the largest boar she'd ever seen crashed from the bushes. Even though she had her sword drawn she'd never be able to reach Jena in time.

At Cwen's shouts, the rest of the warriors headed for Jena. The young one let loose with the arrow. It bounced harmlessly off the boar's tough hide.

Cwen suddenly froze with the knowledge that Jena was to be gored to death. Her sword fell uselessly to the ground as she stretched out her hand as if to touch Jena for the last time.

Without warning an energy surge assaulted Cwen's brain, bringing with it a terrible pain. She didn't know what was happening as her jewelry became red hot, as did her outstretched hand. All at once, a green flame shot from that hand like a flamethrower spewing fire at the wild boar. It squealed horribly as it was consumed by green flames.

When the horrible noise ceased so did the green fire emanating from Cwen's hand. All stared at her agape as the boar roasted on the ground.

None were more surprised than Cwen herself. She didn't know what the hell had just happened, expecting her hand to be burned to a crisp. Cwen couldn't believe it when she looked at her hand. It was the same as ever.

Cwen clenched her fist as she looked into the eyes of the others. If they weren't impressed by her healing powers, this certainly got their attention. The fear level was tangible. She didn't know what to say to them.

Kendra moved closer to the burning boar and looked at it a while. She turned to Cwen. "I've had a yearning for roast pork," she shouted.

Everyone laughed nervously.

Cwen didn't know whether to laugh or cry.

D

In the dark of night, Cwen sat with her back up against a log, Jena asleep at her side. The child was the only one who wasn't afraid to get near her. But they had eaten the boar for dinner. At Kendra's urging, Zeda had skinned the animal and cooked it further with some herbs she'd picked from the forest. The boar was so huge that there was plenty of meat left for smoking, which solved the problem of the diminishing rations.

Cwen didn't know whether to bless Otas or curse him. Why didn't he warn her about this, this green fire stuff? She still didn't know how she'd done it. Terror for Jena had activated it and the green fire had saved her.

Sashna walked silently up to Cwen and knelt beside her. "Uh, could you stop doing that thing with your eyes? Everyone's jumpy enough as it is," she whispered.

"My eyes?"

"You don't know?"

Cwen shook her head.

"They're glowing in the dark. Green to be exact."

"I don't know how to stop it."

"This and the green fire are things you got during *Kyol-hon* with the Overlord?"

""You make it sound like I've contracted a disease," Cwen hissed.

"You may as well have. I wouldn't be surprised if they all bolted."

Cwen thought about that for a while. "Bring Kendra to me."

When Kendra arrived, Cwen knew what she was going to say to her. "Kendra, do you fear me?"

"'Tis a good thing to fear you, I think."

"Do you think I would do you harm?" Cwen now understood how Otas felt.

Kendra thought about that for some time. "Nay."

"'Tis well." Glowing or not, Cwen focused her eyes on

Kendra. "Tell the others that I'm the Queen of the Faeries. We go to Liambria to meet the King. My husband."

Kendra was thoughtful. "What do I say happened to the boar?"

"That, Kendra, was faerie fire."

"That's what I thought it 'twas." She moved away to do Cwen's bidding.

Cwen sat astride Samson, surveying her rearrangement of the column. She had positioned Ting and Raslen to ride behind Sashna, Jena, and Kendra, with Zeda between them. Her purpose was to protect the weakest daughter along with Jena.

Cwen nudged Samson into a slow walk and halted him beside Ting. "Zeda, I have put you here lest you be tempted to flee in the event of trouble." Cwen was tired as hell, which was reflected in her harsh tone. "If Ting and Raslen hadn't found you in time, you would have died. Staying with the group will keep you safe. I may be capable of healing, but I cannot raise the dead." Cwen wasn't sure if that was true or not, but it sounded good.

Zeda lowered her head and mumbled, "Aye, Queen Cwen."

Cwen stared at her a second, not believing what she'd just called her. "Ting, when Sashna and I need to confer, you'll move into her position alongside Jena. The young one must be protected at all times."

Ting nodded gravely. "As you wish, Queen Cwen."

For a moment Cwen was puzzled, then she looked to Kendra, who sat straight in the saddle, gazing ahead. She moved Samson to Kendra's side and leaned in the saddle. "Queen Cwen, Kendra?" she whispered.

Kendra turned her slanted dark eyes on Cwen, the expression on her pretty brown face serious. "To call you anything less 'twould be an insult. I told the others so."

D

Cwen scanned her mind quickly. Kendra truly believed what she had told her. Their leader was indeed the Queen of the Faeries. Cwen nodded to her. "Kendra, I thank you."

"I only do my duty, Queen Cwen."

There was nothing else for Cwen to say, so she moved to the head of the column and motioned Sashna to join her. Without a word, Ting moved into Sashna's place. The daughters moved as one when Cwen gave the signal to ride.

Cwen and Sashna only moved a short distance from the rest for they dare not risk a repeat of the surprise attack of the day before. Besides, the daughters wouldn't understand their conversation anyway. None of them knew the syntax of 21st century English but for Jena, who wasn't inclined to tell the others anything. Odelia had raised her child well.

Cwen played with Samson's mane as she said, "I don't like the fear I sense coming off the daughters. Maybe this Queen of the Faeries thing wasn't such a good idea."

Sashna laughed. "I think it's perfect. Instilling fear is a part of commanding. None of them would dare go against you."

"I'm beginning to understand how the Overlord must feel. It's a lonely sensation."

"A sensation that will only intensify once we reach Liambria."

"Explain."

"Hasn't it occurred to you that you command not just the daughters, but all Liambrians?" Sashna asked.

"Otas' power and strength of will are so huge that any role I play in leading our people is secondary."

Sashna looked at her askance. "You haven't fully accepted who and what you are, have you?"

"No one's really given me a chance to reflect on it. Things have been constantly changing. I haven't had time to seriously think about my marriage to the Overlord." Cwen cursed in exasperation. "Am I making any sense?"

"Completely. Besides watching your back in combat, I don't really know what I'm supposed to do as your second in command."

"I guess we'll both find out what our duties are when we reach Liambria." Cwen chuckled. "Until then, we'll just make it up as we go along."

"As you command, Queen Cwen."

Five more days passed before they reached the last stretch of forest before the mountains. Cwen and the daughters had just traversed a long series of open fields, which took them most of the day. Without the cover of dense foliage, Cwen felt they were too vulnerable to attack, so she had pushed the females and the horses to the limit. Her own fatigue was rapidly catching up with her as night began to fall.

A soft "Halt," came from Sashna before Cwen could enter the forest.

Cwen held Samson still while Sashna reined in beside her. "What's wrong?" Cwen said.

Sashna's eyes held a glazed look. "There's something not right about this place."

Cwen stared at the forest before her. It did appear spooky. A thick mist that hung low to the ground had come with the night. "Sashna, don't tell me you're afraid of ghosts."

"That's exactly what I'm afraid of." Sashna turned to look at her. "I thought these ghosts only legend, but now that I'm here I believe them real."

Samson shifted under Cwen as she stared at Sashna with irritation. "Explain quickly. It's getting darker by the minute."

"This area contains the descendants of a survivalists group that formed after the upheaval. They isolated themselves in the woods. When the bullets for their guns ran out, they turned to swords, daggers, bows and arrows and such to guard their territory. They kill anyone who trespasses."

D

"Just how much of this forest is their territory?" Cwen wanted to know.

"Fifty kilometers east to west. And what's in front of us."

"Liambria and Otas are in front of us. We can't go around. We're low on provisions. The horses and the daughters won't last that long," Cwen insisted, for she felt so close to her husband with her mind it was as if she could touch him.

"Don't say I didn't warn you," Sashna grumbled.

"Ride back to the others. Tell them not to speak. We ride in silence."

When Sashna was back in place, Cwen gave the signal to enter the dark forest.

Two hours had passed since they'd entered the eerie forest. Along with the thick mist the gnarled branches of the trees made the place look downright scary. Cwen kept her mind focused on the essence of Otas, ignoring the niggling thought in the back of her mind that a trap was closing behind them.

Through a thinning of the mist, Cwen could see the base of the mountains in the near distance. Her relief was quickly quelled when her brain sensed the minds of a large number of people. Their thoughts were crazed. Murder their intent. How many? Cwen's mind screamed. A hundred. No, more!

"Run!" she yelled with all she had. Samson bucked into a gallop at her frantic kicking of his sides. She could hear the others thundering behind her, Sashna, Jena, and Kendra were close on her heels. Cwen flung off the black cloak as she drew her sword.

A loud scream forced her to whip Samson around. Raslen was falling from her horse with an arrow protruding from her chest. Then she saw them, the ghosts. They jumped from the branches of the trees, some seeming to come out of the thick trunks.

"'Tis spirits!" Zeda screamed as she looked desperately

for a place to hide.

No, not ghosts, Cwen thought. Camouflage. Their attackers wore dried mud upon their faces, dark clothes on their bodies. "They're men!" she shouted. "Fight back!"

No one hesitated. Not even those weaker. It was fight or die. Cwen hacked a path to Jena, who sat frozen on her horse's back. This was too much for the child.

Just as Cwen reached Jena, she was knocked off Samson from a heavy body launched from the trees. The heavy man pinned her sword arm to the ground. With her left hand, she freed a dagger and plunged it to the hilt into his throat. Shoving the deadweight with all her might, Cwen rolled to the side as the attacker went into his death throes.

More attackers advanced on her, keeping her from getting to Jena. A quick glance told her that all of the daughters had been knocked from their steeds, battling for their lives upon the ground. There were too many! *Sa-Jang!* Cwen screamed with her mind.

Swords clashed, arrows flew as Cwen fought as hard as she could. The soil grew slick with the blood she had spilled, causing her to slip. Cwen spun about, but kept her balance. What she saw made her heart freeze. Jena stood on the bank of a stream with a terrorized look on her face. An attacker was aiming his bow right at her. "No!" Cwen screamed as she ran to Jena.

Cwen placed herself in front of the young one, her intentions to deflect the arrow with psychokinesis. Before she could, her boot soiled with gore lost purchase on the soft mud of the stream bank. The arrow pierced her black tunic and buried itself in her side.

Cwen didn't even scream as she rolled down the bank and landed in the icy water, facedown. Jena did the screaming for her as she skidded down the slope after Cwen.

Jena pulled Cwen's face from the water. "Cwen!" Jena pleaded.

D

Cwen opened her eyes for a second, but she really didn't see Jena. The pain in her side was like nothing she'd ever felt. "Shit," she gasped as her eyes closed shut.

# Chapter 25

Sashna had lost sight of Cwen some time before while she fought for her own life. They all did. Those weaker joined the battle with their bows, the arrows knocking the men from the trees. Only Raslen was down. The rest battled on. But for how long? Sashna thought fleetingly as she slashed her sword across yet another throat. The odds were against them. Thirty-two to a hundred or more. She was tiring fast. Death loomed in front of her.

Before Sashna could fall to despair, there was a great stirring of the air. The blast was so forceful that all fighting ceased. When the whirlwind died, the combatants found themselves surrounded by tall, angry males on big horses. The sheer size of the meanest looking one marked him as the leader.

When the leader's eyes began to glow a hot green in the darkness, Sashna knew who it was immediately. "Hit the ground!" she screamed to the daughters. Even though she had spoken in 21st century English, the daughters didn't hesitate and followed her lead.

Sashna couldn't help watching as the Overlord let loose with a stream of green fire launched from his fist. The power behind that emerald flame made Cwen's earlier demonstration look pitiful. The ghosts had no time to flee as they caught fire instantly. Their howls of pain were horrifying, the stench of burnt flesh even worse.

The battle the daughters had been fighting ended in seconds. Otas stopped the flow of green fire when the terrible

D

cries ceased. He dismounted from his black horse and walked over to the fallen Raslen. He touched her neck with a gentle hand, then nodded to the male nearest to him. He lifted Raslen up to the waiting arms of the rider. When she was secure, the male and horse disappeared.

Otas looked at the daughters spread upon the ground. "Rise."

They all looked to Sashna to see what to do. She stood slowly for her body ached all over, but adrenaline was keeping her going. The others followed her suit.

"'Tis the King of the Faeries?" Kendra asked softly.

Sashna jumped. She hadn't been aware that Kendra was so close to her. Her answer was only a nod as the Overlord approached her.

"Where is my wife?" Otas' eyes were now doing a dance of orange flames.

"I—I don't know, *Sa-Jang*." Sashna was scared to death of him and his anger. "I lost sight of Cwen during the battle."

"I cannot feel her with my mind," he said low. Then louder, "You were to watch her back!"

Sashna staggered back when the blast of anger struck her.

"*Sa-Jang*, over here!" came Jena's small voice. "In the water!"

Otas headed for the stream, Sashna on his heels. When they reached the bank, he cursed. "*Daul-mae!*"

Cwen lay in the cold water with an arrow in her side. Jena was holding her head above water. Otas scrambled down the bank and lifted his wife in his arms. He told Jena to hold onto his shirt as they climbed to dry ground.

"Vlad, see to the child!" Otas called.

A tall Liambrian male took Jena in his arms and popped from view.

The Overlord said nothing as he dematerialized, taking Cwen and Sashna with him.

*Liambria 2*

Sashna sank to her knees with dizziness as they materialized inside a stark white room. There were four Liambrian females waiting for him. Each wore gold collars and bracelets set with blue sapphires. Shaking her head to clear it, Sashna figured them to be healers.

Otas laid Cwen upon a platform that floated in the air. Monitoring devices set in the walls came to life. "See to her," he ordered as he turned to leave.

Sashna knew she was risking his rage, but she asked, "Where do you go?"

His eyes were still doing that frightening dance of flames. "There is another near death. Only I can stop it." With that, he passed through a door that slid open by itself in front of him.

Sashna tried not to gawk at her surroundings, keeping her eyes focused on Cwen, who hadn't so much as twitched. The four females were looking at the arrow in her side. When one of the females touched Cwen's wrist, she gasped and backed away from the floating table.

All of the healers started talking at once. It took Sashna a minute to realize they were speaking in Liambrian.

"Help her!" she shouted at them in Liambrian.

"We cannot," answered the tallest of the four with a quavering voice. She pointed to the bracelet on Cwen's wrist. "She's the Overlord's Queen. Only he may touch her."

Sashna cursed under her breath. Cwen was soaking wet and needed to be out of the waterlogged battle gear. "Move aside," Sashna ordered.

None of them argued with her for Sashna still wore her sword and blood-spattered battle outfit. She took out her dagger and quickly cut away Cwen's clothes, taking care around the arrow in her side. One of the females had the good sense to hand her a blanket made of shimmering, white fabric.

Sashna laid the U-V Laser weapon she'd taken from Cwen's breeches on the pile of sliced clothing at her feet.

Sashna had just finished taking off her boots when the Overlord returned.

The four healers didn't have to be told. They left without a word. Sashna stood where she was.

Otas stared at her some seconds. "Leave us!"

Sashna started to argue that she didn't know where to go in this place, but his look was murderous. She backed to the door and practically fell through it when it opened.

Otas' hand shook as he touched the area around Cwen's side were the arrow was imbedded. Inwardly he sighed, for he could easily heal the damage done by the projectile. But there was no way he could stop her pain when he pulled the arrow free.

"Forgive me, *Katai*," he whispered as he took a firm grip on the arrow. With one powerful jerk, the arrow was free. Cwen didn't scream as he'd expected. She only moaned softly.

Blood flowed freely from the wound. Otas placed his hand over it, trying to detect if the arrowhead had been dipped in poison. He sensed nothing and began healing the puncture. He took his time for the arrow had gone deep, healing each layer of flesh thoroughly before moving on to the next.

When he was done, he waited for Cwen to come around on her own. Slowly, her eyes fluttered open, the irises a clear green. He said nothing as she focused her eyes on his face.

Cwen's eyes turned to pure smoke as she gazed at her husband. She inhaled sharply and yelled, "What took you so damn long?"

Otas didn't answer his wife. He was silent as he gazed down at her. Cwen was aware of the emotions running through him—intense worry, rage, pride, and something she couldn't identify. His feelings were reflected in his eyes. One second they were the gold of worry. Then bright orange raging with the golden flames of anger. Next they were red with star bursts of gold and orange. Cwen had no idea what that meant, but she didn't care. At the moment she was so angry with Otas she would have choked him if she had the strength.

Silent still, he moved away from her, bent down, and picked up the U-V Laser weapon. Holding it firmly in his grip, he came back to her, touching a hand to her shoulder.

Cwen opened her mouth to yell at him again. Before she could, Otas teleported them from the white room. They materialized inside a large chamber. At a fast glance, it looked like the Overlord's *Chim-dae-bang*, but it wasn't. The position of the furniture and the door to the outer chamber were the reverse of his.

Cwen lay on a huge bed with the white blanket still covering her. Tired though she was, she wrapped the large cloth around her and stood on shaky legs. She knew the arrow was gone, but a residual ache pained her side.

Otas nodded his head towards the bathroom.

Cwen knew what he was trying to tell her. Take a hot bath. Although the idea was immensely appealing, her anger was not diminishing.

He was intensely aware of her feelings, saying, "This is the *Chim-dae-bang* of *Ku Yo-Wang*."

"Hmm," was all she said, thinking, So I'm to have my own private chambers.

"Correct."

Cwen shot him a scathing look. Maybe this Mind-Link business wasn't such a great thing after all. Sometimes a person's thoughts should be private. What the hell, Cwen thought, moving to the bathroom.

Once the door had closed behind his wife, Otas went to the outer chamber of the Queen's suite where Vlad awaited him. He listened with his mind to assure himself that Cwen was preoccupied with her bath and wouldn't overhear the words he would speak to Vlad, who sat a glass and a pitcher of *Ma-shil-kot* on the round table in the corner.

"Cwen's really angry this time," Vlad stated. "Even with her Mind-Shield I can sense it."

"Her ire comes from more than fatigue of battle and being shot with an arrow." Otas wasn't inclined to explain more.

Vlad didn't question him. He himself didn't know what the red hue and bursts of gold and orange pulsing in Otas' eyes meant. His thick black hair was unbound, falling wildly about his broad shoulders. Vlad quietly awaited his friend's orders.

"Sashna sits alone on the floor outside *Pyong-pang*, sick bay. She does not know what to do or where to go." Otas shoved a clump of hair from his eyes. "I'm afraid I was overly harsh with her. Take Sashna to her quarters. She needs rest. When she has recovered, take her under your wing."

Vlad nodded and silently left the chambers.

When Cwen finally emerged from the bathroom with a towel wrapped around her, she found the room empty. She didn't care. She wasn't too thrilled about seeing her husband right now anyway. But he had been thoughtful. A dark-green *wanpisu* lay on the bed. Cwen quickly put it on, fluffing out her freshly washed and dried hair. It had taken her awhile to get all of the dirt and mud out of it.

The door to the room whooshed open and Otas entered, carrying the glass and pitcher of *Ma-shil-kot*. Without a word, he poured a glassful and handed it to her.

Cwen chugged it down in a few gulps, holding the empty glass out to him for more. If she were to engage in a battle of words with him, she would need all of the strength she could get.

Cwen observed Otas for several minutes after she'd downed the *Ma-shil-kot*. His eyes were still doing the crazy jig of colors. She couldn't read his mind, but the realization of an important fact occurred to her. "You knew."

He said nothing.

"You knew, didn't you!" This time she yelled.

"If you are referring to the ghosts, as Sashna calls them, yes."

"You let us go into dangerous territory with no thought for our lives! All of the daughters could have died!" Cwen found herself breathing rapidly. "Your lack of concern is appalling!"

Otas' eyes switched to a raging storm of orange fire. "I remind you that the decision to enter the forest was yours! Sashna warned you of what lay ahead."

Cwen snarled. "And travel fifty kilometers out of our way? We were running low on food!"

"You could have hunted. Vlad taught you how to survive in the wilderness!" His deep voice dropped low. "I repeat. The decision was yours."

Cwen stomped away from him, then came back. "Why didn't you stop me if I was making such a stupid mistake?"

"Mistakes are made when one is learning how to command."

Cwen sucked in her breath. "You were testing me?"

"You and all of the daughters."

"Goddamn you!" She slapped him with all of her strength. Otas didn't even blink at the sting of the blow. "Well, what grade did we get, you son of a bitch? Did we kill enough men for you? Did we bleed enough for you?" Cwen couldn't stop the tears of anger from falling. "I don't even know which of the daughters survived. Who died?"

"No one died."

Her anguish was so great she couldn't think clearly. "You lie!"

"If you were in control of your emotions, you could *Dut-da*. Then you would know that I speak the truth!" Otas forced himself to soften his voice. "Only one, Raslen, was seriously injured. She lay near death, but I was able to heal her."

"And Jena?"

"She is well."

Cwen sighed in relief.

He studied her for some seconds. "You still don't get it."

"What?"

"The daughters survived because they fought for their lives. Every single one of them." The red was back in his eyes. "Those females took the lead from you. It was out of respect for you as their commander that they struggled to live."

"You're saying that I have good command skills?"

"You surpassed my expectations." The pride in his voice was unmistakable.

Cwen was still uncertain. "Then I did it right?"

A nod was his answer.

She thought for some seconds. "Your ways are harsh, Sa-Jang."

"I don't deny it. For the daughters to win my acceptance they had to learn to fight or die. That is what my goal is for all Liambrians. The survival of our species depends on it."

"But what did all of this killing do to Jena?"

"The little one learned courage from you." He shuddered at the memory. "After you were shot with the arrow, Jena stayed in the cold water with you, holding your head above the surface so you wouldn't drown."

Cwen was so shocked she couldn't speak.

Otas stared at her for some time. Finally, he pulled the U-V Laser from his pants. "Why didn't you use this? It would have evened the odds."

Cwen shrugged her shoulders. "I don't know. I guess it was unfair to use against the Earthlings."

"You are more like me than you know." He laid the

weapon on the bedside table. "Is that why you took the arrow for Jena?"

"Actually, I'd intended to deflect it with psychokinesis, but my foot slipped. It was my own clumsiness that got me wounded."

Otas fought to keep his expression serious. "However it happened, you did all Liambrians a great service."

"By saving Jena?"

He nodded gravely. "You saved the life of the future mother of the next Queen."

Along with fatigue the shock of what the Overlord had just said sent Cwen into a dead faint.

# Chapter 26

Cwen lay on her stomach when she awakened, smoothing hair from her face. She didn't move her head from the pillow as her eyes focused on the black bedside table. At first she thought she was in Otas' bed, then remembered she had her own chambers. The digital clock sitting on the table confirmed what she had surmised. There wasn't a clock in his *Chim-dae-bang*.

She had to rub her eyes before the blue readout on the timepiece became clear. 0900 hours it said. She couldn't believe she'd only slept for a few hours, feeling refreshed and immensely hungry. It had been very late when she and Otas had argued.

Cwen sat up abruptly when the memory of her husband's last words surfaced in her mind. Jena was to be the mother of the next Queen. For some reason she couldn't remember anything after that. How had she gotten to bed? Vague recollections of getting up to use the bathroom came to her. Sometimes the window had reflected light. Other times the room had been dark.

Frowning, Cwen realized she must have slept for more than a few hours, but for how long? Her full bladder wouldn't let her ponder the question. She slid out of bed and went to the bathroom.

When she finished her business, she noted that although her bathroom looked just like Otas', it had something his lacked. A mirror. Cwen moved to it and gasped at the sight of herself. She looked as grungy as she felt. Her hair was a black mass of snarls and tangles, the unmistakable scent of sweat reached her nostrils. Cwen figured she must have perspired quite a bit during her long sleep. She turned on the shower while thinking, I better clean myself up before Otas shows up.

When she finally emerged from the bathroom with a towel wrapped around her and her clean hair falling to her hips, she held the offensive *wanpisu* with two fingers. There was no way she would put it back on.

Cwen smiled with relief when she spied a clean one draped across the back of the curved chair. She put it on quickly. It was the same as the dirty garment, sleeveless, falling to mid-thigh, and dark-green in color. There were no shoes in sight, so she padded barefoot to the door of the *Chim-dae-bang*. It whooshed open and she stepped into the outer chamber, which was similar to the Overlord's except the slate desk was smaller and had no computers resting on it.

Cwen only gave the gaily wrapped box sitting on the desk a cursory glance. She was hungry and wanted to see her husband. She didn't know the layout of this place, but Cwen hoped someone could tell her how to find Otas. She walked right into the automatic doors for they did not open at her approach. Hands on hips, she said, "Damn!"

Look as she might, she couldn't find a way to activate the door sensors. Did Otas intend to hold her prisoner in her chambers?

Cursing still, she went to the desk and sat in the chair behind it. Cwen stared at the wrapped box awhile before deciding to open it. With a few rips and tears of the paper, she lifted the lid off the box. She smiled in surprise. The box contained a laptop computer with a note taped to it. Cwen gingerly lifted the laptop from the box and sat it on the desk.

She frowned as she read the note. *Welcome home, Cwen.* It was signed by Jal. Who the hell is Jal? she thought as she pulled the note free and opened the computer. It was the same as the one Professor Pimbleton had let her use for her homework. With that not so pleasant memory in mind, she switched the unit on.

Fortunately, it had a menu, so she wouldn't have to do any hacking. She highlighted the selection titled novels and hit the enter key. Scrolling through the directory, Cwen discovered there were over thirty stories to choose from. She was delighted as she decided to start at the top of the list. Moving the cursor there, she hit the enter key again. The screen lit up with words. The page said: "The Green Sapphire by Jal."

Her curiosity was peaked as she scrolled to page one. For every line of English, there was a line of Liambrian symbols beneath it. She noted the acceleration bar at the bottom of the screen. It gave her two choices, sound and silent. Mystified, she chose sound. A pleasant feminine voice began to read the lines of the text. Each English line was repeated in Liambrian.

Whoever had programmed this computer was a genius. She could enjoy a good story and learn Liambrian at the same time.

Cwen was on page ten when there was a stirring of air in the room. She didn't even look up, expecting it to be Otas.

"I've brought your breakfast, *Yo-Wang*," Sashna informed her.

That made Cwen look up. Sashna was wearing a V-necked jumpsuit made of brown shimmering fabric and a teleportation armband. She now wore the gold collar and bracelets set with emeralds.

Cwen switched off the laptop. Feeling very grouchy, she asked, "How long was I out?"

Sashna set the tray of food on the desk. "Four days, *Yo-Wang*."

"Call me Cwen," she growled. "Where's Otas? And why am I locked up in these chambers?"

"He's in conference with Vlad." Sashna found she couldn't look Cwen in the eye as she answered her second question. "You're here to keep you safe until the Overlord tells everyone the Queen has arrived. He's been very busy making preparations."

Sashna was trying to hide her thoughts but Cwen could read them easily. Cwen stood. "He's been doing *Chi-u-da*."

"Uh, yes."

"Why?"

"Vlad told me that you were aware of how much hatred those who are flawed held for Otas."

Cwen gave a slight nod.

"The Overlord feared that they might try to harm his Queen. You're his only vulnerability."

"How many went through *Chi-u-da*?"

Sashna hesitated.

"Answer me, damn it!"

"One thousand."

"My God!" was all Cwen could say. So many. How had they felt having their psychic receptors atrophied? What did they do after they stepped through the Doorway with no memory of who or what they had been?

"I was appalled, too, when Vlad explained to me what *Chi-u-da* was. Then he told me the story of Taki." Sashna opened her hands. "It's the only way to prevent that kind of catastrophe from happening again."

"I know. I know." She sat in the chair and pulled the tray toward her. What Sashna had told her was horrible, but she was weak from the lack of food. The plate held what looked like orange scrambled eggs with meat resting on top of the blue rice. Cwen took a test bite. It was delicious. She was halfway finished when she realized her friend was still standing. "I'm sorry, Sashna. Please sit down."

Sashna smiled at her as she sat on the futon.

Cwen cleaned her plate in a matter of minutes. There

was a glass of juice on the tray as well. She took a sip, then said, "Mango nectar."

"Vlad said you liked mangos."

"I do." Cwen drank the glass down, studying Sashna as she did so. She wondered if Sashna was aware that every time she said Vlad's name she blushed. "So, what have you been doing while I was sleeping?"

"Vlad has been teaching me what my duties are as your second in command." The blush again. "Making sure you eat is one of them."

"You like Vlad, don't you?"

"Of course. He's smart and strong. I find him handsome." Sashna sighed wistfully. "I would've loved having him as my Trainer for twelve years." Realizing what she'd just said, Sashna turned scarlet.

Cwen chuckled. "There's no shame in being attracted to a male."

"I don't know. Well, maybe it's okay." Sashna had a horrifying thought. "Do you think he knows?"

"He knows. As second in command he takes over *Dut-da* when the Overlord is, um, otherwise occupied." It was Cwen's turn to blush.

"Shit," was all Sashna said.

Vlad and Otas had spent the morning reviewing the status of each Liambrian starship. All were now fitted with the Inter-Dimensional Leap processors. There was nothing left to do but wait for word from Raynar.

Vlad observed him as they now relaxed on the futon. One would never know that the Overlord had spent the last days doing *Chi-u-da*. His friend seemed energized. The only odd thing was his eyes. They took on that red hue with the splashes of orange and gold more frequently. Otas still hadn't told him what it meant.

There was some portion of his mind locked away from

Vlad. He could feel that it was some kind of emotion, but he didn't have a clue as to its nature. Vlad was so deep in his thoughts, he didn't hear Otas.

"Vlad," he said again.

"I'm sorry. I was thinking. What did you say?"

"I asked you what you thought of Sashna."

Vlad tried to hide his reddening cheeks and failed. "She, uh, has wonderful muscles."

"What about the rest of her?"

"She's smart and eager to learn."

The Overlord just stared at him with those red eyes.

Vlad cursed under his breath. He of all people knew it was useless trying to hide thoughts from Otas. "I find her appealing."

The Overlord didn't smile. "That's good, for Sashna is to be your wife."

Vlad jumped up. "What?"

"The two of you are genetically matched."

Vlad opened his mouth to argue, then shut it. Although it had been said in a tone that was relaxed, Otas had just given him an order.

"I leave the time of your *Kyol-hon* up to you."

"As you command," Vlad said stiffly. "May I take my leave of you?" He had some serious thinking to do. A wife? He couldn't believe it.

Otas nodded.

Vlad quickly left the Overlord's chambers.

After the door had closed, Otas lay on his side and curled into a tight ball, his forearm pressed tightly to his lower abdomen. He held back the groan that would escape him if he let it. Thank *Ha-nu-nim* Vlad had left so fast. It had taken all he had not to let his friend know of his pain.

The pain was intensifying with each passing hour. He wondered if his wife knew why she had sweated so much while she slept. His body had been aware of the cause. His

Queen was entering estrus and his *Gew-Seen* had come alive. The time for *Bal-Dar* had come.

Cwen didn't know how long she'd sat upon the bed with the computer in her lap, staring at the screen, seeing it, but not concentrating on it. Night had fallen some time before, but she was wide awake. At first she'd thought perhaps she had gotten too much sleep, then the strange spells came over her. For a time her body grew intensely hot. Next it would return to its normal temperature. Her mood was odd as well.

Logically, she understood her husband's reasoning for keeping her hidden. But when she thought about it she grew irritated. Sighing, she switched off the laptop and laid it on the bedside table. She slid from the bed and walked to the window. Of course she could see nothing in the darkness but the starlit sky. Of their own volition her feet began to pace the *Chim-dae-bang*. She felt restless and needed to see Otas. It wasn't that she wanted to speak to him about anything in particular. Her desire was to touch him, feel the strength of his arms, smell the scent of earth, grass, and male.

Cwen wanted to scream her need to him with her mind, but she could sense nothing from him. It was as if the Mind-Link had been severed.

Vlad was frantic as he hurried to the Overlord's chambers. Not once since they'd touched minds as children had Vlad lost complete contact with Otas' mind. Something was seriously wrong. He'd assembled the Circle of Twelve, for he was certain the Overlord was incapacitated.

Vlad tried to slow his breathing as he stood for a second outside the Overlord's suite. Slowly he moved forward and entered. Otas wasn't in the outer chamber, so he went immediately to the *Chim-dae-bang*. What he saw scared the life out of him.

Otas lay on the bed, nude, the blanket tossed aside on

the floor. His head was moving side to side as low moans came from his lips. His eyes were shut.

"*Sa-Jang?*" Vlad said softly as he moved to the big bed. No response.

"Otas!" he said loudly.

No reaction came. His body was covered in a sheen of sweat. When Vlad reached his side, he looked the Overlord over, seeking some kind of injury. Then he saw it. Otas' lower abdomen was flaming red. Vlad knelt by him, reaching out a shaking hand. Before he could touch the Overlord, a strong hand gripped his wrist.

Otas' eyes were now open. They held the red color with orange and gold strobes. The hue remained constant as he looked at Vlad.

"What is the date?" he asked in a raspy voice.

Vlad was confused for a second.

"The date!"

"April sixteenth."

"No!" Otas was unaware that his grip was like a vise. "The date of the past."

Vlad computed the time quickly in his mind. "December fourteenth, two thousand."

"Her age? What is Cwen's age?"

Knowledge dawned in Vlad's mind. "The Queen has been twenty for two weeks."

Otas released Vlad. "I had to be certain." He groaned as he sat up. "She will ovulate soon. *Bal-Dar* must be done before that occurs."

Vlad asked no questions as he quickly found the black robe Otas rarely wore, helping him into it. He steadied the Overlord as they walked to the hidden portal between the Queen's and Otas' chambers.

Otas pushed him away. "Stand guard. I go on my own."

Cwen spun around at the sound of the hidden door

opening. She gasped as Otas stepped forward and stood still while the door slid shut. There was something about the way he looked in the floor-length black garment that scared her. As he stared at her, she saw that his irises were stark red with flashes of gold and orange. Cwen backed up involuntarily, bumping the back of her legs against the bed as Otas moved to stand in front of her.

"We need to talk," he said.

She was about to ask him about what when a low groan escaped him. Cwen saw that he was clutching his belly. It was obvious to her that he was in great pain. Taking his arm, she gently nudged him to the bed. A gentle shove sent him flat on his back.

The sides of the robe opened, exposing his abdomen. At the sight of the inflamed flesh, Cwen gasped. She put her hand on his belly. His skin was hot. She could feel his *Gew-Seen* pulsing beneath her hand.

"*Bal-Dar?*" she asked, although she knew the answer. Her own body was behaving so strangely that she wasn't frightened.

"I . . . wanted to explain." He clamped his lips tight, keeping the moan within as a spasm assaulted him. "There . . . is no time. It must be now."

Cwen silently pulled the *wanpisu* from her body. Nude, she climbed upon the bed and lay next to him. Running her fingers through his long hair, she said, "Do what you must."

It took him a while, but he got himself out of the robe. He positioned himself in the center of the bed, sitting cross-legged. He lifted her as if she weighed nothing. "Open yourself."

When she did, he impaled her with a hot erection that seemed to have come from nowhere. Cwen couldn't stop the loud gasp that came out of her mouth. The sensation was sizzling. There had been no foreplay, yet her body was ready to receive him. She wrapped her legs around his hips as her insides pulsed with the rhythm of his *Gew-Seen*.

He held her face so that their eyes met. The Mind-Link took hold again as he began the process of *Bal-Dar*. His pain became hers when his *Gew-Seen* activated her *Lun-Chow*. The feeling hurt so much she found she couldn't scream. She had no breath for it. Her neck arched with the strength of the agony. He supported her head with one strong hand while holding her close with his other arm.

Through the Mind-Link she could see what he was seeing. His RNA and DNA helixes appeared alongside hers in brilliant colors as though projected on a black screen. One by one strands of genes and traits disappeared from the matrix. New ones rapidly filled the void left behind.

On and on it went with both locked in the throes of pain until she saw nothing, felt nothing. Gently, he laid her limp body on the bed as his *Gew-Seen* contracted. His groin grew heavy with the new seed of *Bal-Dar*.

Otas stayed within her while he waited for her to come around. He wanted her awake when he let this new semen flow into her womb. He placed a hand on her belly sensing her *Lun-Chow* release the ova—two transformed eggs created with *Bal-Dar*.

When Cwen opened her eyes, she looked straight into his, which had returned to normal. The pain had been replaced by intense arousal as if he'd been thrusting into her for hours. A few strokes of his hand across her breasts brought on a powerful orgasm. As pleasure rushed through her, she felt the hot bursts of his seed shooting inside her.

Neither one fell to *Ju-Gum*, but this was the most pleasurable joining they'd had yet. They stayed together. No words needed to be spoken.

Otas placed a hand on Cwen's belly and felt the new life there. His wife had conceived from *Bal-Dar*. Twins. A male and a female. Staring into her green eyes, he decided he wouldn't tell her yet.

The next morning, Otas was already up when Cwen awakened. He sat in the chair by the bed. The expression on his face was one that Cwen had never seen before. Purposeful intent was the only way to describe it.

"Take a shower, *Katai*. It will refresh you."

Cwen stared at her husband. He was wearing the black robe, his hair damp and combed back from his face, falling past his shoulders. Apparently he'd already washed.

She said nothing as she slid from the bed. She sensed that Otas was not in a mood for talking. Cwen now noticed the pitcher of *Ma-shil-kot* on the bedside table. Strangely enough, she had no appetite. She went to the bathroom to do as he'd said, closing the door behind her.

When Cwen emerged with a towel wrapped around her, Otas stood naked outside the door. His bold stance and intense expression made her nervous. Unconsciously, she moved back from him until her back touched the wall.

A few purposeful strides brought him to her. He reached out and ripped the towel from her body. Cwen's breath came in hitches. She felt completely vulnerable and defenseless against his obvious intent.

He reached out and kneaded her breasts with purpose. "Forgive me, *Katai*," Otas said as he moved her thighs apart with his powerful hand. He leaned in close to her face, his lips not quite touching hers. "*Bal-Dar* produces a great amount of seed," he whispered. The Overlord gave her no chance to comprehend what he'd just said as he quickly pushed two fingers within her. "I must have you. Now!"

His hot mouth latched onto hers, cutting off the cry of surprise that came from her. The kiss became molten as he slid his fingers in and out of his wife.

Cwen's knees weakened as her body responded rapidly

to his assault. He broke the kiss as his wife began to sag to the floor. Swiftly, he picked up his Queen, carrying her to the bed. Otas laid her on her back, her legs dangling over the side of the bed.

Cwen was in mild shock for she knew her husband had no intention of asking for permission to do what he intended. Right now, in his mind, Cwen was simply his to take. It was the Overlord's right. Her own mind and body were unable to resist him.

He lifted one of her thighs with each hand, spreading her legs with his strength. A mewling sound came out of Cwen for she was totally exposed to him. He knelt between her legs. Without a word, he pushed himself quickly inside her hot and moist sheath. Cwen cried out his name at the strength of his powerful entry, her insides stretching to take all of him.

Otas waited just long enough for her to become accustomed to the size of his shaft before moving in and out of her with an arousing rhythm. Cwen clutched the blanket with her outstretched hands as her body responded to his sensual invasion. With Otas holding her thighs spread so strongly, she couldn't move. She was forced to take all that he gave and powerless to stop her own rising arousal.

He pounded her that way for some time, grunts of satisfaction came from his mouth. They rapidly reached the crescendo of pleasure. He pushed himself deeply within her as he could hold back no longer. He threw back his head in ecstasy while his body spasmed and his sizzling seed shot forth.

"*Sa-Jang!*" she screamed as her pelvis convulsed with the power of her release. Again, neither fell to *Ju-Gum*, but this mating was even more powerful than falling into blissful darkness.

Otas still held her thighs as he gazed down at her. She looked back at him wondering what in God's name had just happened. Her husband's eyes were raging with orange flames.

The purposeful look had not left his face as he gently lowered her legs.

Cwen found that *Saeng-Gan* was not on his mind as he slid himself out of her. She felt like a rag doll as his powerful arms moved her to the center of the bed. After he'd climbed upon it, he rolled her to her stomach. Cwen wanted to ask him what he was doing, but he gave her no time.

Otas pulled on her hips until she was on her knees. Nudging her thighs apart with one of his own, he entered her swiftly from behind before she could protest. He wasted no time starting his powerful thrusts. His thumb massaged her nub of feminine pleasure as he pounded her.

Through a haze brought on by the enjoyable sensations she was experiencing, Cwen thought, My God! My God! What's happening?

Night had descended while the Overlord still mated with his Queen. He sat back on his heels after experiencing yet another intense orgasm. This time his wife suffered *Ju-Gum*. Unconscious though she was, her hands still gripped the black bars of the headboard, her thighs resting on his.

Otas gazed down at her naked form, placing a hand on her abdomen. Now that he was spent, he wondered if his powerful mating had harmed his children. How many times had he taken his wife? The memory was vague. Fifteen times? Twenty times? He didn't know. Otas felt the energy of the life-forms in his Queen's wombs with his palm. The children were unharmed, thank *Ha-nu-nim*. He kept his hand on Cwen's belly.

He looked to her face when she sighed loudly, her eyelids opening. Her smoke-green eyes held worry. He knew of her fears for he was still within her. They were now deep in *Saeng-Gan*.

"I can bear no more," she said.

With his hand still on her belly, he could feel the pain

radiating from her female's sheath. The tissues were swollen and extremely tender. Part of him regretted using her so roughly, but he had no control over the aftereffects of *Bal-Dar*. "I am finished. I have spent all of my seed."

"Thank God."

Otas smiled down at her, massaging her belly with a soothing touch.

"*Sa-Jang*, what happened to us?"

"Husband."

She said nothing as she gazed up at him. After *Bal-Dar* with Otas and his repeated taking of her, Cwen could only view him as the powerful Overlord that he was.

"We're alone, *Katai*," he persisted, reading her thoughts.

"All right, husband." Cwen combed her tangled hair from her eyes with her hand. "Why did we make love so much?"

"You truly do not know?" Otas scanned her mind. She was totally ignorant of the ways of being a Liambrian female. "You were in estrus."

She thought about that for a second. "I was in heat?"

"That's what triggered *Bal-Dar*. The effects caused my need to mate."

"Then I've ovulated."

"Correct, *Katai*."

"I wonder if I'm pregnant," she said, more to herself than to him.

Otas remained silent. The time was not right to tell her she was.

Cwen's thighs and hips began to spasm from the muscle strain caused by the action of keeping her legs open to receive him.

Sensing her discomfort, Otas slowly pulled out of her. She visibly flinched from the pain that brought her. He lay beside her, turning her face to his. He stared into her eyes for some seconds. "You please me, *Katai*."

"Because I behaved like a wild animal?"

Otas smiled. "Because you didn't fight me during *Bal-Dar*."

"Then we were successful?"

Rubbing his palm across her pelvis, he said, "More than you know."

Cwen sat up and gasped at the throbbing ache in her feminine folds of flesh. All of this mating hurt worse than when she'd lost her virginity.

Otas raised up on an elbow. He knew where her thoughts were going. "This time I will not heal you."

"But why not?"

"The pain will remind you of what has passed between us in the last twenty-four hours. You must accept the fact that you are my wife and the Queen of all Liambrians."

# Chapter 27

$M$accus sat back and admired the rectangular black box he'd just finished constructing. He had no doubts that it would work, but he had to test it first. The subject of this experiment would be himself.

Maccus depressed the black button with a white circle on it. The green operating indicator light had barely come on when his head jerked back from the force of the high-frequency waves radiating from it. Maccus heard no sound, but the energy output of his psychic receptors became disrupted. He tried teleporting away from the thing. Nothing happened. Next he attempted to read the minds of the Trexrans moving about the castle. Again, nothing.

It was sheer torture having his powers of the Gift neutralized. Despite his discomfort, Maccus smiled as he switched the unit off. The Scrambler was a suitable name for the device, for that was precisely what it did—scrambled the neuro-receptors of anyone possessing the Gift. Maccus' intended victims were the Queen and his blasted twin. The problem was to locate them. Otherwise, the Scrambler was useless.

Maccus stood and stretched in the underground room of the north tower. Since this was where the Liambrians had last been, he felt it a perfect place to set up his laboratory.

He looked to the corpse of Lord Ware. Maccus frowned at the memory of killing the hapless Earthling. He'd interrogated the former Baron of Acwellen on the whereabouts of the Liambrians. Lord Ware had laughed at Maccus, showing no signs of fear for his life, telling him that there was no such thing as a Liambrian and that Liambria was a mythical land in the north where the people were faerie.

Maccus had assured him that faeries were no myth, proving it by suffocating Lord Ware to death with the power of the Gift.

Now Maccus ran a hand through his long hair. He'd sent the starship as far as the northern pole of this planet and they had detected nothing. No power surges indicating Liambrian ships had been found. The tracker he'd devised showed no signs of the Liambrians. But Maccus was certain they were still on Earth in this time-frame. How he knew this, he couldn't explain to the men under his command. It was pure instinct.

Cwen held back her groans as she climbed out of bed, trying not to awaken Otas. She felt like she'd just spent an entire day at the gym instead of making passionate love with her husband.

Cwen moved to the other side of the bed where Otas slept. She need not have worried. The Overlord lay on his stomach, eyes closed, soft snores issued from his mouth. By all indications he was dead to the world.

With the shuffling gait of an old woman, Cwen made her way to the bathroom, thinking a hot bath would ease her sore muscles and the persistent ache between her legs.

An hour had passed when she finally came out, wearing nothing but her jewelry and the curtain of black hair falling to her hips. She moved to the curved window and stared out at the morning light. It felt odd being so warm and comfortable when the peaks of the mountains were covered in snow. Cwen recalled that Otas had told her that the temperature was kept at eighty degrees inside Liambria.

Unconsciously, Cwen ran her hands over her breasts, then down her abdomen. She felt different. Strange even. She could feel the changes that *Bal-Dar* had produced. Her breasts tingled constantly as if being bombarded with minute electrical charges. Deep within her belly, her *Lun-Chow* pulsed steadily, mild cramps assaulted her double womb.

She shook her head at the wonder of *Bal-Dar*. Otas had warned her there would be pain. There wasn't a word to describe the tortuous feeling that had gripped her insides like a giant fist. Thank God she only had to go through *Bal-Dar* once.

And then there was yesterday. Otas had been right. The ache between her legs was a constant reminder that she belonged to the Overlord. With all that had happened so far since she'd arrived in this time-frame, she didn't feel so much like a Queen, but the vessel to ease the Overlord's passions.

*Na Sa-rang Tang-sin*, I love you, came to her thoughts. Otas had said it to her more than once with his mind and with his voice. Did she love him was the question. Her behavior of the day before proved that she at least held *koi* for him. The sight of his naked body always sent little shivers running through her. Just the sound of his heavily accented deep voice produced a feeling she didn't have a name for inside her. Was it love? Cwen just didn't know.

Otas gazed upon his Queen. He kept his voice and mind silent while he observed her. Thank *Ha-nu-nim* he was empty of seed. When his wife had run her hands over her body, he had almost come undone. Mating now was out of the question. Cwen wasn't the only one in pain. His genitals pained him from the abuse he had put them through. Otas refused to use his self-healing power to end his torment. He, too, wanted to remember what had passed between him and his Queen.

He gingerly moved to a sitting position. "Come here, *Katai*."

Cwen obeyed him instantly, climbing on the bed beside him. "Good morning, husband."

Otas ran a hand through her unbound hair, still not believing that she was actually his. "What were you thinking?"

"Don't you know?"

He turned her face and stared into her beautiful eyes. "Even though our minds are linked, I don't always read your thoughts. Everyone needs moments of privacy."

Cwen kept the relief from her face. It would not do to have him know that she didn't love him as he did her. "I was thinking how strange I feel. Is the cause *Bal-Dar*?"

"Yes." He gave a definitive nod. "I feel the changes within myself. In fact, all Liambrians are feeling it. They are now aware that *Bal-Dar* has occurred."

"So now I'll be able to leave my chambers."

"Not yet." Otas didn't explain further.

Oddly enough, she wasn't angry. Cwen wasn't in the mood to play Queen just now. Her eyes were locked on his muscled chest. She had an urge to run her hands across his breasts, but she held back. She didn't dare arouse him for she couldn't take anymore lovemaking.

"You may touch me, *Katai*." His orange eyes held amusement. "Nothing will happen. I'm as sore as you are." He placed her hand on his breast.

Cwen smiled at the feel of his smooth skin. Stroking him still, she asked, "Why do I have my own chambers? Is it to keep me from you?"

"The reason is because of me. I find I need to spend a great deal of time alone. I've been that way since I was a child."

Cwen only nodded in understanding, occupied with running her hand over his chest.

Otas took her hand and kissed it. He rose slowly from the bed and put the black robe on. "I will leave you alone for the remainder of the day. You need rest after *Bal-Dar*."

"What of you?" She looked at him with concern. "Don't you need rest?"

"I do. But there are things I must attend to." He moved to the wall with the hidden portal. The door slid open, but he didn't pass through. He stared at her a while.

"Can I open that door?"

He shook his head. "Only I can operate it with my mind."
Otas continued to stare at her. "*Na Sa-rang Tang-sin.*"

"I know," was her answer.

Apparently, that was enough for him for he passed through
the doorway, the portal sliding shut behind him.


He found Vlad waiting for him in his *Chim-dae-bang*, holding his black pants across his arm. The Overlord said nothing
as he sat on the end of the bed, careful not to jostle himself
too much.

Vlad had noticed his friend's stiff walk. "I guess the pants
are out."

Otas shuddered at the thought. "I could not bear the tightness of those things."

Silently, Vlad returned the garment to the open closet
and activated the button that would close it. After the wall
had slid back in place, one would never know what lay behind
it. He observed Otas for some time. "Are you all right? I
didn't know that you would be in such pain before *Bal-Dar.*"

"Nor I. My father told me there would be discomfort, but
I had no idea it would incapacitate me." A shiver passed
through him. "No wonder Raynar forced Taki. If I had delayed another moment going to Cwen, I don't know what
would have happened. I felt as if my *Gew-Seen* was about to
explode."

"Thank *Ha-nu-nim* your Queen was willing." Vlad rubbed
his own abdomen. "By the way I feel, your *Bal-Dar* was successful. I'm aware of the changes in my germ cells. What
new traits did you create?"

"All Liambrians conceived from this time forward will
have my self-healing powers and the ability to teleport without a device. None will be born that are evil. The females
will be like my Queen. They will have her strength and courage in battle. Her intelligence. And most important, her

unpredictability. The husbands of the next generation will not find their lives boring."

"Speaking of husbands," Vlad said. "I fully accept my duty to perform *Kyol-hon* with Sashna." He thought about Sashna's pale blonde hair, dancing brown eyes, and well-formed body. "You could have paired me with an ugly female."

Otas chuckled. "After your bonding, you must teach Sashna how to touch minds with Cwen so that she will remain in constant contact with her, and show her the ways of *Dut-da*. After you, Sashna has the next highest number of psychic receptors."

"As you command." Vlad stared at him for a second. "But you forgot one thing."

"What's that?"

"You didn't tell Sashna. I know she likes me, but she won't let me perform *Kyol-hon* with her unless you order it."

"*Daul-mae!*" Otas cursed. "I will see to it immediately."

"I thank you, my friend." Vlad smiled as he stared at the Overlord. He was aware of what had occupied his friend the last twenty-four hours. Since he himself was feeling the effects of *Bal-Dar*, Vlad was eager to perform the bonding with Sashna.

Cwen sat at her desk, reading the story she'd started two days earlier. She was enthralled. Whoever Jal was had written a tale about the Liambrian Overlord and his Queen. What Jal had written was her own biography, but the characters had different names. Somehow this was even more exciting than reality for Jal's Queen loved the Overlord passionately.

Cwen frowned when her stomach growled yet again. Where the hell was Sashna? She was starving. As if on cue, Sashna popped into view, holding a tray with her breakfast.

Sashna placed the tray before Cwen, then stood at attention.

Even though she was hungry, Cwen didn't touch her food.

There was something wrong with Sashna. Her face was ghost-pale. Cwen stood and moved around the desk, touching a hand to her friend's shoulder. She could have read Sashna's mind, but she felt she could be of more help if she let her speak her thoughts.

"What's wrong?" she asked quietly.

"I ... I ... " Sashna couldn't get the words out.

Cwen pulled her to the futon and sat her down. "Take your time."

Sashna looked at Cwen for a long time. Finally, she answered, "The Overlord just told me that Vlad is to be my husband."

"Why, that's wonderful news."

"That's easy for you to say," Sashna snapped.

"The hell it is."

Sashna noted the smoke in Cwen's green eyes. "I'm sorry. I forgot that you had no choice in going through *Kyol-hon* with the Overlord." Sashna popped up off the futon. "What am I going to do?"

"What Otas ordered, of course." Cwen stared up at her. "Has it occurred to you that Vlad has no choice either?"

Sashna paced for a few seconds. "That's the problem. Otas only matched me to him because of my infatuation."

"You're wrong, my friend." Cwen laughed mirthlessly. "Selections for the bonding are made solely on genetic compatibility."

"You're certain?"

"How do you think I landed in this mess I'm in?"

The color returned to Sashna's cheeks as she sat down again. "Do you love Otas?"

It was Cwen's turn to jump up. How could she explain her feelings and have them make sense to Sashna? "Not yet," she said simply. "But I do like him a lot." Cwen cocked her head. "You have an advantage over me. You're already smitten with Vlad."

Sashna blushed to the roots of her hair. "Okay. Okay. Maybe this isn't so bad." She rubbed her chin thoughtfully. "Maybe you better explain what happens during *Kyol-hon* and this business of sex."

Cwen turned scarlet at the memory of what had occurred the day before.

Looking at her, Sashna commented, "This ought to be good." She crossed her arms. "Spit it out, Cwen."

Cwen did, her face retaining the red heat of embarrassment.

"Rise and shine, sleepyhead!" Sashna's voice boomed.

Cwen groaned, pulling the pillow over her head. She'd been up late reading. She willed Sashna to disappear.

Bright light hit her eyes as the pillow was yanked from her. She could see Sashna beaming down at her. I guess I can't teleport anything yet, Cwen thought. She looked at the digital clock. 0700 it read. She sat up and scowled at Sashna. "Why the hell are you getting me up so damn early?"

"Why, it's the day of your coronation, *Yo-Wang*!" Sashna dragged her from the bed and shoved her towards the bathroom. "It's time for spit and polish, soldier!"

Cwen spun on her. "What the hell are you talking about?"

"You're to be presented to the Liambrians in two hours. Shake a leg, *Yo-Wang*."

"Cwen!" she growled. "And why are you so damn cheerful?"

A wistful look crossed Sashna's face. "I'm a wife now. I know what you mean about Liambrian males. Vlad's body is magnificent."

"Shut up," Cwen said as she went into the bathroom.

When she came out, Cwen was shocked to see an opening in the wall that revealed a closet. "How did you open that?"

"You don't know how?"

Cwen glared at her.

Sashna glanced at the clock. "I guess we have time. Liambrians don't like clutter, so the necessities of living are hidden from view." She pulled Cwen along the wall, pointing out recessed black buttons. Each had a different symbol on it. She opened closet after closet. "This one has your *wanpisus*. This one your *Yang-boks*. This one your shoes. And finally, your washing machine."

Cwen stared at the black square that indeed looked like a washer. "I'm to do my own laundry?"

"Of course, not. That's my job. This thing is great. It doesn't use water. The Overlord doesn't want water wasted on cleaning garments." Sashna frowned. "I'm not sure what the cleaning source is. Vlad told me your father invented it."

Sashna's rambling was giving her a headache. "That's enough of a tour." Cwen rubbed her forehead. "What am I supposed to do at this coronation?"

"Nothing. The Overlord will introduce you to those that matter. You're to play the demure Queen." Sashna laughed at her own joke. Then she sat Cwen on the bed and began to brush out her hair, talking all the while.

Cwen wasn't listening to her. She was scared to death. She'd been wondering when her husband was going to get around to making her presence known. But now that the time had come, she'd just as soon remain anonymous.

Cwen looked at her clothes in the open closets—dark green all. The Queen's color, her father had said. But that didn't include her shoes. They were all black.

After Sashna had finished with her hair, they had time to kill. Her friend told her about the joys of *Kyol-hon* with Vlad, but Cwen only pretended to listen, nodding and making grunting sounds at the appropriate places. Her nerves were screaming.

Finally, it was time to dress. Cwen was shocked by her outfit. Two panels of fabric covered her breasts, barely. The pieces of material came to a vee at her navel. The skirt portion of the garment had slits on both sides that went to her hips. She might as well have appeared naked before the Liambrians.

"Are you sure this is what I'm to wear?"

Sashna plopped a pair of black slippers at her feet. "Oh, yes. The Overlord was very explicit in his instructions."

"I look like I belong in a brothel."

"Liambrians aren't ashamed of their bodies. Vlad said so."

Cwen glared at her. If she heard Vlad's name one more time she would scream.

"You don't get it, do you?"

Cwen was trying to keep her breasts from spilling out of the dark-green dress. "Get what?"

"All know that Otas' mother was a coward." Sashna nodded at the dress. "The Overlord is showing off your warrior's body. With those muscles, no one will doubt what he claims about his Queen."

"Terrific. I'm a showpiece."

Sashna pulled her to the outer chamber, moving quickly to the main doors. Cwen was surprised when they slid open. Once outside in the corridor, she was entranced. The walls were a lighter grey than her chamber walls. Bright lights ran along the floor and ceiling. Some pathways were straight. Others seemed to curve in a circle.

Sashna hurried her along the hall, giving Cwen no time to gape. A double panel of doors slid open and they stepped inside a square compartment. After the doors closed, a voice out of the air said in Liambrian, "Destination?"

"Level fifteen," Sashna answered.

Obviously it was an elevator, Cwen thought, as it began its descent. "How the hell am I supposed to find my way around this place? I don't speak Liambrian."

"Most of the time I'll be with you. However, your father is modifying all of the elevators to speak English too."

Goodness, her father was a busy male, Cwen thought. "Where are we going?"

"To the Overlord's audience chambers."

When the lift stopped, they stepped out. Sashna led her along a curved hallway and stopped in front of a large black door. She held Cwen back so that she wouldn't activate the sensors.

"Why don't we go inside?"

"Not until Vlad gives the signal." Sashna cocked her head and listened with her mind. "Otas is telling everyone of your exploits. Killing a Trexran in the past. Commanding Sevea's warriors to kill the Trexrans. Your fight with Maccus. Our journey here when you killed twenty marauders single-handedly. Saving Jena by taking the arrow yourself. All of it."

Try as she might, Cwen could hear nothing from Otas' mind or his voice. He was purposely keeping his thoughts from her. "How do you know that? I can't hear anything."

"The chambers are soundproof. I'm listening to Vlad's mind. Our minds are linked now, you know."

Indeed, Cwen thought. She hoped her husband hurried up. She was about to break out into a sweat from anticipation.

"Otas just told them he performed *Kyol-hon* and *Bal-Dar* with you. He commands them to give you the respect that is your due as the Queen. Okay, that's our cue."

Suddenly, Cwen found she couldn't move. Sashna got behind her and gave her a shove. Cwen's warrior's training was the only thing that kept her from falling flat on her face after the large door whooshed open.

Cwen had never seen so many Liambrians in one place before. She forced her feet to move toward the dias where her husband stood, Sashna following a respectful distance behind.

Otas looked bigger than life and scary. She realized she'd never seen him in the act of commanding his people. As she got closer to him, she became intensely aware of his black outfit. It was as sparse as hers. Two black panels of material covered his breasts, the opening between gave a good view of his flesh down to just above his groin. The pants portion of his attire left little to the imagination. The muscles of his legs and arms seemed to bulge even though he stood motionless.

When he gave her a stern look, she stopped a few feet in front of him.

"*Ku Yo-Wang!*" his voice boomed.

There were murmurings going on around her. Unconsciously, her mind slipped into *Dut-da*. She didn't understand the Liambrian words of the thoughts flowing around the chamber, but she had no trouble interpreting their meaning. They thought that she was evil like Taki. Despite her warrior's body, they believed her a coward. She was so angry her temples throbbed. After everything she'd been through, this is what she got? Doubt?

Cwen wasn't the only one that was angry. The Overlord's rage made the air seem thick in the chamber. "Your thoughts insult me!" he shouted in Liambrian.

Cwen didn't understand what he'd said, but she could read the emotion of hurt coming from his mind. The rage built up in her so quickly she had no forethought of what she was about to do. Cwen raised her arm and stretched out her hand as her jewelry became red-hot. Without even thinking she blasted Otas with a stream of green fire.

When the green flames hit him, his hair flew wildly about him, emerald electrical arcs danced along his huge body as he shielded himself from her blast. He was surprised, but it didn't show on his face.

The collective gasp of his subjects was tangible, their thoughts even more solid. The Liambrians gathered couldn't believe that she'd had the courage to attack the Overlord, much less possess the power of the green fire.

Otas looked down at her, his eyes churning with orange and gold flames.

Cwen lowered her hand. "Forgive me, *Sa-Jang*. But could you tell me what that was? I don't seem to have any control over it," she said innocently.

Enough of the Liambrians spoke English so that what she had said was immediately translated amongst them.

The look on Otas' face was murderous, but with his mind he said, *Don't look at me, Katai. You'll make me laugh.*

Cwen lowered her eyes to the floor, trying not to laugh herself.

"That was *Cho-rok Bul*, the Green Flame, *Yo-Wang*. It was fortunate that it struck me instead of another. They would have been killed," he said sternly.

The fear level was rising with each passing second as she said, "I beg you to teach me how to control it. I do not wish to harm anyone accidently."

Otas said nothing to her as he scanned the room with his mind. The terror around him was palpable. "All but the Circle of Twelve are dismissed."

There was shoving and shouting as the frightened people tried to pass through the doorway at once. The noise died abruptly as the last Liambrian fled the chambers.

Cwen became aware of Sashna trembling behind her, and Vlad who stood on Otas' right. There were twelve Liambrians in white robes on his left. Cwen recognized her mother immediately, but didn't acknowledge her.

The sound of the Overlord's booming laughter made her look to him. He could hold it back no longer. Everyone except Cwen and Vlad were surprised, they being the only two who had ever heard the Overlord give way to humor.

When Otas could finally speak, he said, "You please me, *Yo-Wang*."

"I told you she was smart, *Sa-Jang*," said a tall Liambrian male in a white robe. "Now no one will question her authority."

That voice. It couldn't be, could it? Cwen thought. She walked up to the male and stared at his face. His brown hair had always been long, so that didn't help. But if she imagined him in an Earthling suit and phony glasses, this could only be one person. "Professor Pimbleton?"

The male pressed his fist to his chest. "I am Jal, *Yo-Wang*. Vlad's father."

"Then you're my uncle."

"Correct."

Cwen had not heard Otas move up behind her. "There will be time enough later for reunions," he said. "My wife has not eaten and she needs her strength." He placed his hands on her shoulders.

Before they dematerialized, Cwen caught the tears of pride that shone in her mother's eyes.

# Chapter 28

Otas and Cwen materialized inside his chambers. He led her to the round table in the corner on which sat dishes with metal domes covering them. A pitcher of *Ma-shil-kot* and two glasses sat beside the covered plates. He sat her down first, then took the chair opposite her.

He uncovered the dishes, and the aroma wafting from the food made Cwen weak with hunger. She smiled. A platter, not a plate, was filled with the breaded shrimp-tasting morsels. Until she looked upon it, she'd hadn't known that the dish was just what she was craving. Beside it was a large bowl of what looked and smelled like dark-green cabbage.

"What's the name of this seafood? I forgot," she asked her husband.

"*Sae-u.*" He looked at her sternly. "Would you please eat. Your hunger is making my stomach growl."

Cwen didn't need encouragement. She was starving, attacking the food with relish. The *Sae-u* sat on a bed of the blue rice. She sighed at the wonderful flavor of it. The vegetable was tasty as well.

Cwen was two-thirds of the way finished when she noticed her husband wasn't eating. He quietly sipped on a glass of *Ma-shil-kot*.

Cwen rose her brows. "All of this was for me?"

"Finish it. You need the nourishment."

She didn't argue, polishing off the food in a matter of minutes. Cwen smiled at him when she was done, but she wasn't quite satisfied yet. He said nothing as he poured her a glass of *Ma-shil-kot.*

Cwen sipped the drink while regarding her husband. "What's this blue rice-looking stuff and the vegetable called?"

"It's not Earthling rice, it's Liambrian *Chin-ji.* The vegetable was *Siu-choy,*" he answered absentmindedly, staring at her with orange eyes that sparkled.

After Cwen finished the drink, the empty space inside her stomach was finally filled. "If I keep eating like this, I'll grow fat."

"No you won't. *Bal-Dar* uses up all stored nutrients. They need to be replaced." He reached across the table and touched her face. "Our *Bal-Dar* has changed you. Right now your metabolism is accelerated. When you feel hungry, you must eat."

"Is that why I feel so strange?"

"Yes," he lied.

Cwen cocked her head at him. "But what about you? You ate nothing. Don't your nutrients need replacing?"

"No. I am male."

That told her nothing, but she wasn't in a mood to argue. Otas kept staring at her so hard she got fidgety, then looked down to see if one of her breasts had spilled from the fabric of her sparse garment. No. That wasn't it. She was fully covered. "Why are you staring at me?"

He smiled slowly. "Queen of the Faeries, *Katai*?"

Cwen flushed. "You didn't read that from my mind?"

"No. I told you I don't always read your thoughts. Just knowing you are well is enough." Otas couldn't help it. He started laughing.

"Well, I had to tell the daughters something. I wouldn't blindly follow anyone unless I knew where we were going. I couldn't tell them they were extraterrestrials, now could I?"

He finally stopped laughing. "No, I don't suppose you could." His look held false seriousness. "But no matter what

I do, I can't get Kendra to stop calling me King *Sa-Jang*. She's entirely convinced that I'm the King of the Faeries."

It was Cwen's turn to smile. "How *are* the daughters?"

"I have fully accepted them as true Liambrians, *Katai*." This time his serious expression was real. "Kendra, Ting, and Raslen have been given the rank of warrior class. They're slowly being trained in what it means to be Liambrian. The others have yet to discover what contributions they will make." He looked at the empty plates. "Except Zeda, that is. She's now in the kitchens. I gave her amber jewelry, and she prepared your meal."

Inwardly, Cwen was tickled pink. She had been right about Zeda. She gazed at Otas for sometime before asking, "Just what happened after I was shot with the arrow? I don't remember anything until I woke up here."

"I did hear your telepathic call for aid. I teleported Vlad and twenty Liambrian males to your location." He suddenly frowned. "When I could not sense you with my mind, I became enraged, and . . . "

"And?" she prompted.

Otas inhaled. "I killed all of the ghosts with *Cho-rok Bul*."

Cwen gasped.

"I, too, was angry at myself at first, for they were defenseless against my power. But rationally, I acted wisely." He passed a hand through his thick hair. "Those men deserved to die. Isolated as they were, inbreeding became common. The result was twisted minds. I did the Earthlings a favor by ridding them of that threat."

Cwen just stared at Otas, thinking he was a hard, hard male.

"I know your thoughts, *Katai*." He sighed heavily. "While you were in that audience chamber, you read the thoughts of those I command. There's always doubt among them because I'm Taki's son. I've had to prove myself to them from the moment I was born." Otas stood up in agitation. "They insulted you and me with their thoughts. If you had not let loose with *Cho-rok Bul*, I might have." Looking down at her, he asked, "Why did you come to my defense?"

Cwen wanted to lie, but their minds were linked. "I felt your hurt caused by their thoughts. It angered me. They have no right to treat you less than what you truly are. The Overlord."

"Until you arrived in this time-frame, only Vlad knew of my emotions. All thought me made of stone." He walked to her side of the table and pulled her up from her chair. He kissed her tenderly for a long time. When he lifted his head, he whispered, "You please me, *Katai*."

Cwen touched a hand to his cheek. "Sometimes you scare the daylights out of me, but you please me too, husband."

She hadn't said that she loved him, but it was close enough. Smiling, he said, "I have a gift for you."

Cwen looked at him questioningly.

"With everything going on around us, we forgot your birthday. What I give you is a belated gift, as Vlad calls it."

She quickly looked around for a wrapped present.

"No." He touched a hand to his heart. "What I give you comes from here. I would not deny you what was denied me. The love of a family. When you're in the privacy of your chambers with your relatives, you may dispense with Liambrian protocol."

"Thank you, husband." Her eyes filled with tears. "Have you no family living?"

Otas laughed harshly. "I have family. My father. His parents. And their parents before them. But none hold love for me because I am the son of Taki."

What he'd just said made her cry harder. "Y—you have no one?"

"I have you, *Katai*." He rubbed at her tears with his thumbs. "I'll return you to your chambers now. I will come to you later." Otas kissed her forehead. "*Na Sa-rang Tang-sin*."

"I know," she responded just before she dematerialized.

When she materialized in her chambers, there was a loud "Surprise!" that scared the life out of her. Smiling at her were her mother and father, Vlad, Sashna, and Jal. Cwen was so startled she didn't know what to say.

Sevea went up to Cwen and hugged her daughter. "Don't be so serious, *Tanim*. This is a birthday party."

"Oh," was all she said.

"My present to you is all of the clothes in your closets. Otas had no idea of your size, so I had them made for you." Sevea smiled. "I designed that dress you're wearing. I know it's outrageous, but that's what the Overlord wanted."

Cwen reddened, looking down to see if her breasts had come free. Before she could say anything, Jal lifted her and spun her around. "Professor Pimbleton, put me down," she stammered.

He did. "It's Jal, Cwen. Correction. Make that uncle." Beaming at her, he asked, "Did you like the computer?"

"It's a stroke of genius."

"Well, Hebron did the programming. I just wrote the stories."

"Thank you, father."

Hebron moved Jal aside and hugged his daughter. "You won't need to recharge the unit. I altered the power supply to self-energizing crystals."

Before she could ask her father about these crystals, Vlad and Sashna were pulling her to the *Chim-dae-bang*. Cwen's mouth dropped open. There sat her thirty-five inch TV with the digital video disc player and the speakers. A futon had been set up before it.

"Vlad brought the TV from the past," Sashna said. Opening yet another closet, there stood the file cabinet with her video discs. "I organized the files."

"And I altered the power source on the TV as well," Hebron added.

Cwen could only gape at the people around her, all talking at once. She burst into tears.

"Now look what you've done, husband," Sevea scolded Hebron.

"It's okay, mother. For the first time in my life, I'm truly happy."

The party would have lasted into the wee hours of the morning if the Overlord had not ended it. He told everyone that his Queen needed to rest.

Soon Cwen and Otas were in his big bed. He watched her intently as she ate all of the midnight snack he'd brought her. There had been food at the party, but he felt she hadn't eaten enough.

After he'd removed that scandalous dress, he'd placed her in the bed naked. He wore nothing. He'd assured her that lovemaking was not on his mind for he didn't have the strength. He'd just wanted to feel her next to him.

Cwen yawned and whispered, "Goodnight, husband." Then lay on her side.

Otas lay behind her, placing a hand on her belly. His wife was sleep in seconds.

Before he entered *Dut-da* for the night, he checked on the small life-forms in Cwen's wombs. His son and daughter had received enough nutrition for the day. Even if he had to hand feed his Queen, his children would receive all the nourishment their growing forms would need.

Otas kept his palm on Cwen's belly as he entered *Dut-da*.

After Otas had stuffed her with breakfast, he'd returned Cwen to her *Chim-dae-bang*. She was actually shivering with excitement. At last, she would get a tour of her husband's fortress. Of course he wouldn't be her guide. Vlad and Sashna held that honor. Otas had instructed Cwen that once outside her chambers she was to behave as the Queen she was.

Which caused her present dilemma. All of her closets were open. Cwen had no idea what she was supposed to wear. Somehow the short *wanpisus* didn't seem appropriate.

She sighed with relief as Sashna breezed in wearing her sword.

After the door slid closed, Sashna nodded towards the outer chamber. "Vlad awaits us," she informed Cwen.

"Sashna, as Queen I don't know what I'm supposed to wear."

"Why, your *Yang-bok*, my friend."

"My what?"

Sashna reached in the open closet and pulled out a dark-green jumpsuit. "This is a *Yang-bok*."

Cwen took the garment from her, then frowned. "I just realized something. Not once since I've been here have I worn underwear. Is this common?"

"Liambrian females believe in freedom of movement. However, your mother anticipated this." Sashna opened a drawer in the chest that lay within the closet, pulling out a small garment.

Cwen took it from her. The underwear looked like bikini briefs. Dark-green of course, made of the same shimmering fabric. Cwen slipped them on. "No, bra?"

Sashna shook her head. "There's no such word in Liambrian."

Cwen sighed as she put the jumpsuit on. There was no zipper, but the fabric had elasticity to it. It was easy to shimmy into it. She looked down at the low V-neckline which exposed her cleavage. "Is Otas mad? I'm supposed to walk around this fortress, showing off my . . . "

Sashna giggled. "As Queen, you're the symbol of fertility to the Liambrians." The fit of the *Yang-bok* left nothing to the imagination.

Cwen snarled in irritation as she went to the shoes closet.

"How am I to be taken seriously when I'm dressed like a harlot?"

Chuckling, Sashna reached around her and pulled out a pair of wedge-soled black boots. "Believe me. After your little demonstration of *Cho-rok Bul* at your coronation, no one will view you in any other way than serious. Everyone's talking about it."

Cwen sat on the bed and pulled her boots on. "What about my hair?"

"You're to wear the warrior's braid."

Cwen quickly plaited the length of her hair, securing the end with a strip of green leather Sashna had handed her.

"So. How do I look?"

"Delicious," she answered mischievously.

Cwen scowled at her as they walked to the doors.

Vlad tried to hide the shock on his face as he looked upon his cousin. Why hadn't he noticed it last eve? His former charge no longer looked or acted like the immature child she had been. Indeed, in the sleeveless *Yang-bok* she had the ambiance of a full-grown sensual female. Words failed him as he sensed her accelerated metabolism. The Queen was pregnant!

*Say nothing, my friend,* came Otas' voice in his mind. *Cwen does not know.*

*Other males will sense it, especially her father.*

*I'll talk with Hebron. The others will dare not speak of it.*

*As you command.* Vlad ended the conversation with the Overlord. By all indications, *Bal-Dar* had produced more than wild passion in all of the Liambrians. His and Sashna's *Kyol-hon* had been unbelievable. He shook himself as he heard Cwen's voice.

"Vlad, I asked you if I look all right?" She stood tall with her hand on her hip.

"More right than you know, *Yo-Wang,*" Vlad answered.

The tour started on the first level where Cwen's chambers

lay. Vlad showed her the way to the Overlord's suite without having to use the hidden door. Sashna's and Vlad's quarters were across the hall, their rooms also connected by a hidden portal.

Vlad informed the Queen that the fortress had twenty-five levels, but time didn't permit him to show her all of them. Right now they were descending to level six, which contained the rooms that Otas used for recreation. So he does have fun, Cwen thought.

She was surprised when they reached the level that only contained two rooms. On the left was the large war room where Otas, Vlad, and a select group of warriors practiced combat. Vlad told her that she and Sashna could utilize the room for the same purpose. They proceeded to the right-hand doors.

Cwen was surprisingly shocked when the doors slid open and revealed an exact duplicate of the waterfall and pool on Hyu-shik. Palm trees and real tropical plants grew in the soil. The humid temperature was reminiscent of that isle of passion. Vlad told her that the water was recycled. Waste of the precious liquid was a thing Otas abhorred. The replica of Hyu-shik was for the sole use of the Overlord and the Queen. However, if the Overlord was not with Cwen, she was to bring Sashna along for protection.

"Vlad, we've yet to meet any other Liambrians," Cwen commented.

"I was to show you where you would be spending most of your time first."

"Hmm," was all she said.

"You'll meet some people now. We're headed for the Agro-deck."

After they entered the lift, Cwen asked, "We grow all of our food?"

"Yes. We also have a level for the sole purpose of raising livestock. One level is also a seafood farm."

"Interesting." Cwen was impressed. Liambria was self-contained. They needn't bother the Earthlings for anything.

When the doors to the Agro-deck slid apart, Cwen's mouth dropped open. Huge was an understatement for the size of this inner farmland. She judged the diameter to be several kilometers across. Frowning, she turned to Vlad. "Just how big is Liambria?"

Vlad felt beads of sweat pop out on his forehead. Cwen didn't realize it, but she had blasted him with her mind as well as her voice. She was learning the Overlord's ways quickly. "Liambria is ten kilometers in diameter."

"You're joking."

"I assure you I speak the truth."

Cwen automatically started to do a *Dut-da* on Vlad, then stopped herself in time when his eyes widened. "Forgive me for doubting you, Vlad."

He nodded nervously in acceptance.

God, she couldn't believe what she was about to do to her own cousin. Her thoughts of shame were interrupted when a group of ten Liambrian males approached, led by a female in a red *wanpisu* with flowing blonde hair.

When they stopped in front of her, they placed their fists over their hearts and said in unison, "*Yo-Wang.*"

"This is Narda. She's in charge of the Agro-deck," Vlad informed Cwen. "Her skill at growing any kind of plant is remarkable."

Cwen just stared at Narda, for she could sense the hatred radiating off this female without trying very hard. She tuned Vlad's ramblings out as she did a *Dut-da* on Narda. Cwen kept her face expressionless as she read the female's mind. Narda's thoughts were in English and she didn't even try to hide her hatred for Cwen.

So this was the female who had coupled with Otas. Narda hated the Queen for ending her prestigious position as the Overlord's paramour. Cwen boldly stared into the blue eyes that held intense jealousy. Cwen herself didn't feel jealous. The emotion running through her was disgust for her husband and this whore.

"Would you like a tour of the Agro-deck, *Yo-Wang?*" Vlad asked.

When Cwen turned her eyes on him, they were pure smoke. "No. I've seen quite enough." She turned on her heel and exited the Agro-deck.

She was halfway down the corridor when Vlad and Sashna caught up to her.

"Is there anything further I should see on this tour?" Cwen asked irritably when they reached her.

"We saved the best for last, *Yo-Wang*," Vlad said.

Cwen only glared at him.

"Don't you want to see Samson?" Sashna asked.

With everything that had happened in the last days, Cwen had forgotten about her faithful horse. She nodded to Sashna.

They took the elevator to level ten. When the doors opened, Cwen was surprised when they walked into the largest stable she'd ever seen. Vlad led her down the length of stalls, stopping before Samson. The horse whinnied at the sight and smell of his mistress.

Cwen patted his nose quietly as she took in the sight of the huge animal in the stall next to him. The black beast looked like a horse, but his large head was square-shaped, the ears blunt. "What is that, Vlad?"

"That's Targ. Otas' Liambrian *mal*, horse." Vlad kept his distance. "Only the Overlord can ride that animal."

Cwen said nothing as she opened Samson's stall. She could see a large field outside the stable, intending to ride off her anger on Samson. Cwen mounted him without a saddle or bridle.

Frightened for her safety, Vlad grabbed her leg. "Have a care, *Yo-Wang*."

Cwen slapped his hand free and took off on Samson at full gallop.

"*Kom-un Chi-ok*, Black Hell!" Vlad swore. "Follow her, Sashna!"

As she ran to her own horse, Sashna asked, "Why's she angry?"

"I'll explain later." Vlad popped out of view.

Sashna raced behind Cwen on her bay stallion, trying to close the distance. The field was three kilometers wide and four kilometers long, surrounded by a high wall made of alloy. Cwen's manner of riding was reckless. Sashna hoped she could catch her before something disastrous happened.

Cwen urged Samson to greater speed as the visions of Otas wrapped in Narda's embrace assaulted her mind. Without warning, Samson began to fight her, bucking in a circle, then veering to the right at a fast gallop. Cwen tried to stop him by tugging on his mane. It had no effect. Samson ducked his head with a snort, freeing his mane from her grasp.

Cwen was panicked for the horse was heading straight for the wall. She had no doubts that Samson could clear the barrier, but she had no idea what lay on the other side.

As horse and rider approached the wall, Cwen had a flash of precognition. This fortress was on a mountain. What lay on the other side was a long, long drop. Frantic, she grabbed Samson's mane again, tugging with all her strength.

Samson halted abruptly just short of the wall. Cwen kept going, sailing over the wall into space.

For those who witnessed it, none could tell who's scream was louder. Sashna's or the Queen's.

"I shouldn't have taken Cwen to the Agro-deck," Vlad said as he paced in the Overlord's chambers. "It never even occurred to me that she would figure out who Narda was."

Otas, shirtless, had his back to Vlad, staring out the window. "What's done is done. I'll just have to deal with it."

"But the way Cwen took off on Samson . . . " Vlad ran his hand through his brown hair.

"She can ride like—" Otas broke off and spun around quickly. His eyes turned pure gold as he raced to the center of the room, holding out his arms. "*Daul-mae!*"

Vlad started to ask him what was wrong when suddenly a screaming Cwen popped into view just below the domed ceiling. She landed in Otas' arms, but her momentum sent them crashing to the floor.

"*Ha-nu-nim!*" Vlad shouted as he ran to the couple crumpled on the floor.

Cwen continued to scream, not realizing where she was. Otas kept repeating "*Daul-mae!*" over and over.

Vlad knelt down. "Cwen! Cwen! You're safe!"

Through her screams, she recognized Vlad's voice. She shut her mouth when she saw where she was. Cwen was on Otas' lap. Her husband's face was as white as *Ma-shil-kot*, his eyes wide and gold.

"*Daul-mae! Daul-mae!*" he swore as he placed a hand on her belly. His children were all right. But that didn't stop his terror. "*Daul-mae!*"

Cwen slapped at his hand but he refused to move it.

"*Daul-mae!*" came out of Otas again.

"Vlad, what's he saying?"

"Um, there isn't an English translation," Vlad answered.

Cwen looked at Otas. "Is it anything like *shit!*"

"Close enough."

"*Daul-mae!*"

"*Sa-Jang!*" she yelled.

"*Daul-mae!*" he said, his hand still on her tummy.

"Husband, look at me!" Cwen grabbed his face. "I'm safe. You teleported me to safety!"

That got Otas' attention. "*Katai*, I did not teleport you here."

"Then, how—"

"You did it yourself." Finally he removed his hand from her abdomen, and ran it through his hair. "*Daul-mae.*"

She slapped a hand over his mouth. "Don't start that again!"

Otas just stared at her, the color returning to his face.

"I—I saw the ground coming up at me real fast. All I could think about was never seeing you again. I guess that activated my teleportation receptors."

Suddenly his eyes began to churn with orange flames. "*Kom-un Chi-ok*! What made you ride out like that with no thought to your safety?"

"I've ridden Samson like that many times. It was like something took over his mind. He was a completely different animal."

Vlad and Otas stared at each other in silence so long Cwen became nervous. "What? What?"

"Narda," they said together.

"You mean to tell me that she has the power to—"

"*Tat-da Wi-e*, Shut up, *Katai*!" Otas said as he pulled her up and gently sat her on the futon.

Vlad cocked his head. "Sashna says the horse is calm now."

Otas only nodded as he sent a telepathic message to the guards.

Cwen kept her mouth shut as her husband had ordered. He looked gigantic in his rage. No. He was more than angry. The Overlord was fit to kill.

With a stirring of air, two bulky Liambrian males appeared with a struggling Narda between them. She spotted Cwen instantly. "You live?"

Otas stepped in front of her. "The Queen is alive!"

Trying to free herself from the guards, Narda shouted, "No! You belong to me! She should be dead!"

"You are evil and insane! You have no knowledge of what power *Ku Yo-Wang* possesses. She saved herself!" Otas turned to look at Cwen.

On instinct alone, Cwen rose and stood next to her husband.

"What is your wish, *Yo-Wang?*"

Only for a second did Cwen hesitate, the memory of the rocks flying towards her face surfacing. She looked Narda directly in the eye. "I demand *Chi-u-da*!"

Narda tried to shrink back from the Overlord, but he grabbed her neck and gripped her head between his thumb and forefinger. Cwen couldn't see his eyes turn into pie-wedges of yellow, gold, orange, and red. But she could hear Narda's screams of agony. They were nauseating and terrifying, but Cwen forced herself to stand erect and watch Narda's tortured expression.

It was over in seconds. Narda's lips flapped soundlessly. "What time-frame do you want us to send her to, *Sa-Jang?*" one of the guards said.

"I care not! Get her out of my sight!"

The guards wasted no time doing as the Overlord ordered.

The Overlord turned to his Queen. "*Katai*, I—" Otas caught Cwen before she hit the floor. Lifting her in his arms he said, "*Daul-mae!* This is too much excitement for a pregnant female."

"*Daul-mae,*" was all Vlad could add.

# Chapter 29

Otas was worried. Cwen had been unconscious for thirty minutes, and even his healing powers could not awaken her. He continued to cool her sweating body with wet cloths. Something was wrong. Very wrong.

His eyes gold with concern, he placed his shaking hand over her belly. Perhaps damage had been done to her wombs during the long fall over the wall. If a miscarriage was at hand, the time to act was now.

Otas frowned in puzzlement for the cervixes of her wombs felt intact, the embryos firmly implanted. He almost pulled back his hand in fright as he became aware of a consciousness in the right womb. Formation of the brain with its psychic receptors was the first stage of fetal development in Liambrians. Completion ordinarily took up to two months. Not so with this new life-form created by *Bal-Dar*. Though microscopic in size, the brain of his child was fully formed—the male, his son, the next Overlord. Until this moment Otas had not been certain.

*Father.*

"*Ha-nu-nim*," Otas breathed. He'd heard the thought projection clearly in his mind. What kind of creature had been created from *Bal-Dar*? Even at this early stage, Otas was certain his son's powers exceeded his own. But by how much? He knew the life-form was waiting for a response. *Son?* he answered telepathically.

*I am Sogon.*

He inhaled sharply. The life-form had named itself.

Consciousness, thought, and language. What else did it—no, not an it, his *son*—know? *Mother. What's wrong?*

*Brain function suspended.*

Otas stopped himself from cursing. It was like talking to a computer. *Cause?*

*I.*

The Overlord tried not to project his shock. He must find out what Sogon had done to his wife. *Why?*

*Necessary. Sister in distress.*

Then Otas felt it. A small, but unmistakable contraction in the left womb. *Abortion imminent?*

*Time remains. Analyze system.*

With his free hand, Otas placed his hand over Cwen's heart. Counting quickly, he gasped as her pulse was nearing two hundred. Then he felt the amount of adrenaline running through her. Otas immediately formed a Mind-Link with Cwen. Even though her brain function was suspended, her visual last thought was of the fall that should have killed her. Using a mild form of *Chi-u-da*, he wiped the memory from her mind.

Cwen's pulse immediately slowed and the flow of adrenaline ceased. A soft sigh came out of her as if she merely slept.

Otas could feel the left womb stabilizing, the contractions halting abruptly.

*Sogon. Your sister?*

*Safe now. She sleeps.*

*Resume brain function.*

*Not yet. Must talk.*

Otas rose his brow.

*We effect mother. She effects us.*

*I understand. Sogon, future avoidance?*

*Alleviate stress input.*

*Explain.*

*Stress derives from fears of the unknown.*

*Continue, Sogon.*

*Insufficient time given to assimilate new data. Mother of high intellect. Complete information necessary.*

Otas smiled to himself. It was the same thing Hebron had told him on Hyu-shik. *Thank you, Sogon.*

*We love. Father love us.*

His heart melted. *Anything else?*

*We hunger.*

The life-form that was his son grew silent. Otas kept his hand on Cwen's belly, not believing what had just occurred.

"Husband?"

Otas started and looked to his wife. Her eyes were a clear green.

"What are you doing?"

He removed his hand, his face reddening with embarrassment. As Sogon had said, it wasn't time to tell her yet. He couldn't very well explain to her that he'd been talking to their son. "I, uh, was making sure you're all right." He lay beside her, stroking her face. "How do you feel?"

"Tired. Like I've been running a race with myself." She frowned. "I fainted, didn't I?"

"Yes," he answered cautiously.

"I guess I couldn't handle seeing you do *Chi-u-da* on Narda."

Frowning, he asked, "What else do you remember?"

"Samson going wild on me. Then I actually teleported myself here before I fell off his back. You and Vlad saying Narda took over Samson's mind. Then *Chi-u-da*. After that I'm blank."

Good. She didn't mention falling over the wall. The memory was gone. "Are you hungry?"

"I'm hungry and queasy at the same time."

Otas reached across her and picked up the inevitable glass of *Ma-shil-kot*. He handed it to her.

"What's this stuff? A cure-all?"

He chuckled. "No matter what shape your stomach is in

you can handle *Ma-shil-kot*. Besides, you need your nutrients because—"

"I know, I know. My metabolism is accelerated." She drank the glass down.

He took it from her. "Rest now. You've had a busy morning."

"But I don't want to sleep. I have many questions to ask."

Otas touched his fingers to her forehead. "*Ja-Da*, sleep." Cwen went out like a light. "Later, *Katai*," he whispered.

As he walked to his own chambers through the hidden door, memories so old that he'd thought he'd lost them came to his mind. Sashna and Vlad awaited him. The strain on Sashna's face was unmistakable.

"Are the babies all right? You were in there so long I became worried," Sashna said.

Otas looked to Vlad with irritation.

"You forget. Our minds are now linked. What I know, Sashna knows."

The Overlord nodded. "The children are fine, Sashna. Stay with Cwen, but when she awakens tell her nothing about being pregnant and don't mention the fall."

After Sashna left the chamber, Otas sat heavily on the futon, shaking his head in wonder.

"You look perplexed, my friend," Vlad commented as he sat beside him.

Otas loosened the leather thong that bound his hair, passing a hand through it. "Cwen carries the next Overlord."

"That's wonderful news. You succeeded on the first try."

"You don't understand." Otas inhaled. "I just had a telepathic conversation with my son."

Vlad stared at him with astonishment. "I know a Liambrian male is aware of his child, but to actually speak to a four-day-old embryo?"

"That's my point. I was concentrating so hard on the

evolutionary process of all Liambrians that I have no idea what kind of creature I created as the next Overlord."

"I think you better explain."

"My son's brain is fully developed, although it's microscopic. He possesses the power to send his mother into a faint." Otas looked into Vlad's startled brown eyes. "That was my reaction, too. He's even named himself. Sogon."

Vlad was thoughtful for several minutes. "Has it occurred to you that this may be normal for the Overlord to communicate with his heir?"

"I have no way of knowing for certain. Remember, my mother and father were separated."

"Yes," Vlad said. "But Raynar knew of your existence and was there at the time of your birth. He was there because of foreknowledge."

Otas leaned back on the futon. "I had almost forgotten that I had awareness while inside my mother. I knew about Maccus and what the Trexrans were doing to him, but I didn't have the power to stop them."

"What you're saying is that you've created an even more powerful Overlord than yourself."

"Without a doubt."

"Hmm. When do you plan on telling Cwen she's pregnant?"

Otas smiled at the memory. "Sogon scolded me because we've been pushing my wife too hard. Everyday we tell her something new, but don't give her the chance to fully comprehend and accept the new knowledge."

"That's true enough."

Otas stared at Vlad for some time. "I'll tell Cwen about the children after I've explained what Liambria truly is and that we'll leave Earth in the near future."

"Good idea. It will take her days to become accustomed to that information."

Because of Luca's urging, Maccus had let the men take shore leave in shifts. His second in command had insisted that the men needed sexual release or else there would be mutiny. Not that Maccus couldn't control them with his mind. The village that lay to the west had plenty of willing Earthling females to slake the lusts of the Trexrans. Maccus himself was randy, which puzzled him. Until now, he'd been able to ignore the sexual side of his nature. Yet he had no desire to couple with an Earthling. On supposition alone, he was certain that it would be as unsatisfying as his liaisons with the Trexran females had been. He wanted—no, needed—the Queen.

"Commander Maccus," said Luca from the doorway of the laboratory.

Maccus had his back to the door, admiring the Scrambler. With irritation, he responded, "Not now, Luca!"

"What I have here may interest you."

Curious, Maccus turned. What he saw startled him. Luca was holding the arm of a female with hip-length blonde hair and slanted blue eyes. Her features were unmistakably Liambrian. Her grey woolen dress was of this time period. "Where—"

Luca ordinarily would not have cut off the Commander, but his excitement was great. He was sure to be rewarded. "I was in the bushes behind the village, uh, relieving myself, if you understand my meaning. Out of nowhere a Time-Jump window opened up and out she stepped." Luca nodded his head toward the blonde. "She fell to the ground because of the pain of time travel. At first that was why I thought she couldn't speak. Long after the pain should have stopped, she still didn't talk. There's something wrong with her, but I don't know what."

Maccus walked to the female and lifted her chin. Her blue eyes were lifeless. When he tried to read her mind, Maccus found it was a void. Complete memory loss? How had it occurred? Maccus pulled the female toward him. "Luca, take care of that," he ordered, pointing to the corpse of Lord Ware. "I'll take her aboard ship to sick bay." With that, Maccus and the female disappeared.

Luca's reward was the task of disposing of the putrefied body of Lord Ware.

*Earth's Orbit*

"Just what are you looking for, Commander Maccus?" the ship's surgeon complained. "This is the third scan of her brain you've had me run. I see nothing unusual."

Maccus practically had his nose pressed to the monitor above the bed where the female lay. "But you should see something unusual. I am Liambrian. You've scanned my brain many times for study. What's missing in this female?"

"Ah." The surgeon focused the probe on the female's forehead. At first he thought he'd found nothing, but on closer inspection the surgeon saw minuscule dark shapes in the frontal lobes, where the psychic receptors should have been. He magnified the image. "Is this what you're looking for?"

"Yes." Maccus studied the screen. "The receptors look like they've been charred."

"Or more like cauterized."

Maccus was thoughtful. "But that doesn't explain why she has no memory."

"True. The rest of the brain looks intact." The surgeon rubbed his chin. "Perhaps some form of psychological trauma caused her amnesia."

"Do you think you can restore her memory?"

The surgeon began to sweat. Although, Maccus had spoken in a quiet voice, he knew that if he didn't repair whatever damage had been done to this female, the consequences would be enormous. Without a word, he clamped a device to her temples that would look like a set of headphones to an

Earthling of the past. He activated a switch on the connecting bar of the unit. A humming noise emitted from the thing. Several minutes passed before a low-toned beep sounded from it. The surgeon sweated profusely as he removed the device from the woman. He stood back as the Commander stared into the female's face.

Maccus saw the light of awareness come into the female's blue eyes. She looked directly at him, her eyes widening with fear.

"Please, *Sa-Jang*!" the female screamed. "I don't deserve *Chi-u-da*!"

Maccus frowned at the Liambrian word. His twin did this to the woman? His brother was *Ku Chi-u-gae*? The female was frantically trying to move away from him. Maccus held her in place with ease. "I am not *Sa-Jang*."

She stared into the orange eyes churning with yellow fire. "You lie! Only the Overlord has such eyes!"

"Untrue." Maccus smiled maliciously. "His twin has the same eyes."

The female's eyes widened even more. "M—Maccus?"

He nodded. "What are you called?"

She wanted to lie, but if this was truly Maccus he would know. "Narda."

"So, Narda. The Overlord did this to you?"

"Y—yes."

"Why?"

Narda clamped her lips shut. Instinctively, she knew Maccus would not like what she had done anymore than the Overlord did.

Maccus painfully gripped her chin, probing Narda's mind. She had no barrier hiding her thoughts. His eyes flared bright orange as he picked up the visual image of the Queen falling from a great height. *Chi-u-da* wasn't good enough for what Narda had done. She deserved death. Without thought, Maccus backhanded her.

Although she saw stars, Narda yelled, "She lives! The Queen lives!"

"How can this be?"

"I—I don't know, I swear! I saw her with my own eyes!"

A low chuckle escaped Maccus. He knew how. He did it himself several times a day. The Queen had the ability to teleport herself without the aid of a device just as he did.

He moved away from Narda. Maccus didn't like her. No, he didn't like her at all. But she would be of use to him. "Tell me, Narda. Where may I find the Overlord and the Queen?" Maccus stared at her some seconds. "If you do not answer, you die."

Narda didn't need the Gift to know that he meant it. She began to tell Maccus more than he'd asked for.

# Chapter 30

O tas gazed out the window in his chamber, not really taking in the view for his father-in-law stood behind him waiting for an acknowledgement. He hated telling Hebron the news he bore with the formality of Liambrian protocol. But he was what he was. The Overlord.

"Hebron, I have summoned you here to tell you something of vital importance."

"My daughter bears your children."

Otas turned to look at him. "You knew?"

"You forget, as her father I'm acutely aware of Cwen. With the exception of yourself, I can sense changes in my daughter that will take other males longer to detect." Hebron smiled. "I sensed her condition the night you allowed us to celebrate her birthday."

Otas stared at him some seconds. "Yet you said nothing to her."

"I know you better than you think I do." Hebron nodded with certainty. "You have your own reasons for keeping my daughter ignorant of her condition. The stress it would cause her at this time being the primary one."

Otas was speechless. Was he so transparent to his father-in-law?

Hebron moved closer to the Overlord, who backed up automatically because of conditioning. "Can't you do for yourself what you have done for the Queen?"

"Explain."

"Your gift to Cwen that she could dispense with protocol

and behave as herself while with her family in private was a gift to us all." Tears shimmered in Hebron's green eyes. "You don't realize what that meant to Sevea and myself. The years without Cwen that were lost can never be regained, but we intend to take advantage of your generosity." Hebron moved forward another step. If he wanted to, he could touch the Overlord. "Don't deny yourself the love of family."

Otas laughed without mirth. "My family cannot stand the sight of me."

"I don't speak of Raynar and his cold-blooded relations. *Sa-Jang*, you have not just gained yourself a Queen, but all of us. We are your family."

"Are you saying that I am one of you?"

"Exactly. I've watched you all of your life. The treatment you received as a child from Raynar was inexcusable, Overlord or no. When I can cut through the surface of all of that hardness that surrounds you, I like what lies beneath." Hebron straightened himself to his full height. "I am proud to call you son-in-law."

Otas observed Hebron for some minutes. The emotions he had expressed were pure. "So be it."

Hebron hugged him even though the Overlord stood rigid. He stepped back. "I will say nothing about her pregnancy until you tell me otherwise."

He started to say "dismissed," but Hebron was already on his way out of the chamber. Otas stood where he was, a single tear sliding down his cheek.

Sashna was taking her position as second in command most seriously. She stood guard at the foot of Cwen's bed, periodically glancing over her shoulder to check on the Queen, who was so deeply asleep she hadn't moved in the last hour. Needless to say, when the rectangular blue-violet light of a Doorway opened in the Queen's chambers, Sashna was immediately on alert.

Sashna stood before the Doorway with her sword drawn. Whoever stepped through had better speak quickly and justify their reason for being in the Queen's chambers.

Sashna's eyes widened as a fifty pound bag of clumping cat litter slid from the Doorway. Next came a grocery cart filled with cases of Whiskas cat food. Sashna smiled at what came next. A laundry basket with four sleeping cats inside. Finally, Amma stepped from the Doorway, her fists clenched at her sides as the pin-prickling sensation ran along her nerves.

Amma's torment ceased the very second the Doorway winked out of existence. She checked her watch. "Perfect. A full minute to spare." Amma's blue eyes scanned the *Chimdae-bang* and took in the sight of a sleeping Cwen. Then her gaze shifted to Sashna. Speaking in a hushed tone, Amma said, "Do you intend to skewer me with that sword, child?"

Sashna hadn't seen her since she was seven-years-old, but she recognized Cwen's aunt as if she'd only seen her yesterday. Sheathing her blade, she said, "Welcome home, Amma."

Amma stared at Sashna for several seconds. "If not for that pale hair of yours, I wouldn't know you. You've grown quite beautiful."

"And you're unchanged." A thought suddenly hit Sashna, causing her to flush. Vlad was Amma's son. She was speaking to her mother-in-law.

"But you have," Amma stated as she scrutinized Sashna. "You've had *Kyol-hon* with my son."

"You don't sound surprised."

"That match was made while you were still a child. I wasn't certain if Otas would follow his father's orders." Amma tilted her head. "Whatever you do, don't call me *Chang-mo*, mother-in-law. I know by Liambrian standards I'm still young. But at the moment I feel quite ancient."

"As you wish, Amma."

Amma grunted as she gingerly lifted each sleeping cat

and placed them on the bed with Cwen. "I had to put the little beasties to sleep. The aftereffects of passing through the Doorway would have upset them." Amma placed a hand on Cwen's forehead. "Hmm. Metabolic acceleration. I'm surprised Otas would be so virile. He's impregnated her. Twins yet."

"How do you know this? I sensed nothing. I gained the knowledge from Vlad."

Amma removed her hand. "I forgot, you know very little about me. I sit on the Circle of Twelve. My contribution is my healing powers. They're equal to the Overlord's."

"Impressive."

"No. Just genetics." Amma turned to Sashna. "Cwen will wake soon. I would be alone with her."

"I'm here by command of the Overlord."

Amma ignored that. "I will protect her." Amma settled herself in the chair by the bed. "Although he already knows it, tell Otas I've arrived."

Sashna had forgotten how authoritative Amma could be. Nodding, she said, "Say nothing about the babies. The Overlord doesn't want her to know yet."

Amma only raised her eyebrows as Sashna left the *Chim-dae-bang*.

Cwen sighed as the soft feel of cat paws touched her cheeks and whiskers tickled her nose. She thought she was dreaming until she opened her eyes. Her cats! All four of them were trying to get her out of bed. Cwen sat up quickly. "Rocky, Bandit, Sassy, Spice. I can't believe you're here." Cwen tried to hug them all at once, but cats could be slippery when they were frisky.

A thought suddenly occurred to Cwen. If the cats were here, then Amma was somewhere around.

"Greetings, *Yo-Wang*."

Cwen turned to the sound of Amma's voice. Her aunt

looked exactly like she had when she'd pushed Cwen through the Doorway, wearing the dark-grey jumpsuit, her blonde hair in the warrior's braid. Cwen stared at her for some time before saying, "I don't know whether to hug you or curse you."

Amma chuckled. "You can do either. You're the Queen, after all."

"You could have at least warned me about all of this." Cwen swept her arm in an arc.

"I did what I had to for your own protection," Amma said in defense. "By now you know what *Chi-u-da* is and why it's necessary."

"I know it's purpose," Cwen responded with irritation.

"Then you know that I shielded you from those that would harm you. Since you were ignorant of who and what you are, you couldn't have inadvertently given yourself away."

Cwen picked up Rocky, a twenty-two pound orange male. "Perhaps," she said as she stroked him.

Otas entered through the hidden portal, interrupting their conversation.

Amma stood. She hadn't seen him since he was a child, not bothering to hide the surprise on her face at the size of the Overlord. "*Sa-Jang.*"

His ire with Amma showed in his orange eyes. "I will speak with you another time. I wish to be alone with my Queen."

Amma said nothing at his dismissal, leaving through the *Chim-dae-bang* doors.

Otas looked down at his wife and the cats frolicking on the bed. "Little *mows*, cats."

"Little?" Cwen held up Rocky. "This cat weighs over twenty pounds."

Otas laughed. "Even so, he is still small compared to Liambrian *mows*. I have several."

"So you like animals, too."

He sat on the bed and began stroking the tortoiseshell

cat that came up to him. "Most of the time I prefer them to people."

"I know what you mean."

Otas looked at the cat supplies, the TV, and the futon. "Your *Chim-dae-bang* is becoming crowded."

Cwen remembered what Sashna had said about Liambrians not liking clutter. "Are you saying I can't keep my cats with me?"

Otas looked to Cwen. He could feel the happiness that the little *mows* brought her. At the moment he could deny her nothing. "The *mows* can stay. We'll have to do something about all of these supplies."

"Thank you, husband."

He touched a hand to her cheek. "How do you feel?"

"I guess I did need a nap. I'm less tired now, and hungry."

"What do you wish to eat?" Otas asked although he knew.

"*Sae-u* and *Chin-ji*."

"You're forgetting something, *Katai*."

"I am?"

"Your diet must be balanced. You need a vegetable."

Cwen thought about that for a few seconds. "I don't suppose you have any broccoli?"

"We have something similar. How do you wish it prepared?"

"Steamed and not overcooked. I like it crunchy."

Otas nodded, but he didn't move. He continued stroking the cat.

"Aren't you going to order the food?"

He raised a brow. "I just did. I spoke telepathically to the cook."

"You're spooky sometimes."

He smiled for a second, then his look became serious. "You said that you had questions to ask of me. I've decided that I will only answer one. Everyday we've given you new information without giving you time to fully comprehend it. I will not have you overburdened."

Oh, this is good, Cwen thought. She wanted to know everything about Liambria. How could she possibly narrow it down to one question? Then she discovered there was one question that needed immediate answering. "Why Narda?"

Otas cursed inwardly. That was the one question he'd hoped his wife wouldn't ask. He stood and paced, gathering his thoughts. "Narda was Raynar's idea."

Cwen didn't miss the fact that he didn't refer to Raynar as his father. "Go on."

He ran his hand through his thick hair, looking at her. "I'd passed the age of sixteen and I showed no signs of interest in females. Raynar viewed this as a weakness. A male with no sexual appetite, and the next Overlord at that. He thought me impotent. So he sent Narda to me. She was instructed to teach me the ways of being a male.

"When I was with Narda it was the only time I ever felt anything. I believed what everyone thought of me. That I was cold and emotionless. My liaisons with Narda were done more out of habit than need. Plus, Narda had a big mouth. Our joinings were no secret. My people were assured of one thing—that the next Overlord could do his duty of *Kyol-hon* and *Bal-Dar*." He stared at his wife to gauge her reaction. Only one thought remained in her mind. "I hadn't touched Narda for a long time before your arrival in this time-frame."

Cwen said nothing. Her husband's answer to her question left a bad taste in her mouth.

Otas and Cwen dined in the Overlord's chamber. As she'd expected the meal was delicious, the Liambrian broccoli was cooked to perfection. Her husband had surprised her with mangos for dessert. Neither spoke while they ate. At the moment, Cwen was trying to read the thoughts of the pensive

Overlord, but his mind was closed to her. He just stared at her with those fascinating eyes of his.

She couldn't help staring at Otas either. His black hair hung past his bare shoulders, his handsome face was supported by a strong fist. Even from across the table Cwen could smell his scent of earth, grass, and male. As she gazed upon him, Cwen felt a measure of guilt for making him explain his relationship with Narda. Telling her the tale had obviously pained him. He'd only become involved with Narda to please a cruel father and to prove his virility to his people.

The worst of it was that Otas doubted he had the ability to feel anything except pain and loneliness. In the short time that Cwen had known him, she'd discovered that he was a male of deep emotions and passion. Looking upon her husband, she wondered how anyone could believe him impotent. Just the sight of his bare chest sent little shivers up her spine as she recalled what had occurred the day after *Bal-Dar*. The soreness between her legs was now gone, but the memory of their heated mating was fresh in her mind and was reflected in her green eyes.

Otas reached across the table and took her hand. "Our thoughts run the same course, *Katai*."

Strangely enough, she wasn't embarrassed. "Are you reading my thoughts?"

His blue-black mane shifted with the shake of his head. "It's the way you are looking at me."

"I like what I see. The outside and the inside."

He flushed slightly. "So I please you?"

Cwen nodded definitively. "More than I thought possible."

Otas turned her hand over, rubbing his thumb across the calluses left on her palm from wielding her sword. "Then you have gained acceptance to being my wife."

"I just realized I have." Cwen frowned. "I can't say when it happened."

"*Bal-Dar*, perhaps?" He slowly smiled. "Or the next day?"

She stared at the thick bracelet on his wrist for a time before answering. "*Bal-Dar* was duty." Cwen gazed into the shifting patterns of his orange eyes. "At first your aggressiveness frightened me. But at your touch, I found myself unable to resist."

"You find me sensual?"

"Very," she answered breathlessly for his blunt question lit a flame within her belly.

"And I, you." His eyes brightened. "It's more than *koi*." He rose and stood behind her. "It's who you are in here." Otas touched her forehead. "And here." He placed his large palm over her heart.

Cwen sucked in air. His warm hand made her left breast tingle, and the nipple hardened.

He kneaded her breast as he said, "I cannot make love to you now. I've yet to replace my seed." Curious, Otas formed a Mind-Link with her. He wanted to know what effect his touch had on his wife.

Cwen leaned her head back against his hard stomach. She didn't care what he'd just said as long as he continued to play with her breasts.

He did, using both hands. "*Katai?*"

"Umm?"

Otas smiled down at her. His wife was becoming aroused quickly. "I fear I've neglected you."

Cwen found it hard to think with the way he was touching her. "H—how?"

"It's past time that I show you the proper way to teleport and use *Cho-rok Bul*." He lifted her and moved to the futon. He sat and laid her across his lap. He pulled the top of the *wanpisu* down, exposing her breasts. The Overlord resumed his play.

His touch was making her crazy with desire, yet he wanted to talk. "I thought I knew how to use them."

"Not so. You teleported from fear. The first time you used *Cho-rok Bul*, you feared for Jena."

Cwen was practically panting. "You knew I b—barbecued a boar?"

"Every time you use the Gift, I am aware of it." He raised her *wanpisu*, exposing her tangle of black curls. "Tomorrow I'll begin your Training."

Cwen only half heard what he'd just said. "H—husband, if you can't make love to me, then you better stop what you're doing."

Otas ignored her and began to rub her belly. If what he was doing would harm his children, Sogon would let him know. Nothing came from the mind of his son.

He raised her chest so that he could capture an engorged breast with his mouth, sucking hard. His wife gasped with the strength of it. He parted her legs and slid two fingers gently inside her. Moving them slowly in and out, he rubbed the flower hidden in her female folds.

She grabbed his head, raking her fingers through his hair, saying "*Sa-Jang!*" over and over like a litany. Her arousal became great as he continued his play. When the powerful orgasm came, she slipped quietly into *Ju-Gum*.

Her release was his for their minds were linked. "*Ha-nu-nim*," he said. Otas was astounded at the amount of pleasure he gave his Queen.

# Chapter 31

It was the fifth morning of Cwen's Training by the Overlord. They were in what her husband called *Ku Hyu-ga-bang*, the vacation room. This location was perfect for her instructions in the use of *Cho-rok Bul* and teleportation. The replica of the clear pool of Hyu-shik had served as a flame retardant for the green fire. Otas had had her aim her bursts of the emerald flame into the water.

Cwen now used her fist instead of her open hand to aim the Green Flame. The force she wielded was indeed powerful, but it would never equal that of the Overlord's, which was just as well. Cwen felt she could not turn *Cho-rok Bul* on a humanoid. The boar had been bad enough.

Otas had surprised her for he was a patient teacher. *Cho-rok Bul* had been easy to master, but teleportation was an entirely different matter. Her husband had informed her that it was blind luck that she had materialized under the ceiling in his chambers. He'd scared her when he told her she might have appeared within the walls. When she'd asked him what would have happened to her, he refused to answer.

She had listened carefully to Otas' instructions. Teleportation was not only visualizing where one wanted to go, but mathematical calculations had to be made quickly on the exact coordinates. Longitudinal and latitudinal degrees were of vital importance.

Thanks to Jal's teachings of math, Cwen's ability to calculate the coordinates soon became equal to Otas'. She practiced teleporting herself and objects around the *Hyu-ga-bang*.

By the fourth day, the Queen could teleport at will. On this, the fifth day, Otas had turned the lessons into a game of teleportation tag. Cwen was it.

Cwen used the Mind-Link to sense Otas' location, but before she could touch him her husband would disappear.

Cwen now sat in a cluster of bushes, not without frustration. She knew that Otas was hiding behind the waterfall, but if she teleported to him he would just pop out of view again. With chin in hand, she tried to figure out what she was doing wrong. Cwen pondered her dilemma for some time. After a while she had the answer. There was always a stirring of the air before Otas appeared before her. Her husband had told her that it was a displacement of the surrounding atmosphere that caused this effect.

Cwen inhaled deeply, then vanished. She reappeared underwater behind Otas. Slowly she rose from the pool, careful not to make any splashing noises. The Overlord wasn't aware of her as he peered through the falls, seeking signs of his wife.

Cwen fought hard not to giggle. She reached out a hand and slapped Otas between the shoulder blades. "Tag! You're it!"

"*Ha-nu-nim*!" Otas spun around and lost his balance, sailing through the waterfall and sinking into the pool.

Cwen thought the look on his face was priceless. She passed through the falls and tried to swim to him, but she was laughing so hard she did a poor job of it.

When she reached shallower water, Otas picked up his giggling wife. "Come. You'll drown yourself." He deposited Cwen on a bed of grass. Otas stared at her seriously while he twisted water from his thick hair.

"Forgive me, h—husband." Cwen couldn't stop laughing. "But the look on your face was so funny."

"Your laughter does not offend me. The sound pleases

me." Otas kept his eyes on her as he slowly slipped out of his wet pants.

Cwen stopped giggling at the sight of his huge erection. Keeping her gaze fixed there, she removed her wet *wanpisu*.

Otas knelt beside her and pushed his wife on her back. His eyes glowed bright orange as he took in the sight of her body.

Cwen inhaled sharply at the intensity of his visual appraisal. He wasn't even touching her, but she felt herself responding to his magnetic perusal. She'd learned a few phrases in Liambrian from Jal's book. This was the appropriate time to use her favorite. *"Man-ji-da Goh,* Touch me."

The muscles in his belly twitched in reaction to her words and his shaft grew in length. He said nothing as he ran his hand along her flank, then smoothed his hand over her abdomen.

*Sogon*, Otas said with his mind. *I would mate with your mother.*

*Not harm us.*

With his son's go ahead, Otas placed his hand on Cwen's mound. At his touch, she moved her thighs apart. He slid a finger within, finding his wife hot and ready to receive him.

Laying his weight upon her concerned him. *"Wenjo u-ru du-sa"*, he whispered, gently nudging her onto her left side. He stretched out alongside her, lifting one of her legs. Otas placed the head of his shaft at the opening of her sheath. With deliberate slowness, he entered her inch by slow inch.

Cwen clutched his shoulders at the titillating sensation of his entry. With a gasp, she sighed, *"Sa-Jang."*

The Overlord took his time pleasuring them both. Several minutes passed as Otas made gentle love to his Queen. When they reached the summit of ecstasy, they fell into the darkness of *Ju-Gum.*

*Liambria 2*

Brilliant, Maccus thought as he stared around him. Absolutely brilliant. The Liambrians walking about the large field mistook him for the Overlord, which is what he'd intended for he was dressed in a black tunic and breeches, his twin's color, Narda had informed him. He could tell by the frightened expressions on the faces around him that the Liambrians feared his brother. Maccus had no way of knowing that it was the grin of triumph he wore that was the cause of their uneasiness. The Overlord never smiled.

Brilliant, Maccus thought again as he stared up at the enormous fortress. He of course knew it for what it was—camouflage. This was the tactic the Liambrians had used to hide from the Trexrans on their home planet. The dampening field surrounding the entire area was the reason his men couldn't detect the location of the Liambrians from the starship. But the shielding wasn't capable of preventing him from teleporting to this location.

Grinning still, Maccus checked the amplifier wristband. The device didn't detect the *koi* of the Queen from where he stood. Considering the ten kilometer range of the wristband, Liambria must be huge indeed. Maccus began to move forward toward the stable, watching the amplifier all the while. The Queen was here somewhere in the complex. Now all he had to do was locate her with the amplifier. Then his plans would be set into motion.

Cwen sat at her desk, staring at the screen of the laptop, her expression dreamy. Cwen's memory of what had just occurred between herself and Otas was interfering with her concentration. The words of Jal's novel were a blur. It wasn't just the fact that the Overlord had made love to her that preoccupied her mind. It was the way he had done it—with extreme tenderness. Cwen sighed. She now had no doubts that when her husband said he loved her he really meant it.

Which brought her around to her own feelings about the Overlord. There was such sadness and loneliness within him. Remnants of his life before her arrival. His emotions reflected her own. Although he'd terrified her in the beginning of their marriage, Cwen now experienced a strange sensation in her heart when she thought about Otas. Was this love she was feeling? Cwen just didn't know for she had no point of reference. However, she did admit to herself that whatever emotion she was feeling went beyond mere lust.

Cwen smiled without turning when the air stirred behind her. She inhaled deeply, expecting Otas' scent of earth, grass, and male. Cwen gasped when the pungent odor of spice and rubber hit her nostrils. Maccus! she thought with terror. Before she could turn and defend herself, a hard chop to her neck sent her into darkness.

Even though they were working, Otas, Vlad, and Hebron were sitting relaxed in the Overlord's chamber. What they were doing concerned all Liambrians, but they attended to details as a family.

"Hebron and I have finished the census, the tally on the animals, and inventory in ships' stores. We're in excellent shape," Vlad informed the Overlord.

"When we get word from Raynar, I estimate it will take two hours to get all of the animals sheltered, the crews and passengers to designated ships, and the domes secured over the open fields. We're prepared to launch on your order," Hebron added.

Otas was sitting with his feet propped on his desk. "So now we wait."

"Correct," Vlad agreed.

*Father!* screamed in the Overlord's mind. Otas shot to his feet, his eyes bright gold.

Vlad recognized the sign of deep concern in the Overlord's eyes. "*Sa-Jang*, what—"

The Overlord held up his hand for silence. *Sogon, what's wrong?* he asked with his mind.

*Danger! Mother danger! Brain function suspended!*

*By you?*

*Not I. Something, no, someone.*

Otas tried to sense Cwen with his mind. He panicked when he heard nothing of her thoughts. He raced through the hidden door between their chambers, Hebron and Vlad behind him. She wasn't in the *Chim-dae-bang*, so he continued on to the outer chamber. There her laptop sat, still in operation. But no Cwen. *Sogon! Where are you?*

*Unknown. Far from father.*

*Sogon. Keep sending your thoughts.* His brow furrowed as he concentrated on the location of his son. The Overlord's eyes turned from gold to flaming orange as he triangulated Sogon's coordinates. *I'm coming, Sogon!*

*Hurry! We fear!*

Hebron could hold back his fright no longer. "*Sa-Jang*, please. What's wrong? Where's Cwen?"

Otas cursed himself for not foreseeing this event as he ran back to his chambers. When Hebron and Vlad caught up to him, he turned to them. "Maccus has taken the Queen to Castle Acwellen!"

Hebron was too terrified to speak, but Vlad wasn't. "*Daul-mae!*" he cursed.

Cwen groaned as the throbbing pain in her neck brought her to consciousness. Whatever she was lying on felt like cold concrete. Shivering, she opened her eyes. The memory of Maccus' unpleasant scent caused her to jump to her feet despite her pain. Cwen recognized her surroundings immediately—the underground room of the north tower at Castle Acwellen. It was now filled with Trexran technology. There in front of a rectangular black box sat Maccus, who smiled at her maliciously with his hand perched upon the black object.

Cwen cursed inwardly. She had been wrong. There was one humanoid she would blast with *Cho-rok Bul.* She raised her fist. At the same time Maccus depressed the switch on the black box.

Immediately, Cwen's psychic receptors began to vibrate, disorienting her. She tried to teleport herself away from this place, but nothing happened. What was Maccus doing to her?

"Your powers have been neutralized, my Queen," Maccus informed her. "The Scrambler is most efficient, don't you think?"

Cwen said nothing as Maccus rose and moved to her. She was scared, but Cwen forced herself to formulate a plan of escape. She had to get away from the beast!

"I know you're wondering how I found you." Maccus went to a large oak door and opened it. Narda's dead body hung from a hook on the back of the door. "The ship's surgeon restored her memory. It didn't take much to persuade her to give me the information I needed."

Cwen was thinking furiously. If she was affected by that blasted black device, so was Maccus. His powers of the Gift wouldn't work either. Cwen had no weapons. But she still had her skill of martial arts. She tried not to let Maccus' size scare her. Vlad had always told her that the size of your opponent meant nothing. Her muscles tensed in readiness.

"I know Narda tried to kill you," Maccus said as he came back to her. "My brother is a weakling. She deserved more than this *Chi-u-da.* Death is more permanent." Maccus touched her cheek. "I killed her for you, my Queen."

Cwen slapped his hand away. She kept her mouth shut for Maccus was insane. Words would be useless against him.

Maccus stared at her for a long time. "I know you expect your *husband* to come for you."

Still Cwen said nothing.

Orange and gold shifted in Maccus' eyes. "When my twin arrives, I will decapitate him. You and I will rule the Liambrians."

Otas opened a hidden compartment on the wall in his chamber. Inside rested several U-V Laser weapons. He grabbed one and turned to Vlad and Hebron. "I go to get my Queen."

"Not without me!" Vlad insisted. "She's my cousin."

"And me!" Hebron's eyes were dark smoke. "Cwen is my daughter."

Otas started to argue with them, but stopped. This was a family matter. He handed each of them a U-V Laser. They stood close together as the Overlord activated his teleportation powers.

They only faded from view for a split second, then reappeared. Otas gripped his head as pain shot through his brain like lightning. "There's some kind of energy field surrounding her. I can't get through."

"Where in the castle is she?" Hebron asked frantically.

"The north tower."

"We have to teleport outside. I know the way in. I—"

Before Hebron could finish, Otas plucked the coordinates from his mind. In the next second, they vanished.

Sudden insight hit Cwen. "Maccus, the Overlord won't be able to teleport here with the Scrambler on."

"I'll turn it off when I'm finished."

Finished? Cwen thought. She was blind without the power of *Dut-da*.

"I intend to have you." Maccus' smile was a leer. "After being with me, you'll see that I'm the better choice."

It was now or never. With a quick snap-kick of her leg, Cwen nailed Maccus right in the groin. He bent low and howled in pain. She then kicked him in the head, knocking him over. With Maccus down, she raced to the Scrambler so that she could switch it off and get the hell out of here.

Before her hand could touch the black box, Maccus grabbed her around the waist. Cwen didn't have the time to wonder at his quick recovery. She slammed the heel of her hand into his mouth. She knew that she'd hurt him, yet Maccus' hold on her strengthened. He ripped the front of her *wanpisu*, exposing her breasts.

Cwen became frenzied as she hit him again and again about the head with no effect. Maccus was impervious to the pain she was inflicting. His mind was intent on one thing— raping her. Cwen screamed as his hand clamped onto her breast. Maccus lifted her so that her feet flailed in the air. He knelt, laying her on the floor none too gently, holding her down with his strength. Cwen kept beating him about the head and face, twisting her body every which way to prevent him from taking her.

Maccus grabbed her thick braid, practically snapping her neck. With another powerful rip of the *wanpisu*, she was naked. She'd stopped screaming some time before, for she needed all of her breath to fight him off. But battle as she might, Cwen realized Maccus would have his way. He began to run his hands over her body, grunting like an animal.

When Maccus freed his penis from his breeches and tried to part her legs, Cwen finally screamed, "*Sa-Jang!*"

Otas blasted the door to the underground room to atoms. At the sight of what Maccus was about to do to his wife, the Overlord lost his reason. Dropping the U-V Laser, he attacked Maccus, grabbing him by the genitals and throat, lifting him off Cwen. He slammed Maccus into the wall and locked both hands around his neck. He squeezed and squeezed. Maccus' face turned purple and his eyes bulged. Even at the sickening sound of his twin's larynx being crushed, Otas still choked Maccus.

Vlad found the source of the Gift disruption and switched it off, shaking his head to clear the effect of the thing. In his rage, the Overlord had been immune to the psychic disruption.

Hebron moved behind Otas and placed a hand on his shoulder. "Cease. There's nothing more you can do. See to your wife."

Slowly, logic returned as Otas released Maccus and let him fall to the floor. He looked to Cwen, who was trying to cover herself with the shreds of her *wanpisu*. His wife's face was pale as death, her hands shook uncontrollably.

Otas knelt beside her. "*Katai*, how did he find us?"

Her husband's eyes churned with the red flames of violence, but he scared her less than Maccus had. With a shaking finger, she pointed to the hanging corpse of Narda. Cwen found she couldn't speak yet.

Otas spotted Narda. "*Daul-mae!*" he cursed as he teleported the dead body miles away.

"*Sa-Jang.* We must leave," Vlad hissed as he picked up the weapon the Overlord had dropped. "Trexrans are coming."

"I—is Maccus dead?" Cwen finally said.

"No, *Katai.*" Otas went back to Maccus. "His body is in stasis while it repairs itself."

"Shit," she said quietly.

"Hebron, take that device." Otas placed a thumb and forefinger on Maccus' forehead. "I'll wipe the memory of our location from his mind." He was finished in seconds.

He went back to Cwen and lifted her from the floor.

They all stood close together as the Overlord teleported them back home.

# Chapter 32

*Liambria 2*

When Otas, Cwen, Hebron, and Vlad materialized in the Overlord's chamber, they found Sashna, Sevea, and Amma awaiting them. Still holding his Queen tightly pressed to his bare chest, the Overlord was in no mood to speak with anyone for the lingering rage within him burned his blood like lava. He knew what was on the minds of the three females before him. The thoughts of concern coming from Sevea and Sashna did not increase his anger. But what he read in Amma's mind fueled the red flames raging in his orange eyes.

Otas nodded to Sevea, who moved forward and covered Cwen with the green robe she held. When the tattered *wanpisu* and Cwen's naked flesh were shielded, Sevea silently moved back to her place beside Sashna.

"*Chang-in*," the Overlord quietly said.

Hebron quickly sat the black box on the slate desk, then moved in front of Otas, who silently passed Cwen into her father's waiting arms. Hebron said nothing as he took her into the *Chim-dae-bang*, the door sliding shut behind him.

Vlad stood straight at the Overlord's side, saying nothing for he knew his friend well. The females had no idea what was about to occur, but he did.

Otas turned his eyes on Sevea and Sashna. They visibly flinched at the rage radiating off the Overlord. He stared at them some seconds before speaking. "*Chang-mo*, Sashna, I understand why you are here. Through the Mind-Link with your husbands, you knew of Cwen's abduction." His voice was soft, conflicting with the expression on his face.

Both females nodded.

"Sashna, there is no need for your guilt. There was nothing you could have done to stop Maccus." Otas' eyes shifted to Sevea. "Your worry for your daughter pleases me. She is safe now." His eyes now fell on Amma. The one person in this room he held immense dislike for. "Why are you here, Amma?"

"I was with Sevea when she received the telepathic message from Hebron. I knew my healing powers would be needed." Amma stared up at the Overlord with arrogance. "And I was right. By the look of her, the child has been raped."

"My Queen is not a child!" The volume of the Overlord's voice rose steadily. "And she was not raped!"

Amma raised her brows in doubt.

"You thought I would fail my Queen, didn't you?" He didn't wait for an answer. "I have known which people harbored dislike for me and doubt in my abilities of the Gift since the day I was born! Even now I can feel your hatred for the son of Taki!"

"You're weak! My powers of healing equal yours and they shouldn't. If you were the right kind of Overlord, Maccus wouldn't have been able to steal Cwen from right under your nose!"

Otas let loose with a psychokinetic blast that sent Amma sailing. She landed on the futon. "*Tat-da Wi-e*! Never speak to me so again!"

Amma couldn't respond for the Overlord held her lips locked shut with the power of his mind. Her blue eyes were so large from surprise and fear they looked magnified.

"You kept the Queen ignorant of who and what she was not to protect her, but to keep her under your control!" It took all Otas had not to wrap his hands around her neck. "If

Cwen had known of her importance, she never would have met those Trexrans in the past. If she had not killed one of them, Maccus wouldn't have known she was the Queen!

"As for your healing power equaling mine." The laugh that came out of his mouth was terrifying. "That was true when I was six-years-old and still learning the ways of the Gift. You know nothing about me. I am no longer that confused child. I am a full-grown male and the Overlord!"

He finally released the hold on her mouth. "B—but your father thought enough of me to place me on the Circle of Twelve."

"I am not my father," Otas said quietly. "Have a care, Amma. You are not above *Chi-u-da*."

Amma knew of this mind erasure, but had not believed him capable of it until now. She was convinced that the Overlord could kill her with his thoughts alone. "I—I beg forgiveness."

"Leave my chambers! The sight of you sickens me!" The Overlord meant it, moving to the window and standing with his back to the people in the room.

Amma stood shakily, taking in the look of disgust on her son's face. "Vlad?"

"As second in command, I stand with the Overlord." Vlad turned his back on his mother.

"Sevea?" Amma implored.

"I see it clearly now. To think I defended your actions to the Overlord." Sevea looked upon Amma with immense anger. "I wondered why Cwen had no sense of self when she arrived here. No thanks to you, she's strong and resilient. Despite you, she's a good wife to the Overlord. What you have done is unforgivable. I no longer call you sister." Sevea turned her back on Amma.

The only one left was Sashna, who said nothing and joined the others in their dismissal of her. Amma quietly left the Overlord's chambers.

Otas stood silent for several minutes, then he said, "I would be alone with my Queen."

The three of them left the Overlord, saying nothing.

Otas went to the *Chim-dae-bang* and found Hebron sitting alone in the chair by the bed.

"My daughter is bathing. She wished to wash away Maccus' touch," Hebron informed him

Otas only nodded.

"I heard all through the Mind-Link with my wife. I thank you for making things clear to us." Hebron clasped his shoulder. "I'll take that disruption device and see how it operates. The knowledge may be useful." Hebron left the *Chim-dae-bang*.

Anger raged within Otas because of the fact that Maccus couldn't be killed. Taking his twin into captivity and confining him was also useless, for Maccus would simply teleport to freedom. Otas sat heavily in the chair and awaited his Queen.

An hour passed before Cwen finally came out of the bathroom. She had scrubbed herself until her skin stung. She spotted Otas sitting in the chair. She couldn't look him in the eye as she tightened the robe around herself and climbed on the bed. Cwen lay on her side, facing away from her husband.

Only seconds passed before she felt his weight upon the bed. He lay behind her, stroking her clean hair. Cwen inhaled deeply, smelling his unique scent, which gave her comfort.

"Do not shut yourself away from me, *Katai*," he said.

"I—I have shamed you."

He nudged Cwen on her back. "It is I that feels shame, *Katai*. I should have foreseen this."

Cwen stared up into his yellow-orange eyes. "You can't always read Maccus' thoughts."

"I should have known that Maccus would be affected by

*Bal-Dar* as all Liambrians were." He clawed a hand through his hair. "Maccus was driven by lust."

"I kept hitting him over and over. But he didn't feel the pain."

"He felt it. Remember, Maccus is insane. To him pain is excitement."

Cwen was quiet as she pondered his words.

He was pleased at the direction his wife's thoughts were taking. Her shame turned into disgust for Maccus. Anger had now replaced self-recrimination for what had occurred. He felt it safe to open her dark-green robe and place his hand on her belly.

Cwen sighed. The warmth of his hand somehow soothed her. She felt protected by his touch. "Why do you keep doing that?"

Otas stared at her some minutes. "I intended to wait a while before telling you. But now seems like a good time."

Cwen looked at him with questioning eyes.

"*Bal-Dar* was more successful than you know." He smiled. "You carry the next Overlord and his sister."

Cwen stared up at a smiling Otas while his palm still rested on her bare abdomen. She couldn't believe what he'd just told her. "Are you saying that I'm . . . I'm . . . "

"You're pregnant."

Cwen found that she could say nothing. How did her husband know what she did not?

Reading her thoughts, he said, "Sevea told you that a Liambrian male is aware of his child from the moment of conception while you were at Castle Acwellen. Don't you remember?"

Cwen nodded while a strange feeling coursed through her. She gazed upon the Overlord, taking in the sight of his long black hair, handsome face, beautiful eyes, and his powerful bare chest and arms. The fact that he had impregnated her made her feel excitement and a growing warmth for her husband. "When did this happen? The day after *Bal-Dar*?" She recalled Otas' unbelievable sexual prowess on that day.

"Right after *Bal-Dar*. While we were in *Saeng-Gan* I knew that you had conceived from the process."

"The next Overlord and his sister," she said to herself. "Twins." Cwen fell silent while she absorbed this news.

Otas decided to say nothing as he began a clinical examination of his wife. Through his hand on her belly, he could feel that his children were safe and sleeping. He knew that Sogon would tell him if any harm had been done during Cwen's fight with Maccus.

His wife lay still as he parted the robe over her breasts. Otas' touch was not sensual while he examined her breasts. Good. No bruising had occurred. The areolae were darkening from her condition, the breast tissue was becoming firm, preparing for the production of milk. Instinctively he knew that her breasts were becoming tender. He closed the robe and placed his hand back on her tummy. He propped his head on his hand, watching Cwen.

Her green eyes stared back at him. Cwen was in somewhat of a daze. She knew what Otas had been doing. While he'd examined her, she began to see him in a different light. Cwen may have called him husband, but the fact that he was the Overlord never left her mind. That was how she'd viewed him. Until now. "Husband, am I all right? Maccus didn't harm your babies?"

"*Our* babies are fine, and so are you." He frowned in thought. "I hope my rage didn't frighten you."

"The way you attacked Maccus scared me. But now that I know I carry your children your actions are understandable."

There was a slight brightening in his orange eyes, indicating irritation. "I have shown you caring and passion, yet still you don't understand."

Cwen kept her mouth shut, fearing to make him angrier.

"I did what I did to Maccus because he had taken *you*

from me. The fact that you're with child was secondary."
Otas took a deep breath. He didn't want to lose his temper.
Cwen had been through enough this day. "You are my wife.
What Maccus was trying to do to you was the cause of my
rage. Now, do you understand?"

"Yes, husband." Cwen ran her hand across his chest to
calm him. It had always worked before. She hoped it did now.

It worked. He sighed heavily. "Forgive me, *Katai*. I am
still tense."

She continued to stroke him for the muscles of his chest
were still bunched for battle. God only knew what was going
on with the power of the Gift in Otas' mind. "There's nothing
to forgive."

He rolled to his back, laying Cwen on top of him. Her
head rested on his chest. He was silent some minutes, thinking how to tell her what he must. Stroking her back, he finally said, "*Katai*, I would tell you about the life-form that is
our son."

"You said that he was the next Overlord."

"Yes. But you should be aware of what he is now." He
inhaled deeply. "Our son's brain is fully formed and functional. He has consciousness, thought, and language. He has
named himself. Sogon."

Cwen raised her head and stared at him wide-eyed.
"You're joking."

"I wish that I was. Sogon will be more powerful than I.
Already he speaks to me telepathically." He purposely left
out the fact that Sogon had the power to suspend her brain's
functions. He watched the shocked expression on her face.
"I was surprised as well. But if not for Sogon, I wouldn't have
known where Maccus had taken you. Our son told me of
your danger because you were unconscious. His thoughts
reached me all the way from Castle Acwellen."

"My God," was all she could say. What kind of creature
lay in her womb?

"I heard your thought, *Katai*." Otas pushed her head back to his chest. "During *Bal-Dar*, I was concentrating so hard on improving the species as a whole I had no idea what I created as the next Overlord."

Cwen lay quiet for some time, listening to the steady rhythm of Otas' heart. "Well, when Sogon is born our lives will be far from boring."

The Overlord chuckled deeply, the tension finally leaving his body. He lay quietly stroking Cwen's back. He was amazed there was no stress in her mind after her encounter with Maccus. All that he read there was a determination not to fall into his twin's hands again. A degree of calmness settled around his wife.

"*Katai*?" he said.

"Yes, husband?"

"Because I'm Overlord, I know all there is to know about pregnancy and birth. But I'm a male. I think it best that you talk with a female who has been through it. Preferably, one with the healing powers of the Gift."

Cwen raised her head and gazed into his eyes. Hers turned to green smoke. "I don't want Amma to come near me."

Otas cursed at himself silently. Of course she had heard all that had occurred in the outer chamber with Amma for their minds had been linked. "I'm sorry. In my rage, I neglected to shield my thoughts from you. I had intended to tell you of Amma's misdeeds at a later time."

Cwen reached up and touched his face. "The timing was perfect. All of this time I blamed myself for what occurred in the past. Amma said that my running into the night without Vlad precipitated Operation Scramble."

Otas said nothing, letting his wife speak her mind.

"All of those years I spent with her were wasted on learning the ways of Earthlings. I should have been given full knowledge of who and what I am. I've been doing *Dut-da* on Amma. Her intent was to confuse me." She frowned. "But more important Amma wanted me to hate you as she does. It worked to a certain degree. After our first time together, I hated you out of ignorance. Liambrian ways are so foreign and alien to those of Earthlings. I apologize for giving you such a hard time. Can you forgive me?"

Otas' eyes brightened with his emotions. "*Katai*, there's nothing to forgive."

Cwen looked down, rubbing her hand across his bare chest. When she raised her eyes, she said, "*Na Sa-rang Tang-sin.*"

"I know," he answered softly.

Cwen lay her head back on his chest. "I wish Sevea to attend me."

"I've already summoned her."

"What of Amma? Do you plan to do *Chi-u-da*?"

"Only if you order it. The damage was done to you. As *Yo-Wang* it's your right to decide her punishment."

"Hmm," was all Cwen said as she formulated plans of what to do with Amma.

Sevea stood in the Overlord's outer chamber worried to death. Otas' telepathic summons had sounded urgent. She moved to the *Chim-dae-bang* doors, stopping just before the sensors were activated.

*You may enter, Chang-mo*, she heard telepathically.

Wiping her sweating palms on her burgundy *Yang-bok*, Sevea stepped inside. What she saw melted her heart. Her daughter lay comfortably on Otas while he lazily stroked her back. There was much love between them. She could sense it.

"*Chang-mo*, your daughter is pregnant," he informed Sevea.

Sevea looked stunned. "Hebron knew this, yet he said nothing?"

"I asked him not to." Otas smiled. "Cwen wishes you to attend her and teach her what she needs to know."

Concerned crossed Sevea's face.

"I know your thoughts. There was no damage done during Cwen's struggle with Maccus." Otas gently lifted his wife and lay her upon the bed. He stood and moved to the *Chim-dae-bang* doors. "I have examined my Queen. I would like to know if you concur with my assessment." That said, he left the chambers.

Sevea sat on the bed and quickly examined her daughter. "Twins!"

"The next Overlord and his sister."

Sevea stroked her forehead. "Do you have any questions?"

"I have no idea what the gestation period is for Liambrian females."

"Usually eight months. But your babies are developing at an accelerated rate." Sevea was thoughtful. "My guess is that it's a result of *Bal-Dar.* An evolutionary advancement. In a month, I'll be better able to determine the time of birth."

"What causes this metabolic acceleration?"

"In Liambrians there isn't a placenta. At implantation the embryo's umbilical cord melds with the blood vessels of the womb. The result is that the mother's liver and spleen create more blood cells to send nutrients and oxygen to the baby."

"Well, that explains why Otas has been stuffing me with food." Cwen frowned for a second. "I'm going to get fat."

Sevea chuckled. "Not with the metabolic acceleration. The only thing that will grow is your tummy."

Cwen sat up and smiled at her mother. "So, how do you say grandmother in Liambrian?"

Sevea flushed slightly. "That thought never did occur to me. The word is *Hal-mo-ni.*"

*Earth's Orbit*

Luca stood to the side as the ship's surgeon worked on Commander Maccus. He'd thought Maccus dead when he'd teleported him to the ship. When the surgeon had informed Luca that Maccus was merely in stasis, he was immensely disappointed, for part of him wanted the Commander to die. Then this nightmare chase across galaxies and time after the Liambrians would end. Unfortunately, Maccus was the only one who knew how to work the Time-Jump unit. Luca and his men needed the Commander alive if they were ever to reach home again.

A raspy groan came out of Maccus. "He's coming around," the surgeon said, who waited until the Commander opened those strange eyes of his. "Commander Maccus, can you hear me?"

"Yes," Maccus rasped.

"Do you remember how you got injured?"

The Commander frowned at the pain in his throat. Try as he might he couldn't remember what had happened to him. "No."

"Memory loss," the surgeon whispered to Luca. He attached the memory restoration device to Maccus' forehead and activated it.

Three attempts achieved no results. The surgeon pulled Luca some distance from Maccus, and whispered, "His amnesia is the result of traumatic shock. It's understandable the way his larynx was crushed."

"But no one has that kind of strength except the Commander himself."

"Well, he didn't do it to himself." The surgeon moved back to Maccus, Luca followed.

"Commander, what's the last thing that you remember?" the surgeon asked.

Maccus thought about that for a while. "I was going to construct a device to disable the powers of the Liambrians."

"Hmm," was all the surgeon said as he checked Maccus' throat again. The bruises had almost faded away.

Luca stood where he was, saying nothing. If the Commander didn't remember the Liambrian female he'd brought to him, Luca had no intention of telling him otherwise. He would make sure the surgeon kept his mouth shut as well. Maybe, just maybe this nightmare would end and they could return home.

Cwen and Otas sat upon his big bed playing with the cats. Her husband had insisted that she sleep in his bed every night, so he'd left the hidden door between their chambers open so the "mows", as he called them, could have the run of the place.

Cwen watched him tickle the tummy of the tortoiseshell cat she'd named Spice. Her husband and the cat had formed an immediate bond, which pleased her.

She lay on her back and stared through the curved skylight above the bed. The night was clear. Millions of stars pulsed their brilliance. She sighed at the sight.

"What are you thinking, *Katai*?"

"I've always wondered what it was like traveling through space." She reached up a hand and stroked his black mane. "I now realize that you and everyone else here have done just that." She smiled at him. "Space travel has always been a secret dream of mine."

Otas debated with himself for a few seconds. Despite what his wife had been through this day, she was calm and free of stress. He reached out a hand and placed it on her abdomen. Sogon was silent, within the dreams of babies. He made his decision. "I'm glad to hear you say that."

"Why?"

"Because we will leave this planet soon."

Cwen stared at Otas. He wasn't joking. "Leave Earth?"

"This planet belongs to man. We have no right to be here."

There was logic in what he said. When she thought about it, everyone she'd ever known was Liambrian. Now that she had her cats, Cwen would be leaving no one behind. "Where are we going?"

Good, he thought. His Queen was resilient. "Raynar is searching for a suitable planet to be our new home. Once he sends word, we launch."

"Hmm," was all she said for some time. "And where are these starships we're to travel in?"

"You're sitting in one."

Cwen couldn't help laughing. "You're joking."

"I assure you I'm not."

Cwen sat up as facts came to her mind. Her mother had told her that the Liambrian starships were ten kilometers in diameter. The exact size of the Agro-deck. On her tour with Vlad and Sashna she'd been told that Liambria was self-contained. It had to be if it was a starship. "You said this is one of them. There are more?"

"Counting this one, there are nine docked on this plateau. What you took for mountain peaks are the tops of our starships."

Cwen suddenly became so excited she couldn't sit still. "Tell me everything. No. Show me everything. How does something this big get off the ground?"

He laughed as he laid her down. "Not tonight, *Katai*. You've had enough excitement for the day."

Cwen gave him a false pout.

Otas ran his hand along her thick braid. "We'll start with the bridge in the morning."

Cwen turned pensive. "There's something I must attend to first."

"Amma?"

"Yes. I've decided to strip her of her diamonds. She doesn't deserve to sit on the Circle of Twelve." She looked to him for his approval.

"I have no say in this. The decision is yours, *Yo-Wang*."

Nodding, she said, "I need you to teach me how to remove her jewelry."

He let her practice opening and refusing one of his bracelets. Within a half hour, his Queen had mastered that particular power of the Gift.

# Chapter 33

Sashna stood to the right of Cwen, who faced the window with her back to Amma and Jal. If the Queen only knew her silence and stance were as intimidating as the Overlord's. Since she and Cwen had risen early to perform the Mind-Touch ceremony together, Sashna realized Cwen knew exactly what she was doing.

Vlad had taught Sashna the ways of *Dut-da*, which she now used on Amma. She remained silent as she read Amma's thoughts, although they angered her. Despite what had occurred the day before in the Overlord's chambers, the Queen's aunt still clung to her arrogance and sense of superiority. Sashna kept herself from smiling for she knew Cwen's intentions. Sparks would soon fly in the Queen's chamber.

Cwen slowly turned, her smoke-green eyes glared at Amma. Her aunt stared back at her with an air of authority.

"I now understand why you kept me ignorant of who and what I was during my time with you," Cwen stated bluntly.

"As I've said, it was to protect you. It was to ensure—"

"You still think me that stupid child, don't you!" Cwen blasted her aunt's ears as well as her brain. The look of shock on Amma's face was a sight to behold. The Queen didn't give Amma a chance to speak. "I have been doing *Dut-da* on you since your arrival here. I know exactly what your motives were for keeping me ignorant."

"I thought the knowledge that you were an extraterrestrial and the Queen of that species would drive you mad."

"My ignorance almost accomplished that!" The Queen stood right in front of Amma. "Which was your intention. You believed that I would come to you for comfort and guidance in my fear of the Overlord."

"That's not true!"

"You persist in thinking me an idiot." Cwen laughed. The sound was not humorous. "What you hoped to gain was control over me, and by doing so have influence with the decisions of the Overlord." Cwen leaned in her face, saying quietly, "You thought Otas weak and malleable. You were wrong, Amma. You have no concept of what my husband truly is."

"He's the son of Taki."

"True. But you have no idea of what powers of the Gift Otas possesses, or what kind of male he is." Cwen stared at her a long time. "You know nothing of me, either."

Amma went rigid as the Queen's powers of psychokinesis held her in place, her blue eyes widening with fear of Cwen.

"I know from the Mind-Link with the Overlord that he sent instructions back through time with Vlad at the time of his coronation. I was fourteen then. The Overlord had rescinded Raynar's order that I be kept ignorant of my identity. You were to teach me all before I came to the future." Cwen was so angry she felt like slapping her aunt, so she clenched her fists. "I've read Vlad's thoughts as well. He said nothing about your deceit to protect me from the confusion the strife between you would have caused. Vlad focused all of his efforts on teaching me to be a good warrior. And he succeeded. I'm not afraid to kill, Amma."

Amma started to scream when the Queen fell upon her, but the wife of Otas moved so quickly there wasn't time to get the sound out. In a matter of seconds, Amma was stripped of her diamond jewelry.

Cwen kept her psychokinetic hold on Amma. "You don't

deserve to sit on the Circle of Twelve. Your thirst for power marks you as flawed."

"But look at all that I did for you," Amma pleaded. "The romance novels, the video discs, and the cats."

"As the Earthlings say, like feeding candy to a baby. Give a child sweets and he'll follow you anywhere." Cwen flung the jewelry to her desk, ignoring the clanking sound it made. "From this point forward you will serve us by tilling the soil on the Agro-deck. When we reach our new home, you will farm the land."

"But I'm a healer," Amma whined.

"I don't trust you to touch anyone." Cwen looked her over for some time. "I've yet to decide if you're truly evil. Tread lightly, Amma. I'll be keeping track of you. If you're like those that have gone through *Chi-u-da*, I will not be merciful. I'll kill you myself with *Cho-rok Bul.*"

Amma almost sagged to the floor when the Queen released her. By the look on Cwen's face she meant every word. Amma looked to her husband for help, but Jal refused to set eyes on her.

"Jal," Cwen addressed her uncle. "I know why you spent all of those years teaching me about Earthling matters. However, I will let you have your say."

"If you've been doing *Dut-da*, then you know my marriage to Amma was arranged because we carried the right genes to produce Vlad." Jal wiped the sweat from his brow. "It's not without embarrassment that I tell you that my *Kyol-hon* with Amma was incomplete. A Mind-Link was never formed between us. The only thing that came out right from that joining was the conception of my son. I knew nothing of the Overlord's order that you be trained in the Liambrian way."

Cwen's heart pained her for Jal's disgraceful confession. "I know that there's no such word in Liambrian for divorce, but today I set a precedent. If it is your wish, the *Kyol-hon* between you and this female is dissolved."

"It is my wish, *Yo-Wang*." Jal straightened his shoulders. "I stand with Vlad in this matter."

"Your choice is wise." Cwen nodded to Jal. "Dismissed."

Her uncle left the chamber with a spring in his step.

Cwen looked back at Amma, who hadn't been reduced to tears from what had just occurred. "Leave my chamber, Amma. You're not welcome here."

Amma opened her mouth to plead again, then shut it. She turned to leave.

"Amma," Cwen said, stopping her in her tracks. "Never cross my path. I just may kill you on principle alone."

Amma wasted no time removing herself from the sight of the Queen.

Otas and Vlad sat in the Overlord's chamber awaiting the Queen. Even though they were eager to show Cwen the bridge, they'd been curious about what punishment the Queen intended to mete out to Amma. The two of them had eavesdropped on the goings on in the Queen's chamber by *Dut-da*. The two males had been shocked by Cwen's decision, staring at each other in silence.

"And I thought you were hard and cold," Vlad finally commented. "It's the perfect penance for Amma. She hates getting her hands dirty."

Otas nodded his agreement. "Cwen did not gain this ability from our *Kyol-hon*. Her lack of mercy for her aunt is entirely her own."

Both males fell silent as the Queen swept into the chamber, Sashna on her heels. She stood before the Overlord, who sat on the futon beside Vlad. "I would see the bridge now."

Otas took in the sight of his wife's flushed cheeks and her eyes, which held the dark smoke of rage. He rose and pulled Cwen to the table in the corner, forcing her to sit. "If the bridge crew sees you in your present state, they will flee."

Cwen wasn't aware that she was scowling at him. "I'm angry inside, but it's not showing on my face."

"At the moment, even I fear you."

"So you heard."

"Your imagination of appropriate penalties is far better than mine." With a slight glowing of the green sapphire in his collar, a glass of *Ma-shil-kot* appeared at Cwen's elbow.

The tension left her face as she smiled up at her husband. "I take it this is to cure my anger."

"And to feed our babies. It's been hours since you've eaten." Otas sat beside her at the table, motioning to Sashna to sit next to Vlad.

Cwen finished the *Ma-shil-kot* in seconds. "I don't suppose you have another glass handy, do—"

A second glass materialized before she could finish her sentence. She sipped slowly this time, regarding Vlad. "I hope you don't hate me for what I did to Amma."

"On the contrary. You did me a favor. Matricide is forbidden."

"Hmm," was all Cwen said as she sipped her drink. Now that she was calmer, Cwen noticed that Otas wore a black *Yang-bok* designed like hers, sleeveless with a low V-neckline. The sight of his pectorals and muscular arms would intimidate another Liambrian. Not her. Cwen's thoughts were running in a different direction.

*I like your thoughts, Katai*, Otas said with his mind. *I will see to your needs after we inspect the bridge.*

His visual thought made Cwen turn scarlet. She looked quickly to Vlad and Sashna, who were immersed in their own telepathic conversation. Now assured that their mind-communication was private, Cwen sent Otas her own visual thought of what she would do to him.

His eyes turned bright orange as a red heat burned his cheeks. "I think we should get on with the tour."

Cwen smiled as she finished her liquid snack.

They didn't take the elevator as Cwen had expected. Otas led them along a curved corridor. He stopped before a double set of doors that were not far from his chambers. He gave her a quick smile before his face assumed the pensive expression of the Overlord.

Otas stepped forward, and the bridge doors whooshed open. Cwen stood next to her husband with Vlad and Sashna behind them as the doors slid closed.

Hebron jumped up from the command chair on the left. "*Sa-Jang wi-e ku Ta-ri, Sa-Jang* on the bridge!" The bridge crew of twenty joined him in standing at attention.

Otas walked forward and went down the two steps that brought him to Hebron's level.

Cwen stood where she was, gaping around her. The Liambrian bridge bore slight similarity to what she had visualized. But this was even better. The command center of this Liambrian vessel was more oval than circular, and the computers and monitors sounding off their operating blips and bleeps were the real thing. She was entranced.

Cwen jumped when the crew shouted, "*Yo-Wang!*" holding their fists to their chests. She just stared around her at the males and females wearing grey *Yang-boks* with sleeves, not knowing what to say.

*They're waiting for you to give them an order*, Otas said with his mind.

*Me?* Cwen was suddenly terrified. *I don't even speak Liambrian!*

*My crew speaks English.*

Cwen thought about it for some seconds. She didn't want to sound like an idiot. "At ease," she finally said.

The crew went back to whatever they had been doing before their arrival. Cwen moved down the steps to Otas' side, who was talking softly to Hebron. She heard her father tell him that the crew didn't know Cwen had never been on a bridge, or on a starship, for that matter.

Nodding, Otas said, "Leave us. Stay, Hebron, Vlad, Sashna."

In less than a minute, they were alone. Cwen only glanced at her father, who wore a *Yang-bok* that was the color of bright-green leaves, before staring around her again.

"You may inspect each station, *Tanim*," Hebron said.

"Okay," Cwen answered absentmindedly as she moved four feet forward to a module that stood in front of the left-hand command chair. Cwen was fascinated by the technology. The module had Liambrian symbols written on it. Of course, she didn't know what they meant. The unit operated by a combination of a plasma screen with multicolored boxes for different functions and keypads like the one she'd seen Vlad use in the laboratory in the past.

Cwen started to touch one of the plasma boxes, then stopped. "Father, are the, uh, engines on?"

Hebron smiled. "No. And the docking moorings are fully engaged. We won't go anywhere."

"Hmm," she said as she sat in the chair bolted to the floor in front of the module. For five minutes, she touched the plasma screen, activating different functions. Then she did the same to the keypads. In the center of the desk was a blank screen that came to life with numeric values as she activated the buttons. Cwen turned in the chair and stared at Otas. "This unit is for navigation."

His eyes widened. He was stunned.

"Correct, *Tanim*," said Hebron.

Cwen then moved to the module to the right of navigation. It, too, had plasma screens and keypads, but with different symbols. For another five minutes, she played with the module. "This is the helm."

"Correct, *Tanim*."

Otas leaned close to Hebron. "How does she know that?" he whispered.

"Shhh," Hebron hissed as his daughter moved up the steps to the far right station.

After staring at the monitors and manipulating buttons, she said, "This is ship's communications." She didn't wait for her father's response and moved to the next station. After another five minutes, she turned to Hebron. "This is ship's monitoring or the engineering station."

"Correct, *Tanim.*"

And so it went for the next twenty minutes with Cwen testing and identifying each of the stations. She was now at the third station to the left of the bridge. After experimenting, she commented, "Good. You have a deflector array." She looked to her husband again, who was becoming more flabbergasted by the minute. "We can move meteors, asteroids, or other space debris from our path." At her father's nod, she moved on.

When she was satisfied with what the function was on the next station, Cwen came back to Otas. "It just occurred to me that I don't know how the ship is powered. By fusion reactor?"

Otas and Hebron stared at each other for a second. Neither had anticipated this question. There were no English equivalents to explain it. Both shook their heads.

"Matter and anti-matter?" she persisted.

"No," they said together.

"Well, does it at least have warp capabilities?"

Otas was totally confused. "What is this 'warp?'"

Hebron laughed for he knew Cwen was getting her ideas from Earth television and movies. "The ship is designed to deform at light-speed."

"300,000 kilometers per second?"

"It can go faster than that. We have ten levels of light-speed, which we call *Pal-sok-do.*"

"Great," Cwen said with enthusiasm. "But we must have the equivalent of impulse power."

Otas was totally lost on the conversation, so he let Hebron answer her questions.

"We have sub-light speed. It's called *Ton-din*."

"Hmm," Cwen said again as she looked to the large blank wall space between stations. "How do you see where you're going? There's no viewer."

"Oh, but there is." Hebron moved to the left command chair, activating a switch.

Cwen's mouth dropped open when the grey wall became crystal clear. She could see the mountains beyond, or rather the other starships. "A window? Won't it shatter at high speeds?"

"None of the windows on Liambria are made of glass. They are the same as the walls. A blending of *tol* and alloy with a slight altering in the molecular structure that allows us to adjust them from opaque to transparent."

Cwen giggled with delight. This was so wild! Then she had a thought. "It also operates as a communications screen, doesn't it?"

"Good insight. It's also a projection screen. It can display whatever is on the monitors of each station."

"Hmm." Cwen moved back to the final station on the far left. After a few minutes, she said, "This is a weapons console, but it's off-line." Cwen placed her finger on what could only be the firing mechanism. "Is it malfunctioning?"

"Uh, not exactly," Hebron answered, counting the seconds to when the Queen would realize what was wrong with the console. He only reached ten.

Cwen placed a hand on her hip as she turned to face Otas and Hebron. "This ship has no weapons?"

They both shook their heads.

Cwen moved to stand before them, both hands on hips. "Stop me if I'm wrong. When you were hiding from the Trexrans on Liambria, you were hidden from them by a dampening field. Correct?"

"Yes," Hebron answered.

"So I'm assuming this vessel can be similarly hidden."

"Correct. It's called *Man-to*."

"Whatever power source this ship uses, the Trexrans can detect its energy signature even if the *Man-to* is engaged. Am I right?"

Hebron shot Otas a glance that said, "She's your wife. You answer her."

"You are correct," Otas said flatly.

"The Trexran ship has weapons, of course."

A nod from the Overlord.

"What kind?"

"A pulsar beam based on the Ultraviolet principle."

Cwen rubbed her forehead. "So when we launch into space, Maccus will be on us in minutes." She paced for a few seconds. "Does this thing at least have a force-field?"

"We have *Him-tul*, shields," Otas answered.

"Hmm." She was silent for a second. "Will it stop this pulsar weapon?"

"Unknown. When we launched from Liambria, we immediately time-shifted to the next day. No Trexran ships could find us." Otas felt smug as he dragged her to the helm desk. Finally, he knew something she didn't. "Your father has added a new element to time travel." He pointed to an orange square on the plasma screen. "This is the Inter-Dimensional Leap unit."

Cwen's eyes widened with interest. "You're talking about topology, aren't you? The fourth dimension of time. You intend to evade the Trexrans by shifting into the fourth level of spacial extension."

Otas couldn't help smiling. Cwen's intellect was impressive. "Correct."

Cwen rubbed her chin. "How far from Earth do we have to be before we can make a dimensional leap?"

"One hundred light-years," Hebron answered.

"Then we have a problem. The Trexrans can fire on us before we reach the coordinates for the leap. We have to have a weapon." Cwen stared at Hebron a while. "That console is there because you were developing some kind of armament before you fled Liambria."

"Your intuition serves you well, *Tanim*. I had invented an *O-Roe*, torpedo, utilizing the intensified force of U-V lasers. But I don't think it will penetrate their protective shield."

"You're familiar with the concept of balance of terror?" At Hebron's nod, Cwen continued, "How many of those torpedoes did you make?"

"One hundred. They're still aboard ship."

"Then we must make them more powerful." Cwen stared intently at Otas. "What about *Cho-rok Bul*?"

Otas scowled. "Forgive me, but I don't see how throwing green flames at the Trexrans will be of any use."

"What I have in mind is condensing *Cho-rok Bul* and containing it." Cwen smiled. "When I hit you with the Green Flame at my coronation, I saw green electrical arcs bounce around you while you defected my blast. My guess is that *Cho-rok Bul* is negatively charged."

"Brilliant!" Hebron picked Cwen up and swung her around. "I can have the Overlord aim the Green Flame at self-energizing crystals. They can absorb the energy. Along with the U-V lasers, this mix will be extremely potent."

"But how will you contain it?" Cwen wanted to know.

"In positively charged canisters that will fit inside the *O-Roes*."

"What about a detonator?"

Hebron kissed her forehead. "That part is already done. The *O-Roes* detonate on impact." Hebron hugged the Overlord, who was taken by surprise. "Forgive me, but I must get started. Give me three hours, then meet me in Engineering." With that, Hebron was gone from the bridge.

Otas stared at Cwen so long she became fidgety. "What?"

"Even if you didn't favor Hebron, I could not doubt that you are his daughter." He ran his hand along her braid. "Your father was only fifteen when he invented all of this technology you see around you. It has nothing to do with the Gift. Hebron is a genius."

Cwen was astonished. "My father is responsible for all of this?"

"Yes. And that's not all of your inheritance." Otas led her to the right-hand command chair and sat her down. "You're like Sevea as well. Your mother is Captain of *Liambria Five*."

"Mother commands a starship?"

He nodded. "Sevea commanded *Liambria Five* on our journey to Earth. You favor your mother's way of thinking. The two punishments you doled out as Queen to Narda and Amma are signs of a leader." He sat in the other command chair.

Cwen remembered her mother's tale of the exodus from Liambria. "She was carrying me during the flight here."

Otas grimaced as he remembered Sogon's words of caution about Cwen's stress level. He was pushing his wife too hard. Her expression was one he was unfamiliar with. "Forgive me, *Katai*. I am overwhelming you. Perhaps it's best that we stop for the day."

"Oh, please. Don't stop. I wish to know everything." Her green eyes pleaded with him. "All of my life I've been kept in the dark. I can't bear anymore secrets."

"You're sure you feel all right?"

"I wish to know why there are two command chairs," was her answer.

Otas decided that ignorance was more stressful than knowledge to his wife. "We will lead the Liambrians to our new home."

"We?" Cwen shot him a glance. "I thought the Overlord had the final say."

"Not in space." Otas took her hand. "We command *Liambria Two* together."

"Then you better teach me how to fly this ship. I've never even been in an airplane."

"By the way you knew all of the functions of the stations, I assumed you had an idea how this vessel operates."

Cwen smiled. "For one thing, I can't read Liambrian. Second, my knowledge is conceptual, not experiential. I don't want to look like an idiot in front of the crew."

"How did you learn these concepts?"

"Most of the theories I learned from Jal. The rest were from watching sci-fi videos."

"What are these videos?"

Cwen started to explain, then gave up. "I'll have to show you."

He stared at her some seconds. "I will make a deal with you. Everything you need to know about *Liambria Two* is on the computers in my chambers. We'll review the schematics tomorrow. While I'm with Hebron in engineering, you will eat lunch and rest afterward."

"Another nap?"

"Yes. I won't have you tiring yourself because—"

"I know. I'm pregnant," she said with slight irritation.

"After you've rested, you may show me videos. I would understand what this balance of terror is."

Cwen couldn't help laughing. Otas had no idea how many video discs she possessed. "We can't do it all in one night, but I'm going to show you how to learn something and have fun at the same time."

The look he gave her was dubious.

# Chapter 34

## Liambria Two

It was late afternoon when Cwen finally awakened from her nap. She had been so excited about *Liambria Two* being a starship that she just knew sleep wouldn't come. But it did. That was after Sashna had stuffed her with a big meal. It was some kind of red meat stir-fried with Liambrian broccoli in a flavorful sauce served over *Chin-ji*. Sashna told her that Otas has ordered the cuisine for he felt a diet of *Sae-u* alone wasn't balanced. Of course, there had been a glass of *Ma-shil-kot* to rinse her lunch down with.

Cwen smiled as she climbed from the bed and stretched. Liambrian babies must need a lot of nourishment, she thought. Even after that heavy lunch, Cwen felt she could eat something now. The cause must be the accelerated metabolism of pregnancy, she supposed, rubbing a hand across her abdomen. Cwen decided she would eat soon after she'd set things up for her husband to view the sci-fi videos.

Hebron had sat the universal remote on top of the TV where she couldn't miss it. Cwen went to the wall and opened the closet that contained the video files. She picked one of her favorites about an interstellar war and laid it on the futon. She frowned. There was one thing missing in this entertainment area—a coffee table to sit food and other important items on.

Cwen would worry about that later. Right now her attention was focused on the thirty-five inch screen of the TV. There was a bright glare obscuring the screen from the afternoon sun. Cwen moved to the window, looking for some way to stop the light from beaming through. There were no shades or drapes. She slapped her thigh in frustration.

Cwen was scowling at the window when Otas entered.

"You look troubled, *Katai*," he said.

"This brightness coming from the window will never do. To fully appreciate the colors and special effects of the videos requires a dim room." Cwen gestured to the window.

"All of our windows are the same as the one on the bridge. They can be darkened." He reached around her and pointed to a black recessed button on the sill. He pressed it, and the window dimmed to a smoke-gray. "Enough?"

Cwen glanced at the TV. "Just a touch more."

And that was all he gave the button. The window was close to being opaque.

"Perfect!" Cwen grabbed his hand and led him to the futon. She practically vibrated with her anticipation of her husband's reaction.

Otas sat, rubbing his forehead. "I need to sit for a minute, *Katai*."

Cwen now noticed the haggard look on his face. She'd completely forgotten what he had been doing the last three hours. "Did blasting *Cho-rok Bul* into my father's canisters exhaust you?"

Otas freed his hair from the leather thong. "No. That only gave me a headache. It's just that I haven't quite . . . how do the Earthlings say it?"

"Shifted gears?"

He nodded.

Cwen sat beside him, placing a hand on his shoulder. "Sometimes talking about what's on your mind will clear your head."

Otas smiled at her. "As always your wisdom surprises me."

"Thanks, I think."

He chuckled as he ran his hands through his hair. "It was a compliment." He lowered his hands and rubbed his face. "I'm as confident as Hebron that the *O-Roes* will work. It's the preparation that I'm thinking about. I've ordered the crew to inspect all launch tubes to be sure they are ready for firing the *O-Roes*."

A thought suddenly struck Cwen. "How many torpedo tubes do we have and where are they?"

"Two fore. Two aft. Two starboard. And two port."

"Good. We can fire in every direction."

"Yes, we can." Otas looked thoughtful for a few seconds. "This ship carries twenty thousand Liambrians. I've ordered that the knowledge that we have armament capabilities only be known by the crew."

"Just how large is your crew?"

"Five thousand. Most of them male. One thousand are females."

Cwen wasn't a feminist, but she felt the number of female crew members low. "Why so few?"

"It's the aggression factor. Remember my father's *Bal-Dar* was faulty. Not enough females are like you and your mother."

Cwen knew that he spoke the truth for she'd discovered the same thing during her journey with the daughters. "I agree. But I bet that the ones on the crew are courageous and ruthless."

"That they are." Feeling more relaxed, Otas stood for a second and stretched. He looked down at his wife. "Now I'm ready for this ritual of video viewing."

"It's not a ritual. It's fun."

"Not according to your father and Vlad." Otas' green sapphire in his gold choker glowed brightly for a few seconds. The first thing that materialized in front of the futon was an ebony coffee table. Next came glasses and a pitcher of mango nectar. He held off teleporting the last item to gauge his wife's reaction. "Vlad tells me that the last thing I'm about to teleport is essential."

Cwen just stared at him. She knew what should be included as a snack, but there was no way he would find it in this century.

Smiling still, he said, "I know what you're thinking." With that, a two gallon bowl of steaming popcorn appeared before her.

Even though she was delighted, Cwen asked, "Where did you get that?"

Otas sat beside her, taking a kernel of popcorn and tasting it experimentally. "It is good." He chuckled for a few seconds. "I was so concerned with other things, I had no idea how many TVs and video disc players were brought from the past. Hebron and his engineering crew have converted all to self-energizing crystals." He shook his head at the wonder of it all. "Apparently, popcorn became an obsession with Liambrians. You'd be surprised how much of this food is stocked in the galley storeroom. There are even seeds to grow a crop on the Agro-deck."

Cwen couldn't help laughing. The Liambrians may be leaving Earth, but they would take a piece of the culture with them. When she could breathe, she asked, "Are you ready now?"

"You may begin." Otas sat forward, elbows leaning on his knees as the title flashed across the screen, his eyes glued to the set.

When the story ended, Cwen realized she'd eaten the entire bowl of popcorn. Otas hadn't moved the entire two hours that the disc played. The booming sounds coming out of the speakers didn't seem to bother him. Right now her husband was staring at the FBI warning about copyrights. "So what did you think?"

He didn't look at her when he answered. "The Earthlings have incredible imaginations. There were some inaccuracies about traveling across the galaxy, but they were trivial. I now understand this balance of terror. In war, enemies must have equally powerful weapons. What captured my interest were the battle tactics." Otas gazed at her now. "I sat in your command chair on the bridge during the flight to Earth. All of my life I was taught how to command a starship. But the only tactics I was ever instructed on were methods of evasion."

"Since the people of Liambria were non-aggressive, I assume there were never any wars," Cwen surmised.

"Correct. But when we leave Earth the Trexrans will be right behind us."

"That concerns me, too. Is their ship as fast as ours?"

"I'm afraid so." He rubbed his chin. "Maccus will catch up to us long before we reach the dimensional-leap coordinates."

"What you're saying is that we have a war now."

"Yes. And I intend to win it."

"Do you have a plan?"

"Not quite." Otas took her hand with the remote in it. "Can these videos be played at a faster speed?"

"No. But on the box there are chapters you can select. Say, a battle scene." She pointed to the listing on the box.

"Vlad said that you have all of these videos memorized."

"It's true."

He was silent as he sent a telepathic message to Vlad. Then he said, "Pick all of the videos with battle scenes. I would view them all." He leaned over and gave her a quick kiss. "I've asked Vlad to join me. You and Sashna will have dinner together in my chamber while we do so. Neither Vlad or I have given the two of you time to discuss feminine matters. I know you would like to discuss your pregnancy with a female rather than me."

"Thank you." Cwen rose and went to file cabinet, pulling out video disc after video disc. She stacked them neatly on the coffee table. "There. That should hold your interest for a while."

Otas didn't smile, his expression serious. "You know, I've just realized I was somewhat prejudiced against the Earthlings. I considered Liambrians far above them. But now I understand that when it comes to methods of aggression, the Earthlings are far more superior." That said, he began to read the video boxes.

Without a word, Cwen left her *Chim-dae-bang*.

Otas studied his wife as she stared at the parabolic space maps that he'd pulled up for her on the computer at his desk. He knew her quietness wasn't caused by intense concentration. The Queen's mind was elsewhere.

It's no wonder, he thought. He'd spent the last five days teaching her everything she would need to know in order to give commands on the bridge. He smiled as he thought of his wife's intelligence. Cwen had learned every functional capacity of all the bridge stations. She could now interpret the Liambrian symbology written on the plasma screens and keypads.

He hesitated in speaking to her for he wondered if he'd oversaturated his Queen with knowledge. Then he decided he hadn't. Cwen wanted to know everything about the starship—how the engines worked and where they were, the internal location of the *O-Roe* tubes, the technological aspects of liftoff, and so forth. But he'd held firm, telling her that for now the bridge was all that mattered because he expected word from Raynar any day now. Otas wanted her sufficiently prepared for immediate launch.

He inhaled deeply of her scent of roses. He couldn't help

it for she sat on his lap. He stared at the back of her head, then reached out a hand and ran it down her thick braid. "Have you had enough?"

Cwen abandoned the computer and leaned back on her husband's chest. "The maps are fascinating. I've just got something on my mind."

He didn't need *Dut-da* to know what was troubling her. It was the same thing he was concerned about. "Maccus?"

Cwen sighed heavily. "I know you wiped the memory of our location from his mind. But won't his replicating abilities eventually repair the damage?"

"I'm uncertain." He wrapped his arm about her middle. "When I did *Chi-u-da* on Maccus, I didn't harm any of his brain cells. And there wasn't much to erase from his mind." He smiled even though she couldn't see it. "I guess my attack on him was so traumatic that his own mind buried the memory."

"But we don't know how long he'll have amnesia."

"True."

"I can't bear the thought of falling into his hands again." She rubbed a hand on her thigh. "This *Yang-bok* isn't suitable for carrying weapons. There's nowhere to put them."

"We have weapon belts."

"Can they hold U-V Lasers?"

"Yes."

"Then I would have one, please."

"*Katai*, I don't think that would be wise."

Cwen became irritated. "You weren't the one having that beast pawing at you. I refuse to go through that again. The only way to stop Maccus is to stun him with the laser weapon."

Otas found that he couldn't argue with that, setting her on her feet. He moved to the hidden cabinet where he kept the weapons. After he opened it, he pulled out a black belt with several storage pockets and a U-V laser. He said nothing as he gave them to her.

"Thank you," Cwen said as she buckled the belt around her waist, slipping the laser weapon into the appropriate slot.

Otas opened his mouth to speak, then closed it as he received an urgent telepathic message from Vlad. "Come. We must go to the bridge." He was halfway out the door by the time he'd finished his sentence. Cwen hurried after him.

Cwen could feel the tension of the crew on the bridge as she stood beside Otas while Vlad updated him on some new development. Since they were speaking rapidly in Liambrian, Cwen had no idea what was going on. "Could you two speak English, please?"

"Forgive us," Otas said as he moved to the sensor station where a dark-skinned female was operating the controls. "This is Oanh, Kendra's mother. She's been monitoring an energy surge that appears for a few seconds, then fades. Next, it reappears in an entirely different position in the orbit around the planet."

Cwen only gave Oanh a cursory nod. This wasn't the time for social amenities, she thought as she stared at the monitors. "Oanh, can you tell the difference between a Liambrian energy surge and a Trexran ship output?"

"Aye, *Yo-Wang*. Trexrans still use fusion reactors when traveling at sub-light speeds."

Vlad slapped his forehead. "I know what you're thinking. This idleness is making me stupid." He touched a hand to Oanh's shoulder. "Do a sensor sweep on the last known position of the Trexran ship."

Oanh rapidly manipulated buttons. The monitor screen was blank. "They're gone."

"I doubt if they have left this time-frame. Do a scan on the stratosphere of the planet," Otas said.

After five minutes a distinct energy signature appeared on the left screen. "The Trexrans are moving toward the south pole," Oanh informed them.

Otas grunted. "They are physically chasing this echo we're monitoring. Keep tracking the Trexrans on this screen. Use the other for the unidentified pattern."

"Aye, *Sa-Jang*."

While Oanh continued to monitor, Vlad whispered to Otas, "The last position of the elusive energy signature was north of the equator."

Otas stared at him for a second. "It's Raynar."

"You're certain?"

"Evasive maneuvers are all Raynar knows. He's using the Doorway to move in and out of this time-frame to keep Maccus from triangulating our position."

"His return can only mean his mission was unsuccessful," Vlad surmised.

"Perhaps."

"There!" Oanh pointed to the screen excitedly. "Right above us! That's a Liambrian vessel!"

They all stared at the screen. The starship was in stationary orbit, giving them enough time to be certain of the energy signature generating from it.

"Vlad. Signal that ship," Otas ordered.

Moving to the communications console, Vlad opened a scrambled frequency. "This is Myong-Yong. Identify."

"This is *Liambria Eleven* requesting immediate docking procedures."

Vlad recognized Raynar's voice and immediately sent him the coordinates to land.

"*Yo-Wang*, accompany me." When his wife had moved to his side, he said to Vlad, "Signal Raynar to come to my chambers immediately." That order given, the Overlord and the Queen left the bridge.

Cwen stood at the windows in Otas' chamber watching *Liambria Eleven* land. She heard no sound coming from the starship, but the room vibrated with the power of the vessel's retro-thrusters. Cwen was amazed that anything so big could actually fly through space. *Liambria Eleven* landed smoothly between two docked starships.

Cwen's gaze slid to the side, settling upon Otas. Her husband's expression showed annoyance. He hadn't said a word to her since they'd left the bridge.

A stirring of air announced Raynar's arrival, but Otas didn't turn to face his father. Although tempted, Cwen followed the Overlord's lead, keeping her back to Raynar.

Several minutes passed before the Overlord finally turned about. Cwen followed suit. Still Otas said nothing as he looked at Raynar. The tension between the two males bounced between them like a ball.

Cwen unsuccessfully tried to keep the surprise from showing on her face, for Otas looked nothing like his father. Raynar was dressed in a dark-blue *Yang-bok*, his thick hair a yellow-gold pulled back into a ponytail. His height appeared to be four to five inches shorter than the Overlord's, but he was still powerfully built. The only thing these two Liambrian males had in common was their eyes. Yellow and gold still swirled in Raynar's orange eyes, but not with the brightness of Otas'.

Cwen forced herself to stand still as Raynar's gaze moved from his son to her. While he stared at her, Cwen tried to read his thoughts, but Raynar still possessed the Mind-Shield of an Overlord. She couldn't break through it. Of one thing she was certain, the former Overlord was assessing her as his eyebrows rose in surprise.

Cwen became irritated at this silence. Were they going to stand like this for the rest of the day? Before she could break the silence, her husband finally spoke.

"Raynar," the Overlord said simply.

"*Sa-Jang.*" Raynar placed a fist on his chest. "*Yo-Wang.*"

The Overlord stared at his father for a long time. "I would

know why you have returned. Did you not find a suitable planet for habitation?"

"I found us the perfect home." Raynar looked to Cwen, then back to Otas. "However, the course is quite complicated. It's filled with hazards that must be avoided. Transmitting the coordinates wouldn't have given you sufficient information." Raynar lifted his shoulders in a shrug. "It was a wise judgement. When we came within two thousand light-years of Earth, I knew the Trexrans had found the Liambrians."

"How?" Cwen asked.

"Even though he's twisted, Maccus is still my son. I'm always aware of my two sons."

Otas ignored that. "Explain the complications of reaching the planet you've discovered."

"The planet's solar system lies on the opposite side of the central bulge of the Milky Way galaxy. Because of the intense gravitational pull and turbulence of this area, I had to plot a course around it. We were only able to travel ten thousand light-years inside the galaxy. There's a temporal rift in this region. We made four Inter-Dimensional Leaps, but the effect remained." Raynar loosened the thong on his ponytail and ran his hands through his blond hair. "We had to travel the rest of the distance through intergalactic space. But it was worth it."

Cwen couldn't believe the enormity of what Raynar was saying. "This solar system is 25,000 light-years from the central bulge. Are you saying that you had to traverse through intergalactic space for approximately seventy-five thousand light-years?"

"No. I didn't mean to imply that it was necessary to travel the full distance of the galaxy's 100,000 light-years. Our new home is the same distance from the central bulge as this one, 25,000 light-years."

"Describe this planet," Otas broke in.

"It meets all of your specifications. It's uninhabited with the exception of the simplest microorganisms. There's plant life, oceans, and . . . "

"And?"

Raynar smiled. "The solar system has two dwarf stars. The warmth of the planet should please you."

Otas didn't return the smile. "Did you leave the architects and the construction crews on the planet?"

"Yes. I knew that would be your wish."

Otas moved to his desk and opened a communications link with the bridge. "Vlad."

"Yes, *Sa-Jang?*"

"Assemble all *Hom-Yongs* in my audience chamber at 1500 hours. We launch at 0000 hours. Begin preparations."

Cwen's stomach did flip-flops. It had nothing to do with her pregnancy. The concept of spaceflight was one thing. But actually doing it? Her runaway thoughts ceased when she felt Otas' eyes on her.

"Leave us, *Yo-Wang*. I would speak to Raynar alone."

Cwen said nothing as she left the chamber, thinking at least there wasn't any luggage to pack for this journey.

# Chapter 35

Otas was silent as he stared down at Raynar. He refused to sit in the former Overlord's presence for that would give the appearance of a son talking casually to his father. Otas hadn't considered Raynar as his parent since he was six-years-old. But his hatred for Raynar caused his present dilemma. Only his father could answer the questions on his mind about Sogon. His worry about how to broach the subject was reflected in his eyes. He was unaware that his eyes had gone pure gold.

"May I speak freely, *Sa-Jang?*" Raynar asked.

The Overlord gave a curt nod as his consent.

"Your Queen has exceeded my expectations."

Just for a second, orange fire burned in Otas' eyes. "You thought she would be like Taki."

With a shake of his head, Raynar said, "You misunderstand me. When I first held you after your birth in the Trexran stronghold, I knew that my *Bal-Dar* was successful in the creation of you."

Otas said nothing even though Raynar had just given him an offhanded compliment.

"I was there at the Queen's birth, as were you. When I passed her to you for the Mind-Touch ceremony, I tried to do *Dut-da* on her, but her mind was silent. Just as it was a few moments before. Until now, I had no idea what kind of a Queen she would be."

"Continue," Otas said.

"Although I read nothing from her mind, your Queen holds

great hatred for me. I saw it in her eyes." Raynar cocked his head. "She's very protective of you, as a Queen should be." Raynar smiled.

Otas did not.

"By the metabolic acceleration that I sensed, she didn't refuse *Bal-Dar* as Taki did. I see that I'm to become a grandfather."

"Genetically, yes. But I have no intention of letting you near my children. I would not have them subjected to your kind of parenting." Otas flinched inwardly. He hadn't intended to express his emotions so openly to Raynar.

"I know of your hatred for me. No matter the time or distance from you I'm aware of it." Raynar shrugged. "If I had not raised you in a manner that would benefit all Liambrians, you wouldn't be as you are. An aggressive Overlord."

What came out of Otas' mouth didn't quite sound like a laugh. "Raynar, you know nothing about who I am."

"My powers of the Gift may be diminished, but I do know this. For the first time in four generations there's love between the Overlord and his Queen."

Otas' irritation showed on his face. "Enough! I will not discuss what passes between my wife and myself with you!"

Raynar shut his eyes at the intensity of the hatred blasting his brain from Otas' mind. Opening his eyes, he decided now was not the time to try to have a father and son talk. Raynar changed his tactics to a male to male discussion. "I perceive that you have something to ask of me."

Careful, Otas thought to himself. He didn't want his father to know about Sogon. "Since Maccus and I are identical, how did you choose between us?"

"Why, by the thoughts you sent me."

Otas raised a brow in question. "I spoke with you telepathically?"

"Not in words. But visual images. Don't you remember?"

"My memories before my birth are vague." He couldn't ask Raynar the question on his mind directly for it would give his secret away. Fortunately, Raynar solved the problem for him.

"How could you know this, for I never told you." Raynar paced a few steps. "The Overlord is capable of communicating with his heir. By your visual thoughts, I knew what the Trexrans were doing to Maccus. But their genetic tampering wasn't the primary reason that you are Overlord instead of Maccus. Your twin's half of the egg didn't contain the chromosomes to develop an Overlord. Your's did. Your brain was fully functional within a month of your conception."

Otas kept his face passive. Sogon's brain had reached full capacity long before that time. "So I sent you a message when it was time for my birth."

"Correct. After I freed myself from the Trexran cell, I followed the thought patterns you were projecting. You and Maccus lay side by side. Completely identical externally. But not inside. When I touched Maccus, his mind said nothing. But you." Raynar couldn't help smiling at the memory. "Upon your birth you had the ability of language. You told me you were the next Overlord."

"Is that when you named me?" Otas tried to keep the intensity out of his voice.

Raynar stopped smiling. "I didn't name you. Your exact telepathic words to me were 'I am Otas.'" He stared at his son for a long time. "You were the first Overlord to name himself after his birth."

Otas stood speechless. He remembered it all now. He had named himself, but he'd been a full-term baby. *Ha-nu-nim*, what was Sogon?

When Cwen entered her chamber, she found Sashna waiting for her on the futon. By the paleness of her friend's face, Vlad had told his wife of the liftoff at midnight.

As it was 1200 hours it was time for lunch. Sashna had set out dome-covered plates on the round table in the corner. By the look of her, Sashna wasn't any more interested in food than Cwen was.

Cwen sat next to her. "So you heard."

With a slight nod, Sashna turned her brown eyes on Cwen. "I didn't even know this was a starship until the Overlord took us to the bridge. I thought I'd learned everything Vlad knew during *Kyol-hon*."

"Apparently, males tell us only what they wish us to know. I didn't gain this information from my *Kyol-hon* with Otas either."

Sashna leaned her elbows on her knees. "Unlike you, I've always known I was an extraterrestrial. But to leave Earth and travel to God-knows-where?"

"I'm scared to a certain extent. But I'm excited at the prospect of spaceflight. It's always been a secret dream of mine."

Sashna jerked her head towards the *Chim-dae-bang*. "That's because of all those sci-fi videos you watched. They put strange desires in your head."

Cwen chuckled. "Since we're Liambrians, we don't have much choice but to go where they go."

"Not to mention following our husbands." Sashna stared at the table. "We should eat before the food gets cold."

They both sat at the table. Cwen only stared at the platter of *Sae-u* and *Chin-ji* Sashna had uncovered. Although it was her favorite dish, Cwen had absolutely no desire to eat it.

Sashna was staring at her own filled plate. "I can't eat. Vlad's going to be angry."

"Why would he get mad over something so simple?"

"Ever since our bonding, Vlad's been stuffing me with food and *Ma-shil-kot*. He told me that my nutrients needed to be replaced. Apparently, *Kyol-hon* causes some wear and tear on the body."

Cwen studied her friend. As a female she couldn't tell if Sashna's metabolism was accelerated. But Vlad was doing the same thing Otas was doing to her. A quick *Dut-da* of Sashna told her that she was ignorant of her condition. Cwen would say nothing. This was a private matter between Vlad and Sashna. Using her power of teleportation, Cwen sent the food back to the kitchen, or rather, the galley.

"Thank you," Sashna sighed. "I couldn't bear the sight of that food."

"I won't tell if you won't."

Sashna giggled. "This has been happening to me for the last few days. I don't wish to eat. I don't know why."

"Hmm," was all Cwen said.

Both females fell silent, pondering the enormous journey they were about to embark upon. Neither of them knew that having no appetite was the Liambrian version of morning sickness.

Otas stood in the hidden doorway gazing at his wife, who sat upon the bed, knees drawn up, arms wrapped around them. Her gaze was fixed into nothingness. She was completely unaware of his presence. He quietly moved to the side of the bed.

Cwen jumped when she felt his eyes upon her. "You scared me."

"Your mind was elsewhere." He sat on the bed, placing a hand on her knee. "Are you well? The cooks in the galley told me that the food they sent up to you rematerialized, uneaten."

"I feel okay. I don't know why, but I couldn't eat."

Otas grunted. "I'm surprised it hasn't happened before now. Pregnant females often experience loss of appetite."

"We do?"

He nodded as a glass of *Ma-shil-kot* appeared in his hand. Giving it to her, he said, "But our babies still need nourishment. Drink it all." Then he added, "Please."

Cwen held her breath as she chugged the drink down. For a second, she thought it wasn't going to stay in her stomach, then the queasiness faded.

Otas took the glass from her and stretched out beside her on the bed, encouraging her to lay beside him. When she'd settled her head on his chest he asked, "What were you thinking?"

"This journey to a new planet reminds me of a tale from the Bible. There was to be a great flood. God warned a man named Noah to build an ark. Noah gathered pairs of every kind of animal and his family. The flood came, killing all living creatures on the planet. The ark survived. Earth was repopulated with the offspring of the men and women and animals aboard the ark.

"I realize that's exactly what we're doing. Each Liambrian starship is an ark. And the Trexrans and Maccus are the flood."

"A good analogy, *Katai*. Raynar tells me that our new home will be able to support Liambrian plant life for the soil is similar to ours. The oceans, streams, and lakes have the correct pH for our fish to thrive. And the twin stars are more than I could have hoped for. Liambrians need the warmth and rays of two suns in order to live long lives."

The image of Raynar popped into Cwen's mind. She couldn't tell the age difference between father and son. "How old is Raynar?"

Otas frowned in thought. "Fifty," he finally said.

"Did you tell him about *Liambria Two* being armed for battle?"

"No. Only my crew knows of the existence of the *O-Roes*. I cannot risk a security breach. We'll have to lower the dampening field that surrounds us before we launch. Maccus must not be able to read the thoughts of someone who may inadvertency give away my secret."

"But what of your crew? Can you trust them not to accidently project their thoughts?"

Otas chuckled. "All crew members aboard each ship were selected because of genetics. The fifty thousand that make up our space fleet aren't given to panic, irrationality, and have the strongest Mind-Shields. Can't you tell this from your encounters with Sevea, Hebron, and Vlad?"

"What you say is true." Cwen became pensive for a few minutes. Sevea had told her that 200,000 had escaped Liambria. "How many Liambrians have you performed *Chi-u-da* on?"

He hesitated for a second. "Eleven thousand."

"So 189,000 are left."

"No, *Katai*. You're forgetting the children. The census is 201,000 Liambrians."

"Are any children aboard this vessel?"

"Since we are now a battleship, all of the young ones will ride on the other nine starships."

Cwen became silent for a few seconds. "Do you have a battle strategy in mind?"

"I do."

"Tell me."

"I will not," he said sternly. "But I would tell you this. All of my life we have been fleeing the threat of the Trexrans. I run no more." A fire had lit in his eyes.

Cwen didn't press him. Her husband wasn't in the mood for an argument. Nor was she for that matter.

Otas looked to the digital clock and saw it was 1300 hours. "I must meet with the *Hom-Yongs* in two hours."

"Can I go with you?"

"No, *Katai*. You will stay here and rest."

"But I'm not the least bit tired—"

Otas was startled as his wife fell deeply asleep. He had

planned on touching her forehead and saying "*Ja-Da*," but something else had done it for him. Or someone else.

Otas turned his sleeping wife on her back and placed a hand on her belly. *Sogon.*

*Father.*

*Mother. What happened?*

*I make sleep.*

*Why?*

*Father say so.*

Otas frowned. Did Sogon know everything that they said? Read their thoughts? He suddenly got his answer.

*Sogon hear all.*

"*Ha-nu-nim,*" Otas breathed.

Cwen was curled on her side, sleeping soundly. Suddenly, a voice in her mind said, *Seek Hebron.* Cwen sat up quickly, not quite knowing what had awakened her. She looked around the *Chim-dae-bang.* Except for the sleeping cats, she was alone. Then again, *Seek Hebron.* Cwen gasped at the urgency in the telepathic thought, climbing from the bed. She didn't even know where her father's quarters were inside the starship.

She ran to the outer chamber, sighing with relief. There Hebron sat on the futon.

"Good. You're awake," he said.

"Thank God you're here. I don't know why, but I need to see you."

"I've brought you something." Hebron handed her a gold necklace made of a thickly linked chain. In the center of the piece was a large green sapphire set in an oval of gold. "I was driven by . . . something to make this. Remember the disruption device we took from Maccus?"

"Yes. He called it the Scrambler."

"I tore it apart and discovered how it worked. Behind the gem in the necklace is a miniature Scrambler."

"Perfect." Cwen studied the green sapphire. "How do I activate it?"

"Press the stone once. When it glows, you'll know the Scrambler is working."

"Your timing is impeccable. I have need of this." Cwen hugged her father.

Wrapping his arms around her, Hebron asked, "How do you plan to use it?"

Cwen frowned for a moment. She hadn't known she wanted the device until her father had given it to her. "I'm uncertain." She tucked the necklace into a pouch on her weapon belt and secured the flap.

Still holding his daughter in his arms Hebron ordered, "Go back to bed. You need to rest. I'll see you on the bridge at launch time."

Why was everyone telling her she needed to rest when she didn't feel like it? Cwen thought. Before she could ask her father just that, she fell asleep where she stood.

Hebron picked her up and carried her to the bed, laying her down gently. He stroked her forehead. "By *Ha-nu-nim*, I don't know what force is driving us, or what you plan to do. Have a care, *Tanim*."

Silently, Hebron left the Queen's chambers.

# Chapter 36

Cwen had bathed and dressed in her dark-green *Yang-bok*, her hair plaited in the warrior's braid. She sat on the edge of the bed, waiting for Otas. At exactly 2300 hours her husband appeared in the doorway to the *Chim-dae-bang*. Otas looked formidable dressed in the black *Yang-bok*. His black hair was pulled back into a ponytail. The expression on his face held determination.

"Come," he said to her. "It is time."

Cwen said nothing as she followed him to the bridge. After the automatic doors swooshed shut behind them, Vlad shouted, "*Sa-Jang wi-e ku Ta-ri*!" All of the activity on the bridge stopped as the crew placed their fists against their chests.

Cwen spotted Hebron at the engineering station. She knew the crew was waiting for her to give an order. Since they would launch in an hour, what she needed to say was obvious. "Start the engines, Hebron." That said, she moved down the steps to her command chair. She activated the miniature monitor screens on the ends of the armrests, viewing what each station was doing.

Cwen realized that except for Vlad, Hebron and Oanh, she didn't know the names of the rest of the crew. But now was not the time for introductions. She noticed that Vlad had installed another chair at the sensor station, in which Sashna sat. Her friend's face was deathly pale. Cwen didn't blame her. Now that the time was upon her, she was scared herself.

Cwen listened to the low hum coming from the engines

as she watched Otas inspect each station and say a few encouraging words to each of the crew. Finally, he sat beside her in his command chair, activating his own monitors. His expression was so intense that Cwen decided to hold back her curiosity and ask no questions.

"Vlad. Where is the Trexran ship?" Otas asked.

"They've been orbiting the planet, trying to home in on Raynar's energy signature. They're now approaching the south pole."

"On viewer."

The screen lit up with a colorful schematic of the Earth. Very near the southern pole was a flashing green dot. The question came out of Cwen before she could stop it. "Won't they detect us when we launch?"

"Yes, and they can reach this position in minutes." Otas stared at her a second. "That's why all Liambrian ships will launch at the same time."

"Isn't there a risk of collision if all ships liftoff at once?"

"You must trust us, *Yo-Wang*." Even though he was tense, Otas gave her a quick smile. "The crews are experienced and know what they're about."

"Okay," she said, although a fluttering had started in her stomach. Cwen became quiet as she watched the activity around her. She glanced back at Sashna, who was doing a poor job of hiding the terror on her face. Cwen gave her an encouraging smile. Her attention returned to the mini-monitors on her command chair. She may be going along for the ride, but she wanted to know exactly what was happening at all times.

"Vlad, open a communications link with all starships," Otas ordered.

Vlad did as commanded. In seconds all vessels reported their status.

Cwen recognized Sevea's voice. The confident tone of her mother made her relax slightly. Cwen stared at Oanh, who sat at the helm and turned to look at the Queen. Oanh gave Cwen a cocky smile, which reminded her so much of her daughter, Kendra. The dark-skinned female's assuredness made Cwen relax even more. These people knew a hell of a lot more about what they were doing than she did.

The time before launch was passing quickly when Cwen suddenly had a thought. "Excuse me, *Sa-Jang.*"

Her husband was intently viewing the monitors on his own command chair. "Yes, *Yo-Wang?*"

"Uh, won't we be affected by the powerful gravitational forces of rapid vertical acceleration?"

Otas looked to her. "Don't worry. All Liambrian vessels automatically maintain the correct gravity regardless of what the starship is doing. You will be fine." That said, he went back to his monitoring.

There was nothing left to do or say, but wait for the inevitable, Cwen thought as she straightened herself in her chair and the hum of the engines grew louder. She rubbed her sweating palms together, then placed her hands in her lap, trying to look calm.

"Vlad, secure all domes and hatches," Otas said.

"Aye, *Sa-Jang.*"

There was a slight shuddering of the ship as all of the domes covered the open fields and latched into place.

"All domes and hatches secure," Vlad informed the Overlord.

"Helm, retract docking moorings," Otas commanded.

A loud metallic thunk could be heard as the moorings released their grip on the earth.

Through the communications link, Otas spoke to all vessels. "Twenty seconds. On my mark."

The engines revved at full power while Cwen gripped the sides of her chair.

Vlad was counting off the seconds. "Six. Five. Four. Three. Two."

"Mark!" Otas said. "Full boosting thrusters!"

Oanh punched the plasma screen and up the ship shot. The screen was now transparent, giving them a view of the other starships racing through the atmosphere.

Cwen was amazed that anything this big could get off the ground so quickly. *Liambria Two* vibrated with the turbulence that assaulted it as they passed into the stratosphere. Within seconds they were in space. The sight of the black sky with the flashing white of billions of stars made Cwen's heart race.

"Navigation, set course thirty-three twenty-five mark fourteen," Otas said.

"Course heading set, *Sa-Jang*," said a blond male that Cwen didn't recognize.

"Helm, ahead one half *Ton-din*, sub-light," Otas said.

*Liambria Two* shot forward along with the other ships. Even though the stars were flying by, Cwen thought they were moving too slow. "Won't the Trexrans catch up to us at this speed?"

"That's my intention." Otas didn't look at her. "View aft."

The receding planet that had been their home for twenty years was displayed on the screen. Goodbye, Earth, Cwen said silently to herself. Although everyone of importance to her was traveling with her, Cwen still felt a sense of loss.

"Vlad, any sign of the Trexrans?" Otas asked.

"I have them on sensors. They're leaving Earth's orbit."

"Increase speed to full *Ton-Din*!"

Through the viewer Cwen could see that the Liambrian fleet was flying in a reverse V formation, *Liambria Two* at the point of the V. She didn't know what her husband was up to, but their rear position made sense for they were the only starship with weapons.

"Engage dampening field," ordered Otas.

The vessels in front of them faded from view. Cwen cocked a brow at her husband.

"I don't wish to make it too easy for them," he said quickly, then put his attention back into commanding the ship. "Maximum *Him-tul*, shields!"

Cwen's nervousness suddenly disappeared as she decided to become an active participant in the goings-on of *Liambria Two*. "Vlad, distance of Trexran ship?"

"400,000 kilometers, *Yo-Wang*."

"Time to Inter-Dimensional Leap coordinates?"

"Ten minutes."

"*Yo-Wang*, *Liambria Two* will not make the dimensional leap with the other vessels," Otas informed her.

Cwen only looked at him questioningly.

"I intend to engage the Trexrans in battle." He gazed upon his wife. "I'm teleporting you to *Liambria Five*. You'll be safe with Sevea."

"No."

Otas couldn't believe what she'd just said. "You have no choice."

"I refuse to leave you."

Fire burned in Otas' eyes. What was his wife doing? Now wasn't the time to argue with him. He didn't speak as he turned his full teleportation power on her. Nothing happened. The Queen remained where she was. "What in the Black Hell is going on?"

"I said I wasn't going anywhere."

"How did you resist my power?"

"Not now!" Cwen snapped. "We've got bigger problems. Distance of Trexran ship?"

"One hundred fifty thousand kilometers, and closing," Vlad answered.

"*Daul-mae*!" Otas swore. "Signal *Liambria Five* to make the leap without the Queen."

Two minutes before the other vessels were to make the Inter-Dimensional Leap, they dropped their dampening fields becoming visible.

"Disengage dampening field!" Otas growled.

Cwen knew her husband was enraged, but it would give him an edge in battle. She didn't know herself how she had resisted his teleportation power, but she couldn't worry about that now. The Liambrian vessels disappeared in pairs as they jumped to the next dimension.

"Full stop!" Otas shouted. "View aft!"

The Trexran ship was getting close. Cwen was surprised at its configuration. She didn't know what she had expected, but the vessel was the classic saucer shape of UFO sightings. However, it was big, its diameter equaling *Liambria Two*, but not as tall.

"Helm, on my mark jump three minutes forward in time!" Otas said. "Distance of Trexran ship?"

Vlad responded quickly. "Twenty thousand. Fifteen thousand."

"Now, Helm!"

Cwen tried to ignore the pin-prickling sensation as she stared at the screen. Empty space filled the viewer where the Trexran vessel had been.

"They disappeared!" Luca stated the obvious.

"The Liambrians will be back," Maccus said calmly. "Full stop."

The Trexran ship halted its forward motion.

"Aren't we going to go after them with the Time-Jump unit?"

"What time-frame do you suggest, Luca?"

He thought about that for a second. "I don't know, Commander."

Maccus chuckled. "All the Liambrians know is evasive maneuvers. We'll sit here and wait them out."

"But that could take hours, days even."

Maccus stared at him for some time. "And we will yet be here."

Luca stopped himself before the curses escaped.

"Helm, twenty-five degrees mark ten astern," Otas commanded. "Time remaining?"

"One and a half minutes," Vlad answered quickly.

Cwen smiled to herself. She knew exactly what Otas was doing. When they reappeared, they would be behind the Trexrans.

"Hebron, man the weapons console." When Hebron was in place, Otas asked, "Do you have the last known position of the Trexran vessel?"

"Aye, *Sa-Jang*. *O-Roes* locked on target."

"Ten seconds," Vlad counted.

When the time was up, they were right behind the Trexran ship. Otas wasted no time. "Fire!"

Hebron let loose with four *O-Roes*, each exploding on impact. The Trexran vessel listed dangerously to the left. Before they could celebrate, the Trexran vessel fired two beams of bright blue light as it shot forward. The impact of the weapon shook *Liambria Two* like an earthquake. Those that were standing fell and rolled across the floor with the rocking of the ship.

"So now we know that they have aft weapons," Hebron said.

"They're coming about!" Oanh shouted.

"Hard to starboard!" Otas shouted back.

*Liambria Two* passed to the right of the Trexrans.

"Fire port *O-Roes*!"

Four more *O-Roes* hit their target, but the Trexran vessel had starboard weapons as well, blasting strongly into *Liambria Two*.

The ship titled crazily from the impact. "Starboard thrusters. Level us off!" Otas shouted.

If she wasn't sitting in *Liambria Two*, this battle would have been better than the videos she'd watched, Cwen thought.

"Condition of *Him-Tul*?" Otas asked.

"Shields down to fifty percent." Vlad did a quick scan. "So are the Trexrans'."

"Bring us about, Helm. Hebron, fire as many *O-Roes* as you can when we face them again!"

The two ships were now head to head. Hebron fired ten *O-Roes* while twin beams blasted *Liambria Two*. The engineering console exploded, shooting sparks into the air. A crewman put out the flames with an extinguisher.

"We've lost *Him-Tul*!" Hebron shouted.

Vlad scanned the enemy. "So have the Trexrans."

"Distance?" Otas asked urgently.

"Ten kilometers."

Hebron cursed. "Without *Him-Tul* we can't fire *O-Roes*. We'd be damaged by the explosions."

"Then we're dead," Oanh said quietly.

Maccus could barely see through the smoke on the bridge, but his hearing worked. The amplifier on his wrist was beeping like crazy. The Queen was on that Liambrian ship!

"Shall we finish them, Commander?" Luca inquired.

"Hold your fire!"

"But they're at our mercy."

"And we're at their's, you idiot! I said, hold your fire!"

Otas rubbed the sweat from his forehead. "Why doesn't Maccus fire?"

"For the same reason we don't," Hebron answered.

"Stalemate," said Vlad.

Otas looked to Cwen. He himself was terrified for her, yet his wife appeared calm. "I don't know how you prevented it, but you should have let me teleport you to safety."

Cwen stared at him for a second. Then she stood.

"What are you doing?"

"I'm going to end this madness." That said, she dematerialized.

"*Daul-mae*!" Otas cursed.

*The Trexran Vessel*

Cwen materialized on the bridge of the Trexran ship. All showed surprise at her unexpected arrival. She waved a cloud of smoke from her face as she approached Maccus.

When the Queen stood before him, Maccus found he could only stare. She was magnificent! The tight dark-green jumpsuit outlined her body perfectly. His loins came alive at the vision she presented.

"I would speak with you, Maccus."

Maccus could say nothing because of the sensuous overload.

Cwen looked around the bridge. "Is there someplace where we could speak more privately?" She placed a hand on her hip.

"Uh, yes. Yes." Maccus stepped down from his command chair. "If you'll follow me?" He gestured with his arm.

Nodding, Cwen followed Maccus to his quarters. After the doors slid closed behind them, she quickly looked around, spotting another Scrambler sitting on a table. Maccus was so flustered by her presence that he didn't even move to the device as she'd expected. He stood close, looking down at her. Control was the only thing that kept her from gagging at his foul scent.

Cwen stepped a few paces from him. "Maccus, I've come to a big decision."

"I would really like to know your name."

She clasped her hands behind her back. "Oh, I'm sorry. It's Cwen."

"Cwen," he repeated. "It suits you."

"Look, Maccus. We don't have much time. The Overlord will be here any second."

He frowned. "Continue."

"All of my life I've never been given any choices. It wasn't my idea to marry your twin."

Maccus looked doubtful.

"Your brother is handsome, but he lacks . . . aggression." Cwen stared up at him a while. "I believe I've married the wrong twin."

Maccus puffed up his chest. "You're serious?"

Cwen was counting on the fact that he couldn't read her mind. "Very."

"And you wish to strike some kind of bargain?"

"Exactly." She forced herself to move to him and place a hand on his cheek. "I know you want me. Am I right?"

Before Maccus could answer, there was a great stirring of the air as a murderous-looking Otas appeared. Maccus didn't know why he flinched at the sight of his brother, feeling imaginary pain in his throat.

*Play along, Sa-Jang!* Cwen said urgently with her mind. She raised her fist and blasted her husband with *Cho-rok Bul.* As the emerald electrical arcs danced around his body she said telepathically, *Fall down. Pretend that I've paralyzed you.*

Even though he looked as if he would kill her, Otas did as she'd said.

Maccus' eyes bulged. "Wh—what did you do to him?"

Cwen knelt down beside her husband, quickly forming a Mind-Link with him. *When I give the word, add your teleportation strength to mine!* She touched his cheek lightly before she stood and walked back to Maccus. "It's a power I have as Queen. I've just paralyzed him for a few minutes."

"Interesting," Maccus said, staring at his fallen twin. "So you were saying?"

"You want me to be *your* Queen. Am I right?"

"Yes," Maccus answered cautiously.

"You need me and all of the Liambrians to create a master race. Correct?"

Maccus only nodded.

"You were tracking more than one Liambrian ship. I know where the others are hidden."

Maccus laughed sardonically. "Just what do I have to do to gain what you offer?"

"First." Cwen pulled the necklace Hebron had given her from her pouch. She slipped it around Maccus' neck, fusing the ends solid while she kissed him lightly on the lips, trying not to retch. "Be my new husband."

"What else?" he asked as he pulled her closer to him.

"Kill *Sa-Jang.*"

Maccus jumped back from her as if she were fire. "I don't believe you. It's a trick!"

"Your plans will never work as long as the Overlord lives."

Maccus pondered that for a few seconds. "There's only one way to kill him. I must cut off his head. Otherwise, his self-healing powers will keep him alive."

"Correct." Cwen held out her palm. Her sword suddenly materialized in her hand. "You don't have much time, Maccus. He will be mobile soon."

Hesitantly, he took the sword and moved toward Otas.

*Now, Sa-Jang*! Cwen moved to Maccus and leaned up as if she would kiss him. Quickly, she pressed the green sapphire, activating the miniature Scrambler. The gem glowed bright-green as Maccus yelled and dropped the sword when his psychic receptors became disrupted. Cwen jumped back quickly as he swung his fist at her.

"You bitch! I knew I shouldn't have trusted you!" Maccus tried to yank the necklace from his neck, but her fusion of metal held.

Cwen could feel Otas' strength added to her own. "Goodbye, Maccus!" With the power of her thoughts, Maccus disappeared from the Trexran ship.

Otas was on his feet in a second. His rage that his wife

had taken such a grave risk was radiating off him in waves. "*Katai*, explain yourself!"

"Not now, husband! We have to get back to *Liambria Two*!"

Cursing, Otas teleported them off the Trexran ship.

### *Liambria Two*

When the Overlord and the Queen materialized on the bridge, everyone sighed in relief, until they took in the expression of intense rage on Otas' face.

"Back us off from the Trexran ship!" he bellowed as he sat in his command chair.

Oanh wasted no time doing as he'd commanded.

Otas glared at his wife, who now sat in her own chair looking totally calm. "I would have your explanation now, *Yo-Wang*."

Cwen ignored his rage. "*Sa-Jang*, can you sense Maccus?"

He opened his mouth to yell at her, then closed it as the essence that was his twin came to his mind. "Maccus is suffocating. Dying."

There was a collective gasp from the bridge crew.

Otas' rage was replaced by confusion. "Where did you send Maccus?"

"To M16." Cwen sighed at the perplexed look on Otas' face. "The Eagle Nebula."

Hebron completely forgot about Liambrian protocol at his daughter's words. "*Tanim*, that's 7000 light-years away!"

"I know."

Otas forgot about protocol as well. "*Katai*, even with our combined strengths, we don't possess the power to teleport someone that distance."

"I can't explain it. I didn't even know what I was going to do when I boarded the Trexran ship. I—it was like something was controlling my actions."

Otas looked to Vlad. With silent communication they knew what, or rather who had helped the Queen.

"*Sa-Jang*. The Trexran ship is signalling us," Oanh said. "On viewer."

A Trexran with scraggly brown hair and a sweating face appeared on the screen. "Th—this is Subcommander Luca. We surrender."

"Liambrians have no use of prisoners," Otas informed him.

"B—but we don't have any quarrel with you. We were just following Commander Maccus' orders. And now we can't find him."

Otas listened with his mind for a second. "Maccus is dead."

"None of us know how to work the Time-Jump unit. How do we get back to our own time and home?"

Otas looked to Hebron. "You don't."

Hebron fired a volley of *O-Roes*. On the fifth hit, the Trexran ship exploded in a massive ball of flame, rocking *Liambria Two* with shockwaves.

"Now it is finished," Otas said quietly. "Helm, set course to rendezvous with the Liambrian fleet."

Oanh smiled as she set the ship in motion.

Otas looked to his wife, who was now showing signs of fatigue. He stood and reached out a hand to her. She took it and rose. "Vlad, you're in command. *Ku Yo-Wang* needs rest." That said, the Overlord and the Queen left the bridge.

Otas sat in the chair by the bed in his *Chim-dae-bang*, chin on fist, while his wife scrubbed off Maccus' touch. He himself was dazed. Finally his evil twin was no more, and the Trexrans would have no knowledge of where the Liambrians were located. The trials of a lifetime were finally over, if one didn't count being the Overlord, that is. His concerns at the moment were that of a husband. How could he explain Sogon to his wife?

Cwen emerged from the bathroom, wrapped in her green robe. Silently, she climbed on the bed, laying on her back. Otas moved to the bed and lay beside her. Without a word, he parted the robe and placed his hand on his wife's abdomen.

*Sogon,* Otas said with his mind.

*Father happy now.*

*What happened to Maccus?*

*Maccus bad something. Something need air to live. I make mother send where no air.*

*Thank you, Sogon.*

*Mother happy too. I sleep now.*

Otas looked to Cwen's face. Her green gaze was questioning. Flushing, he said, "*Katai,* I didn't quite tell you everything about our son."

# Epilogue

## Liambria Two

Cwen lazily stretched as she took her time waking up, listening to the steady hum of *Liambria Two's* engines. Otas had arisen hours before, quietly leaving the *Chim-dae-bang* as his wife slept on. She had been aware of his movements about the room in a somewhat hazy fashion. She even remembered the soft touch of his lips on her forehead, something the Overlord did every morning. Her husband insisted that she sleep as long as she liked, not just because of her pregnancy but for all of her actions as Queen of the Liambrians. Otas thought she'd done more than enough to earn the title of *Ku Yo-Wang* and the respect of her people.

Cwen smiled as she watched the myriad of brilliant stars through the skylight. To the Liambrians the Overlord and the Queen were heroes for they'd eliminated the threat of the Trexrans for all time. If only her people knew the whole truth. It had been the fetus that was her son who had done the deed. Besides Otas and herself, only Vlad and Hebron knew what had actually occurred. Sogon, the next Overlord, had ensured the survival of his species.

Otas refused to let Cwen be humble about her role in killing Maccus because Sogon had gained the knowledge of how to get rid of this threat from reading his mother's mind.

A small shudder went through Cwen as she remembered

how close Maccus had been to raping her. By the purple hue Maccus' face had turned while the Overlord was choking him, Cwen had realized then that the replicater twin needed air to live. She'd kept her thoughts to herself as she conjured up ways to kill Maccus. Cwen had thought to drown him, but Maccus would teleport himself to safety before death occurred. Then she'd thought about blowing him out an airlock into space, but the same glitch was present. Maccus would still save himself by teleportation.

Sogon had been the force that solved the problem by taking possession of Hebron's technical skill and driving him to make the miniature Scrambler. Her son had also been the source behind her actions on the Trexran ship. Sogon was the one responsible for preventing the Overlord from teleporting his wife to *Liambria Five* for she was instrumental to his plans. Sogon had used her knowledge of Astronomy to pick the perfect place for Maccus' demise. Cwen couldn't help wondering what powers Sogon would possess when he was full-grown.

She ran a hand over her large abdomen. She was only in her sixth month of pregnancy, but her belly had grown at an accelerated rate during the five month trip to their new world. Sevea had estimated birth would occur in the seventh month.

Cwen couldn't help smiling again. The grateful Liambrians loved spaceflight and delighted in giving their Queen a tour of the galaxy by traveling at sub-light speeds.

Deciding it was time to get up, Cwen rolled to her side, for it was the only way she could get out of bed. She groaned as she stood on her feet because her back began to ache. She supposed that was normal since her belly was so huge.

Ignoring the pain, she wiggled into her *Yang-bok*. Her mother had purposely had the garment made from stretchable fabric in anticipation of pregnancy. The *Yang-bok* didn't hide the contours of her body, for Liambrians believed the shape of a pregnant female an affirmation of the continuance of the species. Owing to this was the fact that other than Sashna, one thousand females had become pregnant following *Bal-Dar*.

It took some effort, but Cwen managed to get her boots on. She drank three glasses of *Ma-shil-kot* before heading to the bridge. When she stepped into the control center of *Liambria Two*, Cwen was greeted with a loud *"Yo-Wang"* from the crew. She tried not to frown because her back was really starting to hurt. All she wanted to do was sit down in her command chair. "As you were."

After she had sat, she sighed. The pain wasn't gone, but it was better than standing. "Good Morning, *Sa-Jang*."

He had an urge to touch her, but held back from displaying his love for her so openly. "We're on final approach to our new home."

In her excitement, Cwen forgot about her backache. "How long before we land?"

Otas smiled at her obvious anticipation. "Thirty minutes." He manipulated some buttons on his command chair and projected an image on the viewer.

Cwen stared agape at the projection of their new world. Twin stars brightly lit a planet that reminded her of Earth. Most of its surface was covered with oceans. The atmosphere turned the sky to aqua, swirls of clouds moving within it. "It's beautiful! I can't believe Raynar found such a world in so short a time."

Otas rose his eyebrows. "It took him over a year Earth time. He surveyed several planets before he found this one. He returned to our time by using the Doorway and the Inter—"

Cwen held up her hand. "Don't try to explain it. I won't be able to absorb whatever you say." She shook her head at the enormity of it. The Liambrian fleet had taken so many Inter-Dimensional Leaps and jumps through the ships' Doorways, that she had no idea what time-line they were in.

Otas chuckled. "I will tell you this. In the time that's passed, the architects and construction crews have completed a landing field."

"Good. I was afraid we'd have to perch on a mountain." The planet loomed larger on the screen as *Liambria Two* made its final approach. Cwen thought their new home looked like a large jewel. "What are you going to name it?"

"Only one name is fitting. Liambria." He turned his attention back to landing the ship. "Helm, slow to one quarter *Ton-Din*."

The noise around her faded as she experienced mild cramps in her abdomen. It can't be, she thought. It's too soon! But her babies had other ideas.

Cwen remained silent during the entire landing procedure. She didn't want to distract her husband at a crucial time such as this. She wasn't even aware that *Liambria Two* had touched ground until Otas called her name for a third time.

"*Yo-Wang?*"

She looked to the Overlord. "Yes?"

"I asked you if you wanted to see our new home."

It took some maneuvering, but she got to her feet. "Of course."

*Father. I come*, Sogon announced.

Otas stood swiftly. "You're in labor!"

Cwen waved him off. "First babies take a long time to be born."

"That may be true of Earthlings, but not Liambrians!"

She started to argue, but a strong contraction doubled her over.

"*Daul-mae!*" Otas swore as he swept her up into his arms, then disappeared from the bridge.

It was all over in twenty minutes. Otas didn't even have the chance to summon Sevea. He'd delivered his children himself. The twins were not premature as he'd feared. Their weights being thirteen and ten pounds.

Cwen was soon resting comfortably on her side with the babies between herself and Otas. Although he was a big baby, Sogon was a miniature version of the Overlord, his newborn eyes churning with the orange and yellow swirls. The girl baby with her cap of wavy black hair favored Cwen, who was trying to think of a name for her daughter.

Otas touched a finger to Sogon's forehead.

*Sister's name Ayana*, he informed his father.

Otas gazed at Cwen, smiling slightly. "Sogon says her name is Ayana."

Cwen stared at her baby girl. "It suits her." Then she frowned. "What else does he say?" She didn't quite know how to handle being the mother of a telepathic-talking baby with powers that exceeded his father's.

Otas listened to Sogon's thoughts for some time. Finally, he answered, "Our son says that he knows he's the next Overlord, but he wants to be a baby first. We're to treat him as such."

"Thank *Ha-nu-nim*," Cwen sighed in relief.

Printed in the United States
2559

9 780738 847